IN PURSUIT OF LIGHT

DISCOVERING KIA BOOK 1

SARAH B MEADOWS

Cover design by Cover Couture

www.bookcovercouture.com

FROM THE AUTHOR

Acknowledgements

Ann Hammond (AKA Gerry) - The first to read In Pursuit of Light from start to finish, and the first to become what is now known as "The Team". Your feedback, guidance and honesty has helped shaped not just these books, but me as a writer/author and helped to keep the characters on track.

Elizabeth - Though you wish to remain anonymous, I know I speak for many when I say your presence within our lives leaves a mark only an angel can make. Your patience is unmeasurable, and your commitment a rarity found amongst people. Thank you for believing in not just the books, but in me, as a person.

My Editor -

Amy Jo Schuster - You have enhanced my writing skills to a level that has given me confidence as a writer and author - a gift that will never be forgotten. Here's to many more early morning and late night editing session to come.

My Alphas and Betas - Autumn Bryant, Coleen Walton, Jennifer Kress, Kim Smith, Linda Lee and Rebecca Aspell.

Thank you for your time, your patience and more than anything, your support.
To my family and friends who have also stood by me from the beginning - Eunice Bourn-Fernley, David Bourn-Fernley, Daniel Adams, Harmony Bourn and Seonaid Mhor.
A special thanks also goes to Anna Crosswell, our cover designer, and Darren Birks, our photographer. Thank you for going the extra mile.

For my Team, who have stood by me from the beginning.

PREFACE

Rolland

This place must be at least five hundred years old, its stone walls are crumbling and only four of the windows still have glass panels in them. The smell of dampness riddles the entire building, although this part seems to be in the worst shape. Heavy with moisture, the air clings to my skin like a wet towel. *How anyone can stay in a place like this is beyond me, although I'm sad to admit I've slept in worse.*

I run my bare fingers along the decrepit walls, feeling the residual energy and emotions that coats them as I allow it all to flow up through my hand. It took a few years to learn how to control this part of my ability, to rein my gift in enough that I could, for the most part, tune people out. For so long, I was constantly being overwhelmed with the emotions of others, either from direct contact with them or from touching places where they had been. Stepping into a room full of humans who have no idea how to form a primary mind barrier was a living nightmare. Having their needs and wants screaming at me was a total mind fuck. Thankfully, my Brothers learned early on how to control their emotions around me and it made everyday life more bearable. Unfortunately, I can never shut it all out entirely and little bits and pieces still filter through if strong enough.

As my hand continues along the wall, I let the energy of the hostages I'm searching for, the reason I'm in this god-forsaken awful place, guide me to them. Their fear, sorrow and anger seeps through my senses, pulling me along the passage and I find myself taking a steadying breath to calm the bombardment that gets stronger as I draw near.

Behind me, I can hear Seb taking out two of the so-called guards. More than likely he's playing with them instead of actually knocking them out swiftly, like he should be. He knows, though, that our window of opportunity to get the innocents out is short, so I'm sure he won't dally too long. That being said, Matt didn't plan tonight's mission as well as he usually does, changing the location on us at the very last moment and pissing Gerry off. All of the boys had to be reorganised and the exit plans revised, but I suppose as long as we find the innocents and get them out safely, nothing else matters.

My Brothers - Sebastian, Gerry, Matt, Brad, and the elusive Jack, who thinks of himself as our leader - as well as myself, have been combining our hidden "gifts" to rescue and set free innocents for hundreds of years. Since the turn of the last century, our focus has been on intercepting human trafficking institutions and organisations. Matt finds the intel through various sources, then hands the info over to Gerry who sets up the missions with "his boys," the only people outside of us that he trusts. Brad, Seb and I get told when and where.

Going in blind like we have tonight is a slight annoyance, but nothing we can't handle. To be honest, it makes things more entertaining and challenging, much like it was back in England in the early eighteenth century.

Needing a break from staving off the crushing weight of the emotions around me, I clear my head and let my mind slip back to those times. Jack hadn't joined us yet and Brad would get Gerry completely wasted trying to help him ease his anxiety. Poor Matt would usually end up drawing the short straw when it came time to wake Gerry at the crack of dawn. Luckily his gift gave him the ability to shield himself from Gerry's mood swings, especially when Gerry decided to take it out on inanimate objects. Unfortunately, the only thing the rest of us could do to protect our arses was to duck and cover.

Poor Gerry, he really does suffer badly from anxiety and trust issues. When he first joined Seb, Brad and I in the early 1700s, he seemed fine. But as time went on, he would get anxious every time one of us left to visit a neighbouring village for supplies, or to scout the hills that surrounded the house we had lived in for a decade. When Matt joined us fifty years later, he got even worse. It took him the longest to accept Jack, the last to join our group, though a part of me still questions whether or not he actually has accepted him.

Thankfully, Brad has a particular way of using his deep voice to calm Gerry, which I'm pretty sure is one of his gifts. Unfortunately, in the past when Brad wasn't able to calm him down, Gerry would end up either going into a full-blown rage, taking it out on the nearest building, or passing out because his heart couldn't take the stress. Over the years we've managed to find other coping mechanisms for him, though they only seem to work for a short period, especially when he thinks people are keeping information from him or when others are around that he doesn't know.

Setting Gerry off is like waking a grizzly bear from hibernation and this thought has me chuckling softly to myself, as he actually looks like a grizzly bear most days. His thick, dark chestnut hair that curls at the ends when in need of a cut, his emerald green eyes, and light skin all make him an excellent mascot of Irish manliness.

Brad is the most grounded one of our group, never batting an eyelash at anyone, even Gerry. With his sturdy sizeable frame, warm impenetrable skin and dark features that soften his face, he reminds me of a gentle giant. He's always level headed and stoic, but this makes it hard to get a reading on how he's feeling. Matt, however, is the complete opposite. His shorter frame, lighter skin, straight jawline and nose, and shining grey eyes combine to give his face the refined appearance of a granite statue. Not that it reflects his personality, though, as he's the softest of all of us. He laughs easily and wears his heart openly on his sleeve. Add to that his exceptional ability to gather information on just about everything, and you have a genuine diamond in the rough.

Feeling a surge of desperation and pain, I shake my head clear of the nostalgia. As I take in my surroundings, I see two doors just ahead of me on the right. The first one is open, and I can easily see that it leads to an empty room while the next one is just a couple of yards further and closed. As I approach the closed door, the fear from what feels like at least a dozen people hits me in the chest like a sledgehammer. But then, just as quickly, it softens... eases... as if it's being muffled... or shielded.

Pushing on the door I find that it opens easily, as it's barely hanging on its hinges, and see steps leading straight down into a passageway that's only just visible, by a small glow of light coming from below disrupting the otherwise overwhelming darkness. Without hesitation, I quickly make my way down the narrow stone steps.

When I reach the bottom, I can see that the light source I

spotted from above is coming from a single torch hanging on the wall. Thankfully the light is bright enough that I can clearly see a holding cellar just in front of me, filled with over a dozen people huddled together in three separate cells. Grabbing the torch so the people can see my face, and hopefully see I mean them no harm, I make my way over to the first barred steel door. As I near them, intense fear, worry and sorrow gush from them like an overflowing river and it threatens to overwhelm me. Pushing through it, I find that my first reaction is to use my gift to reassure them, but I know that in the short amount of time I have, every second counts. Instead, I use my enhanced strength and begin to effortlessly rip the doors off of their hinges, hoping to free as many of them as possible before our time runs out.

"Quickly!" I whisper-shout to what looks like the eldest man in the group. "Head up the stairs and turn left along the corridor. You'll find two of my men waiting there to help get you safely out of here and back to your homes." Jason and Ryan, two of Gerry's boys who are highly trained in military combat, wait at the exit. Gerry himself is waiting just inside the cover of the trees out back where he can mask their disappearance.

With surprising agility, the older man, and two of the women, begin ushering the others out. Most are eager to be free and rush out without too much encouragement, but I notice that a few of them hesitate, looking back behind them to the far-right wall. Wondering what could be more important than escaping, I follow their line of sight and see nothing but a dirty grey wall with shackle hooks along the top and bottom.

My eyes are about to move back to the people when I sense it - a tugging at my heart and my gut, a feeling of something filling every nook and cranny of my body with the contentment of returning home after many years of being away. There's a profound sense of ease within my soul and while I don't remember my homeland, in this moment, I can tell that that feeling of belonging is still deep within me.

Trying to get my bearings, I look back to the old man and see he's holding a young boy, maybe about three years old, cradled in his arms and he doesn't appear to have a scratch on him. A saving grace perhaps that they've not endured any physical harm while being here. As my gaze wanders up to the man's face, I see that he's staring at the wall, his eyes full of tears and having a look about them that I can't quite decipher.

"I do not understand how it is even possible for anyone to do what she did. She has saved so many lives here and we will always be in her debt. We will not forget," the man says through a trembling breath. He turns, making his way up the stairs and out through the broken door, heading in the direction of the waiting men.

Turning back to the wall, that sensation of home hits my soul full force once again. I walk over to the wall, seeing nothing but grey stones. *Who is this 'she'? Maybe a buried body lies behind here*. Intuitively, I know that's not right, and I start moving my hand along the stones.

As I continue to walk along the wall, the feeling grows deeper and impossibly stronger and, rather than hit a corner as I expected to, I find that the wall continues on and curves around into another opening. Moving the torch in my hand slowly around the alcove, I don't see anything at first. But as I move deeper into the space, the light catches on the back wall - and the body that hangs limply on it. At first glance, I would believe the person to be dead - if it wasn't for the tugging at my heart pulling me closer...

Pulling me home.

CHAPTER ONE

*R*olland

　　As I'm drawn closer to the figure, something begins to stir deep within me. I can see that it's a female hanging from shackles on her wrists - her head is drooped forward, and her long dark hair is matted and dirty, obscuring her face. In all of the years of fighting alongside my brothers, I've never seen so much torture inflicted on one body. There's so much blood covering her tiny frame and every single inch of her pale skin is marked or burned.

　　Shaking my head, I realise I've been standing here staring for far too long, stunned into shock by the sight that will forever be etched into my memory and seared like a tattoo into the very fabric of my soul.

　　Gently that same feeling of belonging steels over me as peace and tranquility flow from her followed quickly by another feeling, one that I cannot fully describe. It starts stirring within me slowly, climbing its way up my back - it feels foreign and I can't put my finger on it.

　　Taking a step closer, I run my fingers along her thin neck seeking a pulse. The instant my fingers touch her delicate

1

skin, possessiveness floods my heart and squeezes it like a vice. Shaking my head to clear what I think are her emotions, I quickly realise that it's MY emotions I'm feeling. Not wanting to dwell on that odd occurrence, I force myself to focus on the spot where our skin connects and am rewarded with her strong pulse pushing gently back at me. It's not fast but it's there. *She's certainly still alive with a heart beating that firmly. How she can still be living after this amount of suffering is a testament to her will to survive.*

No emotions emanate from her, but that feeling of home and peace still pulses out of her like a steady drum that won't be silenced. Setting the torch down, I take her weight into my left arm and rest her head carefully on my shoulder. With my other hand I start pulling roughly at the chains attached the wall, but they don't snap as I expected them to. I give another firm yank, but the shiny black chain links don't bend at all, even under the full force of my extreme strength. *What the hell are these chains made of? I don't have time to be messing with this shit.*

Pulling my sword from its sheath, I take a hard swipe at the chains where they're attached to the wall and rewarded with nothing but blue sparks as the sword hits the metal. *What the ever-loving fuck?* Not even a scratch is reflected on the chains.

"What's going on, Rolland?" Seb's distinct voice comes from the entrance of the room. I turn to him taking in his caramel skin that looks even darker in the low light. His ebony hair falls loosely around his jawline, making the stubble around his face seem rougher. His features are a complete contrast to my own lighter ones. Except for our height and build, we look nothing alike. Vigilant, deep cognac eyes run over the girls' limp form where it is draped against my shoulder. *Does he sense it too? Does he feel the draw and instinct to do anything for this stranger?*

Based on the look on his face he appears to be just as confused as I feel. The need to protect the girl grows stronger, encouraging possessiveness to crawl up my spine, burying itself deep within me.

Taking another calming breath, I try to quiet the emotions that grab hold of me.

His eyes find mine and I know he feels it too. No words are spoken between us; there's no need. Before we could talk telepathically, we spent years working together in silence to sneak up on our enemies, forcing us to learn to communicate without words.

From a clip on his belt, he detaches his enhanced whip which has been infused with the same unique metal as my sword. Both weapons were given to us by Jack many years ago when ours were no longer useful. Seb strikes the chains, pulling it tight from the wall, yanking as hard as possible to help weaken the chains links. Aiming my sword, I take another swing at the same area. More blue sparks fly but this time the chains break. Most of the links all fall to the stone floor as though they were never fully attached, with only a few still stuck to the cuffs on the girl's wrists. I watch as the links on the ground glow faintly blue before settling into what look like ordinary black metal rings.

As I place my sword back in its sheath, Seb puts his whip away and grabs the torch off the ground from where I dropped it. I adjust the girl in my arms, so her legs drape over my right arm and her head rests against my chest and I finally get a look at her face. In the dim light, I can just make out what looks to be a fresh bruise marring her left cheek, a cut on her bottom lip and a fading scrape along her forehead. Her features are small and delicate with thin dark eyebrows that peek out from under the dirt that covers her pixie-like face.

"We need to move. I'll keep the path clear, Rolland," Seb urges from my right. Following him back out of the cellar and up the stairway, the need to get out of this hell hole grows heavy.

Our path is clear till we reach the entrance hall. Seb stops. *"Two up on the next floor. I'll redirect them to the right. You take the left passage and head to the chopper. I'll be right behind you,"* Seb speaks through our mental connection.

Warm fluid trickles over my left fingers where I'm holding the girl at the waist. The full moon has disappeared behind the cloud outside, taking with it our only light, meaning I can't see where the blood is coming from. Panic starts to run through me. She's so small and thin, any more blood loss and surely her heart will give out.

I finally make it out and see the chopper. Relief washes over me as I see it's still ready to go. A quick glance around confirms no more so-called guards. As I approach the chopper, I hear footsteps behind me, but I know those footfalls and the energy that's coming from my back, so I don't need to turn to see who it is. With Seb just behind me, I feel a small amount of comfort knowing he has my back.

We're just a few yards away from our chopper when I feel a sharp stabbing pain in my lower right back. I know I've been shot but no other gunfire follows. *Shit, that's going to hurt like a bitch to pull out.*

I keep hurrying forward and jump up into the chopper to a take a seat in the back, hoping it will give me cover from any more bullets. I take a quick glance at the woman still cradled in my arms to make sure she's secure.

"Where's Jack and Brad!?" Seb shouts to Matt through the front seats as he hops in behind us.

"Brad is still 'round front, running the diversion he started up. I haven't a clue where Jack is." I can barely hear Matt's tense voice over the noise of the blades.

Damn, we don't have time for this. My hand is thoroughly coated in her blood now and more panic rises in my chest. My heart rate picks up and adrenaline spikes through my body. Closing my eyes, I try to clear my mind again. Thankfully some rational thought quickly returns.

"Brad! Get your big arse back here now! We need to leave, like yesterday, no more games!" Seb's stern voice comes from inches in front of my face. Peering up at him, I see his cognac eyes have deepened to mahogany and are full of an emotion I haven't seen for many years. Panic and fear aren't emotions I associate with Seb. He's logical, assertive and can stay calm in the most stressful of situations. He's speaking into our comm unit and his voice sounds as panicked as I feel. His full attention is on the girl, so I take another look down, but my eyes aren't as good as his, which means I can't see shit.

"What is it, Seb?" *Do I want to know?*

"She's bleeding out bad and I'm pretty sure it's a bullet wound. How she's still alive is beyond reason. I need to remove it so that I can heal the puncture."

My stomach feels like it's dropped out, giving my body another adrenaline hit. Seb's emotions are leaking through which is unusual for him, most of the time he's in control of them around me.

Torn between pushing him away, in need of protecting her

5

and punching him in the face for not acting faster. *Why is he not moving to do it already?*

"Why are you hesitating, Brother?" I spit out through clenched teeth. His eyes meet mine and despair is all I can see. "Spit it out, what's the problem?" *Damn the man. I swear I would hit him if it weren't for the need to keep a hold of her.*

"I fear that the stress of healing her will be too much for her heart. She's so weak already, forcing her body will put more strain on it... Fuck it, if I don't do anything she will surely bleed out." He moves to stand and switches an overhead light on; its glare blinding me for a few seconds.

After my eyes adjust, I get my first look at her wounds, not just the one that's bleeding out but what looks to be brand marks, lashings from whips around her shoulders and bruises at various stages of healing. The question of how she is still alive keeps going around in my head like it's on repeat.

Seb moves his right hand over the bullet lesion and dips his head in concentration. More blood seeps down my hand as his fingers intrude on the puncture to find the bullet.

I close my eyes, starting a new mantra in my head to stop the ever-repeating questions. *He's healing her, not killing her. He's healing her, not killing her. He's healing her, not killing her.*

"Got it." His voice comes out strained and is barely audible over my heartbeat pounding in my eardrums. He pockets the bullet and returns his hand to her stomach to start healing the gash.

The chopper suddenly lurches to the left - no doubt from Brad's weight. Seb whips 'round into a defensive stance in less than a blink.

"What the fuck, dude? I was havin' far too much fun with them pansies," Brad's low voice grumbles from up front.

With the ceiling of the chopper being so low, it makes it

impossible to stand up straight, causing Seb to stand hunched over in front of me. His back doesn't relax after hearing Brad's voice and I start to wonder if he's feeling the same overwhelming need to hide and protect this girl. To kill anything that comes within a one-mile radius of her. *This is insane.* I try shaking my head to regain some sensibility, but it's no use this time.

"Matt! Get us the hell out of here, now!" Seb practically growls as he hollers over the noise of the blades, making him barely understandable.

"Whoa man, what got up your arse?" Brad calls back. I assume he's turned back round to the controls as he doesn't continue speaking.

Seb returns his attention to the girl, seeming to take a calming breath. *We're both screwed. What and who the hell is this girl? She's got us both acting as though this is our first mission and struggling with the stress of it. This is usually semi-fun once the dipshits have been taken care of.*

Seb returns to his position of squatting on his haunches, placing his hand back on the wound. The chopper ascents sharply, and I realise the side door is open as a blast of wind curls around my back. *Damn, I should have grabbed a blanket to cover her.* I try closing my eyes to find my centre.

Five seconds couldn't have passed when the side door slams shut. Seb spins back into his defensive position. His broad back and shoulders take up my line of vision, blocking out whoever just jumped on the chopper. I run my eyes over his body to see he's already drawn his sword. *Shit, when did he do that?*

"You take one step and I swear I'll remove your head without a second thought," Seb snarls with venom, obviously not happy with whoever it is who has just joined us.

Another wave of panic and possession rears its ugly head

making me curl the girl closer to me. I'm torn between putting her down to aid my Brother in killing this mother-fucker and keeping her in my arms where I know she's safe.

"You're not touching her, Jack." *SHIT!* Silence seems to stretch on as I wait for Seb to be forced to move.

"You have my word that I will not remove her from Rolland's arms, I need to see if she is who I think she is." Jack's cold voice never changes regardless of the situation. He's never ruffled by anything and keeps his mask well in place, so you never know what he's feeling. He doesn't mince his words and to this day he's never gone against them. A fraction of relief comes with his statement yet it's not enough to relax Seb into lowering his sword.

"Jack, I will never forgive you if you remove her from Rolland's arms *or* this craft. You have my word." Seb speaks with such passion it's a wonder he's not raising his sword to Jack's throat at the same time. Seb reluctantly inches aside to allow Jack to move forward, then reaches a hand up to find a blanket before shaking it out to cover her small body.

Jack's tall frame struggles with the low ceiling, causing him to bend over significantly. His platinum blonde hair is pulled loosely back in one of his leather ties, making his high cheekbones more pronounced. He reminds me far too much of an elf most days, so I'm regularly checking to see if he's sprouted pointy ears. Plus, he usually seems to dress like one. Whether he's joining us on a mission, having dinner at home or gallivanting off to wherever it is he goes, I've never yet seen him wear regular clothes. His fighting gear usually consists of leather type material, though it's questionable if it is leather or not. Everything hugs his fit body closely, from his boots that nearly reach his knees, to his dark jacket which he wears under a cloak. If beauty were to be associated with a man and remain masculine, it would be

8

Jack. His icy blue eyes always remind me of the clear skies of Sweden. Cold, crisp, hard, yet stunning at the same time. There's not a mark on his porcelain skin from the sun or the fights he's been in.

He doesn't meet my gaze as his eyes are drawn immediately to the girl in my arms. Drawing her closer to me as he moves toward us, I have to force myself not to turn my back on him.

Following his line of vision, I can see a small mark behind her left ear, about the size of a fingernail. Grime and dried blood cover the mark, but it's there. It looks more like a birthmark than a tattoo. If I had to guess what it is, I'd say it was an atom or particle of some kind. The nucleus isn't round but instead shaped like a small tiny star.

Raising my eyes up to look at Jack, I still see only his usual stoic mask.

"Impossible," he whispers so low that if I hadn't seen his lips move, I would've sworn he had never spoken. The next time he speaks, he does so that Seb can hear him over the noise of the engine. "I need to see if she is unconscious or…" He doesn't finish but raises his hand and places it on her head, closing his eyes. A few moments later he makes a small grunting sound and I see his brow furrow in concentration.

My eyes skip to Seb to see if he's noticed. He's watching Jack's every movement.

"Seb, what the hell is going on? He never takes this kind of interest or reacts like this when he pokes about in people's minds."

"I don't know, but I'm five seconds away from removing his pretty blonde head from his stiff pretty shoulders," Seb grinds out as he continues to glare daggers at Jack.

We hold our breath as we wait to see what Jack will do. He remains stooped over, his hand still on her forehead and as

9

I watch, the line between his eyes deepens further. I've never seen him concentrate this hard on anything before.

He finally opens his eyes, straightening a fraction within the small space. Seb lowers his sword slightly for the first time since Jack has stepped onboard. Jack moves away from us slightly where there is more room for his tall frame, while Seb resumes his stance in front of me, meaning I can't see shit… again.

"She should not be here," Jack begins. There's something in his voice this time, something I've never heard from him; an emotion tinges his words. *Confusion maybe?* I feel no emotion from Jack as usual, no surprise there. So, the slight emotion seeping from his words pricks my attention and I wish Seb would move so I could watch his face for any clues. A useless notion as Jack never reveals anything that he wishes to keep hidden, but it would ease my mind to know what's going on.

"She has built walls within her mind, so strong I have not seen anything like it since… a very long time. What is left of her mind on the surface is just a shell of who she truly is." I know he's leaving out information like he usually does, only revealing what he knows to be certain.

Damn Seb for standing in the way. "*Seb, move your fat arse.*" He doesn't even acknowledge me.

"She has fragmented her mind to protect it from someone or something." Jack must have moved forward again as Seb's back stiffens, his sword raising a few inches.

"Her physical state is part of what keeps her where she is. Do not heal her, Sebastian, as her body does not have enough nourishment or energy to restore itself." There's a small pause before he continues. "Meet me in Sebastian's room, Rolland, once you have returned."

Seb relaxes entirely and spins on the spot, running his

eyes over her as though searching for something. The torture in his eyes is maddening, but Jack is nowhere to be seen, thankfully, as he will have teleported back to the house. I watch as Seb pulls a first aid kit down from a cabinet above. I didn't even know there was one up there.

"Fucking pompous dick. *Do not heal her, Sebastian.* He may as well have told me not to breathe," Seb grits out as he lifts the blanket and starts gently cleaning the other cuts he can reach. I don't feel any more blood running down my hand, so he must have closed the wound up enough.

My mind is still spinning with what Jack said or what he didn't say. *'Has not seen anything like it since,' Since when?* The pompous prick has been with us for just over a hundred and fifty years. He's the oldest of us, so he's probably pushing a thousand years, though he's never told any of us anything about himself. The prick is invaluable and to say he's unreliable is an understatement, but he's never steered us wrong on information.

The remaining ten minutes of our journey feels like an eternity. Once Seb has finished, he sits down opposite me full of agitation as his legs bounce up and down as though he wants to pace but can't. His combat gear is similar to mine, both of us wearing dark leather trousers and long-sleeved tops. The heat from the summer makes it hard to wear anything thicker, plus we heal relatively fast, so there's no need for protective gear over the top. Seb prefers lighter boots to my heavier ones, as they aid him in climbing and balancing along narrow ridges. The look of torture is still within his eyes. Knowing he can heal every broken bone, wound and bruise but not being able to will be tearing him apart. *At least he's sheathed his sword.* His dark hair is taking the brunt of his frustration now. Every time he stops to look up, he runs a hand through his hair as though to give him something to do.

11

I'm thankful that I have her in my arms, like salve on an open wound. *Am I going crazy? I don't know this girl and the feelings are as strong, if not stronger, than those I have for my brothers. Loyalty, protection, familiarity and a sense of home flow from her, yet I haven't even seen her open her eyes or heard her speak.* Looking down at her neck again to watch her pulse, I see several bruises that look like finger marks that travel the width of her throat. *I wonder how damaged her vocal cords are?*

"Rolland, are you hurt? There's still blood dripping onto the floor and I'm pretty sure all her open wounds are covered." Seb's tense voice tugs me from my thoughts.

Damn it. I was hoping to pull the bullet out myself, but I won't get a chance if Jack's going to dive straight into poking around her head. I glower back at him and don't say a word. For the first time since stepping on board the chopper, I see his eyes change from torture to amusement. He knows I hate him poking around and healing me.

"Show me." It's not a request but a demand.

Fucking twat. I swear I'll get him back for this. Turning slightly in my seat, I show him my back where the bullet is still embedded. He steps over and squats at my side. I've had worse injuries but it's still a bitch to have a bullet pulled out without any liquor to dull the pain.

"Don't be such a pussy, Rolland, it's just a flesh wound." Mirth tinges his words, but he's still as full of worry as I am.

"Just be quick about it," I mutter, closing my eyes. I try finding my centre to help distract myself from the pain.

Finding my centre is natural after years of practice. At first, it was like trying to fall asleep while high on twenty shots of caffeine. It's what most people would call meditating, though on a slightly more profound level.

"Rolland, I think the bullet was laced with something, it's

12

different to the one I pulled from her." Seb's husky voice soon breaks through and I find the pain in my side has eased considerably. I open my eyes to find him looking at both bullets with a look of puzzlement on his face. "I'll give them to Matt to take a look at later, see if he can trace them. What's more worrying is what the bullet itself contains. I need to pull whatever substance was in the bullet out of your blood before I can heal it." He finally looks back up at me, scowling with despondence as he runs his eyes over my face. He pockets the bullets while waiting for me to reply.

"Just leave it a few hours, you can play doctor later once we're back at the house." He nods as he runs his eyes over the girl before rubbing a hand over his face as though trying to rid an unwanted thought from it. He then moves back over to the other side of the chopper to resume his brooding.

≈

"That's us home guys." Matt's dry voice comes through the speakers overhead.

Shit, we haven't told Matt and Brad about her. My eyes meet Seb's and a silent understanding passes. Seb has the door open before we touch down, giving me a chance to get ahead before Matt or Brad can ask questions.

From the rooftop where the landing pad is, I make my way down the steps and through the house toward the west wing where Seb's room is. It takes more time than I would like. Opening doors while holding something as frail as her body is harder than I thought. Seb's footfalls catch up with me and he's soon two steps ahead making the process easier. We finally get to his room where Jack is already waiting.

Seb's room is spacious with a king-sized bed in the middle facing the en-suite to the right. It has a cosy feeling with all of the mahogany furniture and the light shades on either side of the bed that give a softness to the room. Soft rugs break the solid wood flooring and the pictures he's collected from travelling dot the walls.

I look over at Jack who's standing by the bay window with his back to us. His head is dipped down to his chest like he's weighed down in thought. His blonde hair is still pulled back into a leather tie, but he's already changed out of his fighting gear into light cotton trousers and a silk tunic.

How that man can do so much in such a short amount of time borders on crazy. His behaviour is beginning to rattle my nerves. He knows who she is, and it scares him.

I make my way over to the bed, sitting on the edge, I wait for Jack to decide how to go about this.

CHAPTER TWO

*J*ack

When they had her in that forsaken place, I could feel her energy from five miles away. Denial is not something I have ever indulged in, yet that energy can only come from something as pure as life itself. Something unspoilt, untouched and still in tune with what it means to be alive. I told myself that there could be no possible way that there was one of her kind there, that perhaps the energy was being emitted from a piece of technology instead. Then it moved and I knew I had to follow it.

Ayrans are close to what humans were before the parasite invasion over seven thousand years ago. History, as humans understand it, was retold and manipulated, making them all feel tiny and insignificant. Memories were erased and the mind was hijacked. DNA was rewritten, and all knowledge of their origins removed and destroyed.

Mid Arch was still free from the parasite the last time I visited, before getting stuck here in Gaia. There seems to be a barrier that it cannot pass. Unfortunately, that could not be said for the scum which would occasionally find their way into Mid Arch. I spent much of my childhood in Mid Arch, growing up with the Ayran children and learning how to move as they do. No other race can move that way. We would visit as often as we could, bringing gifts that they would usually find amusing.

The journey to Mid Arch from my homeland of Fresbeck would take us weeks, but as soon as we stepped across the boundary into their land, time seemed to shift. They have no sun or moon to tell night from day, and it disorients the mind. Many times, I tried to climb to the tops of their Ancient Trees which are taller than any skyscraper in Gaia. The girth of the mature ones is at least a mile wide, and they stretch so high the tops could not be seen from the undergrowth. Their lower branches are so thick you could comfortably fit a village on them. When I came of age, I tried to scale them, to see what was above the dense canopy of thick, lush, colourful foliage. Yet when I reached a particular apex, I would either pass out or forget why I was climbing. After the twelfth time of falling and breaking too many bones, leaving me out of 'The Chase' for the summer, I gave up. I asked the Ayrans what could be seen beyond the treetops, but they only ever replied, 'It is only for those with eyes to see'.

Turning back to face the room, I make my way over to Rolland and look him in the eye, hoping he understands how austere I am. "Be ready, Rolland. I am unsure of how long this will take or even if it will work on the first attempt." Puzzled at my lack of confidence no doubt, he raises an eyebrow in question.

Placing my left hand on her forehead, I take a calming breath and prepare myself for another onslaught of her mind.

Dropping down into her mind... is easy, which it should not be. All Ayrans have natural defences within their minds to prevent intrusion, unlike humans. Humans are only able to

16

muster a small shield which is fragile, even after years of practice. Her mind, however, is nothing like what I expected it to be. There are no memories to look on, no thought paths to see and no emotions to feel. It is empty, though it is clear she has buried it all somewhere.

As I look around me at the beach I stand on, I find it very similar to those found on Gaia, except the sand under my feet which is black and has no softness to it. To my right is the sea, which is an unusual grey colour, with waves that seem to be calming from the storm that just passed. When I dropped into her mind previously, a raging storm greeted me with the full intent of destroying me. I eventually found her, curled up in a cocoon on the clifftop to my left. This time the sky is scorched and torn, most likely from continuous attacks, although I cannot be sure as it is new to my eyes. With no prominent place to start searching for her, I start off toward the same area I found her before.

Following the path I took last time up the cliff, I begin pulling myself up using tufts of grass and tree roots. No other sounds to be heard except the waves that still crash against the giant rocks beneath me as the wind ripples through my hair like a caress.

Finally reaching the top, I pull myself up onto my feet and I begin making my way toward the spot I found her in previously. Long grass taller than me grows to my right and I can see what looks to be a mountain in the very far distance. Nothing here is what can be seen in Mid Arch. Some areas perhaps but not in the heart where all Ayrans live. There are small trees like those found just outside of The Dark Lands, and there are others that look like those from Gaia, all scattered about.

The ground beneath my feet is dry, as though it has not

rained in months, which is a complete contradiction to the storm that was here just a short time ago.

As I pass another blackened tree that seems to have no life within it, I come to the large boulders she was curled up between before. Except now she is not here. My heart skips a beat, knowing I have been here far too long already. Time is elusive within someone's mind. Much like when the mind is in a dream state, it feels as though you have just closed your eyes, but hours have passed. Yet, you could sit and watch a wall, feeling each moment pass, like it is an eternity.

I look at the mountain in the distance, wondering if she has taken refuge there. I begin walking through the long grass, pushing it aside as I go.

After what feels like too long, a noise pulls my attention to the right of the grass. I freeze, allowing my ears to readjust to the silence that now comes from my lack of movement. I wait patiently. Breathing steady.

The snap of a twig pulls at my ears from the right again. Moving slowly, I keep alert, ignoring the snapping of grass under my feet. Eventually, the grass begins to thin, opening out into a clearing that has many boulders off to the right. Another tree that looks more like those found on Gaia stands strong and healthy toward the back. Stepping softly, I begin looking amongst the boulders, hoping she is here. My heart starts to race slightly as time feels like it pokes at my back, reminding me of what happens if I stay too long.

Within the last pile of large boulders, I finally see her. Curled tightly into a ball within her cocoon, my heart breaks for her. Seeing her like this within her mind is beyond a doubt the saddest I have felt for many years. The cocoon is made up of translucent colours that move and swirl amongst each other. An Ayran foetus sack membrane is made up of the same energy and substance as the one she is using. Impenetrable, yet so delicate to look upon.

I crouch down, moving slowly so as not to scare her, and as I get closer, I can see she is trembling, seeming to struggle to take a full breath. Her head is tucked into her chest, with her arms pulled over her head. My foot makes a small sound and she freezes.

"It is just me again," I say softly, but she keeps herself frozen. "I had to leave. But I am not going anywhere this time." Still, she does not move, though a slight tremor makes its way across her shoulders. "My name is Jack, a Tyrian, and you have my word that I would never hurt you or one of your kind," I speak softly to her, hoping some of my words will reach her ears through all her fear. "Just take a deep breath, there is no one else here except us." She does not respond, keeping her body tightly wound up.

Running my hand over her cocoon so she can feel my energy, it pulses back at me, indicating to me that she is exploring me, searching and testing to see if my words are true. Static travels up my fingers and along my arm, searching for falsehood. She finally lifts her head a fraction, but I still cannot see her eyes.

Wind picks up behind me, and I begin to wonder if another storm is manifesting. She shivers as it curls around the cocoon.

"You are going to be fine, sweet Ayran. You are safe now. No one is going to hurt you."

Thunder begins to rumble from behind me and I curse it internally. She trembles harder, pulling her head back within herself.

"Just listen to my voice, not the storm, just my voice," I say to her, keeping my voice as soft as I can. Her shoulders relax. "Good girl. Now take a deep breath and focus on the

air going through your lungs." She takes a small breath, but trembles again.

Another roll of thunder breaks behind me. I feel time closing in at my back and I wonder how long I have been here.

"Can you tell me your name?" I ask gently. She does not say anything, and doubt starts to ebb away at me as to whether I will be able to pull her from here.

"Kia," she finally responds, her voice barely a whisper.

I feel my whole body sigh in relief. Without realising it, my head leans forward to rest onto her cocoon, static washing through my mind. I pull my head back to look at her again.

She finally looks up from her arms and I get my first look at her beautiful blue sapphire eyes. Even though she has been crying the whites of her eyes are still clear. The deep blue of her irises swirl like the wind around us. Stunned at their beauty, I feel myself becoming lost in them. Her soul is still whole, still there, just torn apart. It feels like a thousand years since I have seen eyes of such beauty. All Ayrans have the same multi-coloured eyes that change with their moods, but hers seem so much more profound. I cannot say I have ever seen another Ayran with eyes that swirl like hers as if an artist has dipped its coloured brush into clean water to rinse it.

Internally I shake myself out of it, so I can find my tongue again. "I know how hard this is, but I ask you to trust me." Her eyes search mine.

Another roll of thunder breaks through, and it sounds like it is just behind me now. She trembles at the sound of it but keeps her eyes steady on mine. Rain starts up, along with another roll of thunder, and she buries her head back into her arms again.

"Listen to my voice, Kia, not the storm. I am right here. Just you and me. The storm is just noise, nothing else." I keep speaking softly to her, but she continues to cry into her arms.

My heart seems to hurt, as though someone has put a blade through it. Taking another deep breath, I lean my head onto her cocoon, wondering how I am ever going to get her out of here.

The static barrier between us drops, and I let out a breath of relief, though I do not raise my head yet. A few moments later I hear movement and I chance a look up. She is sitting up straighter but with her arms curled around her middle.

Giving into my desire, I pull her into my arms without another thought. She is trembling but thankfully does not push me away. Stroking her hair as I hold her in my arms, she finally calms down enough to look up.

I could lose myself in her eyes, honestly, lose track of who I am or why I am here. They remind me of my homeland and its people. Clear of any deception or lies. Truth and innocence are all that shine back. The purity of life still within its meaning.

Without realising it, my head has moved closer to hers. My mind has shut down as though it is under the control of my body, with no rational thought remaining, just a single need to taste her lips, to feel home and whole again.

My lips touch hers and the full force of her emotions hit me. Fear is still rolling through her, but desire is right on its heels, giving chase. And simmering just under the surface of it all, the desperate need to also feel complete.

A small thought to stop my foolishness rises but is squashed by the need to feel more of her.

Tracing her lips with my tongue, I hear her breath hitch. Her hand moves up my neck as she opens her lips to me. I doubt I will ever get enough of the taste of her. Warmth spreads through me and I feel her body relax against me completely.

Being switched off to my own emotions and desires for so long, I risk losing myself to her. My own need for more starts to rise and I am not sure I have any strength to fight it, to fight her.

I continue to explore her mouth and hear her breathe deeply as I push some of my energy into her.

I finally find the strength to stop and pull back from her lips. When I do, it is to see her eyes shining with tiny specs of silver stars deep within them. Her pupils are dilated, and I know I have her full attention.

"Listen to my voice, Kia. I am right here with you, angel," I say as I pull her to her feet with me, so we are both standing.

The next part of pulling her back is a lot harder.

"I cannot ask you to trust me, but you can still trust yourself." She blinks but holds my gaze. "Close your eyes and tell me what you can hear?" I ask softly.

A moment passes before she closes her eyes, tightening her grip on my back. I can tell she is hearing the storm around us, not the sounds on the surface.

"The storm is not real, Kia, it is just inside you. Listen to your heartbeat." A small crease appears on her forehead.

Pulling partly from her mind so that my awareness is upon the surface as well as in her mind, I speak to her aloud, pulling her back to her physical body. "Kia, angel, wake up for me."

She lurches awake faster than I expected and jolts from Rolland's arms. Rolland makes a grab for her but is too slow and she falls to the floor, landing on her side.

She recovers fast and begins scrambling away on her

hands and feet. Rolland sounds as though he is struggling to catch his breath after the onslaught of her pain.

"Kia, it is me, Jack," I say, still using my home language to speak to her. She glances at me, but her eyes flash back to Rolland just as her arms give out, unable to hold her weight, and she falls limply to the floor again.

I scoop her back into my arms as I speak. "Rolland, sit on the bed with your back to the headboard. Let us try this again. Perhaps if she does not see you when she first opens her eyes, we may have a chance of keeping her awake long enough to calm her."

Rolland is still hunched over on the floor, trying to catch his breath. He looks up at me with eyes full of questions.

The longer it takes to get back into her mind, the more time she has to run.

"How can someone so small, feel so much pain and still be alive?" His voice is a mixture of disbelief and awe.

Taking a deep breath, I give him the only information that I know to be true. "She is stronger than all of us put together, Rolland. I do not have time to explain... please, I beg of you. Get on the bed and prepare yourself if you want to help or I shall take her to someone else that can."

He's up in a heartbeat, taking her from me. "She's not going anywhere, arsehole. She stays in my arms, or I'll cut your pretty little head off of your shoulders while Seb makes kebab sticks with your eyeballs if you so much as think of moving her from this house." He means every word of it.

"Good. Now please hurry up, you are wasting time." A sharpness comes with my words that I did not intend to slip out, but my heart is pounding knowing she can be anywhere within such a vast space.

He repositions himself on the bed as I instructed him to do and curls her small frame against his chest.

Sebastian covers her with the blanket. I had almost forgotten he was here. His ability to blend into the shadows is exceptional.

Positioning myself so that I kneel on one leg in front of them on the bed, I take another look up into Rolland's eyes.

He stares back with a look of determination this time. Closing my eyes again, I place my hand along her forehead, slipping back into her mind far too quickly.

I land back in the opening with the boulders, but she is not amongst them. Looking up at the mountain, I start running toward it. A part of me knows she is there. Unsure of what going into that mountain will mean, I push harder.

I come to a halt when I find the entrance guarded by two giant lions, closer to the size of heavy weight horses than those of regular lions on Gaia. Their deep, honey colour fur and bronze manes appear a little darker under their wings which are folded high behind their backs, shadowing their head's slightly.

As I come to a halt, they both stand, preparing themselves to pounce. Two sets of eyes glow back, stopping me in my tracks. Their tails flick in annoyance to my presence, daring me to move.

I feel entirely out of my depth with how to proceed. Never in all my life have I ever come across a mind like this. If they strike me, will they have any real effect on me?

One of the winged lion's attention is pulled to the entrance of the mountain, but the other continues to stare down at me with deep golden eyes. I feel as though it is running a claw down my insides. The first winged lion turns and heads off into the mountain, leaving the second to watch me. I keep my eyes steady, hoping with all my heart it sees nothing but the truth within me.

The remaining winged lion sniffs at the air. My stomach

drops out slightly, but I cannot leave her here.

The lion takes a step forward and my instinct is to step back, but I keep my stance steady, yet not threatening. It takes another couple of steps closer, continuing to sniff the air.

My people are all about confidence, never letting the opponent see your fears or weaknesses. Years of practice is put into masking each emotion, controlling the body's urges and needs.

Applying every ounce of control over my body, I remain calm, focusing on getting to Kia, not on the thousand-pound lion that wants to eat me.

I hear a purr as it gets closer, which puzzles me. A few more steps brings the lion within touching distance. It continues to purr as it walks around me, coming to a halt as it stands on my other side.

I take a tentative step forward and since he makes no move, I continue, hearing his purr grow louder as I move away.

Picking up the pace, I move into the mountain's entrance and follow the tunnel around till it opens out into a large pit. My eyes find Kia standing to the side, looking down into the abyss with such longing, I wonder what holds her back.

None of this makes any rational sense. It is more like taking a step into a dream than her thoughts. How has she been able to do this?

"Kia, what is down there?" I question, my voice echoing off of the walls. I would think it would startle her, yet she stands entranced by the pit.

I move closer to her, looking around for the first winged lion, but it is nowhere to be found.

I get within reaching distance of her, hoping to grab her if she steps off. "What is down there, sweet angel?" I ask again, looking down into the abyss. Light flickers off the walls of the cave from torches onto her face, catching on the tears that fall freely toward the ground.

"Me," spoken as a whisper, but its echoes off the walls, seeming to sound louder than my own. I frown, puzzled by her answer.

"Kia, I know you are afraid and looking for comfort, but you are stronger than this, I can feel it." Her foot moves forward an inch. "Just give me another chance, I beg you, Kia... please."

She turns her head to the right slightly. "It hurts and there is so much darkness out there." Another tear tracks down her cheek.

I chance another step closer. Kia looks up into my eyes and it feels as if she is holding me there. "One more chance, Kia, and if I fail you, I will not stop you next time." She looks back into the abyss with such yearning.

I offer her my hand, but she hesitates. "I just want to go home," she says. Her voice is so small, but she turns to me taking my hand.

Pulling her into my arms, I feel her take her own breath of relief. "Let us try this again, angel," I speak into her ear. "Tell me what you feel, Kia?"

I wait for her reply, but I can feel time pushing at my back again.

Moving her head to the side as though trying to follow a sound. "It has a different rhythm to my own." I realise she is hearing Rolland's heartbeat.

This should work.

"Concentrate on that sound and nothing else, Kia. Do not look or listen to anything more. Just the steady beat and rhythm of that heart." I feel her body relax against me and as I start to pull myself back to the surface, I feel her coming with me this time.

CHAPTER THREE

*R*olland

Her pain creeps back slowly this time and I
ready myself for the onslaught. It takes every ounce of my
control not to move or make a sound, afraid I might startle
her again.

I feel every broken bone, cut, bruise, sprain and burn she
has travel through my own body as I pull it all away from her
and into me. There are three broken ribs on her front left side
and four on the back right. The sprains she has in both hands
ache deeply and there's a substantial pulsing on the back of
her head. The fire from her back hits me and a wave of dizzi-
ness rolls over me. I wonder if it's her pain causing it or my
own body trying to give in from taking in too much so fast.
Wanting to confirm I've gotten it all, I continue to search her
body for any part that I might have missed, starting at her
head and working my way down. All is good until I get to her
legs, where ripples of pain shiver up from her knee joints and
sharp stabbing currents come up from her feet.

This piece of my gift took years to master, yet it still feels like I'm missing something crucial. For a while it's easy to take on the pain of another entity, displacing it, however, is far more difficult. The whole process is incredibly draining both physically and mentally, but I eventually found that carrying it as weight seems to work best, although it gets tiring fast. Burying the pain within me seems natural, yet the consequences of doing so means I end up out of it for days.

I feel her head move to the side, but I keep my eyes shut. *Fuck. How can someone so small endure that much pain? Every inch of her body is wracked with it.*

Jack's smooth voice sounds nearby, speaking to her in his language, one that none of us can understand. *Does that mean she's from his homeland?* Her energy is different from his or anyone I've ever met, but she seems to recognise it, as she nods her head once in response to whatever he asked. I hear him say my name and I feel her head turn up, but I continue to keep my eyes closed.

Unexpectedly her emotions come bubbling up, threatening to overthrow my concentration as I continue to work on her pain. With my last remaining amount of focus, I push some calming warmth into her tired, overwrought body. After a few seconds, I feel her relax completely and curl into me. I'm glad for all of the years I've had practising this technique, as I doubt I would've had the strength to do this otherwise.

A few minutes pass and I hear Jack's voice spill through my concentration. I've got a firm grip on the balance now, so it doesn't distract me. "Rolland, her name is Kia and she is in desperate need of rest and nourishment to heal her body. Some of her memories will be buried deep within her mind so she will be acting on instinct alone now. I will be back shortly with some crystals to help heal her mind, so she can understand you." His voice moves to my right as he stands.

"Sebastian, once she has some nourishment in her, you

28

can start to heal her slowly. She has no reserves left, so any extra strain will push her to revert back to the safety of her mind." His voice is further away, but not far enough that I can't hear him. "I will be back as soon as I can." He says something else in his language and I feel Kia stiffen but nod. Fear is still pouring out of her in buckets, but she curls back into me.

Times stretches on and I'm not sure if I've been laying here for five minutes or five hours. Her fear has subsided slightly, becoming more like a dull throb than a sharp ache. Continuing to pull her pain away, I open my eyes to chance a look.

Deep blue eyes look back at me and I'm drawn to the specks of silver swirling within them. They're like two moving marbles in the night sky and I can't help but feel like I'm looking at life itself. Her eyes search mine for something, maybe my soul? I don't fight her gaze - I have nothing to hide except my fear of her leaving the safety of my embrace. My arms tighten a fraction in response to the thought, but her reaction isn't what I expected. Instead of pushing away, she curls herself deeper into my chest and I feel her arm move around my waist.

Closing my eyes again, I feel her relax completely into me. As she does, her hand touches my open wound. She gasps as she sits up quickly. *Damn it, I should have had Seb heal it earlier.*

I open my eyes again to see her staring at me. Her brow is furrowed in confusion and puzzlement, as she looks at her small fingers covered in my blood.

Seb's bed sheets will have my blood soaking through them. *Good! Serves him right for being such a cocky shit earlier.*

The blanket around her shoulders slips down, but she

doesn't seem to notice or care. Moving slowly so as not to frighten her, I pull it back up over her shoulders. Her eyes search mine again. It's as though she's examining my own emotions, but all I feel is the need to protect her, to take away every ounce of pain her body endures. She relaxes and leans forward, resting her head on my chest.

A few moments later I hear Seb's footfalls making their way through the house toward us. Kia stiffens slightly in alarm.

"Shh it's okay, Kia, it's just Sebastian," I reassure her in my quietest voice. Rubbing my hand up her back, I feel a massive wave of pain slam through me. Moving my hand away slowly from her back, I move it to her head and begin to wonder what other marks and bruises she has that we still haven't seen.

Seb appears in the doorway with a tray in his hands. If having skills in the kitchen was said to be a gift, then that would be another of his. I can't cook for shit, but Seb's a natural. The smell of something hits my senses and I can't help the moan that escapes me.

Kia flinches, probably thinking I'm in pain again. I open my eyes and give her a small smile to show her I'm okay, but she just looks back in confusion. Seb makes his way round to the other side of the bed where there's room for him to sit, placing the tray of soups down as he does.

Kia keeps her eyes on me for several more seconds before turning her head in Seb's direction. He freezes in his movements, like a deer caught in the headlights. As a bystander, it's amusing to watch. Seb is just as lost to her as I am.

I'm starving, and my body needs nourishment to replenish the blood loss and the energy I'm using to keep her pain away. My stomach rumbles and Kia's head whips back toward me. *Has she seriously never heard a stomach rumble before?*

Seb releases the breath he's been holding in and moves slowly to pass me a bowl of soup first. Kia's eyes track his movement, looking at it like it's going to hurt me. Her reactions are becoming a little concerning, but I take the bowl from Seb. It smells like his vegetable soup. I haven't a clue what's in it, but it's a hearty meal he saves for occasions when one of us takes a hammering.

Kia still eyes it up as though she wants to knock it out my hand, but after a few spoonful's she looks down at the bowl in my lap. I see the moment the smell hits her senses as I watch her pink tongue sneak out to wet her beautiful lips. I take a spoonful of the soup, savouring the flavours. *Damn that man can cook.*

"Did I tell you how amazing you are, Brother?" I'm still looking at Kia but aim my words at Seb. He moves closer to us, taking the second bowl into his hands.

After a few more spoonful's, I attempt to sit up, but the pain from the still open bullet wound washes over me. I slump back tiredly against the headboard as the bowl gets whipped away from my grasp.

I feel Kia try to get off my lap, but I manage to find her hips, keeping her firmly in place. "My bad, my bad," I say through clenched teeth.

Checking that I still have a good grip on her pain as well as my own, I chance to open my eyes to find two angry sets focused on me. Kia's dark blue ones are like slow spinning marbles and Seb's cognac ones look about ready to knock me out.

"If your done being a spoilt princess, can I heal you now?" Seb says quietly through tight lips.

"Yeah, yeah, just get on with it already," I tell him. I can tell Kia doesn't understand us as I feel her begin to panic. "Kia, you're okay." I point to my side and then to Seb, pushing some more of my comforting energy into her.

She seems to understand as she doesn't go to move away again or stop Seb from coming closer. Seb lowers himself down onto his haunches and lifts my shirt. He rests his hand carefully on the wound and I feel warmth begin to spread up my side. I can feel muscles stitching themselves back together and my skin rebuilding itself.

I let out a deep sigh of relief at the same time I feel Kia's hand move to see if it's healed. I can feel her own relief seep through and when I look up, it's to find her watching Seb, her eyes wide and thoughtful. He sits back on the other side of the bed, passing me back the bowl of soup. Kia looks on with more interest in the soup this time. Instead of mistrust in her eyes now, there's curiosity. I take a spoonful of soup and hold it up to her lips, hoping she'll take some. She opens her mouth and sips the soup tentatively and another spike of pain flares up as she swallows. Just as I thought earlier, her throat and vocal cords are damaged.

Taking the spoon back, I offer her another mouthful which she sips more willingly. The thought occurs that I could pass her the bowl so that she could feed herself, but from what I saw of her hands earlier, I doubt she could even hold the spoon.

I feel her trust build with each spoonful of soup she accepts from me but when a small crease appears on her forehead, I wonder what has her looking suddenly confused. She glances up to meet my eyes again, opening her mouth as though to speak, but nothing comes out.

Pain flares up and I realise she's trying to speak but can't. She closes her eyes and slumps her head and shoulders forward. Frustration seeps through and my heart breaks for her. I sit up without a struggle this time, trying to comfort her.

Taking her head in my hand, I lift it up so she's not bent forward, and I try to get her attention. "Kia, what is it? What has you so sad?" She looks back down at the bowl and then back up at me.

Surely it can't be because she's eaten all my soup. "The soup? Is that what has you so sad?" I look over at Seb who seems just as puzzled as I do. "Pass me the other bowl and please tell me you made more." He passes me the one meant for her then is up and out the door before I finish.

After she empties the second bowl, her eyelids start to droop, so I pull her forward gently and find not much encouragement is needed. She snuggles deeper into my arm, her face buried into my lower chest. One of her hands loops around my back and the other clings to my shirt. Her fingers look black and blue with a couple looking dislocated. *How she's holding onto my shirt is a mystery.*

A few moments later, Seb reappears with more bowls. "I thought your soup was magic before, but now I'm beginning to question if you're slipping something more than food into it," I joke, trying to pull a smile from him.

His lips twitch, but he doesn't laugh. "Don't give me ideas, Brother. I may just do that the next time you decide to refuse to let me heal you," he responds as he takes his former place on the other side of the bed. "Did she eat much more?" he inquires, keeping his voice low, his usual smoky tone more intense.

"She took a second bowl then gave in to her body's need to sleep." My stomach rumbles again, so Seb passes me another bowl. Three servings later and I feel my energy levels begin to replenish.

Closing my eyes to help refocus on drawing her pain

away, I feel Seb climb off of the bed followed by the sounds of him cleaning up. Kia's hand tightens reflexively on my shirt as she burrows herself into my side and I settle us down deeper into the bed.

Something tells me it's going to be a very long night.

CHAPTER FOUR

*J*ack

As I return to Sebastian's room, my hand reaches into my pocket to gently rub the beautiful black gem, known as Gauldrix, that lies quietly within and I cannot help but wonder if Kia will recognise it. Stones, gems, and crystals are not mined back in my homeland and it is considered a crime to remove them.

When my homeland was invaded, all of our homes were destroyed by the same infestation that now riddles Gaia, but I managed to take a few pieces of what remained of one of the last Ancient Trees that had fallen. The Ancient Trees grew higher than any skyscraper I have seen on this plane and could house thousands of families, heal any wound or infection, and held all of the secrets of our ancestors. The Gauldrix still carries the same power as it once did, but it needs the energy of another living thing to power it. Back home, it would have been powered by The Source but now that it is cut off, it sits dormant.

The room is peacefully quiet as I stand there looking at Kia curled up in Rolland's lap, taking in her stunning beauty.

My eyes home in on her small hand as it clutches Rolland's shirt, helping to settle my mind knowing she has found some semblance of comfort whilst I was gone. I also cannot help but hope that some measure of trust was earned as well, even if only a little.

Movement to the right pulls at my attention. Sebastian is staring at me with the same tortured look in his eyes that he had earlier. His dark hair has taken the brunt of his frustration and as I watch, the lines on his forehead deepen and a muscle in his jaw begins to tick. Bowls are piled up beside him, but the water jug does not look to have been touched. Ayrans drink water purified by The Source at the heart of Mid Arch, but the water here is full of the same parasites that have taken over Gaia and there are very few ways of cleansing it fully. I walk over to the water jug and drop a small Brondroll stone into it, which should only take a few minutes to cleanse the water.

"How much longer do I need to wait?" Sebastian's refined tone is tight, yet he is keeping considerable calm given the circumstances.

"How much has she eaten?" I glance over at her briefly before shifting my eyes to meet Sebastian's.

"Two bowls." No emotions come through his words. *I am impressed that she managed so much in her first sitting.*

"See if you can get her to take a bowl of rice. Keep it simple and stick with vegetables. Use one of the Brondroll stones to cleanse the water before you boil it. Once she has eaten that, take her through to your healing bath. Do not overdo it, Sebastian. Just a little at a time, or you will do more damage than good," I inform, while moving back to the other side of the bed, taking the space remaining by Rolland's leg

Sebastian makes his way out of the room but stops at the

door. "Who is she, Jack?" he asks before letting out a breath of frustration, then turns back to me, waiting for me to answer. *Is he ready? I have kept so much from them all for so long.*

"She is what is known as an Ayran, although not much is known about them. Their homeland, which we call Mid Arch, is realms outside the ice circle. The outer area that surrounds their lands is only passable by foot, and for reasons unknown to us, their land is impenetrable by The Swarm. I visited on many occasions whilst growing up, learning the ways to channel The Source. It is her direct connection to The Source that is enhancing Rolland's protective nature, and why you feel the need to heal her more than your need to take your next breath."

I pause as I glance over at Kia before continuing. "They are closest to the origin of all humanoid life as we know it. Their energy is still pure and uncorrupted, attractive to all of the life around them. Unless we can find a way to cleanse her of the infection that plagues Gaia, it will take over her body and mind, destroying her memory and leaving her with no knowledge of who she is or where she came from, just like the rest of human life on Gaia." I look back at Kia. Her eyes are open, as she studying's me.

"Thank you for your honesty, Jack, I won't forget it." He turns and leaves, pulling the door closed behind him with a soft click.

I open my hand to show Kia the Gauldrix stone. She looks on curiously but does not show any signs of being angry with me for having it. Her hand reaches out to touch it, but she quickly snatches it back and retreats under the blanket, her eyes full of confusion. That was not the reaction I was expecting from her and I pause momentarily to sort my thoughts.

"This will help heal your mind, Kia, so you can under-stand Rolland and Sebastian." Her eyes meet mine with trust and understanding as I gently place the stone in her hand. "I will do the work, just do not fight me, alright?" She looks back up and nods. As our hands touch, her eyes begin to swirl and her lips part. The memory of us kissing flashes through my mind and she gasps. *I did not mean that to slip through - what is wrong with me?*

"What are you doing, Jack?" Rolland's hearty voice comes from behind Kia.

Ignoring him, I focus on the Gauldrix in her palm and begin sending my energy through it, which travels up her arm and into her shoulders. I can visibly see her body relax as she folds back into Rolland.

The knock to the back of her head may well be the reason she cannot decipher all languages right now. The area of the brain that is responsible for speech is in the frontal lobe in humans. But an Ayrans' brain is mapped out slightly differ-ently and their speech center is in the back. It is slightly larger, and the neural pathways are always shifting, depending on what language they are listening to.

Finding the part at the back of her mind that needs healing should be easy. The pressure on that one spot from the injury is causing a build-up of energy and the power from the Gauldrix will release the blockage, healing the injury. *If only it could be used to heal the rest of her mind and body*.

"She should be able to understand most of what you are saying now, Rolland. Some words will be unfamiliar to her, but she should pick them up quick enough." I open my eyes to find them both staring back at me.

Rolland looks down at Kia, who continues to watch me for a heartbeat before sitting up and turning to face Rolland. She would be trying to speak if her vocal cords were not so badly injured. Rolland sits mesmerized by those deep blue sapphire eyes, just like a moth drawn to a flame.

"How about a drink, Kia?" I ask in English. She nods in response but keeps her attention on Rolland. I walk around to the other side of the bed, filling a glass with water and passing it to Rolland, hoping he can coax her to drink it.

"Kia, I promised my help to a few people, so I need to leave for a short period. Rolland will not leave your side until I return, and once you have the strength, Sebastian will try to heal some of your injuries." She finally looks over at me and gives a small nod. Grateful for her acceptance, I make my way to the door. But before I can get halfway there, Rolland calls out, "Jack, wait."

When I turn back around, I see Kia, even in her weakened state, trying to get out of Rolland's lap. With one hand still clinging tightly to Rolland's shirt, she uses the other to pull me back to her. I run my hand soothingly down the back of her head, the action calming us both. If I stay any longer, I will not be able to leave her side at all, but I am comforted with the knowledge that there is a trace of my energy left in her mind, should she fall back into its depths.

She finally releases me and I take a step back. Her eyes are swirling fast with her emotions, and in my own language I assure her, "you have my word, I will not be gone long, sweet Ayran." With one last gentle touch on her cheek, I hurriedly make my way out of the room, before I can change my mind.

CHAPTER FIVE

*S*ebastian

My mind is still going over Jack's words about cleansing Kia. The infection that he spoke of is visible, but is often mistaken for rot, fungus, mould or disease as it drains the life out of all living things in Gaia, causing them to die in an unnatural way. Because of it, and the loss of our memories from The Swarm, we're trapped here. Images will sometimes surface, like a teaser in a movie trailer, but then slip away, leaving me with nothing but a headache that lasts for hours.

Jack still remembers a significant amount but trying to get information from him is like pulling blood from a stone. And even when he does share knowledge, it always feels like he's only giving us bits and pieces of the whole. What we do know of our origins is that we come from the lands outside the ice circle that surround Gaia. But between the large amount of armed guards and the deadly snow storms that encompass the area, it's virtually impenetrable and deadly.

We do know that Mid Gaia, which is occupied by Atlantians, is free from the infection because of the barrier that surrounds it and the turning away of those that have been infected. My stomach churns at the thought of Kia being stuck here like us, without any memories, but then the thought of her leaving us makes my heart race faster than a hummingbird's wings. *What the hell is wrong with me?* Jack's words explaining how her connection to The Source enhances our natural traits play through my mind. *Is that really what this is?* Shaking my head to clear it, I turn my focus back to making some food.

The kitchen is the heart of the house, where we all congregate, so I designed the kitchen with an open floor plan. In the middle of the room is a large island with an attached breakfast bar that makes it into a T shape, this is so I can still talk to the guys whilst cooking. A hob with eight burners is located in the middle of the island. As both me and Gerry have a passion for cooking, a regular hob just wasn't going to cut it. A small sink sits to the right of the hob and has instant hot water with a built-in filter to remove the fluoride - though Matt still won't drink it, preferring it bottled. To the far right of the island, from where I stand, is a beautiful, yet solid, long dark wooden table surrounded by a plethora of chairs. The main sink sits to my back, which looks out over the front garden of the house. Patio doors are located to the right of the main sink and open out onto the deck which has light wooden furniture scattered around. Spot-lights give the kitchen a freshness, along with the white doors and sandy tiles beneath my feet. The summer sun is just beginning to trickle in through the windows behind me, bouncing off the black marble worktops.

Halfway through cooking the rice, I turn my head to see Matt amble through the doors from the main dining area, his head down and his focus fully on the phone in his hand. I chuckle quietly to myself. Every time I see him, he either has his nose in a book or his eyes glued to a screen - it's a wonder he doesn't ever run into anything. It wouldn't be the first time he's been in and out of the kitchen without noticing my presence. *With any luck this will be one of those times.*

Matt's the shortest of all of us at just under six feet, but his wide shoulders and chest are strong and solidly built. A sharp jawline and slightly pointed chin give his face a refined, almost aristocratic appearance which is further emphasized by the silver rimmed glasses that rest lightly on his perfectly straight nose. His usually fresh face, however, is still looking tired and a bit haggard from lack of sleep. Ash brown hair, which is still slightly damp from the shower, hangs down just past his ears and is in obvious need of a trim. He's wearing a crisp, light blue shirt that he has rolled up to his elbows and a pair of khakis, his usual attire unless we're out on a job or mission.

My eyes follow him as he makes his way round the breakfast bar, heading toward the fridge on my left and I make sure to be as quiet as a church mouse in order to evade the questions I know he will have. I gave him the smallest amount of information when we got off of the chopper, but I know I'm going to have to tell him more. He grabs a bottle of water with his free hand and shoves it under his arm, before reaching for another, but that must be the last in the fridge as he fumbles slightly. *Shit, that means he has to look up.* As if hearing my thoughts, his head lifts and he finds me watching him. The bottle and phone slip from his grip, but his quick reflexes help him catch both items before they hit the floor.

"What the hell, Seb! Make some noise, would ya?" Matt scolds caustically, running his charcoal grey eyes over me with a glare. *He must be stressed to be using words such as 'hell'. Matt never swears.*

"If you had looked up when you came in, you would've

seen me. You should be more aware of your surroundings," I tease, lifting a brow mockingly.

He's lethal with his fists, but useless out on missions. I've only seen him raise his fist once when he was defending a woman back in America a hundred years ago. The only other time is when he spars with one of us.

Sliding his phone in his pocket, he begins restocking the fridge with water from the cupboard beside the fridge.

"So, how's our guest? Care to share anymore intel, or is she going to stay locked away in your room?" he asks playfully, looking over his shoulder.

Possessiveness rears its ugly head, curling its way up my back and I nick my finger with the knife. The cut heals instantly but that doesn't mean it doesn't sting like bitch. I try to pretend like nothing happened but unfortunately Matt's sharp eyes didn't miss it.

"What's going on, Seb?" he asks with concern, as he quickly finishes restocking the fridge and walks back over to me. His fresh mint shower gel hits my nose. I rub a hand over my face to try ridding myself of the feelings crawling around inside me.

"Jack said she's an Ayran. The closest race left to the origin of all humanoid beings. Every inch of her body is either bruised, burnt, broken or cut, and that's just what's on the surface. I can't heal her because she's too weak and has no nourishment within her. Jack's been in her head twice now, and each time he comes out, he looks more lost than when he went in. Rolland hasn't put her down since he found her, and it's taking every ounce of his concentration to draw her pain away so that she doesn't fall back into her own mind." I take another deep breath and remove the rice from the heat. When I glance over at Matt, he's stunned silent. Remembering I haven't yet given him the bullets that I removed from Kia and Rolland, I dig them out of my pocket and hold them out to him.

"Can you see if you can get a trace on either of these?" I ask. "I think Rolland's was laced with something, but the other looks clean." The last part coming out on a heavy sigh. There's no response from him and he still hasn't moved a muscle. *Maybe I said too much?*

"Matt!" I say louder. He startles, bringing his gaze back from where it had drifted to the floor.

Taking the bullets from my hand, he pushes his glasses up with the other as he takes a quick look at them, then nods. He says nothing as he grabs the bottle of water from the counter and lumbers out of kitchen. *What was that all about?*

I finish putting all the ingredients together for the simple rice dish I've been working on and head back to my room, keeping my steps at quiet as possible, the only sound being the forks moving against the bowls. Light spills in through the front door to my left as I make my way through the corridor to my room.

Thankfully the heavy door of my room is ajar, making it easier to push it open with my foot. Inside, I find the bed empty and my heart bottoms out. Sheer panic rips through me and I bellow, "Rolland! Kia!".

Curses come from the bathroom, and I take a deep breath as my relief floods through me. *What the hell are they doing in there?*

"Seb, quiet voices, Brother! Quiet voices! Your shouting nearly had me knocking myself out." Rolland's deep voice urges me through my head.

I start making my way over to the door to see what the hell is going on.

"It's not what it looks like, Seb, trust me. Well it's kind of what it looks like, but not as bad as you might think. Just

44

don't freak out and scare her to death for fuck sake." His words confuse me even more.

As I walk into the en-suite bathroom, what I see is not quite what I was expecting. The shower takes up one entire right-side wall of the room and standing under one of the many shower heads I see Rolland, shirt off, with only parts of Kia showing as most of her body is obscured by his broad muscular back. As I move closer, I can see that he has one hand on the wall, steadying them both and Kia's got both arms wrapped tightly around his neck, with her head buried deep into his left shoulder, hiding her face.

"Is she okay?" I ask him tentatively. She's shaking and I'm pretty sure it's not from lack of heat.

"You scared her with your big, fat, loud, mouth, you idiot," he bites out, but there's warmth to his words.

"*Sorry, man, the bed was empty. I panicked,"* I explain as I run my eyes over his tall frame that seems especially large with such a small body wrapped around it.

"Kia, it's just Sebastian, look," he speaks quietly into her hair, running his hand gently over her arm. "He didn't mean to frighten you, he's just being a hot head." And with that, she leans back from him to look over at me in puzzlement.

"He means I panicked, not that my head is actually hot," I try to explain as I see her small nose crinkled up.

She looks a lot fresher having some of the grime and dirt washed from her body. But now the bruises, burns and cuts on her arms seem to scream at me, demanding I heal each and every one of them. I bring my gaze back to her face to see it relax as she looks to Rolland for confirmation. He shrugs his shoulders, which must have jolted her, as the next moment his eyes close and his face screws up in concentration.

Grabbing two warm towels from the heater, I head back over to them. *This should be fun.*

45

"How are we going to do this, Rolland? I don't suppose you thought this through, did you?" I tease him lightly, looking him over. His honey coloured hair which just barely brushes his shoulder is sticking to his cheek slightly and he's breathing deeply.

"You wouldn't have either if you'd seen her face when I turned the tap on to wash her hands. Her reaction to the water was complete bliss, despite the amount of pain she is in. I thought she'd enjoy getting some of the grime and dirt washed off of her in the shower. Everything else was insignificant, to be honest," he rambles, his deep tone warming me, as it always does. *Now that I can believe.*

His river blue eyes are full of sympathy, but they've lost some of their shine. He's always so full of life, never able to take anything seriously for any length of time and finding fun in just about everything. You would almost think he's a teenager rather than the four-hundred-year-old man he is.

Kia's head now rests on Rolland's right shoulder, which is closest to me, and I can see her eyes studying me. Deep blue pools of slowly swirling gems look back at me and she truly looks relaxed for the first time since we've met. I find myself being pulled into those blue pools and I feel as if I am falling into a peaceful yet elusive dream. Silver specs glitter back, and my heart begins to race with desire.

"Seb…Seb…if you move any closer you'll be needing to change too." Rolland's voice sounds like it's being muffled, but I can still hear him… unfortunately.

Shit, how did I get so close?

My head is inches from hers and true to his point, I find I was nearly showering with them. Shaking my head to clear my thoughts, I turn my gaze away. It's time to get some food in her stomach, as the sooner she eats, the sooner I can start healing her broken bones.

46

"Kia, I'm going to help Rolland get out of his wet clothes, but he will need to set you down, so he's got better balance. Whatever you do, don't let go of him. He needs to remain in contact with you to keep the pain away, okay?" I explain gently.

With a single nod from Kia, Rolland moves from under the shower toward the marble covered dresser by the door as I turn the water off and follow them. He sets her down gingerly on the marble, careful to keep his left arm in contact with her body while his right hand rests next to her. I can see his arms slightly shaking and it's clear the fatigue of pushing his body and his gift far past what they are meant to endure is getting to him.

Kia has a grip on Rolland's neck and her eyes on his face. His eyes are closed, with his head bent forward. I drape one towel over his back and place another down next to Kia, then get to work removing his heavy boots and leather pants, internally cursing them for being such a bitch to remove. Once off, I grab a pair of cotton pants from one of the drawers and hold them open for Rolland to step into, but he doesn't move to put his feet into them. Looking up to see why he's not moving. I find him staring straight ahead at the mirror hanging on the wall behind Kia's back.

"What is it, Rolland?" I ask hesitantly.

Without answering me, he looks back down at me with glistening eyes and moves his feet into the pants, pulling them up with his right hand. I stand to see what he was looking at, but he picks up the towel I had set on the side and wraps it quickly around Kia before I get a chance to see anything.

"Later, Seb, let's just get her fed so you can start healing her," he says tightly, causing my gut to curl.

He gathers her fully into his arms with one hand under her

legs and the other across her back, before he walks back into the bedroom. Morning light spills in through the window where I left the heavy curtains open last night, bouncing off the deep plum walls and brightening the room.

Rolland takes Kia to the far side of the bed, the side that isn't covered in his blood, and settles down with her. Picking the bowls up from the cabinet where I had set them, I make my way over to the bed. The rice has probably gone cold, but it should still taste okay. Passing one to Rolland, I set the other on the bedside table and pull one of the large cushioned chairs closer.

"What say you to some rice, Kia?" Rolland offers lightly, but I can tell he's struggling to find his words. It could be from what he saw in the mirror, or because he's struggling with her pain levels, but either way, I think she senses it too, because her brows furrow with concern.

She goes to take the bowl from Rolland, but he pulls it out of her reach. "I got this. Let me help you, then we rest. Deal?" he suggests with raised eyebrows. It's clear she's still confused with some of the words he's using, but I think she grasps what he's trying to say.

He begins feeding her like he did with the soup and with every mouthful she takes, I feel my own anxiety lessen. Once she's finished, she drinks a glass of water then curls herself into Rolland's bare chest and turns to face me. Her eyes are slowly swirling, and the silver specs are clear in the bright light as her gaze wanders over my face then down my shoulders. They flash back up to meet mine and I'm not sure what she's thinking, but she doesn't seem alarmed.

Rolland's eyes are shut, and I think he's deep in his centre - not sleeping, but not fully aware of his surroundings either. I sense movement and the sound of metal catches my attentions, and I look over to see Kia's small hand reaching for mine. Her fingers are black and blue with bruises, three of which are broken. She still has the cuffs on her wrists that kept her chained to the wall.

I tentatively take her hand in mine, careful not to make any quick movements. Moving my gaze back to Kia I find her eyes closed. *Did she mean to comfort me?*

I start easing some of my energy into her fingers. But it's like holding back a dam. My energy's been trying to escape to heal her ever since I walked into the cellar she was kept in. Every spike in adrenaline has caused the energy behind my gift to surge.

Careful not to let it flood out. I begin to trickle it through her small fingers. The bones mend themselves back together and the bruises start to fade. Her wrists are also sprained, so I push a little more energy through, feeling the ligaments reattach themselves to the bones.

After a minute or so, her hand looks back to normal. I peek up to find her eyes back on me, searching for something.

"Can I do the other?" I ask quietly.

She pulls her mended hand back under the towel and slowly moves the other forward. I repeat the same process, fixing the bones, ligaments and soothing over the bruises. I go to pull my hand away, but her tiny fingers grasps it to stop me.

When I look back up, she closes her eyes, letting out a soft breath.

I watch her sleeping for a while before deciding to rest my head on the bed beside Rolland. With her left hand curled up in mine, I find some comfort finally.

S urrounded by dry air and sand, I hear voices calling for help somewhere. Looking around I find myself back in my first memory. The Sahara Desert.

So many lives lost, and too many families torn apart.

Making my way over to the village, a family I don't recognise calls to me. A small child lays in his mother's arms, her hands are covered in his blood. She calls to me for help, yet like every other time I have this dream, I try to heal the boy, but it's too late. He's lost too much blood and I can't save him.

The dream changes to another memory. Another life I couldn't save.

A woman lies with a knife deep in her chest. It's too late and her heart gives out. The man who put it there is long gone. My heart breaks and the need to destroy something festers within me.

The next dream slams into me hard, and I struggle to keep focus on my surroundings.

A shipwreck can be seen in the distance on a stormy sea. This memory is from not too long ago, in the turn of the last century. My Brothers and I were traveling by ship, when we came across an island. Another ship tried to berth there too, but the storm took it off course, destroying the whole vessel and crew. Not a single life could be saved.

My heart hurts from the onslaught of my memories. Wishing I could have saved them.

The dream doesn't fade this time, but a disembodied voice pulls my attention away from the wreck – a voice I don't recognise, comes from behind me.

I turn and find a cliff with a grey stone building at the top. I don't recollect the cliff or building, but the screams coming *from it, are enough to have my feet moving without second thought.*

Making my way toward the cliff, I begin my ascent up its side, listening for any more screams coming from the building, but none come. Once I reach the top, I take in the building in front of me. Sections of it are incredibly old, six hundred years maybe. Other parts look brand new. The doors and windows are all in place, but parts of the roof are crumbling. The sound of a door slamming shut comes from the second floor. Screwing my eyes shut to try and wake from the dream, I find that I can't. I'm trapped here. Where am I? This isn't real, I know it's not, but I can't pull myself out of it.

Curious as to what the building is, I make my way over and start looking through the windows. Blackness is all I can see, not even my own reflection. Three windows on the second floor have lights on, so I start climbing the side of the building.

Using the window ledges and old stones that haven't been fixed yet to pull myself up, I get to the window where I think the noise was coming from. Nothing could have prepared me for what I find in there.

It's Kia.

She shackled to the far wall, facing away from me. Her back has lashes from what must be a whip. Burn marks are along her shoulders and four small black circles cover her lower back. She's barely moving, but I can see the rise and fall of her shoulders from where she's trying to catch her breath.

Fear grips at me and dread pours through my stomach. I'm going to be too late. Just like I was with the others.

Using my fist to smash through the glass, braking it easily, I rush over to Kia, taking her small form into my arms.

She doesn't open her eyes, but it looks like she's trying to speak.

Noise from behind me has me up on my feet and my sword drawn. There's nothing there, but the door that was shut, is now open. Darkness creeps in from the entrance to the bare, musty room I stand in. Fear begins to climb its way up my legs, curling around them like snakes. I turn back to Kia, but something catches my eye again, and I whip my sword around trying cut down whatever else is in the room. Fear has made its way up to my heart, and I feel like I'm drowning in it.

Bending down to reach for Kia, I touch her back, and a small amount of relief trickles through. I still haven't turned away from the door, and a part of me knows, as soon as I do, whatever it is, will strike.

The need to see Kia with my own eyes starts to overwhelm me. I take a quick glance at her and find she's got her eyes shut, but she's still alive.

Movement catches my eye again, except I'm ready this time. I turn fast to meet whoever it is.

A set of pitch-black eyes that hold nothing within them, look back at me. The figure is pushing eight feet, and its smirking like it's founds its next meal. No arms or legs can be depicted from its semi translucent black body, which seems to hover just a few inches from the floor.

Paralysed and unable to move, I watch as it starts toward Kia. It says something I don't understand, and I begin to panic. Using every ounce of strength to push against the wall of energy holding me still, I feel myself slip forward.

The energy keeping me trapped breaks and I find myself standing in my room with my sword drawn, breathing heavy with sweat dripping down my back.

"What the hell, Seb!!!" Rolland grunts through clenched teeth.

I look over to see Kia buried deep into Rolland's side, with her arms wrapped around him. She's trembling, and her towel has slipped from her shoulders revealing marks on her back. The same marks I saw on her in the dream. *Did I slip into her dream? Or was it her memory?*

Those black eyes flash across my vision and I still feel the residue of fear clinging to my body; I shake myself slightly to rid my body of it.

"Seb, what happened? Her fear is through the roof and I can't get a grip on it. Put your sword down and try speaking to her," Rolland's scolds still clenching his teeth. There's a fine sheen of sweat across his forehead.

Laying my sword down under the bed. I take the comforter and pull it up over her shoulders. Squatting down beside the bed so I'm eye level with Kia's face, I find she's got her eyes screwed shut, with her chin tucked deep into her neck.

"Kia, it's me, Sebastian," I coax softly, "I'm so sorry." I want to reach out and comfort her, but I'm too concerned that I'll hurt her more, causing Rolland more stress.

I reach under the towel for her hand, which is still wrapped around Rolland's sides. Gently taking it into my own. I ease a little healing energy through her finger and up her arms.

"I had a bad dream and I couldn't wake myself from it. When I woke, I think I was still caught up in my emotions and I just reacted. I didn't mean to frighten you," I try to comfort her, running my thumb over her knuckles.

She nods her head and begins to turn toward me. When she finally opens her eyes, they're not swirling, but a fixed deep blue with no silver specs to be seen. Fear is plainly visible all over her face, but I don't think it's from me.

She blinks slowly, taking a deep breath.

Pushing a little more energy through her fingers, I see her shoulders begin to relax. Rolland finally releases a heavy breath and I begin to wonder if I really was the cause of her reaction.

Keeping eye contact with her, I continue to rub my thumb over her knuckles. "Was it me who frightened you, Kia?" I don't know what made me ask, but the words are out before I can stop them.

Instead of nodding or shaking her head, she turns back into Rolland's chest, and I hear Rolland take a sharp intake of air.

"I swear to you, Seb, if you keep frightening her, I'll remove your tongue and use it to wipe my arse with," Rolland spits out.

Kia sits bolt upright and glares at Rolland. I can't help the chuckle that escape me. From the look on her face, if she had the strength, I truly think she would punch him right now.

At the sound of my laughter, Kia looks around to me in confusion.

"He's joking, Kia, he's just tired and grumpy. He would never hurt me -" That's not true, I rethink my words. "He would never hurt me out of spite, only out of fun," I clarify with a smile playing around my mouth.

She turns back to Rolland, but he just raises an eyebrow. "Fine, I won't hurt him, I promise," he relents, rolling his eyes, then brings his gaze fully to me, a smile pulling at his lips. "You've got a woman fighting your battles for you now, that's kinda hot."

His ocean blue eyes look incredibly tired, and his usual butterscotch skin tone is beginning to fade.

I roll my own eyes at his in response. *At least he's still joking.* I look back at Kia and she's still eyeing Rolland, but her body language has relaxed.

Deciding that sleep would be best to avoid for a few hours, I head into the en-suite, and start preparing the healing bath in the next room.

It's about the size of a small swimming pool, so it can easily fit at least a dozen people comfortable. Adding the healing salts that Jack supplied, and some of the gel that Matt makes, I adjust the setting of the pool to keep it at the right temperature for the next forty-eight hours. The salt cleanses any general infections and the gel relaxes the muscles.

The floor of the pool has crystals embedded into it. Clear quartz and rose quartz, amethyst, citrine, black tourmaline, carnelian, various aventurines, plus a couple of others that Jack provided. But like the Brondroll and Gauldrix stones, they have powers that I don't understand. I tried researching them to find out what they do, but I found nothing. *They are most likely from wherever the hell he came from himself.*

Deciding to get more comfortable, I take a quick shower and dress in some cotton pants and a thin white vest. Checking the pool, I find it's at the right temperature. The crystals and stones shining off the lighting, gives the room the appearance of a lost cave. The thought of getting Kia healed to some degree, lifts my mood as I turn to make my way back to the bedroom.

CHAPTER SIX

*R*olland
My body is starting to shut down from exhaustion after the last spike in Kia's emotions, and I'm beginning to doubt my control over keeping all her pain away. *What set her off? There must be more to it than just Seb moving too fast and drawing his sword. It felt more like she was drowning in her fear.* At least her eyes have regained a few specs of silver, but they aren't swirling like they were earlier.

I pour some of the remaining water into a glass for her and lift it to her lips, but surprisingly her hands meet mine, and she takes it from me gently. Looking more carefully at her hands, I see they're free of any bruising and broken bones, with just the cuffs remaining on her wrists. *Those are most definitely going to be a bitch to remove.*

Seeing that the towel has once again fallen off her slim shoulders, I pull it up carefully around her shoulders then settle back down into the bed to try and find my centre and regain some focus. But whether it's from the lack of sleep or my inability to stop worrying about Kia, I can't seem to settle myself. I can feel sweat coating my head and back, and my body feels like it's been running for days.

A small, cool hand runs along my forehead, but as much as I want to open my eyes to her, they protest and remain closed. This seems to make her anxious and I can feel her panic begin to rise, so I push what little calming energy I can muster through to her. I hear her sigh deeply and a few moments later her head comes to rest over my heart.

Time passes by slowly, marked only by Kia's soft breath as it tickles my chest, her body relaxing with each exhalation. Suddenly I hear Seb's warm voice trickle through my brain, but it sounds like he's talking to me under water. Fighting my way to the surface, I feel a hand on my chest as heat begins to seep into me.

Is he trying to heal me? What a dick. He just can't help himself. He must play nurse at every opportunity.

The warmth that's growing feels different from his healing energy though. It's more like what I felt back in the cell we found Kia in. The memory of her back there crashes into me like a bucket of ice, and I yank myself from my centre a little too quickly. Instinctively my arms tighten around the body in my arms to confirm she's still there, but my head bashes into something hard as I sit up too quickly.

"Fuck, Rolland! Shit! What's your head made of? Stone?" Seb's curses fill my ears. Slightly disoriented, I shake my head to clear it then massage my eyes with one hand. When I finally open them, two pools of sapphire are swirling back at me.

I look over to Seb who's rubbing his head and wincing. "Rolland, you were totally out of it, man. We've been trying to wake you for nearly five minutes. I didn't think you were going to wake up," he chides in his dulcet tone, running his cognac eyes over me. I look away to avoid his questioning gaze. *If I'm struggling with her pain after just a few hours, how did she ever survive it herself?*

"The pool is ready, but I'm not sure you're going to be up for it, Rolland. Maybe we should wait for Jack to return?" Seb suggests as he continues to watch me, still rubbing at his head. *Fuck that, she stays in my arms till this feeling leaves me, or I pass out. The pompous prick can suck on eggs,* I think to myself. Gathering Kia into my arms, with one hand under her legs, and the other supporting her back, a wave of heat rushes through me, sending a shiver through my bones.

Knowing Seb is about to heal Kia urges me on and helps me push past my body's desire to rest. Drawing the pain away from her and burying it deep within me, I make my way through the en-suite without acknowledging Seb's comments. Stepping through the archway and into the room that houses the pool, the smell of the salt and gel hits my nose. The combination is incredibly refreshing and reminds me of the salt lakes of Iceland. I feel Kia's curiosity, worry and a small amount of joy struggling to get through her other intense emotions. Looking down at her, I see her full attention is on the pool, and imagine myself seeing the room for the first time.

Along the right side of the pool itself there are four seats built into the wall, perfect for relaxing into and zoning out. Having fallen asleep in them many times, I know they're quite comfortable. Both the left side and back of the pool have a ledge halfway up to accommodate more people.

As Seb steps up to my right and turns toward Kia, her emotions begin to change. Fear and worry still pour from her, but a trickle of desire seeps through too. *If only I could tell what she is thinking.*

"Kia, the pool will help the healing process, but there could be a slight sting from the salt. Once in, I'm going to start healing your broken bones, and then take a look at your back, okay?" With her full attention now on him, she gives a small nod of confirmation. Seb shifts his deep-set eyes on to me, full of concern. *"Take it slowly, alright?"* he cautions. I nod in response before moving us closer to the pool. Despite her nod of confirmation, however, another spike of fear rears up and Kia turns her head back into me, burrowing her nose in my chest, forcing me to take a deep steadying breath to help process it.

The instant my foot hits the water, the gel and stones get to work, easing the muscles in my legs, and soothing them like a warm caress. I take the next two steps easily and I've still got Kia's small frame above the surface, but as the water continues to soothe my muscles and tendons, my body begins to crave rest and the time to restore itself - my legs begin to shake a bit.

The next step down into the pool seems to stretch as seconds slow down. My muscles seem to have relaxed too much now and my left foot slips. Falling sideways into Seb, I try to regain my footing, but my body doesn't respond and we slip into the water. As Kia comes down with me, the sudden shock of her pain overwhelms me as it fires through my body. Fear engulfs me and I can't separate her emotions from mine.

Flashes of being chased underwater by shadows burst across my vision, followed by a stabbing needle like pain up my back. I try to drag air into my lungs, but all I inhale is water, and as another wave of fear crashes through me, my body gives up and I'm dragged into darkness.

CHAPTER SEVEN

Sebastian

I watch Rolland sink into the water, taking Kia with him, and without thought, I yank her up into my arms. She's gasping for breath and shaking from head to toe. As I settle her into the safety of my arms, fear sets in for Rolland as he hasn't surfaced yet.

"Kia, breathe for me, sweetheart, breathe for me. Deep breaths," I urge her softly.

She's trembling and clinging to me hard, her arms and legs clamped around me like a vice. *Shit, Rolland still hasn't come up yet.* "Kia, Rolland is still in the water, and I need to pull him up. I'm going to set you down so that I can get him, okay?" She shakes her head no, refusing to let go, and I take it that she'd rather stay clung to me like a monkey and brave the water again than be put down and left by herself.

As I step deeper into the water, I hold Kia to me tightly with my left arm and thrust the right one down low, grabbing Rolland's arm. Kia gasps in pain as her body dips into the water with me. I haul Rolland's massive body to the surface quickly, dragging him over to the top step, then feel along his neck for a pulse. *Fuck, it's barely there*. Kia is still shaking hard and her arms tighten around my neck even more.

"Kia, you're okay. I've got you," I speak into her hair while rolling Rolland onto his back with my right arm. "I need to get the water out of Rolland's lungs, but I'm *not* going to put you down." Her heavy breaths are laboured, and I begin to worry she took water into her lungs too. Placing my hand on his chest, I push my energy into his lungs to force them to move and expel the water. He coughs it up but doesn't move or open his eyes. I check for his pulse again and sigh with relief as it beats strongly under my fingers.

Kia's body is still shuddering as she moves in my lap to face Rolland. Letting go of me, she moves to sit next to him. Resting against his broad chest, she places her hands on either side of his head, and I see a small blue light glowing from her palms. Kia slumps to the tiles as Rolland jerks awake and I manage to catch her and pull her into me before her head hits the floor. *Fuck.* She's passed out, and I send out a silent prayer that she's not retreated into her mind again.

I turn to Rolland to see him trying to catch his breath. He looks pale and in need of time in one of the healing chambers. "You okay?" I ask, leaning over to him slightly.

"I'll be fine," he rasps, running a hand through his tangled locks before turning toward us. "Is SHE okay?" His deep voice scratches as he tries to catch his breath.

"She pulled you from unconsciousness, then collapsed." I flicker my eyes over him, watching his shoulders shake as they continue to heave in deep gulps of air.

Rolland moves so he's sitting out of the pool altogether. "I don't understand how it's possible, Seb. She's so small, and she's been carrying all that pain and fear for fuck knows how long. The fear alone is so overwhelming that the other emotions that trickle through are like grains of sand in comparison." The crackle in his voice eases slightly.

"Jack said she's stronger than all of us put together, so don't be so hard on yourself," I try reassuring him. He rests his head in his hands for a moment, causing his shoulder-length hair to fall over his arms. Suddenly, Jack appears in front of us, covered in dust and grime and looking like he's been walking through ankle deep mud. *Where the hell was he?* There's not a spot of dirt on his face, though, nor is there a hair loose from his tie, yet his fingers are layered in soot. *This man is a never-ending puzzle.*

"Speak of the devil," Rolland mutters as he turns to look up at Jack's tall frame.

Jack lowers himself to his knees, bringing him to eye level with Rolland. "Be ready," he says, the only warning he gives before he places his hand on Kia's forehead and gets to work pulling her back. Rolland laces his fingers with Kia's as he rests his head back down on his knees.

I glance up at the clock on the wall and watch as time drags by slowly. Minutes pass like hours, yet there's still no movement or sound from either Kia or Jack. *How long has Jack been in there now? Something's not right.* When I look over to Rolland, it's to see him watching them curiously.

"What is it?" I ask.

"I can feel her. Her emotions… I don't usually feel them until she wakes up. At first, I thought they were my own but now…" He moves closer, so his shoulders are nearly touching Jack's, then closes his eyes. "She's confused and lost." Rolland takes a deep breath, relaxing his shoulders. His face calms and I see his hand tighten slightly over Kia's.

A few seconds later Kia lurches up and tries to scramble from my lap.

"Whoa, whoa, whoa, I got you, sweetie, I got you," I

soothe, encouraging her back down. "Look, Rolland and Jack are here too." Thankfully Rolland still has a hold of her hand, but as I look to Jack, I find he's already up on his feet with his back to us and his shoulders heaving like he's just run a marathon. *That can't be good.* He starts to make his way distractedly out of the room. Wanting to find out what happened and make sure he's okay, I carefully hand Kia over to Rolland and follow after Jack's receding back.

CHAPTER EIGHT

*R*olland

"That didn't go so well, did it? How about we take it real slow this time?" I say quietly into Kia's hair. She's curled up into me, with her head buried in my neck, legs draped over my right leg, and her arms wrapped around my waist. Her emotions are all over the place, but they don't feel like the heavy weight they were before, they almost feel like they're a part of me. She's trembling, but for the first time I think it may just be from being cold. Worry, and that feeling of being home, safe and secure, roll off her. I push comfort through to her and I feel it come back.

Jack and Seb have left the room, so I inch us forward, shuffling on my butt to the pool. I put my feet in the water but stay on the top step so that our bodies aren't submerged.

"I want you to do this yourself, Kia, but take it slowly, okay? One foot at a time." She gives a small nod and starts to ease one foot in. I can feel her pain bubble up, but it's followed closely by pleasure. As her other foot goes in, another wave of pain rises, feeling much like salt on a friction burn. *Her feet must be blistered or burnt in some way*. Kia

64

begins to turn forward in my arms, causing another influx of pain to rush over me. *That will be from her broken ribs.* Stopping her movements, she looks back up at me.

"Maybe we should keep turning to a minimum till Sebastian returns and heals your ribs?" I suggest. Her eyes are swirling more than they have since she woke earlier, and the silver stars begin to return. Disappointment simmers through as she dips her head to look down at her lap. "I have an idea how to make this easier, but I need you to trust me."

She turns her head up to me, and I watch as her eyes swirl faster, and the blue begins to deepen. They roam over my face as if looking for something, before stopping on my lips. She opens her mouth to speak, but all that comes out is crackle of sound. Her brow creases in frustration, but rather than try again she just gives me a small nod. Making sure my arm is securely around her, I begin slowly sliding us into the pool, allowing the water to lap at her back gently. Her pain swells through me, but it's manageable without the intense effort of keeping her fear at bay.

Once we're deep enough into the water and away from the steps, I stand up slightly to give me more room to maneuver her fragile body. Letting the water take her weight, I slowly turn her to face me completely, sliding her legs around my waist as she moves her arms instinctively up to my shoulders. Her eyes are still watching me, and the silver specs within them seem to be sparking more.

The pool seems to have done its job and relaxed her muscles because she settles easily into a more comfortable position as I shift us over to the left wall, where I can sit back and relax my own body. Looking down at her, I see her eyes are once again focused on my lips. Up until now, I've had no room to feel anything other than HER emotions. There's no room for desire - or lust - when my mind has been focused solely on the task of redirecting her pain and fear. Maybe it's the pool, or it could be because her emotions don't feel so heavy, but there's no denying the desire that's building within me.

My gaze locks on her mouth and I become more aware of my hardness. Her desire floods into me and it's as if we're caught in a bubble. Each of us waiting for the other to make a move. Neither of us blinking or moving a muscle.

Her eyes draw me deep into the blue swirls, daring me to look away.

I'm not sure who moves first, but I suddenly find her soft lips pressed against mine, curious at first. I'm stunned for a second, as Kia stills and retreats slightly.

Checking to see that I still have a firm grip on her pain, I pull her head back to mine, reclaiming her lips. Her desire shoots a fever of need and longing through my body, fueling my own wish to have more of her. Trailing my left hand up her thigh, I feel her tighten her legs around my waist, drawing us closer together.

Thank fuck I'm wearing trousers.

Another surge of desire slams through me, full of hunger and urgency as I slide my tongue along her lips, asking for entrance. One of her small hands tightens on my shoulder as the other slides up into my hair before she opens her mouth to me. The sound of someone clearing their throat comes from the archway to my right, startling us both. Reluctantly, I pull away from Kia's lips, but her eyes pin me to the spot, holding my gaze. Loss and disappointment flow from her, but thankfully she doesn't look hurt. I check my grip on her pain levels and am glad to find that I still have a good hold on them.

"Rolland?" Jack's controlled voice tries to pull my attention away, but I can't release myself from Kia's gaze. Her eyes swirl faster, and a few more specks of silver appear.

"What's going on, Rolland?" Seb's questions in my head, but I still can't look away.

"Seb, see if you can distract Kia for me," I ask.

Seb lowers himself into the pool beside us and stands behind Kia's back. Dropping his head to her ear, he whispers something only she can hear. Whatever he said doesn't seem to work as we stayed locked in the strange trance that neither of us seem to be able to break from.

"I don't think she heard you, Seb," I say sarcastically.

Seb moves his hands, but I can't see what he's doing. He whispers something again, and Kia finally blinks as whatever compulsion was holding us falls away.

Kia turns to Jack, and then to Seb, bringing a small wave of pain from her broken ribs.

Rubbing a hand over my face to shake myself free from the last of whatever energy Kia was using, I turn to face Jack. Kia's head settles wearily against my chest as I see Jack watching her curiously.

"I would advise keeping Kia in Sebastian's room for a few nights at the very least. I will bring down a tray of food for when you are done here. How are you fairing?" he asks as his crystal blue eyes turn to me, searching my face. I start to tell him I'm fine but stop. *Jack will know if I'm lying, he's a bloody walking lie detector, for fuck's sake.*

"I was running on fumes for a while, and I think my body shut down, but since you brought her back from her last head trip, I've been fine," I explain. Jack gives nothing away in response as he nods and walks out, as though I just told him the time. I look over at Seb inquiringly, but he just shrugs. *Damn, that man can be a pain in my arse.*

67

CHAPTER NINE

*S*ebastian
Looking Kia over I can see four deep gashes going down the length of her back, still open, but not bleeding. Several more can be seen underneath those, but they've begun to heal. Her right shoulder has scarring that looks like it may have been caused by a branding iron, and small puncture holes are scattered all over her skin.

Images from the dream I saw her in, flash across my vision, and the need to destroy something surges through my body.

"Seb, you good?" Rolland regards me with understanding.

"Let's get some of these bones healed so you can breathe easier, Kia," I offer.

She lifts her head to look over Rolland's shoulder at the far wall, needing something to focus on, then nods for me to start. Rolland's eyes meet mine, full of apprehension. *"Healing the wounds shouldn't be painful, but it will be draining on her body,"* I project to him. Rolland nods before resting one hand comfortingly on her head and the other on her lower back.

Carefully I trace my hands around her waist and up her belly. I hear her breath catch, and at the same time Rolland makes a strangled noise in the back of his throat. *I assume that is due to his concentration.* Easing some energy into her torso, I find three broken ribs on her left side that have started to set, so I focus there first. But as I begin, Kia startles a bit and tries to move away from me. I glance at Rolland questioningly but don't stop what I'm doing. I feel Kia stiffen, then relax under my hands.

"Is she okay?" I ask Rolland tentatively, flicking my eyes over his face.

"She's trying to take the pain herself. I didn't even know that was possible," he answers, his strong, chiseled jaw grinding slightly.

Once I've healed the three ribs I was working on, I move my energy to the broken ones in the back. Kia's focus has moved from the wall to look down into the water to her right, and she pulls her lips hard into her teeth. I gently ease more energy into her back, focusing on her bones and not the gashes that are screaming at me to heal them.

As I finish up, Kia takes a full, deep breath and sighs in relief as she relaxes against Rolland's chest. I hear him take a deep breath as well, as he settles his head back against the tiles. After a few restful minutes, Kia sits up straight in Rolland's lap and starts to turn to face me, a smile flickering on her lips briefly, before the open gashes on her back cause a whimper of pain to escape. Rolland sits back up in a flash, carefully but quickly turning her back into his chest.

"Are you okay for me to start on your back, Kia? I could sit here for hours healing every inch of you, but your body will need to rest after this," I ask hesitantly.

Taking in Rolland's face as he studies Kia, I notice the golden colour of his skin seems to be fading slightly around his cheeks, worrying me a little. Kia doesn't move or nod, and I begin to doubt she heard or understood me. Rolland's expression shifts to one of concern, as he lifts Kia's head away from his body so that he can see her face.

"Kia, we don't have to do your back now. Do you want Sebastian to work on your throat, feet, or any other part that hurts?" he coaxes, as he assesses her. She shakes her head slowly as she raises a hand and points to her back.

"Are you sure about this, Kia?" I confirm tentatively. She nods her head in affirmation. *"You ready, Rolland? This may trigger some bad memories,"* I warn.

"Ready as I'll ever be. Just take it slowly... please." Damn, he asked rather than demanded, he must really be exhausted.

Placing my hands gently on her shoulders, I begin to trickle energy down her back. Her shoulders tense up under my hands and her breathing becomes more rapid.

I take a quick glance at Rolland, and I see he's in the same trance he was in earlier.

"Everything okay?" I ask carefully.

Rolland doesn't reply so I continue working at Kia's back, hopeful that the gashes seal before it becomes too much for her. Suddenly, her breathing stalls, and her shoulders slump.

"Shit," I hear from Rolland.

Kia whirls around on me with feral eyes, as Rolland tries to keep a hold of her. Not being prepared for her onslaught, I'm shoved under the water by her weight, but she's quickly dragged off me as I push myself to the surface. Taking a step back to give her space, I rub the water from my eyes to see she's still trying to scramble from Rolland's arms.

"Kia, it's Sebastian, look -" His words are cut off as he takes an elbow to the face, yet he manages to pin her arms down and pull her tight to his chest. "Kia, listen to my voice, it's Rolland," he grunts as he closes his eyes in concentration.

Kia's still squirming to get free as her eyes, wild and black, stay solely focused on me. *I genuinely think she would try to kill me if Rolland let her go.*

"Kia, please… It's just Sebastian. There's no one else here. Just you, me, and Sebastian. He's not trying to hurt you." Rolland tries to appease her, but she's not hearing him as she continues to struggle in his arms. I begin to worry about how much more damage she's causing her frail body.

"Rolland, I think she's more worried about you than she is herself."

"What?"

"Just tell her I'm not going to touch you, trust me."

"Kia, he's not going to hurt me, or touch me, sweetheart," Rolland's speaks firmly to her. There's a small pause, but she continues to try and buck herself from his grip. I step back a few more paces slowly and her struggles ease. Seeing it seems to be working, I continue to back up until I'm at least halfway across the pool. She stops in the battle to free herself but continues to glare at me.

No one moves. All I can hear is Kia panting hard and water dripping. Slowly her face relaxes and it's as if someone has lifted away whatever it was that was triggering her reaction. Her eyes begin to lighten from the dark pits they were and the blue returns as they start to swirl. She slumps back against Rolland as her body collapses and tears slide down her flushed cheeks. Suddenly she lunges away from Rolland again but in the direction of the steps this time.

"Whoa, whoa, whoa, where are you going?" Rolland's soothes as he drags her back to his chest. She's crying hard now and can't seem to catch her breath. I wade over to them, grabbing one of her hands. She stops fighting Rolland and peers up at me with remorse and shame. Without a second thought, I pull her to me, careful not to touch her back and she comes willingly, wrapping her arms around my neck. This pushes her lush warm breasts against my chest and forces my body into a state that's simply not appropriate for this moment.

I feel her burrow into my neck, and I dip my head down into her shoulders, breathing in her exotic scent. She leans back slightly to peek up at me so I kiss her forehead reverently, hoping she understands I'm not upset with her. I look to Rolland and see he's resting one hand on Kia's leg and the other is rubbing his eyes.

"That was unexpected," he says as he watches us, lost as to what to say or do.

"Do you want to get out, Kia, or shall we try your feet?" I suggest as I study her face. She lets go of my neck, easing her way back into Rolland's arms. *Shit, we really need to get some clothes on her.*

Kia's eyes are swirling and a few more specs of silver have returned to them. Keeping eye contact, I carefully ease myself toward her, squatting low when I get near, letting the water cover my shoulders. Reaching my hand down to find one of her injured feet, I lift it onto my lap, and run my thumb over the sole, assessing the damage. Something sharp protruding from her heel catches on my thumb, and she tugs her foot back slightly, stilling me in my movements. An idea begins to form in my head but I'm unsure of how Rolland will feel about it.

"You trust me, right, Brother?" I don't look to Rolland, but keep my eyes locked with Kia.

"Of course, why would you question that?" Rolland's perplexed voice seeps through my mind.

"There's a shard of glass embedded into Kia's foot and

72

I'm going to distract her while removing it. Just don't hit me, okay?"

"*O-kay...*" he replies uncertainly, but I trust that he won't react with her in his arms. Kia's still studying me and the swirling becomes faster as a few more silver specs appear. This could go seriously wrong, but I'm willing to try anything to heal her with as little stress as possible.

Edging closer so her face is inches from mine, her ankle still in my hand, I watch as her eyes flick over my face curiously. I hear her breath catch as she zeroes in on my mouth. Her wet, pink tongue darts out and she sucks her bottom lip into her teeth softly. Tentatively, I touch her lips with mine, then draw back just a fraction to see if she's about to bolt. Instead, I find that the tiny silver specks have multiplied, like the stars coming out on a dark night.

Grabbing me by the neck, she tugs me to her, and I hear Rolland grunt from behind. She's already seeking entrance to my mouth and I give her the freedom to explore at her own pace. As she clings tighter to me, I feel myself growing harder, and my restraint begins to falter. Unable to hold back any longer, I brush my tongue against hers, and I hear a small noise coming from the back of her throat. She carries on searching my mouth as my need to touch her grows heavy.

Releasing some of my pent-up frustration through my fingers and into her feet, I feel her hands tighten on me. Wanting to keep her distracted, I curl my tongue around hers and suck at it. That seems to do the trick and she draws in a sharp breath and delves deeper into my mouth. Desperation takes hold and I can feel us both fighting for control.

Before I get too lost in the moment and while she's so thoroughly distracted, I quickly force the shard of glass out of her foot, being sure to keep her focus on the dance our tongues are doing. There's a sharp sting in my lip as she bites down on it, and a growl finds its way out from deep in my throat. Pushing more energy through her foot, I heal the remaining bruises, tears and blisters, then continue on up her leg, stopping at her knee. I can feel that it's bruised considerably and may well have a few chipped bones.

She frees my lips and I open my eyes to find her breathing just as hard as I am. My brain is no longer functioning as everything else around us disappears and the need to have more of her becomes almost painful. Unable to hold back, I reclaim her lips once again, plundering her mouth firmly, and am met with equal abandon. Warmth starts to trickle its way into my chest, and I realise it's her energy, driving its way into my heart and burrowing deep within me. Someone calls my name, but it's too muffled to recognise or hear.

Kia continues to her exploration and her raspy breaths are like music to my ears. Her hand tangles into my hair at the back and she tugs hard, dwindling my restraint to mere ashes. Of their own accord, my hands draw her body even closer to me.

"Sebastian!" Rolland's deep voice drills through my mind, snapping me out of the fog that was clogging it up. Reluctantly and with great effort, I lean back and the see specks have completely taken over her irises. Remembering what I was meant to be doing, I grab her left foot, and I see her brow furrow. I retake her lips, trying to keep my head clearer this time, but I find her slightly more reluctant.

She's caught on to what I'm doing and I'm not sure if it's going to work again.

"Rolland, help me out buddy."

"And how might I do that, 'Buddy?'" he jests, full of amusement.

"Use your imagination. I don't think she's going to be so

easy to distract this time. She knows what I'm doing, and I think she might stop me."

"Oh, she's figured out that you're trying to eat her?" he questions sarcastically.

"That's rich coming from the man who was just doing the same thing," I mock.

"Touché." I see Rolland give a tiny nod from behind Kia.

Trailing my lips across her face, I start tracking my way down her neck and across her shoulder. She relaxes as I lick away the droplets of water that cover her skin.

I run my fingers along the sole of the remaining foot, thankful she doesn't pull back or flinch this time. Releasing energy into her, I thankfully find no shards of glass, but there are quite a few tears, bruises and deep cuts.

Gingerly feeling her toes, I find that two are broken. Knowing this will hurt, and that she will need serious distraction, I glance up to find Rolland kissing her deeply. He's got her full attention, and trusting him to keep her that way, I aim my energy into the space above the tiny broken bones and release it steadily. When it's done, I look up once again. *Shit.* Rolland is breathing heavily, his head resting in the crook of Kia's right shoulder. She's panting equally hard and as her gaze fully locks on me, I see her eyes are nearly entirely silver now, only tiny specks of blue showing through.

"No more, Kia-" Rolland continues to drag air into his lungs. "Please-" he takes a breath before he finishes his words, "just give me five minutes, I beg you."

Releasing my gaze, Kia turns her head toward Rolland, raising her hand to stroke his jaw. The metal cuff dangles from her wrist and I'm reminded of why she's in so much pain. Rolland twists her back around, so she's tucked into his broad chest again, then leans his head back against the tiles, his eyes closed.

"You'll be the death of me, woman," he says, his voice raspy and deep. Startled by his words, she jerks in his arms. I roll my eyes at his idiocy.

"It's just an expression, Kia. He's fine. Better than fine I'd say, by the looks of him. He's far from death just now." Kia turns to me with puzzled eyes, clearly needing to understand. *Fuck, how do I explain this in simple terms?*

"You've got his heart and body running on a lot of emotions, mostly pleasure, and he's struggling with where to put it." I watch as she processes this information.

Apparently appeased, albeit still slightly confused, she curls herself contentedly up in Rolland's lap. Sighing deeply, her dark lashes sink slowly down until they finally rest delicately on her soft skin. A deep groan comes from both Rolland and I at the same time...

We are totally, and utterly, screwed.

CHAPTER TEN

*R*olland

Struggling where to put the pleasure? No, not really - I know exactly where to put it. The taste of her sweetness is still on my lips and I want more. I could never get enough. Still resting my head back against the tiles, I continue drawing Kia's pain away, knowing that with the help of the gel and crystals, I could sit here for hours with her tucked safely into my chest.

Kia settles deeper into my lap and I wonder if she can feel my hardness pushing insistently into her hip. Counting to ten is useless and trying to think of other things is just plain stupid. Her energy lingers in my chest, and I can feel it seeping deeper, warming me from the inside. The water begins to undulate around us as Seb wades over to the steps, but I don't open my eyes to see what he's doing.

After a few minutes, I hear his feet padding toward us then stop by my head.

"Rolland, Kia needs to eat a little after all the healing I've just pushed her body to do. Once she's eaten a little then maybe..." There's a long pause which perks my interest, so I

open one eye to find him looking down at Kia with lust filled eyes.

Yeah, I could have guessed that. "Maybe what, Seb?" He doesn't respond as he continues staring at her and I begin to wonder if she's pulled him into another trance. *This is all very amusing, wish I had some popcorn.* I lift my head up to see if she's awake, but she's not. Frowning slightly, I look over at Seb again.

"Seb, what were you going to say?" I ask in a loud whisper. Seb shakes his head slightly, rubbing a hand over his face.

"I need some sleep, man," he mumbles. "Maybe we should see if we can put some clothes on her. As much as I appreciate the view, it's just not morally right, plus, I don't think Matt, Brad or Gerry are going to be quite as understanding if they see a naked woman walking around the house. Whenever, or if ever, that happens." His brows pull deeper as he speaks.

"Agreed, though I'm not sure how that's going to go down with her." Her disregard for showing her body is evident. I wonder if it is due to her time spent in captivity or if it's perhaps just the way she is. We both quietly watch her for a moment as she sleeps peacefully. My gaze runs over her body, taking in the finger marks on her neck and all of the bruises that are still present. Cuts streak all the way up her arms, interlaced with burn marks in various places. The cut below her thin bottom lip, however, has nearly healed and is barely visible.

Wishing Seb could heal her faster, I drag my thoughts away and wade over to the steps. Seb is waiting with a large towel, so I ease Kia into his arms gently, careful to maintain connection with her body. Her emotions have settled down, and there's this strange feeling of home flowing soothingly through her. I'm not sure that's the right way to describe it, yet it's the only thing I can equate it to - a sense of contentment, calmness, tranquillity and the feeling of knowing you're safe.

Climbing out of the pool, we make our way through the archway and back into Seb's en-suite. It's a warm, well-lit room, with a window high up that lets in just enough light to make it cozy but doesn't allow for any drafts. Seb leads us past the long shower and over to the cabinet that stores loads of cotton trousers. Grabbing a towel from the heated rail nearby, I awkwardly dry as much moisture off my body as I can using only one hand. Dropping the towel in a heap at my feet, I snatch a pair of the trousers from the cupboard, careful not to tug on Kia, as I pull them on.

Once done, I stand up to find Seb watching Kia with an emotion I've never seen in his eyes before - serenity - and a part of me wishes I could leave her in his arms. He raises his eyes to me and an understanding passes between us. *No matter what it takes, she stays with us.* He passes Kia back to me carefully, then turns to grab a shirt for us to use to cover her up. *"I think it would be better if we dress her in a room that will be more familiar to her."* Seb nods his head in response and we make our way into the bedroom.

As I make my way to the bed, I see that Seb has changed the sheets to a deep maroon coloured set and with the sun still coming up, light pinks and yellows bounce off the walls. There's a tray of fruit on the bedside table that I assume was brought in by Jack, as well as a freshly cleansed jug of water. Going to the side of the bed closest to the door, I sit with my back to the headboard, easing Kia into a more upright position as Seb sits on the opposite side, facing us. I don't want to wake her, but she needs to eat.

Preparing her for the transition to wakefulness, I begin

pushing calming energy into Kia as I speak quietly in her ear. "Kia, sweetheart, I need you to wake up for us." A slight frown appears on her forehead, but she doesn't stir. I take a deep breath and speak a bit louder. "Kia, I know you can hear me, sweetie. Open your eyes so I can see you."

A small amount of pleasure, desire and a bit of annoyance trickles from her, as she turns her head entirely into my side, squirming her way deeper into me and pulling her arm over her ear. I try not to laugh as I look at Seb, who's clearly fighting his own need to chuckle at her response. Smiling, I decide to up my game.

Running my hand up her arm, I let a small amount of desire trickle through, followed by pleasure, and I'm rewarded with a small moan, but she still doesn't move. I do it again, and I feel her squeeze her legs together as she peeks up at me through her arm. Her eyes look like two silver pools of pearls glowing in the shadows of her arm, and it feels like she's shot a zap of her energy straight through to my cock. I hear myself make a deep, guttural noise in the back of my throat.

"Seb, I think we're in trouble, Brother." His response is to let out the laughter he's been holding in for the last minute.

Kia's eyes furrow and she moves to sit up, causing her towel to fall and expose her beautiful breasts that are just begging to be appreciated. She looks incredible with her wet ebony hair falling around her shoulders and her big eyes that seem to hold the whole world within them. Seb's laugh cuts off abruptly, drawing my attention to him. He's clearly as stunned as I feel.

Kia raises a thin eyebrow at me in question, but my brain seems to have stopped working because I can't remember what we were doing. *Tasting her lips...yes, tasting her lips again seems like what I should be doing.* Anything else would be just be stupid.

"Kia, we woke you so that you could eat something to help your body replenish after the intense healing." Ignoring the voice that dribbles on from across bed, I let my gaze leisurely peruse her body. She looks so beautiful, despite the bruises and cuts still covering it, and all I want to do is trace every inch of her with my tongue. My body clearly agrees as my hardness begs for attention. My fingers start tracing up her arm and I hear her breath hitch. My eyes flick to hers, and she's looking back at me with desire and want.

"Rolland, I hope the silence means that you're both eating," Seb says sardonically.

"Eating, yeah eating her lips and tasting her skin sounds like a fantastic idea."

"No, Rolland. The food, eating the food." I hear him let out a heavy breath. I've still not taken my eyes off of Kia, and her face is inches from mine. "Nope. No, no, no." A hard hand pushes me back against the headboard, and I hit it with a thump.

Shit, that hurt. Kia sucks in a painful breath, jerking me back to reality. I must have lost my grip on her for a split second and guilt riddles me. Looking down at her face, I see she's scowling at Seb, but he's up and off the bed. He picks up the plate of fruit, then settles back down.

My cock stirs again, and my focus is brought back to the situation at hand. *A shirt. She needs to put a shirt on before we have another repeat of whatever the hell that was.* Looking around, I see the one Seb brought in from the en-suite resting nearby. Grabbing it, I show it to Kia. "Sweetie, this may, or may not sound strange, but we need you to put a shirt on, okay?" I explain cautiously.

She had turned her head to scowl at Seb but as I speak,

81

she turns back to me. Her brow furrows even deeper as she looks down at her chest, and then around the room. Confusion and worry start to bubble up, and I'm not sure what to say to make this easier.

"Kia, your body is beautiful, but your nakedness is a distraction, and neither of us can focus. All we want to do is touch and pleasure you, but your body just isn't ready for that yet," Seb explains tactfully. *Huh, I suppose saying it like it is, is a good way to go.* More puzzlement trickles through, but thankfully her worry has dissipated.

Taking the shirt from my hand, she looks at it in bafflement, clearly not knowing what to do with it as she moves it around in her hands. Taking it back from her gently, I pull the neck hole open and cautiously ease it over her head. She raises one eyebrow at me inquiringly, and a smile plays on my lips as my suspicions are confirmed. *I don't think she's ever worn a top before.* Laughing quietly to myself, I carefully show her how to push her arms through the sleeves, then tug the shirt the rest of the way down. Kia looks down at it briefly before dismissively turning her head toward the food, clearly done with the whole mess.

Jack has put together an elaborate spread of various fruit and vegetables. There are strawberries, grapes, pears, apples, perfectly ripe bananas and a whole, unpeeled mango sits to the side. Seb, clearly starving, starts shovelling a handful of grapes into his mouth, and I grab a banana and begin peeling it. After watching us, Kia reaches out and picks up the mango. Bringing it to her lips, she takes a big, full bite out of it, and makes a tiny noise of appreciation. Seb stops chewing, and I pause in my actions, as we both watch her curiously. Kia continues to munch on the mango without a second thought. *Does she not know that she needs to take the peel off first?*

Deciding it's best to show her, I gingerly take the fruit from her hands and begin peeling it with a knife that Jack had thought to put on the tray. As she watches me, she picks up a piece of skin and pops it into her mouth.

"Erm… there are some fruits that have to have the outside shell removed from them, Kia, as they are not easy to digest and often taste badly. For this fruit, called a mango, let's stick to the fleshy part on the inside." She continues to watch me work away and removing the skin. It's a messy job, and I wish Seb had done it, because he can peel and chop one of these with little to no waste.

Once done, I pass the cut-up pieces of the juicy inside over to Kia, then start to lick my fingers clean. Kia dives into the mango slices and she watches me in fascination as I work the juice off my fingers. Seb passes me a warm damp cloth and I want to keep teasing her, but I think better of it and finish off with the cloth. We sit in companionable silence for a bit as we have our fill. Kia gulps down two full glasses of water, then curls herself up into the space between me and Seb. With her back against my chest and her hands in Seb's, I feel her contentment flow through me as I close my eyes and ease down into my centre.

With some hope, we can get a few hours of rest.

CHAPTER ELEVEN

*J*ack

After leaving food for Sebastian, Rolland and Kia, I teleport to the Ketil Mountain in Greenland, to see if Jerhaner can help me sort through my quagmired thoughts. I arrive on a large outcrop about halfway up the mountainside. It is only accessible by those who can teleport and cannot be seen from the ground below. Taking a deep cleansing breath, I enter through the tall stone doors and into the large open common area. Thankfully, no one is about as I walk over to the lift, which is the only exit from this space, and head down to see Jerhaner.

A few hundred years ago, my kind and a few other races claimed this space for ourselves and turned into a home and a safe haven. The inside was carved and created by the Krish-yarn's, a race that has the ability to move and remould solid matter, making building and restructuring any given space, easy and effortless. The entire ground level is the landing bay, with gigantic doors that slide open to allow large ships to fly in and holds everything needed to maintain the ships and build new ones. The first floor above the landing bay is open air and allows you to see down into the area below. All of the remaining space above the first floor is made up of living quarters, with each level varying in height and size depending on which species is living within them. The natural light that comes in through various sized holes throughout the mountainside was created by the Sealeek's, who have the ability to channel currents of energy.

I step out of the lift and make my way along the well-lit corridor. The air is dry, not damp as you would expect inside a mountain due to the system of ventilation shafts that was created. As I walk, I take note of how quiet it is this time of night. Usually the mountain is buzzing with noise, but now it is just the sound of my footfalls which ricochet off the dark, bare walls. I begin to wonder if my friend may have turned in for a few hours. We do not need as much sleep as the other races do, but unlike the Ayrans, who *never* need sleep, we do require some to replenish our bodies.

Rounding the last corner, I find Jerhaner's door open and relief washes over me as I realise I will not be disturbing him after all. Pausing when I reach his office, I find his face to be relaxed, as he sits at his smooth stone desk looking down at his comms device. His office is a dimly-lit and somewhat small room, just big enough to comfortably host a handful of people, but not so large as to feel the cold that can sometimes creep in during the long winters. Even with the bare walls of the mountain, the room still has a warmth to it, with Jerhaner's colourful wall hangings and the various pictures he has collected since we have been here.

"Why are you covered in dirt, Jack?" Jerhaner asks mildly. He has not looked up, so I assume he is smelling it from the clothes, as I have not yet changed.

Trying to find the last of the races and species that are stuck here, is becoming harder each day. With nothing but instinct to guide us, it is growing increasingly apparent that we may not find everyone. I would not have left Kia earlier if I had not given my word to Kerboran that I would return to him to cut off an exit point in one of the tunnels of a mountain in Russia. I had to go back to Kia when I felt her mind slip so I am sure Kerboran shall surely curse my name when he sees my face next.

"I need a few moments of your thoughts, Jerhaner," I state, stepping into his office.

Like all of our race, Tyrian's have features that bear a close resemblance to the human's impression of elves. Jerhaner is just slightly shorter than me in height, but his build and hair are the same. He usually spends more time braiding his at the sides, much like I would have done back in our homeland. Now, it just seems tedious and idol, so I wear it back in a loose tie. Jerhaner's clothing is the common attire for Tyrian's and is made of a plant-based material that looks similar to the leather that Rolland and Sebastian wear. Close fitting trousers and tops keep the warmth in but are also incredibly light and breathable.

Jerhaner's emerald eyes flash up to mine, taking quick note of any minor tells that I may be showing. He squints his eyes at me, telling me he knows what I am about to say to him is austere. I trust him explicitly, as he is one of the few who knows my true identity and real name, and if I did not have full confidence in him, I would not be willing to speak openly with him regarding Kia.

"Pull the door closed - it feels far too long since we spoke," he suggests as he puts away the comms device in the draw of his desk. I do as he requests, then take a seat in one of the high wingback chairs opposite him, considering where best to begin. "I can tell your thoughts are deep and troubled.

What has you in such a quandary?" His voice, though steady, carries concern.

"Jack," he continues, when I do not respond, "I have known you since before we could climb the Trees of Fresbeck. You are - how do they put it here - oh yes, you are an open book to me." His oval-shaped face and refined jawline remind me so much of his father. A familiar crooked smile tugs at his lips, and I feel mine mirror his. That is, until I remember why I am here. I feel my face begin to falter, and I look down at my knees, contemplating how I can explain Kia to him.

"Jack?" he coaxes with concern.

"We found an Ayran a few hours ago," I finally divulge, though I still do not look up at him, which no doubt is a clear sign of the uncertainty of my knowledge. A silence hangs in the air after my disclosure.

"You are not certain, are you?" he asks hesitantly.

"I was completely convinced until I stepped into her mind," I admit, looking up him. "I have never seen a mind like it in all my existence. It bears the resemblance of a Haoghvan, though how that is even possible, I am not sure," I ponder in ambivalence.

His eyes seem thoughtful as a small line deepens across his forehead. "What leads you to suspect she might be an Ayran?" he asks.

"Her birthmark is similar to Melana's, sitting behind her left ear, and I could feel her energy within a five-mile radius of where we found her. I could never mistake the signature of one of their kind, just like you," I emphasize. His face echoes my thoughts and I feel my body relax slightly, knowing I can speak openly to him.

"Why do you question your knowledge then?" he puzzles while lifting a hand to trace a slender finger over his lips.

"She does not respond or behave like one," I explain, as my thoughts return to her behavior in the pool with Rolland, then my own when I kissed her. Though it was only in her mind, guilt still grows within me, knowing how my people would frown so severely upon me.

"How so?" Jerhaner's voice pulls me from my thoughts again.

"Her lack of reaction to a Gauldrix stone, for one, and she was-" I cannot bring myself to tell him. Even though I trust him undoubtedly, something holds me back.

"She what, Jack?" His interest has undoubtedly increased at my hesitation, yet he remains well in control of his emotions.

"Just her general behaviour. Perhaps it is from her time spent in isolation," I say, trying to appease him. He knows I am holding back, but also knows better than to push me.

"I would be more than happy to meet her, to help settle your thoughts," he offers kindly.

"I will consider your offer, though at the moment what she needs is nourishment to enhance the healing process. Her state of mind is working purely on instinct right now. Plus, with The Source pouring directly through her into Rolland and Sebastian, they are not so pleasant to be around," I reason to him, rolling my eyes slightly.

"Conceding that she is an Ayran, how did they even get her here? Though, more importantly, she cannot stay here on Gaia. The completion of the craft we are building below is just about done, with the final tests being completed in the next few weeks, but perhaps it would be wiser to speak to the Atlantians," Jerhaner suggests, leaning forward on his desk with his arms folded.

"My thoughts exactly," I agree, raising my eyebrows a fraction. "Would you coordinate a meeting with one of them as soon as possible? They may even be able to shed some light on who she is, if she is not an Ayran."

"Of course," Jerhaner nods deeply.

Our conversation turns to organising our jeanarms and other preparations that still need to be done, yet I find my thoughts drifting back to Kia's mind and how she was able hide her thoughts like she did.

Even I could not establish such a vast plane within my own mind.

CHAPTER TWELVE

*M*att

It feels like I've been staring at my computer monitor for hours. The bullets still sit on the side of my desk where I placed them hours ago, taunting me to confirm what I already know to be true. I've been following the scum bags for months, maybe even a year. Every time I made a move, they were already gone. Rubbing my hand over the back of my neck to try and relieve some of the tension, I gaze back at the screen in front of me. *It's feels like I've been chasing a ghost. As for the girl, surely she can't be the same one I've been seeing in my nightmares?*

I squeeze my eyes shut, rubbing them with my thumb and fingers under my glasses. *This is mad. Absolutely, unequivocally stone, crazy, mad.* Moving over to the other side of my desk, I take the bullets and begin the process of analysing them. Placing the shell found in the girl under the microscope first, I'm not surprised to find it's completely clean.

The bullet pulled from Rolland, however, shows its dirty side beautifully. The rifling is the same as the one I've got stored away, the one from the same dweeb who shot me when

I got close a few weeks back in Paris. I take a swab of the fluid remaining in the cartridge and prepare to send it to a friend who works at a lab. He's incredibly efficient, given the right money, and has never led me wrong before.

Glancing up at the clock on the wall it reads 5:48 am. There's no point trying to sleep now, I'm too geared up on the possibility that it's the same girl I've been seeing in my night-mares for the last several months. Curiosity overtakes my need to give her space and I decide to find out.

Making my way out of my room and down the stairs, my mind starts to replay the nightmares. They've felt progres-sively more real and I'm beginning to think I *am* losing my mind. The last one was bad enough that I almost talked to the guys about it.

I see her being held up against a wall by a man twice her size, his hand locked tightly around her throat. She can't lift her hands to push him off and chains pull her back against the wall as her legs kick out. The man slams her head hard against the wall as he shouts at her in a language I don't understand. She shakes her head frantically and opens her eyes, pleading with him. She turns her head toward a group of people who are huddled tightly together against a wall behind bars. A small boy is screaming in the arms of a woman, as he tries to reach for the pinned girl.

She closes her eyes and the boy calms. I see a tear begin to fall down her bruised cheek and my heart breaks. I try to move forward, but I'm stuck like a granite statue, as always, a bystander made to watch. A large shadow looms to my left, but I can't turn to see who, or what, it is, and fear starts to crawl up my legs, leaving cold shivers in its track as it makes its way slowly to my stomach.

The girl opens her eyes and I can clearly see the terror etched deep within them. The man holding her laughs

91

throatily and licks her tears away as he runs his hand up her slender arm. She seems to barely notice, her full attention focused on the looming shadow. The fear working its way up my body has now reached my chest and is suffocating me with its stone grasp.

I sense the shadow moving closer, but I can't make out details except that it has a pitch-black tall frame which is easily two feet taller than mine. The man holding her says something else I can't understand, and a look of determination suddenly passes over the girl's face. The shadow moves closer to her, placing itself in front of me, which blocks my view of what's going on. A child's scream pierces my eardrums just as the shadow disperses and I can now clearly see the girl's lifeless body hanging limply in the chains.

I shake myself out of the memory as I amble through the open layout kitchen toward the fridge and grab another bottle of water. As I drink, I glance around the modern space, taking in the black worktops that contrast beautifully with the white cupboard doors, giving it a fresh look that I can't help but appreciate. The sun is coming up, washing some reds and yellows through the kitchen window, lighting up the room. Seb's dirty dishes from earlier still lay beside the sink and I'm struck by this oddity as it's unusual for him to leave a mess, being such a neat freak.

Making my way out of the kitchen through the light entryway toward Seb's room, I hear a crash followed quickly by a thud. I pause to see if I can detect if the sound came from Brad's room above, or from Seb's room in front. I wait for a few beats and no other sound follows. But the feeling that something isn't right sends creepy shivers up my back. As I begin to move again, I hear another thud directly in front of me. Turning right into the hallway that leads to Seb's room, the shivers intensify as I sprint to his door. It's part way open and as I look inside, time pulls itself to a stop.

Rolland is sprawled on his back on the floor next to the bed with his eyes closed and Seb looks to be sleeping on the bed, facing me. My eyes flash down and impossibly I see the girl I've watched being tortured repeatedly in my nightmares half slumped over, trying to pull herself up on her elbows. I sense a movement to my right and, acting on instinct, I throw a shield up around her.

Turning my gaze away from the girl, I look to my right and see a tall and lanky figure, close to eight feet tall, with tendrils of smoke slithering like snakes where its feet should be. Its form appears to be semi-solid and moves as though it has no physical body. The smell of decay hits my nose, making me want to heave as I take in the gangly arms draped loosely next to a body that is covered in black, translucent skin. No mouth or nose can be seen on its decaying face, but its empty black eyes bulge slightly as my gaze locks with it.

Something tells me it's the same shadow that I've seen in all of my nightmares.

Dropping down to the floor, I move over to the girl and pull her small frame into the safety of my arms. She wraps herself around me and energy zaps through my chest and arms, causing the shield to double around us as we lay cocooned safely inside. Her body is shaking, her breathing ragged.

"I've got you, little one, shh," I whisper gently, trying to calm her. With a sob she buries her head into my shoulder and shakes her head. My attention is torn from the beautiful girl in my arms as the floor suddenly begins to vibrate. A heavy thud shakes the ground as I try to look through my shield, but its dense multi-colored glow makes it impossible to see anything.

I shake my head in confusion. My shield is usually white or transparent, not this strange array of multiple colours, nor is it ever as dense and quieting as it appears to be now. I find I can only just make out the voices moving around us. Drawing my attention back to the girl in my arms, I do a quick check of her body. She's wearing nothing but a white shirt that is cumbersome on her tiny frame. There are dried patches of blood along the back and she looks only slightly better than she does in my nightmares. I feel the arms she has wrapped around my neck tighten and I can't help but breathe in her unique scent.

"It's okay, nothing can touch you in here. Just try to relax and calm your breathing for me," I speak gently into her ear. Glancing back up, I try to lessen the energy running through the shield so I can see what's going on, but nothing happens. *What the hell?* As I try again, I feel her grip tighten as she shakes her head. "Are you doing this?" I ask her, confused. She doesn't reply

"Matt! Drop the shield!" Rolland bellows through my head. *"Whatever it was, it's gone."* Panic laces his words.

"I can't. I think she's controlling it," I confess. *"I'm trying to lessen the energy going through, but nothing is happening."* I try again, but it still doesn't respond to me.

"Whatever that was, it's gone now. It's just Rolland and Sebastian," I say soothingly. She doesn't answer me as her head continues to shake and her breathing becomes more laboured.

"Matt! For fuck's sake drop the damn shield!" Rolland barks. He has definitely lost it and I'm pretty sure I'd be a dead man if it weren't for the shield between us.

"She won't let me! What the hell do I do?" I implore. Silence follows, and I start to panic myself.

"Just speak to her, Matt. Tell her we just want to see that

94

she's okay." Rolland's hard voice rumbles in my head. I gently rub her back and her arms begin to loosen, but her grip on the shield doesn't. Pulling her head away from my neck, I gaze at her small, delicate face. Taking in her button nose and thin, pink lips; absorbing every detail and etching them into my memory.

Her almond shaped eyes are heavy, and she looks dazed. "Listen to me, little one. I'm not going to drop the shield. You can keep it up as long as you want, I just want to lessen the power so that the guys can see you," I try to console her as I run my thumb over her round cheek. She pulls her head forward, back into my neck, but her grip on the shield drops slightly, making it translucent enough for me to see through it.

Rolland, Seb and Jack are all crouched around us, only a few metres away since the shield is not very big. Hugging her gently, I can feel her breathing is incredibly heavy and I worry she's going to pass out any moment. Seb seems to take a small breath of relief, but Rolland doesn't appear to be breathing at all. Jack stands and starts pacing but doesn't stop watching us with his electric blue eyes. *I've never seen Jack pace before. Ever.*

"Kia, I'm so sorry," Rolland begins in a soft tone. "I know you're scared and all you want to do is hide away from the world, but I can't let you do that," he insists thickly. I frown at him as he grunts as if someone has hit him on the back. *What's gotten into him?* "I won't let you hide from the world like this. I see too much beauty in your eyes, and I would be doing your people wrong if I was to let you crumble away into nothing like that thing wants you to," Rolland coaxes deeply. His voice is full of emotion, tightening my stomach, but I feel Kia move her head sideways to look out at Rolland.

95

Her breathing has evened out slightly but it's as if she's having to concentrate on keeping it that way. Her grip on the shield drops a little more and the colours stop swirling as it returns to my usual white translucent shade. I still can't drop it, but I feel like I have a little more control over it now. I try drawing it in, so the guys can get closer but it's harder than it should be, and it doesn't move.

Rolland moves around so he can see Kia's face. "Trust isn't easy when you've been through what you have, but you have my word that it's gone, and Jack is here if it comes back. Just drop the shield so I can take the pain away and if you want to put it back up, then you can do so with all of us in it." His chiseled face is hard with concentration, like he's trying to solve a puzzle. His usual warm beige skin tone has faded around his face and there is a ghost of a shadow under his tired lobelia blue eyes.

Her hold on the shield finally drops completely and I lower it, drawing the energy back. Rolland moves forward faster than someone of his size should be able to and plucks her swiftly, yet gently, out of my arms. I run my eyes over his face and I swear I can see his eyes glistening. I watched as Kia's breath evens out and begins to calm down as Rolland strokes her hair and kisses her temple before running his hand down her arms and along her back softly.

I look over to Jack and Seb who seem to be having a silent conversation, even though I know Jack can't speak through any of our minds telepathically.

"She's too weak, Jack, and I'm not doing it so soon after she was attacked," Seb insists as he mirrors Jack's stance. *What the hell? Have they changed roles or something? And why doesn't Seb want to heal her?* I stand up and move closer to them, wondering what the hell is going on.

"Someone needs to start talking," I demand, looking at

Jack first, though why I do, I haven't a clue. It's like pulling blood from a stone. I turn to Seb, but he just rubs a hand over his face and looks up at the ceiling. "Seriously, one of you needs to explain some of this." *Why are they both acting so weird?*

"Which part, Matt?" Seb grinds out with frustration as he looks me square in the eye. His chocolate orbs glare at me as though he's on his last ounce of patience. "If you want me to explain why you couldn't drop your shield, then ask Jack. If you want to know why I won't heal her, then to put it simply," he pauses as he takes a visible breath and gives a quick glance over at Kia, "I'd rather not trigger another flash-back to a memory that was most likely a result of the thing that was just here!"

Crap, they weren't just nightmares, they were all real. Something must have given my thoughts away because Seb's face becomes questioning. *Bugger.*

"What?" Seb asks tightly as he straightens his body out. I turn away, hoping to avoid his questions a little longer. "What was that, Matt? What was that look?" he asserts with a steely tone. *No such luck apparently.* Screwing my eyes shut and hoping to go unnoticed, I take a step toward the door, but my path is blocked by a hand and I feel a zap of Seb's hot energy shoot through my chest.

"OW! What the hell, Seb!" I hunch over, rubbing my chest. I hear movement, followed by a grunt from Rolland who is still sitting on the floor to my right. Remaining hunched over, I open my eyes to see Kia trying to get up out of Rolland's lap to come to me.

"Woah, whoa, sweetheart, he's fine. He just needs to start talking before Sebastian zaps his brain and renders him useless for the rest of his days."

"ROLLAND!" Seb shouts. Kia tries even harder to get up.

"I'm joking, Kia, joking, joking, I'm sorry. He's not going to do anything to him... much," Rolland placates. Seb lets out a frustrated breath and my head feels like it's going to explode. Kia looks at me as though she wants to comfort me but settles back into Rolland's arms again.

"Start talking." This comes from Jack this time. *Darn, I forgot he was in the room.* My chest returns back to normal and I straighten up to find all the guys waiting expectantly. *Oh man, that door is looking really inviting just now.* As is if reading my thoughts, Jack steps in front of the door, blocking my path entirely. "Start talking, Matt, or I will make you." His steely voice remains flat as always, but his tone has an air of authority to it. *Idiot.*

I take another glance at Kia, but she looks away and hides her face in Rolland's neck. *Not going to get much help there, it seems.* Turning my back on Jack, I walk over to the window and try to think of the best way to put it all into words. Rubbing my hand over the back of my neck, I try to ease some of the tension I can feel building there. My glasses slip slightly, so I push them up with my finger as I turn back to face Seb and Jack. Rolland still hasn't moved from the floor on the other side of the bed, but I can see his head as he looks over at me. His honey-blonde hair doesn't look like it's been brushed, but that doesn't detract from the prince charming appearance that never seems to leave him.

"About seven months ago, I started having nightmares and in each of them, I saw her... Kia. The first few times I couldn't remember much of them, but I would wake up in a cold sweat with the deep need to find her," I start. Jacks eyes close, and his jaw tightens. Slightly confused by his reaction, I continue. "In every dream, I would see her being-" The words seem to get stuck in my throat as images flash across my vision and I feel sick to the deepest parts of my soul. Guilt riddles me for not speaking up sooner and my eyes begin to burn. The need to escape the room overwhelms me and I take a step in the direction of the door, but Seb moves in front of me. His eyes are wild, and his dark features make him look even deadlier as he glares at me. I turn away from him to find Kia trying to pull herself out of Rolland's arms once again.

This time he lets her go as he stands up with her, supporting her weight fully, so her feet aren't touching the floor. He steps closer to me, bringing Kia within reaching distance. Her eyes remind me of the sea at night, reflecting the stars in the night sky. They're swirling steadily, and I feel as though they're tugging at my soul.

Guilt for not getting her out faster moves through my chest and I draw away from her gaze to look down at my feet.

A small hand pulls at my head and I feel energy slipping down my neck. I can tell it's the same energy that was being used to control my shield earlier, but there's something different about it now. The feeling is similar to how I feel when I relax into Seb's crystal pool, but stronger. Energy travels deeper down my neck and shoulders, easing the tightness that's formed in my chest from all the guilt. My head is encouraged up and I find Kia's sapphire eyes swirling slowly. All I want to do is lose myself in them.

Kia pulls me closer, wrapping both of her small arms around my neck. Her energy travels deeper and lower into my belly, as though she's trying to soothe the guilt away. I close my eyes and fold my arms around her gently but find Rolland is still holding her against his chest. Carefully, he eases her into my arms so that I'm now fully supporting her weight, but he keeps a hand on her lower back.

My eyes begin to sting from the relief and overwhelming emotions of having her in my arms. A tear tracks down my left cheek and I bury my head deeper into her right shoulder, breathing her in. She smells like the forest after it's been raining - fresh and clean with the undertone of damp wood. More energy trickles through me, soothing the tension etched within my heart before her head moves, followed by her lips on my cheek.

As I look back at her, I see her eyes flick over my face. Small specs of silver appear within the pools of her eyes and I watch them swirl within their depths. *They're incredible.* Kia's eyes catch on my lips and her head inches forward a fraction.

"Nope," I hear, as she's pulled away from me. "Not now, Kia, that's not happening right now," Rolland's voice warns. Her brow furrows but her energy lingers deep within me as Rolland plucks her gently from my arms and back into his. "Later maybe, but not just now. We need to hear him out, which isn't going to happen with his mouth otherwise occupied," he reprimands softly as he takes her over to the bed. Kia's face is full of frustration.

I look over at Seb and Jack, who are both watching Kia with curious eyes. Not sure as to what the big puzzle is, I turn away from them to walk back over to the window. Looking out over the open grounds that surround us, I see the sun is just coming up, reflecting its colours onto the lake that is to the right of the house. Seb's window opens out onto the side gardens that are enclosed by old oak trees as well as beech and sycamores. I can just hear some of the early birds starting their morning songs and it helps to ease some of the anxiety still crawling its way through me.

Taking a deep breath, I try to find the words to describe all that I've seen happen over the last several months. "In each nightmare…" can't call them nightmares if they are real, "whatever you want to call them, I would see Kia getting tortured, abused, forced to endure things that I didn't think were even imaginable." Images flash across my eyes of a man force feeding Kia some kind of liquid, then her being drained of her energy and injected with black fluid. Sometimes she would spew it up and other times she would pass out straight away.

Nausea begins to bubble up, so I take a steadying breath to calm myself and close my eyes, trying to bring my focus back on the singing of the birds outside. "I couldn't move or speak to her and there were beings in the visions that, according to the information I found on them, aren't from here. Beings aren't even the right name for them, they're more like creatures, part lizard and part humanoid. The lizard-like thing was the worst, but I only saw it once." I hope for everyone's sake that my information on that thing is wrong. "There was another thing, a creature that would return to her repeatedly. That *thing* that was just here looked damn close to it, but it was more solid than it had been in any of the visions. Whatever it was, it always left her weaker than when it first entered."

I take my glasses off, wiping them on the lower part of my shirt, more to give my hands something to do than anything. "On a few occasions, I would get a glimpse of their location, but I had a hard time figuring out where it was. When I did finally find it, I went to check it out but there was nothing there. The buildings and places were just as I had seen them in the dream, but there was no evidence or trace of anyone having been there."

I inhale deeply as I prepare myself to tell them the rest. Placing my glasses back on, I turn around to face them all. "The mission last month that I had no intel on was based on a hunch. I saw a landmark that I knew, and I felt like I just had to go, to see if it was all in my head." I watch Seb's face screw up in concentration as it finally dawns on him which mission I'm referring to.

"Paris? Are you talking about Paris?" Seb asks incredulously as he folds his arms over his chest.

"Yep. I couldn't wait for you all to agree on the logistics, so I just went myself."

Seb runs a hand through his ebony hair and looks up at the ceiling. "Matt, you should have told us. One of us would have come with you without question," he stresses as he lets out a heavy sigh.

"And what would I have said, Seb?!" I seethe. Frustration leaks into my voice as I struggle to keep calm. "Oh, hey guys, I'm going to Paris on a hunch based on a series of nightmares. Do you wanna tag along?" I let out a breath in irritation.

"You would never have agreed to it, Seb. Not without getting more information on the layout of the grounds and then asking a hundred questions. I didn't think you would have believed me. Hell, I didn't believe it myself until I walked in and saw her just ten minutes ago!" I rant. My voice has risen and all I want to do is get out of the room, preferably with Kia in my arms, but that's not going to happen.

I look over at her to see she's fallen asleep and her brow is slightly wrinkled, as though she's uncomfortable. Rolland catches my eyes and I see him make a 'keep it quiet' gesture. He runs a hand over her head and down her arms, drawing her further into his solid chest.

I turn my gaze back over to Jack and Seb, wanting to finish up the conversation as quickly as possible. "The last dream I had of her wasn't far from where you found her. I don't know why, but something told me they knew I was tracing them and that they were going to move. So, I looked for the next nearest abandoned building and found that crumbling heap of stones. When I got there, it was total mayhem. Brad told me to stay in the chopper, while he made a diversion round front, and Jack disappeared once we got within five miles. You both took off before I could even say anything. I was left torn between keeping the craft secure and taking off in search of her. My gut was twisting so much, I was nearly about to abandon the chopper. Then Rolland came walking back and my chance was gone."

I look again at Kia and take in her small form curled into Rolland. Possessiveness settles in my chest and my arms feel heavy with the need to pull her into them.

Shaking my head to clear my thoughts, I use Jack and Seb's silence as an excuse to leave. I make my way toward the door without looking at either of them, but I only get a few paces before Seb's hand shoots out in front of me, stopping me in my tracks. I let out a breath of annoyance and look down at the floor.

"Matt, don't be so hard on yourself. I understand why you didn't speak up, but don't hold back next time, no matter how stupid or crazy it sounds *or* feels. Just promise to speak to one of us." Seb's words lift some of the weight resting heavily on my mind. I look up to see compassion and understanding in his intense, deep-set eyes. I nod in response and he moves his hand away so that I can leave. Making my way back to the kitchen, I pick up the water bottle I dropped earlier as my thoughts return to Kia and the energy - *her energy* - that still lingers deep within me.

CHAPTER THIRTEEN

*J*ack

Matt's words are still bouncing around in my head. Seven months. Kia has been mind sharing with him for seven long months. *How long has she actually been here?*

Seeing a Gjinn, as humans call them, was not expected. The possibility that she has a Draconian looking for her is another matter altogether. A Gjinn can be dealt with, but a Draconian… even I do not have the ability to take one on alone. Gjinn's can be warded off by certain stones, of which I only have a few. The couple I do have we could use to ward Sebastian's room, but it is uncertain how long they will hold.

I need to speak to Kia but Sebastian is right, I cannot push her. Her mind needs respite and her body needs more time to rejuvenate. I look over at her and I can tell she is not sleeping, although I am sure Rolland believes she is. She may be resting her eyes perhaps, but she will not rest her mind, not now. It will take her several hours to calm down after seeing the Gjinn.

I move over and sit on the bed which presses in under my

weight. Turning so that I face Kia, I use my home tongue in the hope that I can ease her with some comforting words. "Kia, I need to speak to you." Kia turns further into Rolland's side. Her obvious dismissal hurts. "Kia, please, my angel, I need you to listen to me." She raises an arm to cover her head.

"Rolland, I will be back in a few minutes with some stones to ward the room. The creature that was here is known as a Gjinn, but it goes by many different names. I have weakened it enough that it will not return for at least a day or two. I will explain more to Sebastian, which he can pass on to you through your connection. Speaking about it around Kia right now is not going to alleviate her fear." I take another look at Kia before I stand, then head for the door.

"Sebastian, if you would help me carry a few stones, I would be very grateful."

Walking through the house toward the other side of the building, my mind returns to Matt and why he did not speak up sooner. *Perhaps my own lack of disclosure is partly to blame.*

"Jack, I know we don't see eye to eye on pretty much everything, but-" Sebastian says, pausing as we arrive at my door. It suddenly occurs to me that none of them have ever stepped into my section of the house. I turn to him fully, so we are face to face, almost eye level. Sebastian is a few inches shorter than I am, but his frame is slightly broader in the chest.

"For Kia's sake, I wish to start afresh and try to build more trust between us. I know you have never lied, but something holds you back from speaking openly with me, or with any of us for that matter," he finishes. His words are full of sincerity as his mahogany eyes remain steady on mine. They remind me so much of his forefathers in Grandor, with whom

I spent many cycles. They were some of the most rational and logical beings I ever met and all of them had varied abilities in healing and the ability to mask themselves in the shadows. Sebastian's skill in transferring pain from one being to another, like he did to Matt, is not common amongst his people, but rather a result of his hereditary bloodline. In regard to their physical appearance, they are similar to the Persian's of Gaia. Most of them have silky, very dark brown or ebony hair, medium skin tone and dark, exotic features.

Opening my door, I gesture him into my room. He hesitates but continues through, then abruptly stops in his tracks. I wait a moment, but he still does not move.

"Sebastian, if you could move over just a little so I can shut the door, I would be very appreciative," I request. He edges slowly to the right which gives me enough room to close the door.

This is where I feel most relaxed and at peace. Large arched windows look out onto the east side of the gardens, letting in the summer light. The cream coloured walls are broken up by the many 'fantasy' paintings, as humans call them, breaking up my cream walls. Wide steps lead up to a separate chamber that I use as my sleeping quarters when I am in need of them. The large black and white marble table which sits in the centre of the main room is used when I am breaking up large crystals. Shelves line the walls and are full of stones, gems and crystals that I have collected from across Gaia. Some are a lot larger than others, but most would fit comfortably in the palm of your hand. Those I brought back from my homeland are kept separately in the room above this one. There is more light up there, which keeps them energised for slightly longer after being used.

The stones required for keeping the Gjinn away come from the Donegal Mountain in Ireland where I shall need to return to soon to find more. Taking two from the shelf, I pass them to Sebastian as his eyes continue to feast on everything in the room.

"Sebastian," I prod. His eyes flick to me, but they are immediately drawn away again, and I watch as his eyes land on the far wall that exhibits the sword that I have carried with me for as long as I can remember. It was passed down to me by my father, who I have not seen since leaving Grandor and the memory of receiving it flashes through my mind.

CHAPTER FOURTEEN

*S*ebastian

I'm not sure what I was expecting when I stepped into Jack's room, but it wasn't the sight that is now before me. Never in all my years have I seen so many crystals in one place. My eyes wander around the room, trying to take it all in and I get so lost in what I'm seeing that I forget Jack is there until I hear him call my name. I look over at him briefly but am immediately drawn away again when I spot a beautiful sword displayed on the far wall. It calls to me to touch it and I almost involuntarily move toward it, intent on feeling its energy run through my fingers, but a hand snags on my right bicep, stopping me. I turn and find Jack's angelic lagoon eyes watching me.

"Please do not make me move it, Sebastian. It has hung there for a hundred and fifty years, and I would like it to remain there," he explains, flicking his glance to the wall then back at me, before releasing my arm. He returns to the far side of the room to collect another two stones. They're incredibly heavy and I wonder where he got them. Jack then waits for me at the door, clearly wanting me to exit first. I manage to get another hard look around, wishing I could poke about for a day or so. *The ever-elusive mystery that is Jack. He has more secrets than any of us will ever know.*

I reluctantly make my way out of his room and down the corridor, taking in the various paintings we've all collected over the years. The dark solid wood flooring and the low light keeps the large house feeling more like a home than the mansion that it really is. Heading back to Kia and Rolland, my thoughts are drawn back to the sword that hangs on Jack's wall.

"You are right again, Sebastian, and I would like to thank you for keeping a rational mind when I did not. I cannot protect Kia if I do not know who, or what brought her here." Jack's modulated voice comes from behind me. "Those that know she is here, will not give up easily in tracking her down."

I stop in my tracks as we reach the entrance hall to the house. The space is a large, open area. Light fills the hall from the large windows behind us on the landing of the stairs. As Jack joins me on the landing, the light from the window causes his hair to shimmer to a near silver tone.

He doesn't meet my gaze where he stands beside me. Compassion and empathy aren't emotions I've ever felt in regard to Jack, but knowing he feels just as helpless as Rolland and me, eases some of the hostility I have toward him.

"She's going to be fine, Jack," I assure him, trying to ease his worries, but he still doesn't lift his gaze. "Isn't she?" My gut begins to twist at his lack of confirmation.

Some of the composure that never seems to leave him, drops, along with his shoulders. "You asked for me to be more open with you, and in light of Matt holding back, I agree. We need to have more trust in one another." He takes a visible breath and finally looks up from the stones. His crystal blue eyes that usually seem so cold, appear almost as warm as Rolland's, though the look in them unsettles me, and I feel like he's about to tell me something dreadful.

"You are not the only people who have gifts, as you know, but there are many more of you all over this plane. In small groups your energy goes unnoticed, but in groups of a dozen or more, your energy becomes like a beacon, and it can be felt from miles around. A few of my own kind, and others with similar powers, agreed to keep you apart and in small numbers. Big enough to keep each other safe, but not large enough to draw the attention of those who wish you harm. Most of my time is spent either coordinating with the others who safeguard the groups, like I do with you all, or looking for others that are stranded here. There are very few of us and they hide deep within caves, mountains and the furthest parts of these lands."

Jack returns his gaze back to the stones. "When we have shared this information in the past, the groups have always sought each other out. So many lives have been lost because one of us gave in to the temptation of revealing the truth."

I turn to him fully and it looks like so much weight has been lifted from his shoulders. Yet, sadness still runs across his face when he looks up at me again. He's carried this for so long and not being able to tell any of us must have been slowly eating away at his conscience. A small amount of annoyance simmers through me, but understanding his need to keep us safe helps to ease more of the hostility I usually feel toward him. *The question remains, what does this have to do with Kia?*

"What else are you not saying, Jack?" I inquire cautiously. He lifts a perfectly plucked eyebrow. *Most likely at my quick thinking.*

110

"Ayran's are stronger than all of us put together when they are not drained and shut off from their own minds. As Kia gets stronger and regains her powers, it will be like having ten, if not more of you, under one roof. We will need to be ready for when she is fully recovered to move her somewhere that is less populated or find somewhere that can mask her energy. Very few places like that remain and even then, I have no idea if that will be enough." Jack starts off in the direction of my room and I'm left with the puzzle of how we will keep her safe, and with us.

Following Jack back to my room, I find he has stopped outside my door. *Fuck, what now?* Surging forward fast and preparing to hit whoever is threatening Kia over the head with these heavy lumps of stones, I discover a completely different scene than what I was anticipating. Kia is sitting on the window seat, looking out over the grounds and the forest surrounding the house. Both windows are open and the bird's morning songs are spilling in on the gentle breeze as it is blown around the room. Rolland sits behind Kia with his arms draped loosely around her stomach, looking incredibly puzzled and almost lost. Jack paces forward and sets his stones in two corners of the room, so I place mine in the remaining two. Taking a seat in one of the cushioned chairs by the bed, I turn it so I can watch Kia. As I do, Jack goes over to Kia and kneels by her legs. The bright sunlight is pouring in through the window like a spotlight, highlighting every one of her bruises, cuts and burns. Moving my study back to Jack, I see more emotions play across his face. *What's up with him now?*

Kia has tears falling silently down her cheeks as she looks out the window. Such sadness clouds her eyes that you would think she was watching the world being destroyed right at that very moment. I'm puzzled as to what has got her so upset. Jack says something in his own language to her as I flick my eyes over to Rolland, but he looks just as confused as I feel.

Jack rests his head on her knee gently and says something else. Kia's small hand lifts up and runs over his hair, but she doesn't take her eyes from the view. Jack captures her hand, bringing it to his lips before Kia pulls her gaze from the window to finally look down at Jack. She opens her mouth to speak, but frustration falls over her features as she screws her eyes shut. The need to heal her throat and vocal cords overwhelms me to the point of near suffocation. But her body still needs time to recover from what I pushed it to do just a couple of hours ago.

A small robin lands on the window ledge and chirps quietly. Kia turns sharply, but the bird doesn't fly off like I expected it to. Instead, it hops forward a few steps and chirps again. Kia's face lights up and she smiles for the first time since we found her. The robin flies off and Kia moves to follow it, causing Rolland to grunt from her fast movement. He eases her back to his lap as she continues to smile gently and inquiringly. When she looks back at Jack again, the smile that continues to play across her heart-shaped face feels like it's soothing every inch of the worry that Jack's words left within me.

"Maybe some more food and rest are in order so that Sebastian can do a little more healing?" Jack offers with a smile playing at the corner of his own mouth. *Which is really strange to see.*

"What do you suggest?" I ask, sitting up straighter in the chair.

"Some more fruit, perhaps another bowl of your vegetable soup. Keep it simple and carry on using the Brondroll stones for washing and cooking. I have left some more on the countertop," Jack directs as he moves to sit on the window seat beside Kia.

I take another glance at Kia and find she's looking back out the window but with more curiosity now. Thankful she's not crying anymore, I make my way out of the room and head for the kitchen, feeling slightly more at ease than I have since we found her.

CHAPTER FIFTEEN

*R*olland
          Kia's emotions are a jumble of loss, sadness and hope. I push some comforting energy into her to help settle the swirling emotions, while feeling hers reflecting back. From Jack's spot on the other side of Kia, he studies the cuffs still in place on her small wrists. There's no lock or seam to be found. His gaze moves up to her face, but her attention is still focused outside, watching the birds flying past. I'm pretty sure if her body was in better shape, she would be trying to climb out of the window to follow them. The thought brings a smile to my face, which catches Jack's attention.

"I shall see if Brad has risen yet. It may take him a few hours, but I have no doubt he will be able to make something strong enough to cut through these," Jack assures, running his thumbs absently over the cuffs. He lifts Kia's hands again to his lips, kissing them gently and more hope swells through her as she turns to him.

Affection and desire run through her, finding their way

into my own body and waking up feelings I've been trying to push down for the last couple of hours.

Kia leans forward and places a soft kiss on Jack's cheek before returning her attention back to the view outside. Jack's eyes are wide with puzzlement and worry, yet the underlying look of desire is unmistakable. *How has she brought so many emotions out from someone so stoic as Jack?*

As I watch, Jack's eyelashes slowly lower to his cheeks, and I can see he's trying to shake himself out of his daze without actually moving. Taking a deep breath, he stands and steps into the centre of the room, keeping his head bowed for a couple of seconds more. I assume he's doing something with the stones he and Seb placed in the corners of the room, as I suddenly feel energy pulse through my arm from where it's touching the wall. Jack's head comes up and without a word, he walks out of the room.

Looking back at Kia I see a luminous smile appear on her pink lips and I'm struck with the knowledge that I would do anything to keep it there. "You, little minx, are a heap of trouble and I'm never going to get enough of you," I tell her through a deep chuckle. She turns her gaze fully to me and I find her eyes swirling with those beautiful silver white specs. Her heart-shaped face is enchanting and is perfectly accentuated by her ebony hair falling down over her shoulders. I bite my lips to keep myself from sealing them to hers and the action catches her attention. Desire slams through me again, and I can't tell if it's mine, or hers. Like a magnet, her lips pull my attention to them and it takes tremendous effort to bring my focus back up to her eyes.

Trying to think of something to distract her before this turns into another battle of wills, I drag my eyes away from her face to look out the window. "This is my favourite time of year. Everything is in full bloom and the morning skies are so beautiful." Her desire is still vibrating through my body and I know that if I look back, I won't be able to stop myself from claiming her. My hardness is growing every second, and I'm in desperate need of a piss, which *really* isn't helping.

Kia turns away to rest her head against her arms over the window frame. I let out a harsh breath in relief, but it doesn't help to alleviate my hard cock that's still in desperate need of release.

A few minutes later, Seb stalks back in carrying a tray of food. *"Seb, I seriously need a piss and I can't hold it any longer."* He stops in his tracks, pulling his lips tightly into his teeth to fight his laughter then continues into the room, placing the tray down on the bedside nearest the door. If I wasn't so worried about her reaction to seeing me rock hard, I might have asked her to just come in with me into the bathroom. After helping her relieve herself and wash up after, I don't think boundaries are an issue between us. But the boner between my legs is another issue that I'm not sure I'm ready to explain.

"Kia, Rolland needs to freshen up really quick. He will only be gone for two minutes and will come right back. Do you think you could sit with me whilst he's gone? He'll just be in the next room," Seb asks softly as he gestures to the en-suite. Kia gives a nod and goes to stand.

"Woah there, little minx, no one said anything about you walking anywhere," I jest, scooping her into my arms. Stepping over to Seb who's waiting on the other side of the bed, I place her in his arms so she doesn't get an eyeful of my hard cock jutting out.

Seb pulls his lips into his mouth again. *"Rolland, do not come out of the bathroom until THAT is taken care of."*

"HA, HA, I'd like to see how you fair with her desire slamming through you randomly, especially after not having

116

taken a piss for ten hours!" My hand is still resting on Kia's lower back, so I've still got full control of her pain. But when I look down to her, I find she's watching us both, as though she knows we're having a silent conversation. As if in confirmation, she narrows her eyes a fraction, then looks directly at me. "You ready for this, sweetheart? I'll be as quick as I can," I assure her, preparing us both. I see Seb look to the ceiling, his eyes full of mirth.

Fucker! That snarky smile will soon be washed off his face when he sees the pain return to her. Removing my hand slowly, I make sure to keep eyes locked with Kia. Her breathing starts to increase, and Seb lowers his head to watch her, his face losing all trace of humour. "I'll be right back, sweetheart," I repeat, then move quickly into the bathroom, cursing my body for needing such inconveniences… and I'm not sure if I'm referring to the need to piss or to the need to relieve the painfully hard cock in my pants.

CHAPTER SIXTEEN

*S*ebastian

Kia stares at Rolland's back as he walks into the en-suite. Her breathing picks up and my heart hurts hearing it. Knowing the worst of her pain is probably coming from her back, I decide to move her into a position that will ensure there isn't anything pressing against it.

"Kia, put your arms around my neck. I'm going to move your body so my arms aren't pressed against your back. Sound good?" I explain, running my eyes over her round cheeks and glistening lips. She nods, then takes a deep breath as she moves her arms up and around my neck. As she does that, I begin to lower her legs, moving my hands so that they're supporting her weight under her bum. Kia takes another audible breath, and I take one myself, both of us relieved that part is over. Her head is about level with my chest and her feet dangling above the floor. Her eyes find mine as I study her, and I desperately wish I could take the pain away.

I turn so the backs of her legs are against the bed. The movement tugs at the shirt she's wearing so my fingers feel the softness of her skin which sends heat up my arms. Kia's eyes intensify and tiny specs of silver appear around the outside of her irises. The blue of her eyes deepens, along with her breathing, which seems to have calmed slightly. It's as if she's falling into another trance again and all her focus is on me. I feel myself falling with her.

A door slams from somewhere in the house and I'm certain it's Gerry coming home. Kia's eyes begin to darken as they stop swirling and the silver specks disappear. At the same time her hands tighten on my neck and I feel my stomach drop out. *Shit. Not again.*

Heavy steps can be heard making their way through the house and the sound of Rolland flushing the toilet is quite loud. Kia's eyes seem to widen even more in response and her fingers dig harder into my neck. *Shit!* Mentally I shout,

"Rolland! Whatever you do, do not come out of that bathroom yet!" Hoping he will hear me before it's too late, I scream, *"MATT! STOP GERRY FROM COMING IN MY ROOM! NOW!"* Louder steps pound through the house and Kia's hands slip from my shoulders, but I don't let go of the grip on her bum. Neither of us has blinked and my eyes are starting to sting.

"Seb, what's going on?" Rolland asks in a tentative whisper from the bathroom.

Voices come from the hallway and I know Kia's about to lose it. Whatever the rage is that takes over is out of her control. Suddenly, a thought sparks, and I jump on it. Not moving fast, I lower my head to hers, touching her lips with mine. She doesn't react at first, so I press firmer. When I feel her breathe slightly, I take that as a good sign and I run my tongue along her lips, kissing her again, coaxing another breath from her. I feel her relaxing more so I continue kissing her, until she opens her mouth and starts kissing me back. Her hands work their way back up my chest and then around my neck, tugging me closer to her. Her mouth and tongue become demanding, as if they've been starved for far too long.

A sound from outside the room pierces through our invisible bubble like a pin. Kia pulls away from me and takes a deep breath as realisation washes over her face of what just happened. Tears begin to fill up in her eyes and she tries to talk, but all that comes out are scrambled noises.

"Hey, shh, it's okay, Kia, it's okay," I reassure her gently. She looks away and starts to pull herself from my arms. "Kia, you're okay, sweetheart, please don't panic," I try coaxing again as I encourage her to stay with me. But she just keeps shoving at me, as she takes in big gulps of air and the tears that were building begin to run down her cheeks.

"Rolland!" I call, hoping he'll be able to calm her. Kia continues to push at my chest with her right hand, trying to make a grab for the bed with the other. Rolland yanks the bathroom door open hard, which bangs against the wall, causing Kia to startle. She gives up trying to push off of me and tries to throw all her weight onto the bed. I pull her back against me as Rolland appears in front of us.

He takes her face in his hands, forcing her to look at him. "Kia! You're okay. Take deep breaths for me," Rolland affirms softly. Kia relaxes for only a second before she starts trying to yank his hands away, but he refuses to let go. With her back to me I can't see her eyes, or see what emotions are playing across her face, but the slightly annoyed look in Rolland's eyes worries me. *What's going on with him?*

"Kia, look at me," he demands softly. She tries pulling her head from Rolland's hands again, but his grip stays firm. "No, Kia, I'm not going anywhere and neither are you," Rolland says somewhat forcefully. "Kia, listen to me. Whatever just happened isn't your fault and no one blames you. Just take a deep breath and give me a minute to speak to Sebastian," he continues firmly, still holding her head steady.

Kia continues to struggle in Rolland's grip, and I begin to think she's never going to stop. I hear him grunt just as Kia finally stops fighting him. "Thank you," Rolland says, satisfied though still sounding a bit annoyed.

"What happened, Seb?" he asks me, though he doesn't look away from her as he speaks.

"The same thing that happened in the pool. She zoned out, then was set off by Gerry coming home. I managed to calm her down, but a noise in the hallway got her riled up again. Once she snapped out of the rage and realised what had happened, she tried to scramble away from me," I explain.

Rolland's eyes remain on Kia as his face changes from annoyance to compassion. "Kia, I know this is frightening and that you don't understand what's going on. Neither do we, but please don't push us away. We will figure this out together," Rolland pleads before pulling his lips into his teeth, his eyes searching her face for some kind of response. "Please, Kia, we know we haven't completely earned your trust yet, but we've not given you any reason to doubt us thus far. All we ask is that you take these small steps with us."

Silence surrounds us as we wait to see what Kia will do. Rolland continues to hold her head, keeping his focus sharp on her face. Finally, Kia's head slumps forward followed quickly by the rest of her. Rolland takes her into his arms, wrapping them around her lower back and behind her head, drawing her into the shelter of his body as he moves them over to the bed. Kia tucks her head into his neck, and I can see her shoulders shaking as she silently cries, but she's a lot calmer now. *Holy. Shit. What the hell are we going to do?* I

rest my hands on my hips as I look up at the ceiling, contemplating how, and what, we're going to tell Jack and Matt.
Fuck, and then there's Gerry to deal with.

I look back over at Rolland, and I can tell he knows
what's going through my mind. Sighing heavily, I slowly
make my way over to the bedroom door, trying to delay the
inevitable. *Damn it, why do I always get lumbered with
having to relay the heavy info? Which reminds me, I still
haven't caught Rolland up with everything Jack said earlier.*
A weight settles on my shoulders as I open the door.

Glancing to the right down the hallway, I spot Matt
holding up one of his shields, blocking Gerry's path. His back
is to me, but he seems to be standing steady, seemingly not
fazed by the death glare that Gerry is giving him. Gerry
stands with his thick arms crossed over his solid chest,
looking about ready to kill Matt as soon as he drops the
shield.

Gerry is just a few inches shorter than me. At six foot
five, he has a sturdy frame and solid shoulders, that, along
with his square shaped head, gives him a roughness that
reflects his moods. The dark combat gear he's wearing makes
the bags under his emerald green eyes look even worse and
the few days of stubble covering his straight jaw and his hard,
angled eyebrows make him look deadly. He's nearly as soft as
Matt on the inside, but no one ever gets to see that part of
him. His need to protect and defend all of us drains him more
than anything, so having someone in our home that he doesn't
know, or hasn't even met, is causing his temper to flare. Matt
stopping him from investigating won't be forgiven easily. The
last time one of us brought someone home without running it
past him, he took half the house out on the far side.

Stepping over so I'm shoulder to shoulder with Matt, I
match Gerry's posture, keeping my eyes on him as I speak to

Matt first. "You okay?" I inquire. Matt's hand holds steady as he too keeps his eyes on Gerry.

"Yeah, I'm fine. Is Kia okay?" His soft voice is full of concern.

Gerry still doesn't move a muscle, keeping his death glare solely focused on Matt.

"She's a little shaken still, but Rolland is calming her," I explain quietly. Deciding to get it over with, I try to find the right words to summarise everything that's happened. "Gerry, there's a girl in there that's been through a hundred types of hell. We brought her back from last night's mission and we're in the process of healing her." Gerry still doesn't take his eyes from Matt, so I continue, hoping that by giving him some information he'll calm down.

"Jack says she's not from here and most likely won't be able to return unless we can cleanse her. You're not going anywhere near her until you've calmed down enough to listen to either me or Jack, and I'm not going to explain it while we're standing outside my door where she can hear us."

He finally drags his gaze from Matt and runs his deep-set eyes over my face and body, trying to get a read on me with his heightened senses. I doubt he will smell much past the shield, but his eyes and ears will be picking up on every detail and sound. "I want to see her," he bites through clenched teeth.

"Not happening. I'll call Jack down here and have him move you. I'm only asking for you to hear us out and calm down," I emphasise with raised eyebrows. His steely glare pins me in place but he says nothing further. A few moments later he turns and skulks off. I let out the breath I didn't realise I was holding, then turn to Matt. "You good?"

"He's never going to forgive me, but I can't say I care, Seb." Shocked at his lack of care for Gerry's rage, I frown at him a little. He drops his shield and faces me fully. "Can I come in and see her?" he asks hesitantly. Concern is plainly evident in his eyes.

"Of course, just keep it quiet and remind Rolland to get her to eat. His mind will be fully on keeping her pain down and her emotions level." He nods and ambles into the room. Rubbing a hand over my face, I realise how mentally tired I am as I make my way through the house in search of either Jack or Gerry. Having Jack back my words up will help, but I'd rather not let Gerry out of my sight for too long in case he decides to return to my room before I've spoken to him. Making my way up the stairs to the second floor, I decide to pop my head into Brad's room, to see if Jack's still there.

I knock first and wait for an answer. Brad's heavy voice comes through, muffled by the thick door, but I take it as an invitation to come in. Stepping into Brad's room, I find Jack is thankfully still there, his back to me as he looks out over the side garden through the room's bow window. Movement to my left draws my attention away from Jack to where Brad's gigantic frame looms. He's pulling a black cotton shirt over his thick muscles. I just catch a glimpse of the dragon tattoo that covers the whole of his back, fully detailed with various symbols scattered throughout it. He turns to me as I close the door softly, running his sleepy amber eyes over me, helping to calm some of the anxiety and tension that weighs on my shoulders.

Where Jack's hair is white, sometimes almost silver in colour, Brad's hair is dark and buzzed. Thick, dark eyebrows frame his amber eyes and warm beige skin oddly reflect his easy go lucky approach to life

Unsure of what Brad knows, I look to Jack for clarification, but he's still got his back to me.

"Jack tells me you're in need of something to cut through

diamond infused titanium," Brad says over his broad shoulder, breaking the heavy silence within the room as he picks things up from his dresser. "I should have something put together within a few hours." His deep bass voice rumbles through my ears.

Wondering if Jack still hasn't told him, I stop Brad as he heads out of the room.

"Hold on, Brad," I pause him in his tracks. "Jack, have you not told him?" I ask hesitantly. Jack doesn't reply as he continues to look out the window.

"Jack!" I say louder, which seems to jolt him ever so slightly. He finally turns to face us. I frown at him, confused as to what the hell that was all about.

"Apologies, my thoughts were elsewhere," Jack says distantly. *What the? Does this have something to do with the others like him?*

Jack looks over at me for a moment, then turns his attention to Brad. "Rolland brought back an Ayran from last night's mission. Her name is Kia and she is under a significant amount of mental and physical stress from the endless months she spent in the imprisonment of a Gjinn and other beings that we do not know the full identity of yet. The blade I asked you for is needed to cut through the diamond-infused titanium shackles that are still attached to her wrists. I am unsure how long it will take for her to fully heal, but I hope you can be sympathetic enough to allow her to stay within our home whilst she recovers. There is also the issue of the Gjinn that knows she is here. They consume and manifest fear whilst weakening the mind. Extended exposure to them will lead to any normal person becoming a shell of what they once were. Kia and her kind have higher brain function and as such, are able to put up some amount of defence. But given the amount of time in which she was exposed to them, she may have sustained some permanent damage. There are stones in place in Sebastian's room to keep it warded off, but I do not have enough to cover the rest of the building. This leaves you all exposed and vulnerable. There are ways you can train the mind to keep the Gjinn out, and I will instruct and show you how this can be done once I have returned with more stones. The Gjinn is too weak to return immediately so you will be safe until this evening when I have returned with more of them." He finally looks back at me, then takes a step in the direction of the door.

"Wait, Jack. There's something I think you should know," I say, stopping him in his path toward the door. I flick my eyes over to Brad, knowing this is going to sound bad to someone who hasn't met Kia yet. "Kia has-" I start, but pause, wondering how to best put it all into words. *Shit, how do I put this so it doesn't sound like we've got a possessed person in the house?... Fuck, maybe she is.* Lost in my own thoughts my eyes drift down to the floor.

"Sebastian, Kia has what?" Jack's polished tone pulls me from my internal festering. I look up to find Jack's face full of concern. *What happened to the stiff-shouldered, stoic Jack?*

"Twice now she has gone into some kind of rage. It's almost like she loses herself to it. I'm certain it stems from defence as opposed to malice or hostility. The first time it happened, I was healing her back, and she seemed to be in the same stupor that we found her and Rolland in when we returned to the pool. She turned on me and Rolland couldn't get her to calm. It wasn't until he told her that I wasn't going to harm him and I moved a distance away from them, that she finally snapped out of it. It just happened again when Gerry came in the front door. I managed to calm her before she went into a full onslaught, but noise in the hallway seemed to breach through the state I had her lulled into. Each time she finally snaps out of this state of mind, she wants to take off. If I had to guess, I think she scares herself more than anything." Jack's face has gone from puzzlement, to worry, and now all I can see is concern in his eyes. He takes a deep breath before releasing it.

"Thank you, Sebastian, I think we should pay Gerry a visit," he suggests before turning to Brad, who's looking stunned and at a loss for words. *Shit.* "Brad, the sooner you can make something to remove the titanium shackles off of Kia the better." Jack declares before stalking out, leaving me with a very confused Brad. *Oh man, not again.*

"Sorry, Brad, but I need to catch up with Jack about speaking to Gerry before another part of the house is destroyed," I explain quickly. Brad says nothing, just raises a thick eyebrow at me and shakes his head a little. I see my chance and head quickly out the door after Jack. *For fuck sake. Which way did he go? This house is far too big to be playing hide and go seek with Gerry.*

Gerry's room seems the wisest place to start, and with any hope, he'll be in there shaving his face and getting cleaned up. Turning right out of Brad's s room, I head to the other side of the house. After winding my way through the gigantic house, I finally get to his room and knock on the slightly open door. There's no response so I poke my head in to see if he's in his bathroom, but no there's no noise coming from it. *Shit. Maybe he's taken to the healing chambers to recharge.*

Heading back the way I came I take the route via the kitchen to make sure he's not there. I hear voices coming from the kitchen and I recognise Gerry's blunt, pissed-off tone. *Bingo.* Stepping into the room, I find Gerry busy chopping what looks to be mushrooms and onions. There are a bunch of eggs set to one side and my guess is he's making an omelette of some kind. His deep emerald eyes find mine as I inch further into the kitchen.

"You know how I feel about people I don't know coming into our home, Seb. I don't care how badly injured they are - I don't trust what I don't know. You have five minutes to explain yourselves before I start throwing knives," he demands firmly. His eyes are still full of fury, but his body language has relaxed somewhat. I look over to Jack as Gerry continues cutting the vegetables. Thankful to Jack for having just explained this all to Brad, I begin sorting it all out for Gerry in the best that I can.

"As I said earlier, Gerry, we brought Kia back from last night's mission. She was trapped deep within her own mind and Jack had to pull her out." I flick my eyes over to Jack and he gives the smallest nod of his head. "Since then, Rolland hasn't left her side other than to take a piss, and it's taking every ounce of his concentration to keep her pain and emotions at bay." I take a tentative step closer to the marble countertop where he's working, hoping to get a better gauge on his reactions to what I'm telling him. "I can only heal small amounts of her body, as she has no nourishment or strength left in her," I continue. Gerry starts to crack eggs into the pan as though he is barely listening.

"So far, I've managed to heal a bullet wound, both hands that were sprained with several broken fingers, two sets of broken ribs, and her feet that she couldn't stand on. She's still got broken bones in her kneecaps and her back is-" Kia's back flashes across my vision and her reaction to me healing it pulls at my heart. *How am I ever going to heal it without triggering a flashback?* My mind wanders off to the dream that I'm sure now wasn't a dream - the one of her in the building with what I think was the Gjinn.

"Sebastian? Everything alright?" Jack's sotto voice pulls

me out of my thoughts. I look over at him and see his stoic mask well in place, but a small crease across his brow is just visible.

"Yeah, I'm fine." I rub a hand over my face, feeling the heavy pull of tiredness crawl over me. "As I was saying," I look back at Gerry to find he's paused in his chopping but continues when my eyes find his. "Kia's back is bad and I'm not sure how long it's going to take to heal it." I take another glance at Jack and hope the next part comes out correctly. "Jack tells us she's not from here and is what is known as an Ayran. They have gifts like us but are a lot more powerful." Gerry is still busying himself with the pan, but I know I've got his attention. "She's also had a Gjinn draining her for the past several months, and we had the pleasure of meeting it just an hour or so ago."

Gerry stops what he's doing to peer up from the frying pan. Ire flickers through his eyes, but he quickly pulls it in, refocusing on poking at the omelette. "Rolland and I were completely paralysed, but fully aware of our surroundings till Jack appeared to weaken it enough to send it back to wherever it is hiding now. Fortunately, Matt came in and put a shield up, keeping it off her till it was gone." Not fully brave enough to share with him how Matt couldn't lower the shield till she let him, I continue on. "Which brings us to you coming in. Every noise has her on edge and she can't talk to ask questions because her vocal cords are too badly damaged." The omelette Gerry is making is nearly done and damn, it smells good. He raises his eyes to me, studying my body language - he knows I'm hiding something but doesn't know what.

"What are you not telling me, Seb? The muscle in your right arm is twitching, and even though you're hiding it well, your voice is strained. Your heart rate has escalated twice since you started speaking. Once because of a visual your mind conjured from speaking about her back. The second time has something to do with Matt," Gerry comments vaguely, taking two plates from the cupboard and serving up the omelette. Hoping the second plate is for me, I begin eyeing it. *He isn't as good as me in the kitchen, but he can still cook, I'll give him that.*

"Going by Matt's behaviour outside your room, I'm guessing he has a little more to do with this than you're letting on," Gerry proclaims. Knowing he has my attention with the bribe waiting for me, he continues as he puts down two sets of cutlery beside the plates and takes a seat. "Now you can either tell me and join me for a bite to eat," he raises a flat eyebrow provokingly, "or I'll find out shortly what you're hiding and give this breakfast to Brad. Your choice, Brother." He takes a mouthful of his omelette and gives me a smug, irritating smile, satisfied that he has me where he wants me.

My stomach rumbles and I become more aware of how hungry I am. You'd think I'd be satisfied after two bowls of soup, rice and fruit, but healing Kia coupled with the lack of sleep has left me starved. Giving in, I walk over to grab the plate, but it's snatched up and held out of my reach. "Now, now, Seb. Once I'm satisfied that you've told me the whole truth, it's all yours," he taunts, bobbing his eyebrows. "I'd hurry up though if I were you, Seb, as it's getting cold quick." Letting out a breath of frustration, I give in and tell him.

"Matt has been seeing her for the last several months in his dreams. He thought they were just nightmares, but it turns out they weren't." I watch him steadily then flick my eyes to the plate.

"And?" Gerry presses. I look at him again, and I want to

punch him for being so clued in to the fact that I'm hiding something. *Fucking dickhead.*

"He tried finding her a few times except he was always too late. Last month when he went to Paris and came back with a gunshot wound, he thinks it's because he got too close. His nightmares were real, and he was slipping into her mind somehow," I ramble out. Gerry stops chewing and hands me the plate.

"Wasn't so hard now, was it," he winks, placing his now empty dish over by the sink as I dive wholeheartedly into the plate of heaven in front of me. Sighing deeply, I bring a forkful of food to my lips and tune out the rest of the world.

I just need five minutes...

CHAPTER SEVENTEEN

*M*att

Stepping into Seb's room, I find Kia sitting up in Rolland's arms. There are still tears lingering on her cheeks, but surprisingly her face isn't blotchy - there's only a shallow line running across her brow which seems to fade when she spots me. I inch further into the room, feeling slightly awkward. Kia's eyes light up and a benign smile forms around her small mouth. *Is she truly happy to see me? How can she be, when it was me who let her down by not getting her out sooner?* Oblivious to my internal dialogue, she just continues to smile at me steadily. Unsure of what to do, I stuff my hands in my pockets and shuffle my feet as I look around the room.

"Really, Kia? That's all four of us now," Rolland laughs from behind her head. Kia looks over her shoulder at him with a puzzled expression before turning back to face me with another sweet smile. Rolland leans back on his hands, shaking his head as though giving up. His gaze catches on something on Kia's back and all humour fades from his face.

"Kia, we need to change your shirt, sweetheart," Rolland croaks slightly. *What? Did I hear him right?*

Kia's features drop as she lets out a small huff of air and lowers her head to her chest. Before I know what I'm doing, I find myself kneeling in front of her and taking her small hands into my own. Brushing my thumb over her knuckles, I peek up at her, wishing I could bring that smile back to her beautiful face.

"Matt, I hate to do this to you, but do you think you could help?" Rolland asks as he lets out a heavy breath. "All Kia's wearing is this shirt with nothing on underneath. Perhaps if we put some shorts or boxers on her before removing the shirt, we may still be able to maintain a shred of sanity," he remarks with a bit of humour back in his voice, though he's not actually laughing.

Still looking down at her lap, Kia's mannerism tug at my heart. "Why do you need to change the shirt, Rolland?" I query, running my eyes over her heart-shaped face. *She obviously doesn't want to, and it seems like such a trivial thing.*

"The shirt is stuck to her back, pulling at the skin every time she moves. The sooner we can get this one off of her, the better off she'll be," Rolland explains tightly. Kia lifts her gaze to me, and I wish I could wrap her up in one of my shields so nothing could ever touch her again. Her hand raises up to gently cup my cheek and I can feel her energy trickling through me.

"Okay, how do we go about doing this?" I ask Rolland while holding Kia's gaze, still full of so much emotion, fast with my own. She reads like an open book to me.

"Grab a pair of shorts from Seb's drawers over to your right," Rolland requests. I place a soft kiss on Kia's knuckles before getting up to walk over to Seb's cabinet. Finding some black boxers in his top drawer, I pluck a pair out and then step back over to the bed. Kia looks at the clothing in my hand with curiosity and just a hint of annoyance. Her eyes find mine and I feel like I'm about to collar a deer.

"Are you sure this is necessary, Rolland?" The words are out before I think them through.

"Yes, Matt. It is definitely necessary to put pants on a woman before removing the only piece of clothing she has on her body *if* you're not about to have sex with her," he says sarcastically. I feel my cheeks heat and I wish my mouth would stop moving. Kia's eyes seem to widen a fraction and her smile reappears.

"Whatever you're doing, Matt, keep doing it," Rolland's voice brightens. *What? Be completely and utterly embarrassed that my mouth has no filter?* "Okay, Kia, to save you from having to bend over any further and to keep me from moving you too much, Matt is going to slide the shorts up your legs while I support your weight from behind," Rolland directs, and though I don't think she understood a word of what he just said, she nods anyway, keeping her attention fully on me. "Matt, bend forward slightly and, Kia, put your arms around his neck," Rolland instructs.

Kia slides her arms up around me as I bend over at the waist and I feel her energy seep into me, tracking its way down my throat and through my chest before finally settling into my stomach. From there, the warmth seems to spread out through my very core, and I hear myself gulp. Shaking my head a bit, as if to clear it, I focus on the boxers that I'm holding out to her, waiting for her to slide her tiny feet into the leg holes. But when she doesn't move, I peek up to find her face slightly flummoxed, her head tilted to the side. Seeing that she's clearly confused as to what to do, I spread wide one leg of the boxers and bring it up under her dangling left foot, lifting it up slightly before doing the same with the other foot, keeping my movements slow and steady. Once both are where they need to be, I carefully and calculatingly grab the waist of the boxers and begin ever so slowly pulling them up her legs.

As I glance down to watch what I'm doing, trying desperately to ignore the hardness growing in my own boxers, my eyes catch on all of the bruises, cuts and scars that wind their way up her shapely legs like a tapestry. Her knees are in the worst shape, both looking badly damaged, with each most likely having a few chipped bones. I look back up to Kia's face and find her watching me expectantly. As I continue easing the boxers up her thighs, my rough fingertips brush along her skin as they make their way up, amazed at how soft it is despite all the damage that has been done to it. Kia takes in an audible breath, which seems to pulse more of her energy into me, making me even harder. *Oh man, I'm in trouble.*

Kia's body is now hanging part way off of Rolland's lap and her eyes have darkened into two discs that resemble the night sky, silver stars sparkling deep within them and sending more desire through my body. As Rolland lifts her slightly so that I can tug the boxers all the way up and over her bum, I straighten my body up, letting go of the boxers and gently supporting Kia under her bum as she comes up with me. I feel Rolland's hand brush against my leg and I assume his hand is on her leg where it meets mine in order to maintain his contact with her.

As she settles into my body, her soft chest flush with the hardness of mine, I

look down to make sure she's okay. I'm captured by her eyes that now swirl like two bottomless pools of ocean water, reflecting the brilliance of a full moon, drawing me in and beckoning me to dive into their depths. The thought of diving into something seems to trigger my body into action and my mouth takes on a mind of its own.

Diving for her lips, I find her eager and waiting, her tongue demanding control, a command I wholeheartedly give in to. I can sense that she wants to get closer and would probably be climbing her way up my body, like a monkey climbing a tree, if her legs were of any use to her at all right now. I keep one of my large hands anchored under her bum as the other moves up her side of its own free will, tracing her thin ribs gently as she leans back slightly to take a breath. I catch a glimpse of her eyes, which are now fully silver.

She abruptly pulls herself back into me and reclaims my lips with even more determination, seemingly searching for something within me. Her energy becomes thicker, and it finds its way to my hardness, acting almost like a hand as it tugs on me. I flick my tongue around hers as I trace my fingers down her sides. One of her small hands burrows its way into my hair at the nape whilst I simultaneously feel a jerk on my energy within my chest. Letting it go freely, I feel her energy spike and hear a small noise from her, followed quickly by a hard grunt from Rolland behind her. *Crap. I completely forgot he was there.*

Kia sags in my arms, pulling her lips away with a look of dopey contentment on her face. "Well now that you've gotten that out of your system..." Rolland says, breathing hard, causing me to wonder what he's on about. "I need another personal minute. I won't shut the door this time, I'll only be ten seconds, um, well maybe fifteen. Nothing can happen in fifteen seconds, right?" he rambles on as he makes his way to the bathroom, pulling the door behind him but making sure not to close it all of the way. Kia rests her head on my chest, and I wonder what the hell just happened as she turns her head to my neck and starts breathing me in. Sounds from the bathroom filter through, but I ignore them, burying my nose in her hair. She smells of the forest and the gel I make, with underlying tones of the sea.

Twenty seconds later, Rolland strolls back in, flops down on the bed so that he's completely flat on his back with his head on the pillows and drapes a weary arm over his eyes. He's in a different pair of cotton trousers now, a white vest, and he looks completely worn out. He points to his lap and I can feel Kia's breathing become slightly strained. "Sit, and behave, Kia, for three minutes, while I get my breath and brains back," Rolland orders lightly. I place her on Rolland's lap and her eyes spring open like I've given her ten shots of caffeine. "No, Kia. It's not happening," Rolland chastises, snaking an arm around her tummy. "Just give my brain a moment to catch up," he tells her sleepily. Kia looks over at him puzzled.

"What did you do to him?" I say, smiling. She looks back at me with a bemused and affectionate smile, seemingly content with her work on Rolland. I perch myself beside Rolland's leg, running my gaze over her delicate features and her gentle smile seems to warm a place deep inside of me. "You have such a beautiful smile." I chuckle in my head, amused that my mouth seems to have no boundaries today.

I wish I could just zip it shut and throw away the key, but then I wouldn't get to taste those honey coated lips again, would I? Her smile grows and I feel the heat return to my cheeks again, so I look away, trying to find something interesting on the wall to distract myself.

I feel the bed dip slightly just as Rolland says, "nope. I said no more, Kia," whilst he sits up, pulling himself and Kia up toward the headboard. He rubs a hand over his face before resting his head on Kia's shoulder. "How one little body contain so much life and trouble all at the same time?"

Rolland mumbles against her skin. She looks over her shoulder at him with a great deal of warmth and affection, then raises a hand to his head and begins to stroke his hair. Rolland seems lost in his thoughts, almost half asleep, and I watch as Kia pulls her bottom lip into her teeth. "You're making me sleepy, aren't you, you little minx?" Rolland slurs, sounding half out of it. Kia pulls both lips into her mouth, then releases them before her face breaks into a full smile.

"Kia, you know I can't leave it on," Rolland pleads quietly. Kia's face falls along with her hand from his head. "Don't be mad at me," Rolland murmurs, his voice full of sadness, making my stomach churn. Kia's face turns to confusion and she turns around in his lap to fully face him. My heart finds its way into my throat and my chest feels like a vice is gripping it, giving me no room to breathe. Guilt slams into me, suffocating me all over again. I can now see the blood that has soaked through Kia's shirt, and Rolland is right, the shirt is sticking to parts of her back where the blood has dried. I look up and find Kia comforting Rolland, as she runs her fingers through his sandy blonde hair and places soft kisses on his head.

"Please don't fight me on this one. Don't block me this time, I beg you, Kia," he urges, pulling from her embrace to look her in the eyes. His own eyes are full of so much sadness that I'm almost blown back from the intensity of it and I can't look away from the darkness there. It's not a look that I can recall ever having seen on his face before. "Promise me?" Rolland pleads quietly, and I can see the tears threatening to spill over. Kia nods solemnly in response and places her hands in his.

"Matt, would you grab another shirt from the drawer?" he asks without looking at me. I do as he asks, while my mind starts thinking of ways to help make this easier.

"Rolland, is there any easier way of doing this?" I ask. He looks over at me and I can practically see the wheels turning in his head. "Perhaps if we wet the shirt she's wearing with warm water, the dried blood will soften and release its hold so that we can ease it carefully away from her skin," I suggest. Rolland's eyebrows raise hopefully at the idea and I can see a bit of color darken his cheeks.

"Yeah, that just might work. But not in the pool, not after last time," he cautions, flicking his gaze back to Kia. "How about a shower?" he asks her with a wry smile and Kia instantly starts nodding. "Sounds like we've got ourselves a plan then. Ready?" Rolland chuckles softly as he lifts them both off of the bed and heads to the bathroom.

What in the heck have I gotten myself into? I wonder as I find myself following them without a moment's hesitation. *Guess I'm about to find out....*

CHAPTER EIGHTEEN

*R*olland

Kia's emotions feel like they've become a part of me now. I don't have to concentrate anymore, and I don't think I'm even using my gift to tune in to her. All of which is brilliant for keeping track of her thoughts, but not so good when she's turned on or climaxing with me sitting behind her like a teenage boy. I had no choice but to climax right along with her. *I can't believe she got me to come like that. She felt all that, in just one kiss, and it wasn't even me she was kissing! I'm so screwed.*

Matt's idea of taking a shower should make this easier, but I very much doubt it's going to keep the memories from surfacing. Turning Kia's body around and maneuvering my arms so that one is under her legs and the other is around her back, I make my way over to the en-suite. I begin to wonder if having Matt in here while doing this is wise, given everything that happened in the pool and when Gerry came home.

I hear Matt is a couple of steps behind me. I stop by the marble countertop, so my back is the the mirror as Matt heads over to the shower, turning it on and adjusting the settings. I hope he doesn't take my words the wrong way. *"Matt, the last time we worked on Kia's back, it set her off and she turned on Seb. I know you wouldn't take it personally, but she will get upset with herself if she does."* Matt continues fiddling with the heat settings, running his hand under the water.

"That's understandable. Is there anything I can do to help make this easier?" Relieved that he hasn't taken it to heart, I release a heavy breath. Kia looks up at me with quizzical eyes so I wink, trying to distract her. Her face screws up even more in response, making me laugh. Matt turns around, probably thinking I'm laughing at him.

"Sorry, Matt, but I do not believe that Kia has ever been winked at before," I say through a chuckle as Matt raises his eyebrows high on his forehead. Looking down at Kia's face and her messy, wild hair all about, it suddenly occurs to me that once that mass is wet, it will get in the way and stick to her back. Reaching into one of the drawers, I grab a hair tie and hold it out to Matt, who grabs it as he nods with understanding. Kia watches me curiously and it's clear she has no idea what the hair tie is for.

"Kia, you have a lot of hair and when it gets wet and we have your shirt off, it will stick to your back and hurt your wounds. Matt is going to gather your hair up onto your head and secure it there with the tie. Just hold still for a second," I explain, seeing her frown a little at me while Matt moves in behind her back. Carefully he gathers her hair in his big hands and pulls it up in a ponytail near the top of her head. He threads it through the tie several times before pulling it through one final time, stopping just before the ends come all the way out, leaving them tucked in and letting the hair fall down just a bit.

"Thank you, Matt," I say, "if you could wait until we're

under the water in case it needs adjusting, that would be appreciated, as I think sitting may work best for this." Matt takes a step back, giving us room.

Stepping forward toward the shower, Kia's emotion changes from curiousness to happiness. The first time I turned the shower on, you'd think I'd shown her a mountain of gold, and it was the first positive change we had seen in her emotion. Now I can feel the excitement run through her and I'm even more thankful for Matt's suggestion. Inching us under the shower heads, the sense of bliss, gratitude and pleasure pour from her.

Thinking that we should make the most of the time spent under the water, an idea pops into mind. "Matt, would you pass me over some products from Seb's cupboard?" I feel Kia fully relax her whole body, her head resting against my chest.

"Sure." Matt heads over to the cabinet and grabs a few different items from the shelves, then sets them on the ground so that they can be easily reached. "Anything else?" he asks hopefully.

"Yeah, there is - don't let anyone distract us. I'm not sure how this is going to go, if I'm honest, but the less noise and interruptions the better," I explain.

Matt chews on his bottom lip as he runs his worried eyes over Kia's face. Concern and empathy for what she's about to go through are written all over his refined features. *"She's going to be okay, Matt, I've got her,"* I assure him, trying to ease his worries. His eyes flick back to me as he gives a single nod of his head.

Looking down at Kia's face, you'd think she was sleeping. She's so relaxed, her body settling into the comfort she's found, and her emotions fall into a feeling of calmness that I haven't felt from her before. I turn so my back is against the wall and ease us down until I'm sitting cross-legged on the floor. Kia is curled up safely in my lap, but I feel a few spikes of pain come through from the movement on the back of the shirt - a sharp reminder of why we're here. As I had hoped, the shower feels more cooling down here.

"Okay, Matt, turn the temperature up, just a little at a time, till I say stop." I see him lean over, turning the controller, and I feel the water raining down on us heat up. This enclosure has six shower heads lining the ceiling with several smaller ones along the side and is big enough for at least four people to stand in comfortably. Matt has only turned half of them on, but there's plenty of water pouring over us.

"Perfect, Matt." He moves away slightly, pausing for a few seconds before he makes his way out, closing the door quietly behind him.

"Kia," I speak softly. She opens her eyes and peeks up at me. Neither of us wants to do this, but we both know it has to be done. "Let's get the shirt off, then we can stay here till you turn into a prune," I offer. Her brow furrows. *I need to stop using human phrases.*

"Sit up and face me, sweetheart," I tell her gently.

She pulls herself up, turning her body as instructed. Her dark hair is a beautiful, wet mess as it clings to her heart-shaped face, framing her soft, delicate features and making her seem so otherworldly that my breath catches in my throat and my heart skips a beat.

Drawing myself back to the task at hand, I use my right hand to pull her left leg gently across my stomach so that she's fully facing me. Instinctively she eases herself closer with her legs, causing a wave of her pain to run through me. She slowly leans forward to rest her forehead on my chest again, and I can feel her emotions begin to shut off as the pain that I've been taking from her gets pulled back to her.

143

"Kia, please don't do that," I quietly beg, running a hand up her arm. Her emotions begin to seep through - sorrow, sadness, guilt and annoyance - but she's keeping a tight hold on her pain. "Do you not trust me?" I ask, now stroking the back of her head. More annoyance comes through, but nothing else changes.

I take her head in both my hands and encourage her to look up at me, but she stubbornly keeps her eyes shut, blocking me out. *Little minx, two can play this game.*

Leaning down, I kiss her lips firmly and push some of my own emotions into her - compassion, empathy, respect and desire - urging them through her, so that she gets a deep understanding of how I feel. I hear her breathing pick up and she begins to kiss me back, but before she can open her mouth and take control, I pull back to see that I've got her full attention, a slight smirk on my face. The desire pulsing from her is strong, but so is her annoyance and frustration and I can't help but chuckle quietly. When she finally opens her eyes, I find them swirling steadily.

"Once the shirt is off, I'll give you more of that," I declare, keeping my focus steady on hers. I can feel her desire and need more intensely as her eyes swirl faster. "Nope, not happening, Kia," I tell her firmly, knowing what she wants to do. Her eyes look sad, and disappointment surfaces as she sticks out her lower lip just a bit in a clear pout. "As soon as the shirt is off, I promise. You have my word," I say, stroking my thumb across her cheek. She studies my face, looking for any signs of trickery, but I know she will find none as I have no intentions of ever going against any promise I ever make to her.

Though thinking them through, they would sound terrible to anyone who didn't know what was going on. 'Once the shirt is off, I'll give you more of that...'. Damn this woman. What has she done to me?

"Can you let go and give me control now please?" I inquire and am rewarded with her trust as I feel her pain ease back into me. I take a good hold of it and check it for any missing pieces. "Do you promise not to take it back?" She pauses for a brief moment then nods as water drips down her face. "A promise is a promise, Kia, you can't break it, or it will break our trust," I remind her as I run my eyes over her small nose and round cheeks. The cut that was along her lip is gone completely and the bruises have nearly disappeared. She skims her gaze over my face, before meeting my eyes once more and nods sharply.

"Okay, we're going to do this slowly, all right?" She nods again as her head meets my chest once more and I take a calming breath, readying myself for whatever comes our way.

Ever so carefully, inch by slow inch, I begin rolling the shirt up, keeping a firm grip on her pain, focusing most of my attention on her back. Pain flares up, followed immediately by a wave of panic. Pulling the pain away as fast as I can, I push some comforting energy through her.

Another inch and her breathing speeds up. I've still got a good handle on the pain, but her emotions flare. Fear and the feeling of being lost run through her.

"I've got you, sweetheart, I'm right here," I speak softly through her hair into her right ear. Another inch up, and an image flashes across my vision. A man is looming over her with a spiked metal whip, dripping with blood.

"Kia, you're not there. You're here with me," I tell her as I push more comfort through her, followed by the feeling of peace. She takes a shaky breath and I feel her head nod.

Readying myself for the next wave, I encourage more energy through her, and it feels as though I'm falling into a part of her. I move another inch, and another swell of pain rushes up, feeling like someone has struck my own back with a whip. I suck in a breath, feeling my body begin to heat. I'm only halfway up Kia's back and from the amount of blood on the shirt I saw earlier, I know the worst is yet to come.

I lift it a bit more and heat whips at my back, followed by the sting of acid. Dragging air into my lungs, I try keeping my eyes open. My hands begin to shake and Kia's shoulders tremble. She's crying, but not from pain. Remorse pours from her and I know she wishes she hadn't agreed to this.

"Nearly there, Kia," I say to her, though my voice trembles slightly. She nods and I hear her sniffle. I take a steadying breath as I pull the shirt up several inches this time, trying to get it done more quickly. More acid strikes at my back and it feels like someone is holding a hot blade to it. The pain is resurfacing memories, and even though she's not feeling the pain with her mind, her body is still reacting to it, causing these visions to manifest. And somehow, I'm tuning into them.

"Kia, baby, I'm right here and I'm not leaving you. I'm never going to leave your side. I'd rather die." I vow, knowing my words are true. A part of me feels like it's attaching itself to her.

She sags into me, pulling the shirt higher with her movement. More pain follows and I see another memory of a different man coating a whip in his hand with a substance. Kia shudders as she takes a deep breath, which she seems to hold. The shirt is bunched up over her shoulder blades now and I can feel the weight of it on my own back.

I've got a hold of every drop of her pain, but she seems to be falling into a memory. Tension and fear fill every ounce of her, so I push some calming energy through her again, but it doesn't seem to do anything. She's not fighting me, she's just lost to it.

Wanting to get this over with, I pull the shirt the rest of the way up her back. Pain strikes at my own skin again and it feels like the whip is stuck there, branded to me. A man's voice trickles through my ears, but I can't understand the language he's speaking. I try dragging air into my lungs, but they don't seem to want to work. The pain doesn't leave me but continues to pour down my back. I close my eyes to shake myself from it, but darkness drags me under and I slide across the wall and onto the floor. Kia moves with me and I fall deep into my centre unintentionally.

Aware, but unable to move, I start to panic for Kia. I feel her pull herself from me, followed by the sound of something heavy with water hitting the ground. I try to wake from my centre, but the pain in my back pulls me deeper. The noise around me fades and I become lost, unsure how to get myself out. I try focusing on what I can feel. The pain in my back is gone, but I can't feel the water from the shower either.

"Rolland?" A voice I've never heard before drifts through me so quietly. *"Rolland, you hear me?"*

Who is that? It's slightly louder, and I want to hear more of it.

"Please wake up, you promise me." It sounds foreign and curls around the r's. *"Rolland, I kept promise, but you not keep yours."* It's as though it's struggling to form some of the words.

"Kia?" It can't be.

Something sparks within me and I grab onto it pulling myself from my centre. Taking a deep breath into my lungs, I feel the water running over me again, and the sound of the shower fills my ears.

I haven't opened my eyes yet, but I can feel Kia's hand on

147

my face. "I'm back, Kia, I'm back," I assure her, though my voice is barely above a whisper.

My body feels drained and all of Kia's emotions flood back, but not her pain. "Kia, give it back, and I'll open my eyes."

Her hand pulls from me, but I can still feel her emotions. Annoyance and frustration come from her. I'm just glad the pain in my back has gone.

I can feel her energy right next to me, so I know she's still there. I want to open my eyes to see if she's okay, but a stubborn part of me wants her to give in first.

"Come on, Kia, I'm fine. Just a little tired," I encourage, keeping my eyes closed. Still nothing. *Damn it.* I open one eye to look at her.

She's sitting with her arms crossed over her legs, which she's pulled up to her chest, her head is turned slightly the other way and I can see she is pouting. Her breathing is somewhat laboured. I feel bad for making her suffer, so I open the other eye and sit up, noticing that her discarded shirt is a wet heap on the floor beside her.

Realising I made her a promise and didn't keep it, I decide to make it up to her. Kissing her forearm that rests on top of the other one, I make my way up her arm, sucking the water droplets away. Kia's breathing calms slightly and her emotions begin to change. She's still annoyed, but desire starts to simmer through.

She continues to look at the wall, so I lean over more, kissing her cheek gently. Her desire heightens, and her head moves to me a fraction, but then quickly moves back as she slams the desire down and tries to focus on her annoyance.

Guiding my fingers up her leg, I push a bit of lust and desire, followed by remorse. It gets her attention as she turns her head in my direction, but keeps her eyes closed. My hand reaches her knee where her arms are folded over. Tracing my fingers down the backs of her thighs, I push my hunger for her through my fingers. She pulls her lips into her mouth then releases the top one.

Running my tongue over her top lip, I push hard so I can feel her teeth. She finally gives in and her hands move to my face as she lets go of her bottom lip to kiss me back. I ease her body to me, so she's sitting back on my lap again, but hear her gasp from pain rather than pleasure as she settles. I stop and lean back to look at her. She's looking back at me and it's like a battle of wills again. Her eyes are swirling fast with the silver specs glittering back.

"Let it go, Kia," I tell her firmly.

Her pain slams into me at the same time as her lips do. Shocked by the double onslaught, I dig my hand into whatever I'm holding and find her hips. It seems to spur her on, as she grinds herself against me while fighting for control of the kiss. Her tongue seems to be searching for something as her energy pours down my chest fast, making its way to my heart. Her emotions flood me, and it's true need and frustration that's coursing through her, making my cock that was already hard seem to grow even harder, and I worry what her reaction to it will be. She grinds on me again, pushing me harder into the wall. Small noises of frustration come from her, which perks my ears.

I start kissing her back firmly, forcing my energy at her along with some of the frustration that is a direct result of the hardness I cannot control. She gasps as she pulls from me slightly. Her eyes are entirely silver, and they seem to lock me into place. We're both breathing heavily, and our emotions seem to be jumbled together – no longer sure which are hers and which are mine. Frustration and desire weave a tangled web together.

Flicking my eyes over her face, I take in every detail. Her small nose, delicate cheekbones and eyebrows that refine her face. Her long, dark eyelashes make her eyes appear larger as they pulse, and her lips that look ripe and swollen from being kissed. She grinds on me again and I want nothing more than to finish her off here. But I know her body needs rest, so I try and calm her down by kissing her gently, making my way along to her ear.

"Kia, sweetheart. We need to stop before your body gives out," I whisper gently to her. Disappointment flows through the both of us, but she turns and kisses my cheek.

Thankful she's not annoyed anymore and feeling like I've got full control over her pain, I let myself relax a little. My eyes catch on the bottles Matt set down for us, and I reach to pick up the shampoo. Sitting back against the wall so she can see what I'm doing, I squeeze some shampoo into my hand. Utter confusion covers her face but instead of explaining it to her, I show her by working it into my hair to get a lather going. My hair reaches my shoulders and can be a pest to keep tidy sometimes, but Seb found some great products on a trip we took over to America.

We've used this stuff ever since. It smells fantastic, plus it does the job of making my hair easier to manage. Kia is looking even more confused and very worried, as she begins to shake her head, moving from my lap. I feel my brow furrow, confused at her reaction.

"Kia, its fine. It's just shampoo. It's for washing all the dirt and grease from your hair," I placate, still working up a foam. She continues to shake her head slowly, but she's stopped moving backwards.

I start rinsing my hair off, working my fingers through it until I can feel all of the shampoo has been washed away, then I grab the shower gel and start rubbing it on my body.

Kia's face continues to contort, moving from puzzlement to worry. *It doesn't look I'll be getting any of this on her.* She looks over to watch the bubbles drain away and then seems to look for something.

"What are you looking for, Kia?" She shakes her head again, giving up her search.

She watches me steadily and the blue of her eyes returns, with just a few silver specs left flittering around.

"Do you fancy some food?" I offer as I rinse the last of the gel off my body. After a long pause, she nods. *This should be fun. Getting us both out of these soaking wet clothes and into fresh ones while keeping a hold on her pain. Yep, sounds like a recipe for disaster.*

"Kia, come sit on my lap again and grab hold of my neck, so I can get us out of here," I explain. She climbs on as instructed and her soft arms slide around my neck as her breasts push up against me. *Yep, this is going to be a nightmare.*

Standing us up carefully so as not to jar her body, I step out of the shower and turn it off. Grabbing a couple of towels as I pass the heater, I set her down slowly on the counter and take a look at her back in the mirror. Blood is trickling from two of the deeper gashes, but thankfully the others seemed to have stopped. They will all need to be dressed in bandages before a shirt can go back on.

Kia starts to shiver from the cold and her pain levels increase from the air hitting her wounds. As I carefully wrap one of the towels around her body, I feel another wave of pain pass through me, followed by another vision - Kia being slammed against the wall by the same man with the whip.

Steadying my breath, I pull her head to my shoulder. "Shh, he's not here. Just you and me, okay?" I tell her, running a hand down the back of her wet head. I get a tiny nod in response. *I think we're going to need help to get through this.*

"Kia," I say softly as I carefully pull her hair out of the hair tie and gently dry it with the other towel, "I'm going to call one of the other guys in to help us, okay?" Another tiny nod.

"Matt!" I call, hoping he's not too far away. The door opens slowly, and Matt's head pops in, followed by the rest of him. He runs his eyes over the both of us.

"Can you find Seb and see if he knows where some bandages are that we can use to dress Kia's back?" Matt's face is full of concern, but he nods and leaves.

"Kia, I'm going to put some dry clothes on, while we wait for Seb. Just be sure to keep a hand on my neck the whole time, okay?" She nods and pulls her head away from my shoulder. She's got her eyes closed, and I hope they stay that way while I change.

I reach out to grab some trousers from the drawer then lower myself until I can step into them, being sure to go slowly so that Kia can keep her hand in place. My thoughts turn over how bandaging her back is going to go after what just happened in the shower. *Fuck, I know I have to keep her thoughts away from those images but I'm not sure how much more my body can take. Aw hell, here we go again…*

CHAPTER NINETEEN

*S*ebastian
        After Jack left to find more stones and Gerry finished eating, I decided a quick tidy up was needed. Throwing some vegetables together for a quick stew doesn't take long, so if I don't have time to make anything later, there will at least be food for Kia, and a peace offering for Brad and Gerry. I take the joint of meat out the fridge and place it in the slow cooker along with some herbs and spices, then set the time on the cooker. Once that is done, I get to cleaning up.

As I finish wiping the worktops down, Matt ambles through the kitchen door looking apprehensive and worried. "What's up?" I ask, frowning a little. *Has something happened with Kia?*

"Rolland's asking for bandages for Kia's back," Matt explains, flicking his eyes over my face, then raises a hand to rub at his neck. "He needed to take her shirt off as it was sticking to her back and pulling at the wounds. I suggested he take her in the shower to make it easier to remove and they've just got out," he finishes, then begins drumming his thumb against his leg. *Shit. How did he manage to get the shirt off without her turning on him?*

"Did you stay with them?" I ask, turning from him.

"No, Rolland asked me to wait outside in case she snapped."

I wonder at that for a minute but then realise Rolland was probably right to keep Matt out. I nod my head in understanding as I make my way over to the cupboard where we keep the first aid kit. Using my gift isn't always possible when we have guests here, or when the guys are being big babies, so we keep the kit around just in case. Grabbing some bandages, gauze pads, clips, and some of the special gel that Matt makes, I make my way out of the kitchen to my room.

When I arrive at the en-suite, I find Rolland is wearing a fresh pair cotton trousers and another white vest. Kia is resting her head on his chest, seemingly calm.

"Everything okay?" I ask, as I move to stand next to him, placing the bandages down on the marble top.

Rolland turns to me, looking exhausted and worn out. "Let's get this done so she can rest," he hints, his voice sounding drained. I run my eyes over him, taking in his normal golden tan that seems to be fading around his cheeks and the shadows that have appeared under his eyes.

"Yes, I'm as tired as I look, but we can't put another shirt on until her back is bandaged, and leaving her topless just isn't an option, obviously," he states flatly.

"You're right, it needs bandaging, but I don't think you're going to be able to focus on keeping her pain level down AND wrap her back at the same time," I press back, trying to think of an easier way to keep her focused on him, so I can dress her wounds. The position he's in now won't work as it will mean one of us is getting in the others way.

"I should be okay keeping her attention on me, but I can't do it standing," he explains, looking back at Kia.

"Really? What happened to make you think you can handle her after what happened in the pool?" I continue mind-speaking with him, not wanting Kia to hear me.

"I'll explain later, but just trust me for now," he pushes aloud.

Taking the stuff off the counter, I head back into the bedroom. I don't see Matt around, so I assume he decided to head back to his room to catch up on stuff rather than follow me.

Sitting down in the middle of the bed, I place the bandages and other items down next to me and wait as Rolland makes his way out of the en-suite, carrying Kia. Her arms and legs are wrapped around him and her head rests in the crook of his neck. Holding her in that position, he sits on the bed carefully before turning to rest his back against the headboard and crosses his legs at the ankles. I hear them both take a deep breath at the same time as he settles them both in, followed by a simultaneously slow exhalation of air.

Rolland places his hand over her head then speaks to her softly. "Do you trust me?" She nods her head. "And you're not going to fight me?" She doesn't respond. "I'll be fine this time. No more dropping out on each other." She still doesn't move. "Okay," he lets out a heavy breath. "We do this together." She nods firmly, and Rolland looks over at me. "Ready?" he asks.

"What was that all about?" I ask.

"I'll explain later. Let's just get this over with quickly so we can rest."

Moving closer to them, I get as close to Kia as I can and wait. Rolland closes his eyes before he takes a slow, steadying breath, then rests his head on top of hers, so I can still see him, but not Kia, clearly and dips his chin at me.

With the utmost care, I begin pulling the towel slowly from Kia's back. When she doesn't flinch or stiffen, I find myself letting out the breath I didn't realise I was holding. I let my eyes wander over her skin as I assess the damage. The wounds that have been torn open are bleeding, although not heavily. I squeeze some of the healing gel onto each of gauze pads, looking up at Rolland as I set them down beside me. His eyes are still shut and both of them seem to be incredibly calm.

"You ready?" I ask, holding one of the gauze pads in my hand, but I don't get a reply. Not wanting to startle Kia, I rest my hand on her lower left hip. "Kia, I'm going to put some pads on your back. There's a healing gel on them that will feel cold, but it shouldn't sting or hurt you," I explain carefully. Still no reaction.

Lifting the pad, I place it gently on her back. She doesn't move or flinch, so I take another pad and set the next one under the first. Kia still hasn't moved, and her breathing is entirely even, as though she's sleeping. After the first wound is covered, I start working on the next.

Kia still hasn't reacted, but I hear Rolland's breathing change slightly. I've just one more wound to cover and then I can begin bandaging. I start covering the last one and notice that, while Kia's breathing has remained steady and there has been no flinching, Rolland clearly is not doing as well. He's sweating profusely and his face is scrunched up in deep concentration. I finish covering the last wound and then pick up one of the bandages. I start at the top and place the bandage over the pad. When that is in place, I reach to grab another and hear Rolland take a deep breath as though he's coming up for air, but he seems to hold it in rather than expel it.

I look up at him from where I'm working on the last wound at Kia's waist to find Rolland's eyes open and tears falling freely down his face.

"Hurry up, Seb," Rolland whispers through a trembling sigh that pulls at my heart. He takes a controlled breath, then speaks into Kia's ear softly. "Just a little longer, Kia and Seb will be done." She doesn't move and Rolland relaxes his shoulders and closes his eyes. I move faster but keep my lines even and firm. One more bandage and I'll be done.

As I reach to place the last bandage, Kia starts to squirm slightly in Rolland's lap, followed by a soft whimper and my heart seems to stop beating for a just a moment.

"I've got you, Kia. It's not real. It's just you, me, and Sebastian," Rolland consoles, his voice faint and scratchy. I finally finish with the last bandage and attach a clip to secure it at the bottom. "I'm done, Rolland," I tell him quickly, sitting back.

Kia takes in a strangled breath and begins sobbing, pulling herself tight against Rolland. "I know, sweetheart, I know," Rolland soothes, holding her against his chest hard, and I worry he's crushing her. "Shh it's over. They're never going to touch you again," he affirms. Kia takes a gasping breath as though she's struggling to find air. "Kia, breathe for me. I'm right here. Listen to my voice. Feel my heart," he assures, taking her hand from his neck and holding it against his chest. "See, I'm right here," he tries to calm her.

"Seb, speak to her, so she knows you're here too."

I move round so I can see her face which is tucked deeply into his neck. "Kia, I'm here too," I say gently, stroking her cheek. "Come back to us, sweetheart. It's just the three of us.

I'm sorry we had to put you through that, but a shirt would have made it worse if we didn't cover up your wounds first. It's over now and whatever you saw was just in your mind. No one else is touching you, just me and Rolland." Kia still doesn't calm as she tucks herself further into Rolland's neck and away from me.

"Kia, please breathe, or you're going to pass out," Rolland begs, sounding slightly panicked and incredibly tired as he strokes her head. Kia takes her hand from his, putting it back around his neck.

I move so my back is against the headboard and tight up against Rolland to try pushing some healing energy through her, but it's like hitting a wall.

"Kia, don't do this," Rolland grunts. His breathing becomes laboured and it sounds like he's lifting weights that are much too heavy.

Matt walks in with a laptop under his arm and his earphones in, then stops in his track when he sees us huddled together.

An idea comes to mind. "Matt, can we borrow your iPod?" I plead, leaning back from Rolland slightly. He whips the earphones from his ears and hands them to me without hesitation. Checking that he hasn't changed his taste in music overnight to rock, or heavy metal, I'm relieved to hear classical music coming through the ear pieces. I pop one into Kia's ear, and after a few seconds, she finally starts breathing easier. Although her body is still tensed up and her arms refuse to let go of the death grip they have on Rolland.

"Rolland, put the other one in," I urge. He struggles to open his eyes but takes it from me, fumbling with it slightly. I'm really beginning to worry about him, but he manages to find her other ear, as he strokes her head. Kia's body is still rigid, but her breathing has returned to normal.

After about five minutes, she finally relaxes her shoulders

and Rolland slumps back into the pillows with Kia still fully attached. His breathing is still a bit laboured, but I can tell that it's slowly returning to normal. Relieved, Matt moves to the cushioned chair on the other side of the bed and sits so he's facing them.

Another five minutes pass and I think they've both fallen asleep, though how that is possible with Rolland keeping a hold on her pain, I'm not quite sure. Thinking I could use a bit of a nap myself, I pull up the blankets from the bottom of the bed to cover all of us and settle myself down beside them. Turning to watch Kia, I find she's turned her head towards me, her face completely at ease. Wishing I could keep it that way, I drift off to sleep, her peaceful features the last thing on my mind.

CHAPTER TWENTY

*B*rad

Finishing up on the blade I've been working on for the past hour or so, I set it aside, sensing it's probably almost time for me to get to my other project. Manipulating metal is one of my gifts, but I also teach others how to defend themselves and I'm due at the training centre at ten o'clock. A quick look up at the clock on the wall tells me I've still got time to get my stuff and grab a late breakfast before heading over.

I run up to my room and snatch up a bag, realising as I do so that I've still the blade I was working on in my hand. *I must have picked it up without thinking as I left the workshop.* Shrugging, I set it down on the dresser then begin throwing a change of clothes into the bag. As I'm finishing up, my phone buzzes and I check to see who's coming today. Four of my clients can make it, one of which has only just started. All the women I train are victims of abusive relationships and want to learn self-defence. I set them up in pairs and work them through a programme I put together. The newest member still has a few bruises visible along her arms and is fairly jittery.

My thoughts turn to Kia and Jack's description of the amount of abuse she's endured. He didn't give any details as to her physical state, except to say that the cuffs are still attached and that her reaction to her back being healed wasn't good. The Gjinn is another issue. And just like those that I teach defence to, it's the mental scars that take the longest to heal.

Looking back over at the blade, I decide to leave it there for now. I'll bring it back to the workshop later when I'm not so rushed for time. Making sure I have my bag and phone, I head down toward the kitchen to see what I can find to eat before I go to the training centre. Dropping my bag by the front door, I step into the kitchen to find Gerry, who's looking incredibly tired and in need of a shower.

He watches me as I head for the fridge hoping to find some leftovers or something quick. I spot some rice, which isn't exactly breakfast, but it's food and it's slow releasing, which will help get me through the morning training session. I can hear Gerry tapping away on his laptop, but I'm guessing he's only giving it half of his attention.

As I turn to the microwave to heat up the rice, I decide to poke the bear. "Ya look like shit, Gerry," I tell him, keeping my focus on the microwave as I start it up. Snatching some fruit to take with me, I set it aside along with a couple of energy bars. Grabbing a bottle of water from the fridge, I take a long drink as I turn back around to face Gerry.

"I haven't slept and having someone in our home who I don't know isn't exactly comforting bedtime material," he grumbles deeply, sounding just like the bear he reminds me of most days. His thick, dark, chestnut hair curls slightly when it's allowed to grow to the length that it is now. He usually keeps it short, but with work being so stressful as of late, he's not had any time to cut it. He's still wearing his black combat gear from last night, along with his heavy boots, and dried dirt covers his shoulders, arms and face. *I'm surprised Seb hasn't ordered him out of the house. Not that Seb minds dirt, he just hates it in the kitchen.*

Placing the lid back on the bottle, I set it beside the fruit to take with me. *Poor guy has serious trust issues and no therapy seems to work on him. That being said, I think he needs to be slightly more understanding, given the circumstances.*

Resting my hands on the countertop, I try to think of how I can help ease the man's mind a fraction. "Gerry, I know how hard this is for ya, but from what Jack and Seb said, she's of no harm to any of us unless provoked. The girl sounds like she has more mental scars than you."

He frowns at me, and I wonder what I've said that he doesn't know already. I know Jack and Seb spoke to him about her, because I heard their voices when I passed the kitchen earlier, but what hasn't Seb told him?

"She's not just a simple girl though is she, Brad? She's an *Ayran*. Not that I know what that means, but she's not from here, just like none of us are. The fact that she managed to pull Matt into her mind for the last several months, goes to show how powerful she is," he grouches, his sardonic tone full of annoyance as he flicks his clover green eyes up to me. *What? They must have left that tidbit out.*

"Didn't they tell you?" he tuts, rolling his eyes slightly. "She has every ounce of my sympathy and I'm not such a dick to kick someone out who has suffered as she has. But having a Gjinn poke about the house as well as whoever else she has on her tail, isn't exactly comforting," he bites out with every ounce of venom the man feels, though his face remains calm. "And what the hell do you mean by, not harmless unless provoked?" He screws his ruddy face up in puzzlement. *Ah, that's what they didn't tell him. How did Seb get away without telling him?*

"She wasn't very nice when they touched her back," I say evenly, still keeping my eyes on him. *It's not a lie, just an understatement. I don't have full details on what happened, but that's not for me to share.* Just then the microwave pings, so I turn to take out the rice, and head over to sit with Gerry.

"A fucking Gjinn, Brad. How do you fight something you can't touch?" Gerry snarls, his face deepening in concern as he returns his attention to his laptop. He's right, but with help from Jack and the stones he's off to get, we might have a chance.

"Jack went to get more stones from Ireland and said he's gonna to show us how to protect our minds from the Gjinn when he returns later," I explain, trying to ease his worry a bit, but it's hopeless with Gerry. The guy has more demons than most of us, which is the root cause of why this is so hard for him. "Gerry, just try and get some rest and think it over. I'm sure Seb will have her patched up in a few days and you won't even have to see her," I say 'round a mouthful of rice.

"Maybe," he mutters, frowning pensively as he looks up at me. "How do you think they got her in here?"

"Who? Rolland and Seb?" *Weird question.*

He rolls his eyes. "No, whoever brought her in from outside the ice circle," he clarifies blandly.

Shaking my head, I realise I hadn't even thought about that. Over the course of the last few hundred years we all managed to find each other but since Jack joined us about a hundred and fifty years ago, we haven't found anyone else like us. Jack has told us small bits about why he thinks we're gifted and how there are other lands outside of Gaia. He also explained how he's tried teleporting out of here, but that something prevents him from getting any further than the ice circle. It's heavily guarded which was confirmed by Gerry and his boys a few years back. Thousands of miles of snow storms encompass the ice circle and can only be passed through in certain crafts. Thinking about Jack and his behaviour in my room earlier, I feel my face start to screw up.

Gerry's gaze is still on me and I begin to feel slightly uneasy. "What is it?" he asks with only a mild amount of attention.

I turn to him and wonder if he's noticed Jack's behaviour lately. "I was thinking about Jack and his oddness," I tell him as I inhale another mouthful of food.

Gerry snorts. "He's a weird guy and he wears his oddness like a second skin," he replies back. "It's the secrets he keeps that you should be more concerned about," he mutters under a breath.

I roll my eyes knowing how much Gerry can't stand Jack. Though saying that, even for Gerry his behaviour of late has been slightly extreme. Jack is just Jack in my eyes. With not much to go on, I decide not to say anything more, and finish off my rice as Gerry continues tapping away.

My thoughts turn to our last mission where they found Kia. So much of that night didn't seem right - Matt having little to no details, the change of plans at the last minute. And I swear a couple of the guys I took out weren't human, although it could've just been the darkness and trick of the light. But it got me to thinking that maybe there are more of us.

Wondering about the people Gerry and his men helped, I decide to ask him about them, hoping I don't regret it. "How did you and your boys get on with the others freed from the cells?"

He continues working away but doesn't snap at me for asking. Most of the people we pull from human trafficking have mental issues on some level, and Gerry and the boys usually have a rough few hours after getting them out.

"The boys got them the help they needed and most of them were fit to go back to the homes that were secure enough. Jack made an appearance, which was a little odd-" he pauses, causing me to look up at him. He's staring straight ahead, slightly lost in thought.

"How so?" I ask, wondering what's playing through his mind.

He doesn't answer straight away, but his brows begin to pull down harder. "It's not the first time he's checked in on those we've taken care of, but he seemed to pay special attention to a little boy," he summarises. Not that odd in the scheme of things, but it was enough to catch Gerry's eye.

"Perhaps he was trying to soothe the boy's mind after the trauma," I try rationalising. Gerry tilts his head in consideration, then goes back to typing.

Looking up at the clock, I see it's time to shift my arse into gear. "If ya see the guys, tell 'em I've finished the blade. Once they think Kia's up for it, I'll come and remove the cuffs," I say, pushing my chair back. Gerry nods, but continues to stare at his screen. I step over to the sink to wash my bowl and then pick the fruit, energy bars and water up as I pass.

Pausing at the kitchen door, I turn to the bear. "Gerry," I call. He pulls his eyes up to look at me. "Go to bed before ya scare your own shadow, would ya?" I jest with a smile. He gives me the middle finger as he returns his attention back to the laptop. I laugh lightly but really hope he does get some sleep. The man is a nightmare when he's on edge - add to it the lack of sleep, and he could easily give a Gjinn a run for its money.

The thought of the Gjinn pulls me to a stop at the front door and I look to the right down the corridor that leads to Seb's room. Sighing deeply, I pick up my bag and make my way out of the house, silently hoping that the stones hold for a few hours whilst Jack's gone. *Fingers crossed.*

CHAPTER TWENTY-ONE

*G*erry

Finishing the last of the data entry that needed to be sent over to Ben, I shut the laptop down and feel my eyes stinging from lack of sleep. *Brad's right, I'm desperately in need of a shower and some shut eye.* My shoulders are tense, and my neck is stiff from all the tension that's built up inside me. As I rub my hands over my face to try and wake myself up, my mind goes back to the girl that's in the house. The need to find out who she is and see her with my own eye's crawls through me.

I trust my senses implicitly. If something doesn't feel right, I listen to my gut without hesitation. A part of my soul is embedded with the need to know not only where my family is at all times, but that they're safe.

Once I've met a person, I can usually tell what their intentions and motives are within a moment of looking into their eyes and reading their body language. Knowing all it would take is a flick of my eyes to quell my anxiety, I look over to the kitchen door with longing.

Shaking my head, I sigh deeply and admit that taking a

shower is most likely a better idea right now than trying to force my way in to see the girl. I stink, and I want to get the filth from those dickheads off of me. Snatching up my laptop, I head out of the kitchen and up the stairs before turning left to head toward my room. The house is incredibly quiet and the only noise creeping through the silence is coming from an open window, most likely in Brad's bedroom.

Setting the computer down on my desk, I head to the bathroom to take a much-needed shower. Adjusting the settings on the nozzle so that it's at full power, I step under the water and instantly feel some of the tension leave my neck. The water runs slightly brown and I start scrubbing hard to get as much dirt and grime off my skin as possible. Seb's pool would do a better job at getting some of these knots from my neck, but the heat from the shower will have to do. Switching the water off and stepping out, I wrap a towel around my waist and face the oval mirror over the sink. *Shit. I look like death warmed over.*

Deep bags sit under my eyes and the hair around my face never looks good when it's at this length. I've grown it out before and it worked for a while. But days on the road without the means of maintaining it, I soon start looking rough. The boys said I was scaring those we were trying to help, so the beard went.

Taking some gel and a clean razor, I start the process of shaving. Not much can be done about the deep bags, so the half zombie look will have to do. Once done, I lean over the sink and zone out for a minute. My thoughts turn back to the time when it was just Rolland, Seb, Brad and me. We hadn't met Matt or Jack, and we had travelled across America, trying to find a place that felt right, like home. We could never stay long in any one place, as people would start to notice that we hadn't aged.

After spending years on my own and not understanding why I was so different, meeting the guys finally gave me a sense of family and normality in my life. But the need to protect them from everything began to overwhelm me and the panic attacks started. With a lot of work and help from Brad, Rolland and Seb, I found ways to deal with them. A slow process, but once we realised what was triggering them, they were easier to deal with most of the time. People I don't know or haven't met being in our home is a key trigger for me. And when information about that person is withheld, it's a recipe for disaster.

Sauntering back to my room, I tug on some comfortable slacks and pull a dark hoodie over my head before turning the tv onto something mundane. My hope is that it will drown out my thoughts so that I can switch my brain off for a few hours. Thankfully, I soon find my eyes drooping, and I drift off.

Glasses clinking against one another stirs me awake, and I drag myself out of the dreamless sleep I was in. Glancing at the clock, it reads 1:22 pm. *Damn, I could so do with more shut eye right now.*

Noise from the kitchen filters up to my room and my senses are on high alert thanks to the stranger in the house. Knowing that I won't settle again now that I've woken, I grumbling as I pull myself to my feet and make my way down to see who the elephant is stomping around in the kitchen. *Most likely Matt. Perfect. Just the boy I was hoping to see.*

Rounding the corner at the bottom of the stairs with my mind still half asleep, I hear the tap running. Pushing the door open, I find Matt filling up a clear glass jug that has a stone nestled at the bottom. He looks up and freezes slightly before looking back at the tap. His heart rate spikes, but he doesn't seem as nervous as he usually does when I'm cranky. *Inter-*

esting, that's the second time he's overcome his jitters around me in the last few hours.

Closing the door behind me, I lean back against it. He's not trapped, but I'm not going to make this easy for him. I want some answers as to why he didn't speak up sooner, and how he managed to keep the Gjinn out of his mind.

He turns the tap off, setting the jug to the side. His thumb twitches slightly on the water jug, as he takes a deep breath before leaning both arms on the counter to look up at me through his glasses. His casual light blue shirt is rolled up at his elbows, highlighting his grey eyes slightly.

"What do you want to know, Gerry?" he sighs heavily as he releases his breath, but his heartbeat remains calm.

That's strange, his heartbeat is usually all over the place. "Why didn't you speak up when you went to Paris? We agreed to have no secrets and to speak openly with each other," I ask mildly. He clenches his jaw when I say he's been keeping secrets, but apart from that, he's still holding it together. *I'm impressed.*

"I wasn't keeping secrets, Gerry. I didn't know what was going on and it was like following a ghost," he says through clenched teeth. His heart rate finally picks up, and I can smell fear coming from him, causing me to narrow my eyes at him.

He continues, knowing I'm picking up on all his body language. "I feel so much guilt that it's suffocating me. You have no idea of the things I saw and then to find out they were actually real-" he pauses and looks down at his feet. Hurt radiates from him, and a small part of me feels bad for pushing the subject. "None of us would have survived that, not even Brad, I don't think," he speaks so softly it's almost a whisper. *What? Hearing Seb's list of her injuries turned my stomach earlier, but to see another one of the guys crumbling like this is even more concerning.*

Feeling remorseful for making Matt feel this badly, I step away from the door and make my way over to him. He looks up and turns his head to me. His light skin looks slightly paler than usual, most likely due to lack of sleep, and I can't help but wonder if he's managed to get any at all.

"I can't put into words why I feel like I do around her, but-" he flicks his eyes over me as though he is unsure of how I'll react to what he's going to say. "Just don't be too hard on yourself for being such a dick." *What the actual Fuck? Is he for real?* My face pulls in, confused at his words.

He lumbers toward the door carrying the water jug and stops, turning to face me. "I'm heading out shortly to meet up with Aaron regarding a lead and drop Gregg off a sample found in the bullet Seb pulled from Rolland. The bullet pulled from Kia was completely clean, not a single trace. Rolland and Kia have both finally fallen asleep and I'm not sure how much longer Rolland is going to hold out. He looks worse than he did back in Korea." *Fuck!*

Matt turns and walks out of the kitchen, leaving me stunned. Rolland in Korea was fucking shit. He nearly pushed himself too far. But he wouldn't stop or listen to any of us as he spent days easing the hurt and emotions from people until his body finally gave out.

My mind is still exhausted, and my body could do with a shit ton more rest. Knowing I'm not going to get answers anytime soon, I grab a bottle of water from the fridge and head back up to my room. *Everything else is just going to have to wait for now.*

CHAPTER TWENTY-TWO

*M*att
Sauntering back to Seb's room with a fresh jug of water, I quietly set it down on the bedside table. The stone won't take long to work, and there's still a full glass left from before. I settle back on the chair to finish up a few emails that need to be sent, being sure to keep an eye on the time. Aware I'll need to leave shortly, I'm hoping that either Seb or Rolland will wake up soon.

As I glance up to check on them, I find Kia's eyes watching me steadily. I offer her a small smile, which she returns, warming my heart. *I wish I could see it more*.

I click send on the last email and shut the laptop down, placing it on the chair beside me before taking the glass of water from the bedside cabinet. I move over to the bed, careful not to shift Seb too much. *The longer he can stay sleeping, the better*.

"Do you want a drink?" I offer lightly. Kia's sapphire eyes look deep into mine, and it's like she's searching for something again. A small perplexed frown crosses her face, and I notice the earpieces are still in, so she probably didn't hear me. Leaning over carefully, I pluck one from her ear to see her eyes widen a little before she sits up.

Rolland stirs in his sleep, reflexively shifting her higher so she's sitting more comfortably. Kia looks down at him as her shoulders relax, letting out a soft breath, she seems to lose herself in her thoughts for a few moments.

I sit back up straighter, my movement catching her attention. "Would you like a drink?" I ask again with a smile. She nods, taking the glass from my hand. Then brings it to her lips, taking a tentative sip. Rolland grumbles, mumbling something under his breath. Kia continues to drink, but very slowly, her face in deep concentration.

"Kia, stop it. I'm awake, so stop trying to cover it up," Rolland mumbles sleepily, throwing a muscular arm over his eyes. Kia finishes the water and passes the glass back to me. I recheck the time and see that I've still got a few minutes before I need to leave.

"Rolland, I need to head out soon with the sample and meet up with Aaron, but I won't be gone too long," I tell him quietly.

Rolland waves a hand. "Seb, wake up. Matt's heading out, and I'm not ready to open my eyes yet," Rolland groans deeply. Seb doesn't move a muscle. "Seb, wake up, your beauty sleep is over," he says a little louder. Still nothing. Kia moves off his lap with a mischievous look on her face.

"Kia, what are you up to?" Rolland's asks curiously. She keeps one hand on his chest, sliding off so she's closer to Seb. "That's just mean, Kia," he chastises lightly. *How does he know what she's thinking?*

Kia runs her hand up Seb's caramel-toned arm. He makes a noise in the back of his throat in response, but still doesn't move. She continues to run her fingers up and down his arm, her eyes changing colour. Seb makes another noise and his hand twitches where it rests on his hip. Kia moves her hand to his neck, running it up the side of his dark stubbled cheek. She stops and pulls in a quick breath.

"You're in so much trouble, Kia," Rolland warns as he takes away the arm resting over his eyes and rubs himself, trying to push down the stiffness in his pants. He turns over, burying his face into the pillow.

Seb finally moves and pushes himself up onto his right arm, so he's face to face with Kia, before he lunges forward to claim her lips, kissing her hard. Rolland tries to pull her back with his left arm that's still looped around her waist.

"Please, Seb, this is so mean. You're both so mean," Rolland whines into the pillow.

Kia's arm leaves Rolland's chest as she tugs Seb toward her. I feel myself getting hard just watching and I wonder what's wrong with me. *Is this normal? Then again, why am I questioning what's normal? None of us are.*

Kia makes a small noise of frustration as Seb moves his mouth down her neck, sucking at the skin there for a moment before pulling away. He gets up off the bed and strolls toward the bathroom, his noticeable hardness mirroring the one in my own pants. Looking back at Kia, I can't help but quietly laugh at the death glare she is aiming at Seb's back.

Remembering it's just about time for me to go, I glance down at my watch before picking up the laptop from the chair and heading over to the bathroom door. "Seb, I'll be back in a few hours. I'm dropping that sample off and meeting Aaron in town. Message me if you need anything," I explain, trying to speak clearly so he can hear me through the door.

The toilet flushes and then the tap runs before Seb

appears in the doorway, looking a lot fresher than he did prior to them all taking a nap. "No worries. You find traces on those bullets?" he queries as he leans against the door jamb of the bathroom.

"Kia's was clean, but the other was a match to the one I pulled out in Paris," I say, watching Seb's face reflect my own thoughts. "Yeah, but it just confirms what we already know, not who they are," I tell him.

"When you get back, we can go over what intel you have and maybe see if anything matches up to Gerry's," he suggests, straightening his solid frame out.

Jerk-brains Gerry. I'd prefer to stay out of his way till he's calmed down some more, but who knows when that's going to happen. Figuring it's better to keep that thought to myself, I stay quiet.

"Have you spoken to him yet?" Seb asks, raising a dark arched eyebrow a fraction.

"Yeah, I think I woke him up. He was slightly more tolerable, but still being sour," I sigh, before glancing over at the bed to see Kia fiddling with the earpieces to my iPod. As I amble over to Rolland's side of the bed, I hear Seb making his way out of the room. Taking earphones from her, she startles slightly but smiles sweetly when she sees it's me. *Each smile feels like it's connected to my heart, slowly mending the pieces that were broken by seeing her in those visions.*

"See this small hole? It has to go to the front and in your ear first," I explain, sliding one into her ear. She looks at the other one with puzzlement and tries herself. It takes her a few attempts, but she manages in the end, and my reward is to get another beautiful, genuine smile from her. I smile back, happy that I've brought some comfort to her.

She tugs at my arm bringing me closer to her face.

Without second thinking it, I accept her gentle kiss as her hand encourages my head closer. I hear the chains on her cuff clink in my ear and my face heats, but another part of me doesn't care. Kissing her back, I trace my tongue over her lips. Her mouth opens, and as she flicks her tongue over mine, everything else around me seems to fade out. Pushing my tongue further into her mouth, she breathes in, pulling harder on my head. My free hand finds her cheek and I stroke my thumb over it, running my finger along her neck. Kia urges me further forward and I hear Rolland grumble something, but I don't listen to him. Kia fills my senses and all I want to do is dive deeper into her. Her tongue traces my teeth and it's almost as if I can feel her tracing the length of my hardness. I make a grunt of appreciation as I try and find my way deeper into her mouth.

"Matt, stop!" The panic in Rolland's voice snaps me out of it.

I ease back from Kia's lips to find us leaning quite far back with her hands around my neck, clinging to me like a monkey, her arms the only things supporting her weight. Any further and we would have lost balance and ended up with her laying on her back. *Bugger, that was too close.*

Kia's eyes are swirling intensely and they're full of silver specs. I can't seem to move and my balance is beginning to tilt forward.

"Rolland, a little help, please. She's got me trapped."

Kia's eyes swirl faster, and I can't help but move torward to her lips again, pushing her further back. Kia tilts to the right before her lips find mine, followed by her energy pouring down my throat and into my chest. She bites my lip, then let's go to turn from me to her right.

Released from whatever trance she had me in, I manage to straighten myself out slightly. Her energy still swirls in my chest, warming my body all the way through as I turn my head to see Rolland kissing Kia's ear and neck. She drops her arms from around my neck, releasing me completely. Taking the opportunity to get out, I make as little noise as possible and slip out of Seb's room.

What in the ever-loving hell was that?

CHAPTER TWENTY-THREE

*R*olland

I kiss Kia's neck as I work my way up to her ear and I can feel her desire pool deep within me. *I'm in so much trouble with this girl. I can't get enough of her, and all I want to do is bury myself deep within her.*

Kia's hand moves up my body as her energy travels faster, sinking into my chest then making its way down to my stomach. It seems to tug on my already hard cock, making me grunt as I pull her on top of me, careful not to move too fast.

Every feeling from her flutters through me, and it's as if I'm hearing her thoughts, but not in words. Her intentions and thoughts seem to flit across my mind like projections, although some of the images make no sense. The first few are of us kissing deeply, but then they change into patterns and colours that fill my head.

I push some of my energy and feelings back to her - my puzzlement at how she's burrowed her way into my heart, and my desire of wanting to give her everything and anything, just to see her beautiful smile. Matt's face flicks across my vision along with more sincere emotions.

Her hands rest on either side of my head as she pulls at my energy, which I give freely. She urges back some more of her own while diving back into my mouth.

"Rolland, need more." It's her voice again, yet it's so quiet still. "*Please, Rolland, it feels like I am chasing something."*

Oh man, she needs a release after all three of us have worked her up.

Kia eases back and I find her eyes glowing silver, pulsing, pulling me in so I can't look away. *Not that I have any intention of doing so.* Her dark hair falls on either side of our faces, cutting most of the light off, and causes her eyes to shine even brighter.

"Kia-"

She plunders my mouth again and I lose track of all rational thought. She grinds her warm sweet body into me, rubbing her clit along my hardness. I hear her sharp intake of breath as she leans back. *Shit. This is it. She's going to snap and run.*

Peeking an eye open, I find her silver gems glowing orange around their edges. *Shit.* She doesn't move, and neither do I, both stuck in this moment of time. Suddenly I feel a warmth around my cock, almost as if she's wrapped her small hand round it and I suck in a breath as I watch more orange seep into her eyes. As we stare at one another, I can feel energy swirl around my hardness, and it feels as if she's pulling on it with the heat of her pussy. *Shit, am I inside her? When did that happen?*

Kia's eyes appear almost fully orange now and we still haven't moved.

"Kia. I'm about to lose my shit, and if I'm inside you, we could have a problem."

Her face furrows in perplexity, but then something seems

179

to dawn on her. *"Inside?"* Her voice, light and silvery, is full of curiousness as she tilts her head a fraction.

More energy surrounds me, and my body moves of its own accord, grinding up into her. She finally closes her eyes, taking her bottom lip into her mouth.

"Please, Rolland, a little more."

Unable to deny her, I pull her down into me. *"Yes, Rolland."* More heat centers around my cock, and I know I'm seconds from coming undone. I close my eyes to try and keep a hold on the little amount of control I have left but I'm unable to stop my body from moving of its own accord. *Not that I'm truly fighting it though.* In response, a noise much like a growl comes from the back of her throat as she grinds hard against me, and just like that, my control is gone.

Capturing her lips roughly, I hear her whimper as her tongue dances around mine and I feel the warmth around my cock give a hard yank. I grunt again, forcing my tongue deeper into her mouth and as the energy pulls one more time, I feel myself come. At the same time, Kia pulls desperately at my head, and I hear her make another noise as she bites my lip. *Shit. What the hell just happened?*

Kia is panting heavily, as she finally let's go of my lip, moving her head to rest on my chest. My breathing is equally ragged, and I feel almost dizzy. As we lay there together trying to calm ourselves, I begin to feel her pain coming through. I can't help but wonder if I didn't feel it for a bit because she was able to control it, or if it was because we were so wrapped up in the pleasure of each other that we were allowed a moment of reprieve.

My mind slowly starts to clear, but my body still feels exhausted despite the nap we had. With my left hand, I quietly stroke Kia's soft hair as my right skims its way up her arm where it rests lightly on my chest. As I continue to soothe her, contentment, peace, and happiness begin to override the pain, and I can't help the smile the spreads across my face. Kia's turns her head to look up at me, propping her chin up with her hand.

Don't look at her, Rolland. Don't look. Just don't. You know she'll be the death of you, and yet you wouldn't regret it. My smile grows even bigger at my thoughts and a small laugh escapes me. Happiness continues to roll through me, and I open my eyes to the perfect vision of Kia's face as it beams up at me.

"Happy?" I ask her cheekily. She nods her head quickly in response as she sucks her lips into her teeth. I lift my head to look down her body and see that she's still wearing the boxers Matt put on her earlier. *How the hell did she make it feel like I was actually buried deep inside her?*

Completely dumbstruck, I flop my head back down on the pillow, and hear Seb's light footsteps returning. "I don't know about you two, but I'm starving," he says as he comes into the room. I throw my right arm over my eyes to block him out as I am in no way ready to face him yet.

"Rolland, you want some soup? It's the last from that batch and there are rolls too," he says as his smoky tone travels across the room, followed by the weight of his body pressing into the bed. "Rolland? Did you fall back to sleep?"

"I wish I had," I grumble. *No, that's not true. That was fucking amazing, whatever the hell that was. What the fuck am I going to do?* Kia's brilliant smile flashes behind my closed eyelids and my heart skips a beat. In response, I feel her happiness, chased by desire, as they play their way through my veins. *Oh man, she's fucking relentless!*

"I'm awake, Seb. I just need a minute alone in the bathroom," I clarify before taking a few deep breaths and removing my arm from my face. Blinking several times to adjust to the light, I sit up slowly, resting my weight on my arms. Kia rises slightly at the same time and while I feel her pain flicker through me, I find it's easier now to process. I'm getting used to its presence, although it still wears on me.

Making sure she's okay, I find Kia is looking at Seb and I know she wants to go to him. "Kia, do you think you could behave while I use the bathroom?" I ask playfully, running my eyes over her body, noticing her skin is looking a lot better than it did before we all took a nap. Bruises still mar the length of her small arms and legs, but they appear to be fading.

She turns, frowning slightly, but a smile plays at the corner of her mouth before she nods and starts to ease herself away from me. Pain flares from her knees with the movement, so I stop her. "I think it would be easier if you take her from me, Seb," I say. Understanding, he maneuvers his body around until he's resting up against the headboard. Snaking his arms around her waist, he carefully eases her onto his lap until she's sitting sideways on him, facing me, my hand maintaining constant contact with some part of her body as she moves.

"Seriously?" Seb says as he shakes his head in disbelief. I find his chiseled face looking down at the wet patch on my trousers and I simply shrug in response.

"You have no idea, Brother. You have no idea." I don't even feel guilty for it. And I can't, not when the result was the way she smiled at me.

Dropping my eyes to her, I see she's looking toward the bathroom as though she wants to go herself. "Kia. I'm going to have to let go for just a couple of minutes to freshen up then I'll be back. We'll get you fed and healed up and then you can go. Do you think you can hold out for that long?" I ask her. She looks at me hesitantly for a moment before dipping her chin slightly in response. Quickly but carefully I pull away from her and head off to the en-suite to clean myself up.

Taking off the now soiled trousers, I grab a clean pair out of the drawer and notice that there aren't many left. *I could seriously do with some of my own clothes.* I throw the dirty pants in the basket, and as I start to wash myself, I feel worry begin to flow through me, causing me to stop and frown. *Am I feeling Kia's emotions from in here?* I do a quick once over, and it's almost as if I can still feel her pain. *Perhaps it's my mind **thinking** it's still in pain, even when it's not.*

Finishing up, I head back into the bedroom and find Seb with his eyes closed and Kia resting her head against his chest. I pause my steps for a moment, wishing I could leave her there in his arms, as I'm loathed to disrupt their contented states. If it wasn't for the small frown on Kia's brow, and the barely visible tremor across her shoulders, you'd think she wasn't in any pain.

I continue on to the bed, and as I sit down, I'm momentarily shocked that I can feel my body taking Kia's pain before I've even touch her. Scooting closer, I ease her legs onto my lap and immediately pull all of her pain away from her. As I do, I hear her release a soft breath and see a smile appear on her lips, though she keeps her eyes closed, and her head turned into Seb's chest. Happiness streams from her in steady waves, and I can't help but savour the moment.

Seb passes a bowl and a warm roll over to me before taking another bowl and holding it out in front of Kia. "Kia?" he asks quietly. She's still smiling but opens her eyes to see the soup he is offering her.

I start tucking into my soup, enjoying it and the bread that's still fresh. Kia sits up taking the bowl from Seb as he picks up another roll and holds it out to her. She looks at it like she did the shirt last night, and shakes her head no, before turning to watch me eat mine, her eyebrows raised.

"It's bread, Kia, what's called a roll and they're delicious. Soft and warm on the inside and slightly crunchy on the outside," I encourage. She shakes her head no again, and I frown. *A no to bread?* With a shrug of his shoulders, Seb begins tearing off pieces of his roll, dipping them into his soup.

"While it's on my mind, Rolland, I meant to tell you something Jack told me earlier." I nod at Seb slightly, confirming to him that I'm listening before returning my attention back to my soup. *"He said that there are more people like us trapped here in Gaia."*

I stop mid-chew and glance over at him. At the same time, Kia peeks up at me, and I realise she must be just as in tune with my emotions as I am with hers. She studies me for a moment, then looks to Seb, but he's a much better actor than I am. I continue to chew and focus once again on my food. *"Go on..."* I say apprehensively.

"Jack and others like him, watch over small groups of people like us. Our energy, when in significant numbers, is like a beacon attracting those that would rather see us dead, or worse."

There's no pause in my eating, but I can't help the feeling of concern and worry about Kia that settles like a rock in my core. I feel her foot move to touch me in order to get my attention and I look up at her - she knows we're talking telepathically and doesn't like being cut off from the conversation, especially when she can feel that it's worrying me. Funny how I was able to get all of that, just from one look.

"Sorry, Kia. We're being rude, but we don't want you worrying more than you already are," I explain. She studies me for a moment, and I can tell she isn't happy. Her head drops, and her emotions hit me hard - hurt, disappointment and fear start to creep back in.

"Okay, I'll make you a deal. You finish eating and let us heal both of your knees, then Seb can tell both of us what Jack had to say," I encourage. From the corner of my eye I see Seb's face scrunch up as though I just punched him. *Shit, it can't be **that** bad.*

"You need to get yourself out of that one, because I am not telling her," he states, glaringly. Luckily, Kia seems content with my offer and has already tucked herself back into her soup, so doesn't see the silent heated exchange between us.

Fuck, fuck, fuck, fuck. Me and my big mouth!

CHAPTER TWENTY-FOUR

*S*ebastian
Rolland and his big mouth. I don't feel comfort-able keeping things from Kia, yet she doesn't need to know how her energy is a beacon attracting all kinds of trouble. Maybe I can distract her from remembering Rolland's deal?

Turning my attention to Kia, I'm happy to see she's busy eating her soup. She seems to struggle slightly with the spoon, and I notice her glancing at Rolland a few times, studying how he is eating. I frown slightly, wondering how her people live and eat. The fruit seemed to come second nature to her, but the bread doesn't. Kia watches Rolland put the empty bowl on the side and looks down at her own.

"Are you still hungry?" I ask her. She shakes her head and then turns to the water jug. Taking the bowl from her, I fill her a glass, which she gulps down eagerly, then passes it back. She fidgets slightly on my lap, rubbing my cock. *Shit. I don't think she meant to arouse me intentionally, but with Kia, it doesn't take much. Just looking at her lips will do it.*

"Ready?" She nods, keeping her eyes on me and her hands in her lap. Rolland's got his hands around her ankles, appearing to be more than happy to let her stay with me. He seriously looks like shit and I haven't seen him this bad in a very long time. His hair is still a little damp from their shower and in need of a comb, but his cheeks have regained some colour from whatever happened earlier. Unfortunately, the rest of him is still pale in comparison to his usual tanned tone. At least he's not sweating like he was last night. I was beginning to worry he was going to pass out.

Looking down at Kia's legs, they're both heavily bruised with far too many cuts and scrapes to heal at the same time as doing her knees. Placing my right hand on the leg closest to me, I start easing some energy into it and I can feel that there are small pieces of broken bones, as well as some substantial ligament damage.

I hear Kia's breathing change a little before she turns into me, burrowing her head into my chest. Stroking her head to comfort her, I hope she feels at least a little safety within my arms.

It feels like most of the bones have healed back together, so I begin working on the tissue. I glance over at Rolland to find his eyes closed and a faint frown on his face. Kia has relaxed into my arms and it feels like she's fallen asleep. I continue to study Rolland as his brow pulls down harder and a sheen of sweat appears across his head. *Is he doing more than taking her pain away?*

With the first knee healed, I move my hand to her left leg and begin easing energy into it. Kia is still relaxed against me, her breathing even, but I keep my eyes on Rolland, hoping this isn't a repeat of earlier. Focusing my attention on her knee, I pull the bones back together - Rolland's jaw clenches as he takes a deep, steadying breath. I keep an even stream trickling into her knee, carefully fixing the tendons and tissue.

With the second knee fully healed, I skip my eyes to Kia, then back to Rolland, but neither of them stirs or reacts.

"Rolland, I'm done," I speak to his mind. He doesn't move or reply. *Fuck.*

"Rolland?" I say just a bit little louder. Still nothing.

I decide to speak out aloud, hoping I don't startle Kia too much. "Kia, Rolland, I'm finished." Still nothing. *What the hell is going on with these two?*

Rolland is sweating even more, and his breathing has slowed significantly. *Fuck, that can't be good.*

I lean over a fraction to try shaking him, but all he does is hold on tighter to Kia's ankle to which she makes a small noise in response. I tilt her head back to find her eyes shut as though she's sleeping.

"Kia, wake up for me. It's me, Sebastian," I speak to her softly. She doesn't open her eyes, but her brow furrows slightly. "Kia, wake up. Rolland needs out of there now," I say more firmly. She frowns harder. "Come on, Kia. I know you can hear me. Wake up!" I demand.

She opens her eyes, pulling herself up a little too quickly which tugs her body from Rolland a little. He holds on tighter to her ankle before Kia moves from my lap, pushing herself closer to him.

Worried that she'll overwhelm her mind again, I put a hand on her arm to get her attention. "Kia, you can't over-strain yourself. When you woke Rolland with your energy before, you fell deep into your mind and Jack struggled to find you," I caution quickly.

Kia turns to me, running her eyes over my face, before placing one hand on my chest and the other Rolland's, closing her eyes when she's connected to both of us.

"Rolland?" Is that Kia's voice? Her accent is unusual and

not one I've heard before. I feel energy get pulled from my chest into Kia's hand.

Observing her carefully, I watch her face for any sign of exertion, but it remains passive though I sense her breathing increase a little.

"Rolland, come back." Her voice is quiet, laced with worry and emotion.

Energy gets yanked from me hard and fast, causing me to close my eyes from the pain that laces through me. A vision of Rolland slumped on a dark stone floor flashes across my mind. I whip my eyes open to see tears rolling down Kia's cheeks, yet her face continues to remain calm.

Another drag of energy gets wrenched roughly from me, tightening my chest, making it hard to breathe.

Rolland finally takes a deep breath in and opens his eyes wide. When he sees Kia, he tugs her to his chest firmly. "It's okay, sweetheart. I'm fine. I'm fine," Rolland soothes urgently, stroking her hair. Kia takes a shuddering breath, but she manages to stay calm and not break down completely. Rolland kisses her head as he takes a few calming breaths.

"What happened, Rolland?" I ask with concern. So much of this is new to us and a lot of what is happening doesn't make any sense, but I haven't questioned any of it. When you see such a small body like Kia's riddled with evidence of serious abuse, you stop reasoning and just start reacting instinctively. But seeing Rolland like this is too much - I need to know what happens when they drop out like that.

"Just give me a moment, Brother," he presses, inhaling deeply. "Just let me catch my breath and bearings." He closes his eyes, burying his nose into Kia. She leans back from him, but Rolland pulls her head back to his chest. "Just let me feel you a little longer, Kia. Please." His voice breaks at the end, and my heart hurts for him.

189

Guilt bubbles up at pushing them both too much and my usual control over my emotions slips, allowing them to leak out to Rolland.

"Seb, you're fine. This is just all new to me. It's not your fault," he assures, looking over at me. As he does, I notice his lake-blue eyes look even more drained, which cranks my unease up further. "Kia can move about without help now. Totally worth it," he approves with a triumphant smile, trying to ease my concerns.

But as I study his eyes and take in his pale skin, the dark bags, and the sheen of sweat across his face, I begin to worry how much this is affecting him.

"You look worse than Gerry," I tell him with a suspicious frown.

His smile broadens. "Now that's just mean," he retorts, some life appearing to flow back into his features. He re-positions himself so he's sitting forward, and Kia moves back to give him room, being sure to keep a hand on his legs.

"Pass me some water please, Seb. It feels like I haven't drunk any in days." His words come out raspy and with a slight croak. Doing as he requests, I pass the full glass over to him. He quickly downs the whole lot, so I refill it and pass it back, but rather than drink it himself, he pushes it into Kia's hand. "Drink up, little minx," he encourages with a wink. She reluctantly takes it as Rolland relaxes back against the headboard, sitting much straighter than he was before.

"Well?" I hint, raising my eyebrows at him. He turns and looks at me, then lets out a puff of air.

"I think it started after I helped Jack pull her from her mind in the pool. I began to feel her emotions a lot stronger. Then when the Gjinn appeared, I could feel every emotion she was feeling. I know it's what I do, but it was so much *more* than it usually is. It was as though the emotions were coming from inside *me*. Then she tried shutting me out, keeping the pain to herself." He turns to Kia, raising his curved eyebrows at her. Kia sticks her tongue out and we both laugh. A small smile pulls at her mouth, but the line across her forehead shows she's still concerned.

"It became like a battle of wills over control. Then when I took her shirt off in the shower-" he pauses, still looking at Kia. As I watch them, I get the feeling that they're silently communicating. "I saw some of the things that happened to her and it began to feel as though I was the one getting whipped." I frown feeling like I haven't heard the worst part. "My body couldn't take any more and it gave out. Then I heard Kia speak in my mind, although it was very faint," he explains looking back over at me. He keeps his gaze steady as he continues.

"When you fixed up her back, I got pulled into her mind, and it was like I was there with her, watching everything, but I couldn't stop it," he laments, blinking hard as he tries to compose his emotions. "Just now it happened again, but I managed to intercept, pulling her out of it. The vision changed, and it all started happening to me. I was being whipped, beaten, whilst Kia had to watch me go through it. Then she disappeared and I thought she had died." His voice is full of the emotions that I know he's trying to keep a tight reign on, but it's obvious it's not working. He looks back to Kia who has her chin tilted low down toward her chest.

Rolland sits forward, pulling her into his arm. "You can use the bathroom now, Kia, without me," he mumbles with amusement into her hair. Kia looks over at the door. "But I'll walk you to the door and wait, just in case," Rolland says as he goes to stand, only to find his legs don't want to hold him up.

I move quickly off the bed and push him back down

before he falls. "You sit your big arse down and I'll wait by the door," I order. He doesn't even fight me, which is so unlike him. "Rolland, you're really beginning to worry me."

Kia rises to her feet and she's a little unsteady at first, so I place a hand on her elbow for support as I continue studying Rolland.

"I'm fine, stop faffing about me," he chides, waving me off as he leans back against the bed once more. He keeps his eyes open though, thankfully, quelling a little of my apprehension.

I step in front of Kia to help steady her as she begins rolling her weight about on her toes, testing her body. Kia looks up at me and gives me the biggest smile I've seen yet and it's like the sun has risen in the sky. She pulls me down, kissing my lips hard, running her tongue along my lips. I move my hands around her waist, chasing her tongue with my own.

Feeling myself grow hard, I start to seek more of her, but she leans back, winks, then stalks off to the bathroom. I'm left stunned, as I stand there for a few seconds.

"You're each as bad as the other, that's all I have to say," Rolland mutters as he tries to hold down a laugh. I give him the finger and head to the bathroom to wait for Kia. *What the hell does he know, anyway?*

CHAPTER TWENTY-FIVE

*M*att
                    After dropping the sample off to Gregg to
get analysed, I head over to the other side of town to meet up
with Aaron. I've known the guy for about ten years, so I trust
him well enough, but it's always a risk meeting people to
exchange information.

Pulling up to our usual pub, I sit and wait for a bit,
looking out for any cars that seem off or unusual. It's a bright
day out, so the only shadows that might conceal people are in
the alleyways between the shops and on the right side of the
pub. I spot Aaron stalking up the path on the other side of the
road, but he keeps looking back over his shoulder. My gut
tells me something is off, but I need this info, and he won't
pass this kind of stuff on over the phone, email, or any other
way that it can get traced back to him. Unease crawls through
my stomach, so I wait a couple of minutes longer to see if
anyone follows behind him.

No one does, so I lock up my car and head over to the
pub. It's a newly refurbished building with light greys
contrasting with deep red fixtures, and it doesn't have that

sticky feel to the floors that creeps me out. Solid wooden tables are dotted around the space as you walk in, looking clean and almost welcoming. I spot Aaron at one of the deep red booths at the far back, tending a pint of beer in a firm fist.

Heading over to the bar, I order iced water, which earns me a look of contempt from the short blonde bar lady. I don't intend to stay long and I hate waste. She sets it down hard, giving me another sour look as she does so. I hand her some money before meandering over to where Aaron sits.

I do a quick sweep of the place, noting that there are only two other tables with people at them. It would be a different story if we had chosen to meet here a few hours ago. But with the lunch rush over, and most people back at their offices or away shopping, it leaves a quiet atmosphere with just the low music playing in the background. I take a seat and notice Aaron looking at the door with hard amber eyes.

Aaron's about the size of Rolland, pushing seven feet and just as broad in the shoulders, but that's where the similarities end. His clean, dark hair is pulled back into a loose ponytail, showcasing his deep-set eyes which, at the moment, look very troubled. His strong jaw clenches hard as he scans the pub intensely. He's ex-military, like Gerry's boys, but has no interest in being on board, preferring his own company. He flicks his eyes over me, pulling them in as though noticing something.

"Everything okay, you seem more on edge than normal?" I ask, running my gaze over him, taking in the tattoos down his neck and the rings on his fingers.

"I'm not sure. On my way here, I swear I had someone following me, but it was more a feeling than anything," he summarises with doubt, causing his deep bass tone to rumble even lower through my ears. A pensive frown mars his forehead as he sips his beer. My stomach knots and the need to take off causes my legs to start bouncing.

Aaron scowls harder at me. "What's up with you?" he questions, jutting his square chin at me. "Even for you, this is more nervous than usual," he says blandly, prying my gaze away from its perusal of the bar.

Taking a calming breath, I try easing my twisting stomach before turning back to him. "Nothing, just a long night," I reply, trying to appease him with an even tone, but clearly, he's not buying it. He raises his bushy eyebrows at me, easily picking up on my lie. "It was a long night and I haven't slept yet. I found out some heavy stuff a few hours ago and it's taking its toll mentally." It's as close to the truth as he's going to get from me. Thankfully he nods in acceptance and takes another sip of his beer.

"I didn't want to give you and your boys half information, it's not my way. But I've checked this building over multiple times and then rechecked all the dates. I've kept my eyes on it for the past three months, and like clockwork, there's a delivery of a shit load of drugs that even my top analyst can't get a fix on. A week later, at least three lorries export people from the building," he says informatively, letting out a heavy breath as he rubs a rough hand over his face. "I know three months is a long time to watch a building and not share this with you, but every time I got close, I always came away feeling like someone was following me." He cruises his eyes over to the door again before taking another long drink.

Thinking back to why I didn't talk to the guys about my nightmares, I look down at my glass wondering what would have happened if I had.

"I don't want shit following you, Matt. You're a good kid," Aaron affirms earnestly.

I laugh quietly at his comment. I have to admit my face

has a youthfulness to it, unlike the rest of the guys, and I can effortlessly pass for being in my late twenties or early thirties. With Aaron being in his forties, I know his remark isn't meant to be derogatory.

I look up at him, offering him a smile. "I know what you mean. Passing on information based on half-truths and uncertainty isn't my style either. Though after last night's revelations, I would rather take a chance and run with it rather than ignore something that could end up saving someone's life." I drop my gaze to the glass of water cupped in my hand, as my mind drifts back to Kia and the Gjinn this morning. Rolland splayed across the floor, Seb still on the bed, both rendered paralysed by the Gjinn. *How she had the strength to fight it off for so long and remain sane, is mind-boggling.*

"You sure you're okay, you look half out of it." Aaron's baritone voice drills me out of my thoughts.

I peer up from my glass of water. "Yeah, sorry," I mutter, shaking my head as I lean forward trying to shake myself out of the thoughts.

Aaron takes another long drink, then pulls a piece of paper from his pocket, sliding it over to me. "I'll keep an eye on things for a few more weeks and contact you if I see anything else, but the last movement was just a week ago, so I don't think there'll be any more activity for a couple of weeks yet."

I open the slip of paper and see that it's a central London address. Not somewhere I would ever choose to stay long, and the address doesn't jog any memories. I pocket the paper and take the envelope of cash from my back pocket, pushing it over to him. When he doesn't reach to pick it up, I look up at him in questioningly.

"Let's wait to see if this comes to anything first. So many things about this feel off. Once you get those people out and take the building down, I'll take the cash." I raise my brows at him. *This is a first.* "Yeah, now you see why I didn't want to share the info with you so soon," he says in reply to my lack of response.

Re-pocketing the cash, I check my phone to find a message from Seb with a list of stuff he wants. I also notice that it's close to four o'clock and admit to myself that I want to get back to Kia to see how she's doing, so I decide it's time to wrap stuff up with Aaron. "You know how to reach me if you hear anything more," I say to him, searching his face and seeing my own troubled thoughts reflected back at me.

Aaron nods then finishes off the last of his beer. We both stand and head over to the doors, instinctively scouring the pub as we move through it. Aaron heads out first, holding the door open for me, then checks over both shoulders. As I do the same, I feel something yank hard at my gut again. I stop and scan the area, but I can't see anything.

I walk over to my car, saying goodbye to Aaron over my shoulder while keeping my eyes alert to my surroundings. I notice a few people crossing the street while talking on their phones but see no one looking my way.

My eyes catch on a black Hilux pick-up truck parked on the other side of the road that wasn't there before. I spot someone sitting in the driver's seat, their head faced down as though they are texting. I narrow my eyes as I unlock the car to get in.

Plucking my phone from my pocket, I connect it to the hands-free system as I start the car. I take one last hard look around just to be sure, but still see nothing out of the ordinary. As I pull away, I keep my eyes on the Hilux, but thankfully it stays where it is. Letting out a breath I didn't realise I was holding, I start for the supermarket.

❧

I'm just pulling into a parking spot at the market when I spot the Hilux from the pub pull in on the other side of the lot. My stomach begins to roll, and I feel sweat beginning to bead on my forehead. Staying where I am, I contemplate calling Brad. If someone is really following me, it would be better to leave my car here. This same situation has happened before, and we managed to lose them, though Gerry still lost it for a few days.

No one gets out of the truck and I decide to call Brad while shopping. Grabbing my phone and the essentials I need, I make my way over to the doors of the shop while dialing Brad.

It rings a handful of times before he picks up. "Hey, I'm just heading out of the gym and getting in my truck," he explains, his deep tone flowing through my ear as I head through the doors.

"I'm just picking up a few bits for Seb. Do you need anything?" I ask as casually as possible.

Silence meets my question and I'm thankful for Brad's quick thinking. I don't usually call for this kind of thing, so he knows something's up. "No, I'm good. How's Kia?" He's making conversation, confirming to me he's twigged.

I start grabbing the stuff that Seb asked for, keeping my eyes peeled to see if anyone's watching. I don't see anyone, but that feeling in my gut is being pulled tight like a tightrope.

"She'd just woken from a nap when I left and was listening to some tunes on my iPod."

I can tell from the noise coming through the phone that Brad is driving, as I keep grabbing stuff from the shelves. Just as I'm reaching for an item, something catches my eye, but when try to get a closer look, there's nothing there. The feeling of being watched crawls down my back like a melting ice cube on a summer's day, leaving trickling droplets in its path. I whip myself around but only see two women reading the packaging on their items.

"How's Rolland holding up?" Glad to have Brad on the phone, I walk round to the wine section, picking up two of Seb's favourites.

"He's seen better days, but I think he'll be okay."

The feeling in my stomach eases, and I breathe a sigh of relief. Carrying all of my items to the checkout stand, I'm just turning the corner when the unease slams back into me like a thunderbolt.

"You on your way here, Brad?" My voice wavers slightly.

"Just pulled up," he confirms. *Thank freaking god.* I look around and see someone sitting on the benches on the other side of the tills, head bent down looking at the phone in his hand. Making my way quickly over to the checkout, I do my best to keep one eye on the suspicious looking guy while placing everything on the conveyer belt. I can see that he's wearing a dark blue cap with sunglasses, so I can't make out his face and I can just barely make out a tattoo on his neck.

The cashier starts scanning my stuff, asking idle questions as she passes my order through. I try to be as polite as possible answering her questions, while at the same time packing the groceries, being careful not to squash the bread and eggs against the wine. Between the chitchat with the cashier and the need to keep the food safe, I can feel my focus on the guy on the bench begin to wane. When I get the chance to look back up, he's gone. *Bugger.* My hands are sweaty, and I can feel my heart pumping in the back of my throat.

I finish paying and grab the shopping before ambling

toward the doors. *If I head over to Brad now, then whoever it is, will just follow Brad's truck.* I spot Brad's green Range Rover in my peripheral vision, but don't look straight at it. Deciding to divert the follower, I head back to my car. I dump all of the bags in the boot then climb into the driver's seat.

Sticking the hands-free on, I immediately call Brad. He picks up on the first ring, and before he can say anything I blurt out, "meet me on Sanders Street. I'll park on the next street up and take the alleyway." I can feel my mouth becoming dry, so I lick my lips and try to force some moisture back into my mouth. *Man, I hate being followed.* I don't expect a reply from Brad, so I end the call.

Putting some speed on, I check my mirror and see Brad behind me, although he's keeping a safe distance between us and as I watch, I see the Hilux pull out behind him, though it keeps a reasonable distance between them. Knowing someone is following me is more straightforward than not knowing.

Soon, I turn onto the road opposite Sanders street, and watch as Brad continues on, the Hilux still a decent distance behind. *Good, that will give me the few seconds head start I need.*

Grabbing my stuff, I turn the car off and quickly get out, briefly lamenting that I have to leave the carefully packed groceries behind. Without looking back, I duck behind the next car next to mine. I can see the alleyway straight ahead, so I wait for the truck to drive by. *It will either cross paths with my car and move past, or it will stop along-side mine, in which case, I'm totally snookered.*

The truck comes to a stop next to my car, and my heart plummets. *Darn it.*

I hear a door open, and realise my time is up so I make a break for it, flinging a shield up behind me as I go. The sound of gunfire vibrate through my ears, though the sound is greatly diminished, leaving me to deduce that the gun has a silencer on it.

I push my legs harder and as I round the corner of the alleyway I spot Brad's truck, the passenger side door flung wide open. Moving as fast as I can, I head toward him and throw myself into the open door.

"Go!" I shout, slamming the door shut behind me, hearing at the same time something hit the truck. My gut twists unhappily in response. *Crud, let's hope that's not a tracker.*

Brad speeds away, tires squealing. After a few minutes he checks his rear-view mirror then lets out a heavy breath. "Friend of yours?" he says lightly with a smile playing around his lips.

My heart is pounding, and my insides have twisted up so much that I feel sick. "You have to pull over as soon as it's safe so that we can check the truck for trackers," I urge, trying to catch my breath.

He nods as he turns his attention back to the road. "You have any idea who that was?" Brad asks as he puts some speed on the truck.

"Not a bloody clue," I answer honestly. *What the heck is going on?*

CHAPTER TWENTY-SIX

*B*rad

Matt's still breathing hard and my heart continues to thud against my chest as I pull us over into a lay-by. We both quickly hop out of the truck and start searching around. After a few minutes, Matt finds the tracker embedded in the back and begins turning it over in his fingers.

"Can you disable it here?" I ask, coming to stand next to him.

"No, not without any tools," he mutters, examining it. *Maybe he's looking for a serial number?* Only a second passes before he drops it on the ground and starts stomping on it. *I could probably have done a better job with my fist, but it seems to have helped him relieve some of his stress.*

"You good?" I ask with raised eyebrows, slightly concerned for him. He's the most docile out of all of us, so seeing him show some temper... is odd.

"Yeah, let's get going. I just want to get back and run this address by Gerry," he says as he heads back to the truck and hops in. I get behind the wheel and get us back on the road, wanting to get as far away as possible from whoever was using that piece of shit to track us. I glance over at Matt and find his eyes closed although I can't be sure if he's deep in thought or just trying to catch up on some sleep.

Before too long we turn onto the drive that leads to our house. It's just under half a mile long, made of stone and has a forest of pine trees growing along both sides of it. As we reach the end, the extensive three-story grey stone house we call home comes into view. The building itself is around three hundred years old but has been refurbished and remodelled in the last five years. Jack lived here by himself before he met us, and then we all moved in together around twenty years ago.

The updating of our home was definitely a group effort. Seb spent hours going over the kitchen design, while Matt spent weeks negotiating with the phone company to get quality broadband put in. He finally found the right guy and got it sorted, but during the down time his stress levels were so high that it was like being around a woman who was being denied chocolate. Jack helped Seb put in the pool and healing chambers, and Gerry had a few of the spare rooms kitted out for when the boys stay over. Rolland seemed happy so long as he got the back room that looks out onto the rear of the garden that encompasses the lake. I didn't fuss too much either. So long as I got my gym, I didn't care about the rest. It's home and I love being here, although I do miss the mountains of Scotland. Our time spent there in the late 1800s was incredible, and thankfully we go back to visit every other summer.

I look over at Matt, and see he's truly fallen asleep, so I decide to give him a few more minutes and leave the car idling. I gaze out at the forest that surrounds us, and my mind wanders back to when we met Matt in Iceland. We had gone over to check out the mountain and its hot spring pools, both of which had drawn my attention for years. One afternoon we were resting at our camp site when we felt an energy that was probably about a mile from where we were. Gerry immediately wanted to take off to see who it was, and as much as we tried to explain that it was most likely another one of us, he wouldn't hear us out - he left, masking himself so we couldn't see which way he went. Assuming he would head toward the new energy signature, we hurried that way in the hope that we could get there before he did.

When we found him, he was locked in a silent stare down with another man who was holding a shield up in front of himself as Gerry pushed his energy against it. They both eased off at the same time, seeming to come to a mutual unspoken acceptance. Gerry then stalked off without a single word, leaving the rest of us to have a slightly awkward conversation. We all introduced ourselves and while the new guy, Matt, didn't seem to care much for Gerry's mood, he was intrigued by our abilities and where we'd been living. We invited him back to our camp and after a few cold beers it felt as though we'd known him our whole lives. Matt brought with him a sense of calmness that we all greatly appreciated, even if it did take Gerry awhile to warm up.

Shaking myself out of my memories and back into the present, I turn and run my eyes over Matt. *He seriously needs some sleep.* Regretfully I nudge him awake, and he jolts upright and looks around. "You ready to face Gerry?" I tease, with a small smile playing on my lips.

"AARRRRGGGG," he moans, turning in his seat. "I've so had enough of him for one day. Maybe I can just avoid him," he mumbles.

I laugh as I climb out the truck. "Come on, Matt. I'll tell him you stomped on the tracker really hard and stuff," I say with a laugh. *Poor guy. A small part of me feels sorry for him, but Gerry won't actually hurt him, he'll just give him shit for a few weeks.* I laugh again.

Matt peers over at me with his granite eyes which look *so* tired and I wonder if he got any sleep last night. "Just tell him they got me and they're holding me ransom," he whines.

I shut my door and grab my bag from the back seat. "You look zonked, man, let's go. Head up to bed and I'll cover for ya." I'm still laughing, but I know he's in no state to deal with Gerry right now. I decide to just leave the truck parked out front, knowing I'll move it later when I head out for a run.

Making my way to the front door, I hear Matt getting out and his footsteps on the stones soon follow. As I trudge up the open grey stone steps to the front door, Rolland's voice floats to my ears from my left. I shake my head, ignoring it as I open the door and head straight up to my room so I can drop my gear off before grabbing a bite to eat.

As I make my way up the stairs, I feel my phone vibrate, so I take it out to check who it is. It's a message from one of my clients, thanking me for today. I smile, glad that she's finding the sessions productive. Pushing into my room, I set my bag down on the floor, closing the door behind me.

Just as it shuts, movement to my right catches my eye. I turn around quickly, ready to take out any intruder - only to come face to face with a girl half my size. She's holding the blade I made out toward me in a defensive stance, her entire body poised to strike. Not a single muscle moves as she holds her posture with complete perfection, although as I look closer, I can see that there's a small tremor running along her shoulders and that her legs have started to tremble ever so slightly. Bandages cover her torso, and a pair of black boxers hang loosely off of her hips.

As I continue to let my eyes wander over her, I'm drawn first to her dark hair where it falls loosely around her small shoulders, looking just as wild and untamed as the look on her face, then to her facial features that seem so unique. She has large, almond-shaped eyes, delicate lips, and a rounded nose that helps to somewhat soften her chin that's currently thrust out in determination. Her gaze stays on mine as she studies my body language. The light is dim where she stands by the wall that leads to my bathroom, making it hard to depict her eye colour, though strangely enough, her eyes do seem to pulse slightly with silver stars briefly before vanishing so quickly I wonder if I imagined it. *Ah this must be Kia, our newest resident.*

I flick my eyes down her legs, finding them full of bruises and cuts. *It's a wonder she's standing.* The hand holding the knife looks fine, but the arm is full of scratches and bruises. She lowers the blade a fraction, inching her right foot toward the window to my left. I flick my eyes across to see it's still open. *She wouldn't? Would she?* I look back and find her eyes are still firmly on me. She moves her other foot as voices from the hallway filter through the door. I quickly glance toward it, but when I look back, she's already at the window, climbing up. *Fuck.*

Rushing toward her, I try to grab her foot, but she's already gone. *How is she so fast?* My bedroom door crashes open and I turn to find that Rolland really does look like shit. His skin is pale and the look in his eyes isn't something I'm comfortable seeing in them. Panic, worry and fear are etched into his eyes and face.

"Where is she?" he demands, panting hard. His blonde hair falls across his face as he leans over his knees to take a breath. Seb steps up next to him looking slightly better. His hair isn't as long as Rolland's, but it still flies in front of his face as he comes to a halt. *They both look half-crazed.*

I point up, unsure how to explain it to them. Both their

faces drop, though Rolland's more so. His fear of heights isn't going to be helpful in this.

"She really will be the death of me," Rolland groans as he straightens. He tips his head back before turning to follow after Seb who's already moving. *Now this, I gotta see.*

Following them through the house, I go over the image of Kia in my head and review what all that the guys have said about her so far. Knowing everything she has been through I'm surprised she stood up to a guy of my size *and* held steady as she did. Most would've felt too intimidated.

Passing through the doors and up the flight of stairs that leads out onto the roof and to the chopper pad, Rolland's curses fill my ears. I can't see anything at first because the chopper is in the way, but when I step around, it's to see Kia sitting on top of one of the old chimney pots. She's got her legs dangling down and her hands resting on either side of her. *Holy, fucking, shit. How did she get over there?*

One side of the house is decked out for the Chopper, but the other half of the original building has steep rooftops, which drain the rainwater away into the gullies. Even though the roof has been recently re-tiled, it's still slippery around the edges and along the sides with the moss that grows up here.

"Kia, please come back inside," Rolland's brash voice is full of worry. I'm not sure who he's more concerned about - himself or Kia. Her shoulders and head drop forward, but with her back to us, I can't see her face. "The house hasn't been warded yet, it's not safe, please come inside," Rolland pleads from beside me. But she still doesn't move.

I look over at Seb who studies the rooftop briefly before he begins making his way across the narrow roof ridges to her.

"Oh man, I feel sick." Rolland bends forward, taking deep breaths.

"How did she climb the wall, Rolland?" I ask contemplatively.

He takes a deep breath in and tries to look up. "That's a stupid question," he replies, as though I'm stupid.

I frown, not understanding him. "How so?" I ask, peeking up to see Seb has nearly reached Kia.

"She's not real. No one can live through what she did and manage to scale a wall with no shoes on," he says seriously. Rolland sits down on the floor, resting his arms on his knees.

Flicking my eyes back up to check on Seb's progress, I feel sick myself. Kia is skittering along the ridges as though they were pavement and not the three-story high roof ridges that they actually are. Her face is full of concern as she hurries over the last of the roof tiles without hesitation.

The rays of the summer sun show more bruising along her arms and legs, yet the glow in her eyes seems to draw my focus to them. I would almost say that they look as though they have lights shining from the backs of them.

Kia passes me without a glance and kneels in front of Rolland, pulling him to her. I watch as his whole body visibly relaxes, as though she's given him a sedative.

"Kia. Stop it," Rolland mumbles into her chest. Seb comes back to where we are and runs his hand over the back of Kia's head, looking full of thought. *What the ever-loving fuck is going on here? I'd love an explanation sometime soon but with the way things are going... oh well, only one way of finding out, I guess.*

CHAPTER TWENTY-SEVEN

*R*olland

Kia's pushing calming energy through me. Hard. Forcing my *whole* body to relax. All I want to do is fall asleep here on the rooftop. *How did she move so fast? And how is she even still walking around carrying so much pain?* I look up at her to see her face is etched with worry. Her emotions are full of remorse, as she pushes more comforting energy through me. Resting my head on her chest, I continue to drag oxygen into my lungs.

"We really should head in, guys. Kia's not wearing much, and her open wounds will attract gnats and all types of other fun insects," Seb's dulcet tone comes from above me. Kia's confusion washes over me as she tries to understand Seb's words.

Realising he's right, I try to stand but my legs wobble, making it hard to get up. Seb steadies me with a firm hand as we make our way to the door. I'm generally okay up here but seeing Kia on the chimney like that triggered my irrational fear.

"You're mean, Kia. Really mean," I tell her, meaning it as

a joke. Sadness and puzzlement floods through from her. I stop on the stairs, turning to her. "I thought you were going to jump," I try to explain. Bafflement flows from her.

"I thought you were going to jump and try to kill yourself," I explicit. All I get is a look of perplexity as she runs her sapphire eyes over my face. I don't know how to put it any more simply. She shakes her head, tugging me to her. Instinctively, I wrap my arms around her body, causing her to gasp. Pain flares up my own back as Kia takes a deep breath of relief. Letting go of her, I sink down the wall.

Kia goes to bend down to me, but Seb places a hand on her shoulder, stopping her. "Kia, you're pulling at your wounds, which isn't helping them to heal," he explains in a placating tone. Annoyance sparks from Kia and my vision wavers.

I blink a few times and find Brad's strong features come into view in front of me. "You okay?" His deep voice rumbles through my head. "You need some help up?" he offers, his hard face full of concern. I don't like it.

Pushing myself up on my knees, I wobble slightly as I straighten up. "I just need some food," I grumble slightly at Brad before looking over at Seb. I find his eyes watching with concern. "I'm going to pick up some clothes from my room as we pass," I comment, tugging Kia by her hand as I head off in the direction of my room. "You're staying with me," I tell her without looking at her. Bewilderment and guilt still run from her, so I push some comfort and affection back through our connection.

I hear the others follow behind us and my mind wanders back to how Kia managed to climb the wall. *Yes, there's ivy growing up the sides, but surely that wouldn't hold her weight?*

Kia comes to a stop beside me and a small amount of pain

flickers across my head. When I look back, it's to find her studying one of the paintings Brad had commissioned. Men with black tattoos covering their blue skinned bodies are working to release a dragon caught by normal appearing men. Another wave of pain washes through my head, as though I have a headache. I look to Kia and see her face is full of concentration as she frowns hard.

As Brad and Seb stop beside us, Brad looks at Kia, and then at the painting.

"Come on, Kia. We need to get you both back to my room before Jack returns, or Gerry makes an appearance," Seb prompts, his smoky voice full of concern. I pull on Kia's hand and she reluctantly comes.

A little way down the hallway, we're just passing Matt's room when Kia comes to another stop. Matt's face flashes through my mind. *How did she know this was his room? I need to stop questioning her. It would certainly make my life so much easier.*

Seb and Brad stop again as well. "We're never going to get back at this rate," Seb mutters through a sigh. "Is Matt even back?"

"Yeah, he came back with me," Brad tells us flatly. Seb and I both frown turning to look at him where he stands to my right.

Kia puts her hand on the door and looks up at me, her beautiful eyes pleading. Unable to resist, I give in. "Okay, but be quick," I say with a sigh.

She opens the door incredibly quietly for some reason before stepping in. Matt is sound asleep on his stomach, covers pooled around his middle, an arm hanging off the bed and his head turned toward us. I can see that he's still fully clothed, wearing the light blue shirt he had on this morning. *Man, he must be shattered.*

211

As Kia stalks over to him, I get a look at her back for the first time since she woke from her nap. Patches of blood are starting to seep through the gauze and bandages. I turn to Seb, who raises an eyebrow at me.

"See, she's been pulling at the wounds from all the movement. The bandages should hold up at least until tomorrow morning though," Seb's says, sounding full of worry.

I look back over at Kia where she crouches down beside Matt's head, running her small hand over his hair. She lowers her head next to his arm, taking in a deep breath. Feeling for her emotions, they come freely - curiosity and affection flow from her, but after a few seconds, a spike of fear rips through. She whips her head up and around to look at Brad. Concern is written all over her delicate features as her almond shaped eyes widen and a frown plays across her forehead.

"What is it, Kia?" Seb asks from beside me. Something has her spooked, and by the way she's looking at Brad, I get the feeling it has to do with him.

"Why did Matt come back with you, Brad?" I ask him, still keeping my eyes on Kia as she moves back to us. Seb steps forward, pulling Kia to him gently, before shutting Matt's door quietly.

Brad and Kia study one another with curiosity. "He was followed," Brad finally discloses. Seb closes his eyes and his shoulders drop, knowing he'll have Gerry and Matt's tension to contend with for the next few weeks.

"He called me up, which was odd, and said he was picking stuff up for you," Brad says, jutting his chin in Seb's direction though keeping his eyes on Kia. "So, I started making my way over to the shop in case something was up." His gaze moves to us as he continues. "I stayed on the phone, making light conversation, and then he asked if I was outside. That made me worry a little more, but I'd already guessed he was being followed. When he came out, he looked nearly as bad as you," he chastises, running his eyes over the length of me. I roll my eyes in return and shake my head.

"I'm fine, just need some more food."

"He went over to his car and called telling me to meet him on Sanders Street. He parked on the opposite street and ran through the alley. Someone tried to shoot him, but he threw up a shield. They shot the truck with a tracker, but we pulled over and destroyed it thirty miles out from our road," Brad's summarises, his face looking as concerned as I feel.

He looks over to Kia again. "Once we *get* to Seb's room, I can take those cuffs off for you. That's what the blade is for," he jests with a pointed look. A small amount of affection trickles from Kia, but her eyes remain steady.

Deciding it would be best to hold off talking about this more until Matt has woken up and can give us more details, I continue making my way through the house in the hope of making it to my room within the next hour.

We finally get there without any more stops, thankfully, so I head straight to my cabinet to grab a few clothes. A couple of moments later I hear a noise behind me. Turning, I find Kia lying flat on her belly on my bed, pulling the dark green bed covers in close to her body. Stunned, I just stand there for a moment and watch her. She seems to be breathing in the smell of my covers, making little noises as she does, then goes still and I wonder if she's fallen asleep. I glance over at Seb and Brad to see them wearing the same expression as I am sure is on my face - wonderment, and a slight amount of worry.

Grabbing a book, my charger and few other bits, I step over to Kia, running my hand down her legs. So many bruises and cuts still run all the way up both the backs and the fronts. Gauging a feel for her pain levels, I find she's got a good grasp of them and isn't letting go. Peace and the sense of home flow from her. *I wish I could curl up with her, just where she is.*

"Kia, come on. Let's go back to Seb's room," I encourage softly, continuing to trail my fingers over her legs, but she doesn't move. "Stop ignoring me. I know you're not sleeping," I prod playfully, pushing some desire into her legs. That desire slams back at me, but it's ten times stronger.

Practically shuddering, I take a deep breath in before letting go of her leg. *Shit. I'm in so much trouble.* I take a step back, unsure of what to do.

"What's wrong, Rolland?" Seb asks with concern from just inside the door. "Is she okay?"

I look over to him, unsure of what to say. "Errmmm… maybe?" I chirp, looking back at Kia, wondering how to get her up without this turning into another session of *Rolland losing his shit like a teenager.*

Seb prowls further into my room and over to the bed. "Kia, come on. Let's go back to my room and you can listen to more of Matt's music," Seb speaks softly.

She turns her head to peek at Seb, and when he pulls a breath in, I know we're in trouble - well, Seb is anyway. I turn my gaze away, keeping my eyes on Seb, not daring to look at her.

"See," I clarify, glad to have him see my point.

Seb doesn't look at me, keeping his eyes on Kia. "Not here, Kia. It's not warded," he says, trying to be firm with her, but his voice wavers and cracks toward the end.

"See! Try having that thrown at you for the past twelve hours or so," I point out, still not daring to look.

I can see Seb trying to pull his face away, losing the battle. "How about we take the blanket with us?" Seb suggests hopefully, moving his hand down his trousers to adjust his obvious arousal.

Finally looking down at Kia, I see she's turned her head into the blanket again. I watch as she takes one final deep breath before letting it out with a big pouty huff. As she gets up, she winces with her movements, so I take her hand, drawing the pain into me. I watch her face relax while Seb takes the items I was holding from me, enabling me to pull Kia fully to my chest. Readying myself for another hit of desire, I'm perplexed when I feel nothing but quiet peace and warm affection instead.

Stepping away from me, Kia starts toward the door and Brad moves out of the way, looking slightly concerned.

"You're fine, Brad," I tell him playfully as we near. "Unless she takes a real liking to you, or you threaten one of us, she's completely harmless," I say with a smile.

Brad laughs, shaking his head before starting off towards Seb's room.

Seb and I exchange a look. "What was that headshake for?" Seb asks curiously, looking at Brad's broad back.

"Nothing," Brad replies with mirth in his tone, but with his back to us, I can't see his face.

I'm not buying it, and neither is Seb. "What happened when she came into your room?" Seb's asks.

"Nothing. She just took the knife and then climbed out the window."

I still feel like I'm missing something, but unfortunately, I'm reminded of what she did, and it jars my stomach, making me nauseous. Yet almost immediately I feel Kia pushing comfort to me. *This girl may truly be the death of me....*

CHAPTER TWENTY-EIGHT

*B*rad

Trudging through the house to Seb's room, I wonder how much Kia knows when it comes to combat and self-defence. The way she held herself, and the agility she must possess to get up onto the roof so easily, demonstrate how well she knows her own body. That being said, I'm still surprised she managed it with such little body mass, and I'm even more surprised she's able to even stand given what she's been through.

Then there's her energy, which is incredibly unique, reminding me of the tranquility and peace I found in Scotland. A few times I think I've seen her eyes change colour, but it could've just been a trick of the light. And on top of all of that, there's whatever happened back in Rolland's room. I felt it from where I stood at the door - curling around my legs like a caress, stirring a part of me that I've craved answers to for as long as I can remember.

Passing a few more of the paintings that I've had commissioned over the past hundred years or so, my gaze hones in on one of my favourites - a mountain I kept dreaming of many years ago. Looking over my shoulder as we pass, I see Kia keeps her eyes on it as long as she can, then turns to find me watching her. I turn my head back around, so I don't walk into any doors as we round the last corner to Seb's room.

The bay window is still open and there are bowls stacked up on the bedside tables. His bed is unmade and there's stuff scattered on the floor. I halt in my tracks, but Seb and Rolland just meander around me. *Seb, the neat freak, has a messy room.* I'm in shock and I want to laugh.

Seb looks up at me from where he's bending down to pick up clothes from the floor, rolling his eyes. "*You have no idea, Brad, you really don't,*" he excuses. A smile pulls at my lips, but I say nothing.

Rolland heads into the bathroom as Kia stalks over to the window, but Seb stands in front of her with his dark eyebrows raised. "Behave," he reprimands playfully, before he walks around her and heads out of the room with the bowls in his hands.

I watch as Kia sits on the window seat, then winces when she turns.

"Kia, I'll be right out. Just sit or stand still, and stop moving," Rolland's warm voice comes from the bathroom. Kia ignores him, positioning herself onto her knees, resting her head on a hand.

I still haven't moved from where I stand at the door as I'm enjoying watching her, studying her body language and getting a better feel for the energy that flows from her. She fidgets again, her back clearly causing her discomfort. Even from here I can see the patches of blood leaking through the bandages. The top edge of one of the wounds is just visible and looks like it's starting to heal.

Her breathing becomes slightly erratic as her shoulders

start to tremble a little. Almost like she can't take a full breath.

"I'm coming, Kia," Rolland soothes as he comes out the bathroom. "Sorry, sweetheart." He strides quickly over to her, brushing a large hand over her head before he sits down to the right of her. She leans against him, taking a calming breath and I notice Rolland seems to do the same thing. *What's going on with the two of them?*

Rolland rubs a hand over his face as he tries to wake himself up before he snakes an arm around Kia's waist, tugging her closer. I head over to the cushioned chair that's between the bed and window, pulling it around to face them. Kia still has the knife, but it won't cut through the cuffs without my energy behind it.

"Would you like me to remove the cuffs, Kia?" I ask gently. She sucks a breath in, looking to Rolland.

He frowns at her. "I'm sure it will be fine. We can just take it slowly," he reassures her. I frown at Rolland's comment. *Does she think I'm going to hurt her?*

Kia turns fully in her seat and I see them both wince. Rolland opens his mouth to say something, but Kia glares at him, to which Rolland then shuts his mouth before looking back to me. I pull my lips in to stop myself from laughing.

"You think this is funny?" Rolland asks lightly with a smile of his own. "Just you wait. It will be you next." I frown at him having no clue what he's on about. "Four down, two to go. I'd say she's winning."

Shaking my head a little, I return my focus to Kia and find her studying the knife with longing, as she runs her tiny thumb over the handle.

"You're welcome to keep it once I'm done," I placate, knowing it'll give her some comfort. She looks up with a smile which reaches her eyes.

"Yep. Another one," Rolland says with mirth. I look at him perplexed, but he just tilts his head and smiles broadly.

I move my chair forward, so I'm nearly touching Kia's knees - they're the only part of her legs that aren't covered in bruises. Seb's footsteps return, followed by the sound of him tidying up the room, though he's not being loud about it. Kia raises her sapphire eyes up to Seb and then looks me right in the eyes. It's like we're back in my room, with her studying me again, searching me for something.

Silently, I hold my right hand out and she hands me the blade. Then I open the other hand and wait for her to come to me. Building trust with an abuse victim is always about confidence. Letting them make the first move is a major key point especially with something like this.

Kia doesn't do anything at first, she just stays focused on me, running her eyes over my face and shoulders. *It's not fear that's holding her back. It's nerves.*

"We're going to go slowly. Just raise your other hand when you want me to stop, okay?" I console softly, keeping my gaze steady on her. She nods, moving her right wrist into my hand.

Energy runs through my hand and it feels almost like a heating pad, soothing the skin where our hands are connected. The cuffs are small but tight against her delicate skin, making red marks where they've been rubbing on the bones. Bruises from the pressure on both sides are visible, though they look to be fading to a light yellow.

Encouraging some energy into the blade, it starts to glow a deep blue, similar to Kia's eyes. She leans forward to watch as I push against one side of the cuff. The metal blade gets to work, cutting through the cuff in just a few seconds. I take a quick glance up, but she's not looking at me now.

Turning her tiny wrist over, I do the same to other side

and the cuff falls off, hitting the solid wooden floor with a clank. I watch as the pieces pulse an electric blue just once before they settle to black again.

Kia takes an audible breath in, pulling her arm against her chest before turning her head into Rolland. He strokes her hair as he kisses her crown as he takes a deep breath of his own. She then turns back to face me, a tear running down her cheek, but a smile lighting up her beautiful face. She pushes her other hand into mine eagerly, so I repeat the process. The cuff pieces fall off and onto the floor and I watch as they glow as the other ones did. I pick them up as Kia shakes her wrists out.

Before I can process what's happening, Kia leans forward and places a kiss on my cheek. Warmth spreads through me, trickling down my neck and I assume what I'm feeling is her energy. When she leans back, I find her eyes are swirling, like crystals flickering in the moonlight. Kia sits back further on the window bench and looks to Rolland and then to me again.

"She's eternally thankful," Rolland's says seriously with a small amount of sarcasm. He hasn't even looked at her, and I don't think he intends to just yet by the look in his eyes. She's still looking at the side of his face, like she's trying to tell him something through her smile.

"Can you hear her?" I ask him curiously, flicking my eyes between them.

"I've heard her a couple of times now, but her feelings are loud and clear." Rolland's mouth pulls into a deeper smile. I run my eyes over his face, taking note of his pale skin colour. The warm undertones of his skin are barely noticeable, and he looks incredibly tired.

"I'm fine, just hungry," he says with a deep sigh, knowing I'm analysing him. I narrow my eyes at him then hand the blade to Kia as promised. Just as I stand to leave, Rolland speaks again. "Would you grab my phone from the chopper? I haven't looked at it in nearly twenty-four hours," he appeals, leaning forward against his knees.

"You shittin' me?" *He's going to have a large number of messages from the farm.* It runs itself, but he usually checks in every morning to see if it's all running smoothly.

"No, my mind has been elsewhere." He finally turns to Kia, who stops looking at the blade and tucks it into her boxers.

"Yea, no worries, I'll go grab the phone for ya now," I say as I head out of Seb's room, my thoughts still on Kia. *I wonder how else I can help make her feel more at ease....*

CHAPTER TWENTY-NINE

*M*att

Waking up and seeing the sun begin to set, I wonder if Jack has returned yet with the stones to ward the house. I haul myself out of bed, then take a quick shower before tugging on some dark, loose-fitting jeans and a white Henley. Feeling refreshed and slightly more awake than I did a few hours ago, I glance over at the clock and I find it's just after eight pm.

I head down to the kitchen in the hope of finding some food, keeping as quiet as possible. *With any luck, I'll be able to avoid Gerry for a few more hours.* The kitchen is empty except for the smell of food cooking. I'm delighted when I discover some cooked meat in the slow cooker, along with cold rice in a large dish on the countertop - my stomach rumbles at the sight. *Oh, Sebastian, you're a god in your own right. How this man cooks and keeps on top of everything is a miracle.* Heating up some rice and serving some of the still warm meat, I tuck in, not even bothering to sit.

Brad lumbers in a few minutes later and heads over to the

fridge. "You're looking better than ya did a few hours ago," he comments lightly, pulling a beer out of the fridge. He's changed into his running gear, which consists of loose shorts and a tank top. The tattoo that stretches the whole of his back is visible when he turns his back to me. Scriptures in various languages and symbols cover both arms, none of which I have a clue of the meaning behind. I think most are either from the ancient books he reads or they're his own design, which he usually bases on something from a dream.

"I feel it," I say after swallowing my mouthful. "How are Rolland and Kia?" I ask before taking a scoop of rice. Looking up from my food, I see him grab some snacks from the cupboard. He has a huge appetite, but then again, he's the biggest of us all. His broad shoulders and solid build give him the appearance of a gentle giant, but there's not an ounce of fat on him. In contrast, his short-buzzed dark hair and tattoos give him a very rough look. *How he gets those abuse victims to stay in the room with him is rather odd. Perhaps it's part of his gift?* His skin is completely impenetrable by bullets, flame, blades, and every chemical that he's tried testing on it. Then there are his copper eyes that almost look amber at times, which have a warmth to them that seems to settle something within others when he speaks in a certain way. He used to do it with Gerry all of the time when he had no other coping mechanisms.

Brad's eyes skate up to mine but return to the crisps in his hands. "After Rolland and Seb got Kia down from the roof, I took her cuffs off without any problem," he comments evenly before shoving more crisps into his mouth. *The roof? What was she doing on the roof?* I feel my eyes bulging. "Rolland looked a little better after eating something, though he still needs more rest," he says flatly, bringing his gaze back to me.

"The ROOF! WHAT was she doing on the roof?!" I don't mean to raise my voice so much, but it just kind of happened.

Brad pulls his lips in to stop himself from smiling. "Yea, she climbed into my room, grabbed the blade, then took off again before I could get a hold of her." He stuffs even more crisps into his mouth and takes his phone out of his pocket, acting as though her behaviour is completely normal. *Am I going nuts? She could barely stand when I left this afternoon. How is she climbing rooftops? More to the point, how did she even climb the side of the building?*

Needing to see this for myself, I take my plate and head out of the kitchen, though I catch Brad's smirk as I pass. *How can he be so cocky about this?*

Poking my head out of the kitchen door to see if I can hear Gerry, I breathe a sigh of relief when no sounds come from upstairs. Carrying on through the house to Seb's room, I keep my steps light.

Ambling into Seb's room, I find him sitting up against the headboard on the far side of the bed with his laptop open. Rolland is lying flat on his back with Kia sprawled across his front. She's got her head turned to Seb, so I don't know if she's sleeping, but Rolland looks passed out with his face turned toward where I stand at the door. Some of the colour has returned to his skin and the dark circles under his eyes have faded slightly.

Seb looks up, bobbing his head in acknowledgement as I step quietly over to the other side of the bed, taking the seat that's by Seb. I start tucking back into my food, finding Kia's eyes closed.

I run my eyes over her body, taking notice of her skin which is looking healthier. It has a different tone to it than all of ours. It's hard to pinpoint, as it seems to change depending on the light, but with the sun going down behind us, and the only light in the room coming from the lampshade on Seb's bedside table, her skin tone seems to match Seb's. A bronze tan covers most of her body, with darker spots in places around her face and hands.

I finish off my plate, setting it carefully on the side table, before speaking to Seb through our connection. *"Brad says Kia was on the roof?"*

Seb looks up at my words. *"Yeah. One minute she was sitting by Rolland, the next minute she was off."* He looks back at his laptop but continues to talk silently. *"All I saw was her foot disappear. By the time we'd got out the window, she had vanished. Brad's bedroom window was open, so instead of taking the short way and disturbing Gerry with the noise, we went the long way."* He flicks his eyes up at me, then looks back at his laptop and continues typing. *"By the time we got into his room, she had taken off out of Brad's window."*

How was she able to recover so quickly? I think to myself. *"Then what happened?"* I ask perplexed by his words.

He takes a deep breath, letting it out slowly. *"Brad said he saw her disappear up, so we took to the roof via the chopper pad and found her sitting on one of the chimneys. Rolland had a slight panic attack seeing her up there and he thought she was going to jump. I went over to her and she seemed so at peace. I hated taking her down, but Rolland was nearly spewing, and her back is still too raw, it would have attracted bugs and whatever else. When I told her Rolland was worried about her, she moved across the ridges as if she did it every damn day. She was quicker than me."* He glances over at her and then back to his laptop before he continues to tap away. A few moments later he shuts it down, putting it away in the bedside drawer.

My thoughts return to Brad and his behaviour in the kitchen. *Why does he think this is so normal? Maybe he sees something that we don't?* I look up to Seb to see him resting his head back, but his eyes are open, staring up at the ceiling.

"What are you thinking, Seb?" I project.

He pulls his head forward to look at me. *"You want to know what I really think?* He moves forward and slides his legs off the bed so he's facing me. *"I think we need to stop expecting her to behave like a human."*

I flick my eyes over to Kia. Every part of her looks human. Except when she opens her eyes. Her eyes are not the normal colour and her irises are always changing. Even when her emotions aren't all over the place, they still seem to move.

"She isn't human, and we need to stop expecting her to behave like one. Even Jack said she's acting on impulses right now," he emphasises.

My mind thinks back to her kissing Rolland, Seb and me. How she has no care for her body being on show. The fact that she was pulling me into her mind for several months should be enough, but seeing her small body sprawled across Rolland like it is, seems to trick the mind into thinking she's human. Shaking myself from my thoughts, I look back at Seb.

He raises his eyebrows and heads to the bathroom. *"What I mean, Matt, is don't lull yourself into thinking she's not strong enough,"* he continues to talk to me while in the bathroom. *"She's scared, and rightly so, but I can see something else in her eyes. A determination, and the need to find the veracity in everything."* His words seem to nudge at something deep within me.

Noises come from the bathroom and then Seb emerges. He stalks over to the foot of the bed, watching both Rolland and Kia. *"And then there's the attachment she has with Rolland. You'd think they had known each other for years, but that could just be his gift and her abilities combined,"* he pauses, folding his solid arms over each other, pulling his lip into his teeth, deep in thought. *"But the way she looks at him sometimes, with so much affection. It worries me."*

I stand and step over to watch him, taking in his dark stubble which is coming through, making him look even more ominous than he usually does. He has the complexion and features of a Persian, with light brown eyes that deepen at times.

"What are you on about, Seb?" He doesn't answer straight away but nods his head for me to follow him. *Bugger. This can't be good.*

We walk through the house, but he doesn't stop like I think he would at the front door, rather he continues through into the kitchen. My heart rate has accelerated slightly, and my stomach starts to churn. No one's in the kitchen thankfully, and Seb heads over to the tap, to fill a clean jug with water.

I wait for Seb to speak, but he doesn't. "Seb! What is it?" I demand, trying to keep my voice down.

"Jack said-" he looks up at me, and then over to the kitchen door, "Jack said that there are others like us, which wasn't a complete shock. But when we are in large numbers, our collective energy is like a beacon." He brings his gaze back at me, placing a stone into the jug. I can feel my face screwing up. *What has this to do with Kia?*

"Jack and others like him watch over small groups of us. Keeping us separated. In the past when large groups have sought each other out, it's always ended in death," he explains, then heads over to the cupboard, pulling some clean glasses out before letting out a deep breath. His head remains dipped low as he says, "when Kia has recovered her full amount of energy, it will be like ten of us standing in the same room." My heart feels like it's stopped, and I can't find room in my chest to breathe. "He said that he would find somewhere that can mask her energy, but very few places like that exist."

My vision seems to blur, and I don't think I've taken a breath yet.

"Matt?" Seb's voice tugs at my attention.

I drag air into my lungs. *What the hell is wrong with me? I barely know Kia, but it feels like she's a part of me.* "Seb, I can't," is all I can get out as I look at him.

"I know. I don't think Rolland, or I could even take that possibility into our thoughts right now," he laments, running a hand through his dark hair, pulling on it slightly at the back. "We'll figure something out. I just wanted to tell you," he sighs, picking up the glasses and water jug then makes his way over to the door, pausing beside me.

"I haven't told Rolland yet. I was going to earlier, but then I healed Kia's knees and Rolland told me that his connection to Kia has deepened," he speaks quietly, keeping his eyes on me. "He's falling into her mind and getting stuck there, just like she does. And I honestly don't know if it's going to have any long-term effects on either of them." He finally drops his gaze to the jug in his hand. "But I'm not willing to take the chance of letting them be separated to find out."

His words lay heavy on me as he heads out of the kitchen, leaving me at a loss for words. My thoughts turn to how we're going to keep Kia with us if it means her being in danger. Even without us around, she's going to be attracting them.

Who was Jack referring to anyway? I go over the conversation I just had with Seb and he definitely didn't specify. I head back to his room in the hope of finding some answers. *What are we going to do?*

CHAPTER THIRTY

*R*olland

Feeling Kia's energy seeping through my chest where her body is touching me, I know I could stay here all night. Somewhere deep inside, it feels like she's healing a part of me I didn't know was broken. The weight of Kia's pain has become slightly heavier, but her emotions don't seem to leave me at all now.

"Sleep, Rolland. I happy here." A smile plays across my lips hearing Kia's voice trickling through my mind. Her words are clear, though they still sound as if the words are slightly foreign to her.

"I am sleeping, and you are dreaming, sweet Kia," I say back to her softly. Confusion comes from her, making me laugh, which seems to have a knock-on effect, creating desire within her. I try to focus on something else. *Count to ten, Rolland. One, two, three -*

"Rolland, that silly. Why I dream you counting? I would dream more happy things if you with me."

I expect to feel more desire, so I'm confused when an

image of beautiful trees, higher than any skyscraper I've ever seen, flash across my mind followed by the feeling of what I think home would be like. The image fades as quickly as it appears, and it slips like a dream from my mind. I feel pain wash through me from Kia's head. I pull it to me, then feel confusion and sadness flow from her.

"Hey, what was that all about?" I ask, my voice coming out groggy. Keeping my eyes closed, I stroke a hand up her arm releasing some comfort into her. She begins to lift her head away, but I'm still not ready to wake up fully yet, so I feel for her head and pull it back to my chest. "You said sleep, remember?" My voice is barely audible, even to my own ears.

A noise pulls at my awareness and I hear footsteps coming up the hall. "Arrgg, they're coming to wake us, Kia, make them stop," I mumble to her. She turns her head and I feel her laugh. Finally opening my eyes, I lift my head to look at her. "Did you just laugh?" She shakes her head at my sarcasm, with a full smile on her lips. Stunning, it is simply stunning - there are no other words for it. I vow to myself that I will make her smile like that – Every. Damn. Day. "You did. You got my joke!" I'm beaming with happiness and push every ounce of it into her.

Another image of a man's face flashes across my mind – platinum blonde hair, and features like Jack, but nowhere alike in resemblance. Pain shoots through her head again, which causes her to frown momentarily. More confusion flows from her before she pushes herself up from my chest.

Seb and Matt walk in and happiness floods from Kia once again. She's up on her feet before I can even sit up. *Damn, she's fast.* She throws herself at Matt, but being unprepared for her, he falls back a few paces and goes to grab her back.

He stops his action at the last second, making his arms wind-mill so he falls backward with Kia. She acts faster, displacing her weight on the ground and grabs for his shirt, stopping him from hitting the floor. A noise comes from Kia and I think she's trying to talk. I feel her remorse, but a small amount of humour simmers up. *Oh wow, she's going to be a handful when those bandages are off.*

I pull myself up, swinging my legs around, continuing to watch the little gem of trouble.

"How are you both feeling?" Seb asks from the other side of the bedroom.

I rub a hand over my face, stretching out my muscles, watching Matt and Kia right themselves. She tucks into him with her arms around his waist as Matt looks over at Seb. Even from here I can sense his worry.

Matt places a hand over Kia's head and one on her waist, then leans down to speak in her ear. "Did you miss me?" He has a playful frown on his face as she turns her head and kisses him. He kisses her back, and like every other time she's kissed him, no jealousy surfaces.

"Much better thanks, and I think the little minx has found some energy too," I say to Seb as he makes his way back over. Kia looks to me with raised eyebrows before she kisses Matt again, then heads off to the bathroom.

Seb sits down on the bed beside me. "Jack should be home within the next few hours. I also think it would be wise to get a good night sleep before we do any more healing on Kia, or mind work with Jack."

He's right. As much as I want Kia healed, and to sleep more soundly, there's no point in working the body and brain to the edge of exhaustion.

"Agreed. Though keeping Gerry out of here for that long

isn't going to be easy," I say as I look over at Matt who's still standing over by the door.

"I'll sit up for a few hours, but I won't manage the whole night," Matt sighs heavily.

"We'll take it in turns. Matt can stay up for the first few hours and then I'll take the rest of the night," Seb offers. *Fine with me, I need more sleep than them.*

I nod, then head to the bathroom to wait for Kia to come out. Leaning against the frame, I listen but don't hear any noise. *She hasn't shut the door completely, though she didn't the last couple of times.* I roll my eyes at my thoughts. *Why do I expect her to do things normally?*

I tap on the door lightly, but I don't feel any of her emotions trickle back. "Kia, you okay?" I call through the door. I don't expect to hear an answer, but I would think she'd push some energy my way. "Kia, I'm coming in," I call again as I push the door open, but she's not there.

My heart skips a beat and falls through to my stomach. Taking a deep breath, I force myself to calm as I make my way through to the pool. I find her sitting on the top step with her feet in, leaning her weight back on her hands as she looks out over the water. Her emotions filter back to me before I've reached her and there are so many are coursing through her at once. Calmness is most prevalent, but curiosity, worry, confusion and desire are all swirling together like a painter mixing his colors.

I step behind her and squat on my haunches so I don't get wet and have to change *again*. She knows I'm there, as she can feel me like I do her. Happiness blossoms through her emotions, making me smile.

Leaning forward into her ear, I speak quietly to her. "What has you thinking so hard, little miss trouble?" I move forward an inch, nipping at her ear.

Desire hits me hard in my cock as though she aimed straight for it. Sucking in a quick breath, I'm not prepared for her to move so fast, as she grabs me, pulling me around and pushes me into the water, but doesn't join me. *Damn, she's strong.*

Fighting my way to the surface I find my feet and stop on the third step. When my eyes clear, it's to see her laughing. She's bent over, holding her stomach, trying to look up at me through the hair that falls across her face. She's trying to fight it because it hurts her throat, but her eyes are sparkling, and her cheeks are full of colour, warming my heart. All I want to do is keep her smiling like that. She's so beautiful and I know a part of me is falling harder for her.

A small noise comes from her throat, and even though it's hurting her, she carries on. I'm soaked and I want to soak her back. She sees the thought cross my vision and runs for it. I take off after her, running through the en-suite. *Shit. This could go so wrong but seeing her laugh like that- so worth it.*

Matt and Seb look stunned as I pass them both sitting on the bed, but I don't stop to explain. Following her wet footprints along the dark solid wood flooring, they take me right out of Seb's room and along the corridor, then past the front door. Her footprints are still visible though they're wearing out as the water dries up. They come to a stop at the bottom step, but a few drops are still noticeable... on the handrails? *What the fuck? Is she WALKING ON THE FUCKING HANDRAILS?!*

Seb and Matt's footfalls come up behind me. "Rolland, we're supposed to be keeping her in the room, not chasing her out of -"

"Shh-" I cut Seb off. "She'll hear you." *They must think I've gone mental. Then again, maybe I have.*

The house is still light as the late evening sun trickles

through the large window on the landing of the staircase, which has two flights and bends around in the shape of a U. The droplets are still distinguishable across the solid dark wood handrails, but they vanish at the landing entirely.

Reaching the second floor; left takes us to Gerry's and Jack's rooms, and right brings us to Brad's and my room. Thinking logically, she wouldn't go to my room because she'd think I'd check there first. I start my mission left, to see if she's gone poking into Gerry's or Jack's room.

Stepping lightly along the corridor in search of her, I come to the hallway which has four additional rooms between the bedrooms. One room is for Matt's computers, one is a storage room for additional equipment that we couldn't fit in the cellar, and there are two other spare rooms that have been kitted out for Gerry's boys when they've stayed.

Keeping my eyes peeled for any more droplets as I make my way past the rooms, I hear a creak from behind me. I turn and glare at them, and then see all the water I'm dripping over the floor.

"Rolland, this is-"

"SHH!" I say to Matt, glaring at him. I turn back to my mission and spot a single droplet of water outside one of the spare rooms. I tiptoe up to it, putting my hand on the handle to open it.

A door from behind me bangs open so I whip round to tell them to shut up, except I find Gerry standing in the door way of his room, looking incredibly pissed. *Shit. Shit. Shit. Shit.* Light streams into the dim hallway and noise from his tv fills my ears.

"What's going on?" he asks, his tone hard and his electric green eyes glowing slightly as he looks me over in absolute bewilderment. He looks right, but Matt has disappeared, just Seb and I remain. "What are you doing dripping wet outside my door?" he demands, stepping out of his room and eyeing me up.

I know if I say anything, he'll know I'm lying. So, I stand there and say nothing.

"Who's behind the door, Rolland?" Gerry presses. I run my eyes over him, glad to see him looking better than he did last night. He's wearing his comfortable black slacks and a dark hoodie, making him look slightly warm, a stark contrast to the death glare he's giving me.

Thinking fast I tell myself she's not there. She could be anywhere. "No one?" it comes out more of a question that an answer.

Gerry's face screws up as he regards me curiously. "Move so that I can see for myself then," he challenges, his shoulders stiffening.

I can't move and my heart drops to my stomach. Gerry raises his eyebrows at me and steps closer, squaring up to me. From the corner of my eye, I see Seb's hand point in the other direction, and he takes a small step back.

Faking giving up, I move aside and let a breath out. "Sorry, Gerry, I was erm... I don't know..." I take another step back. "Drying off a bit?"

Gerry just stares at me and then looks at Seb. My heart is pounding. Gerry moves his gaze to the door and then he opens it to walk into the room. I take my opportunity and sprint off the other way.

"Matt heard something from the direction of your room," Seb urges as we run. Rounding the corner, I find my door open but there's no sign of Matt.

"Do we split up?" I ask Seb with a smile. *The game is on and I'm not going to lose to her. Whatever game this is we're playing.*

Seb runs his eyes over me, and a look I can't decipher

passes across his face, which is then replaced by a mischievous smile. "Yeah, lets split up. You take the top floor and I'll make my way back down again." He skims his eyes about and then taunts, "whoever finds her gets dibs on holding her tonight."

The shithead. "Deal."

CHAPTER THIRTY-ONE

Sebastian

Rolland's gone nuts. Truly nuts. But to see the life back in his eyes again like this, I couldn't care less. He's looked so rough the past twenty-four hours, that I started to doubt I would ever see the sparkle and humour back in his eyes. He's like a big kid. Unable to grow up, full of life and practical jokes. My opposite most days. His passion for his farm shows in every single acre and animal he takes on. The farm is in Dartmoor in the southeast of England, just by the national park. It's a small drive to the coastline, and the beaches and lakes are spectacular. Most of the produce I use in my restaurants comes from his farm, and it's what sets my food apart from the other businesses around it.

Pulling myself from my thoughts, I step off the bottom step, keeping my feet light. *This is crazy. A Gjinn is trying to pull the life out of Kia, the house hasn't been warded, and there's an angry Gerry grumbling around, yet we're playing hide and seek. But the hell with it. Rolland's smiling again, and the look on Kia's face as she flew like a bullet from the room was priceless. I can't say I've ever seen such graceful movements in my life - her feet barely touched the floor.*

A small creak comes from around the corner near my room. I pause in my steps, listening for the most minor of sounds. I hear the movement of clothing and I wonder if it's her shorts. I move my foot an inch and listen for it again. *Fuck, I hope I don't frighten her too much.* I move my feet and go to grab her body around the waist. But the body I catch is too large and fully clothed.

"Arrr, bugger!" Matt swears as he falls on his side, both of us landing in a heap.

"Shit, I thought I had her," I grouch as I get to my feet. Matt is still trying to catch his breath as he straightens his glasses. "Have you seen her?" I ask him desperately. He shakes his head no, so I step over him and begin creeping toward my bedroom quietly.

I hear a loud thump followed by Rolland cursing from the front door. I run through with Matt at my heels and come to a stop when we reach the open foyer. We see Rolland rolling on his side on the floor, with Kia standing over him, looking very proud of herself.

"That was mean, Kia, my heart nearly stopped," Rolland whines as Kia folds her arms over her chest, smiling from ear to ear. Rolland stays on the floor rubbing his ankle.

I make my way over to them and look down to Rolland. "That doesn't count," I tell him, folding my arms over my chest.

He turns and faces me. "Yeah it does, I saw her first," he counters. I raise my eyebrows at him and then look to Kia. She kicks him in the leg lightly. "I did!" he declares, then goes to grab her, but she dodges easily before turning from him and walking past me. She tugs Matt by the hand, poking her tongue out at me as she passes.

My eyes widen. *Did she hear us?* Matt is fully confused but goes willingly. I turn back to Rolland as he gets to his feet.

"She fucking pounced on me!" he says in mock rage, pausing beside me; his face is full of playfulness. "I'll get her back for that. Mark my word, Brother. I'll get her sweet ass back for that." He carries on heading toward my room and I very much doubt his words.

I laugh and decide to head up to check in with Brad. Tapping on the door, I wait this time. A few moments later he opens his bedroom door, spilling light into the now dim corridor. He opens it wider when he sees it's me, then walks over to his dark, oak desk and begins tidying away some books he must have been reading. He's got his dark sleepwear on, so he must be about ready to turn in for the night.

I run my eyes over the dark brown walls and soft leather furnishings, which give a richness to the room. Though his king-sized bed is still unmade from this morning.

"What was all that noise?" Brad asks humorously.

"Kia giving us the runaround. She pounced on Rolland, knocking him flat on his arse," I tell him, closing the door behind me before heading over to his window which looks out over the trees that surround the house. The lake is just visible although the best view of it is from Rolland's room.

I hear Brad give a short, scornful laugh behind me. Turning back around, I peer over at him with a smile, catching his amber eyes flash up to me briefly before he continues to put his books and papers away. Most of his books are hundreds of years old and mythological based. His fascinations for dragons and trolls knows no bounds.

"Her defensive behaviour won't go away overnight and the only way you get through to someone who has walls as high as hers is through building trust," Brad says sympathetically as he puts his phone on to charge. "If I had to guess, I'd say she has plenty of combat skills and muscle memory." He heads into the bathroom and I turn my gaze back to the window to watch the evening rays of sun fall behind the horizon of the fern trees. A figure walks the perimeter of the driveway and I recognise Jack's tall frame, his platinum blonde hair seeming to shine from the last of the light. I lean against the window frame, observing him as he places a few more stones down before continuing his circuit.

"Her footwork on the roof surpasses my own and that's after she's been immobile for months," I say agreeably. I hear Brad brushing his teeth as he steps out from his bathroom to look at me. He's smiling around the toothbrush and bobs his dark eyebrows. I squint back at him, wondering what he's sussed out that we haven't.

"Anyway, it looks like Jack's back. Matt and I will take shifts staying awake to make sure Gerry doesn't go poking his nose about until Kia's healed. We also thought it best to leave any mind work with Jack until the morning when we're fresh," I say, looking back out the window. Jack places the final stones down, then stands with his head bowed for a few moments, activating them all at once.

Brad reappears and looks out the window with me. "Ye, sounds good to me. Now that he's warded the house, we can at least sleep without the thought of any Gjinn knocking on our door." His broad shoulders heave as he lets out a heavy breath with his words.

I decide to leave him to sleep. "I'm going to catch Jack before he vanishes again." Brad nods as I make my way out the door.

"Night." I hear Brad's brass, timbre tone follow me out the door.

"Night," I call back over my shoulder.

Heading down the stairs, I find Jack waiting by the front door looking like Legolas from one of Brad's favourite movies. He's even still got his cloak on. *What happened to the white cotton stuff he had on earlier? Though Ireland is probably a bit cold for that, even at this time of year. Especially the coastline where I think he was. He's just missing a sword and pointy ears, and he could definitely pass for an elf.*

His pale complexion and piercing light blue eyes seem to shine like his hair did outside. He's got it half pulled back with the rest falling over his shoulders that are covered in light mud. His face looks the perfect state of calm, as usual, not an ounce of emotion showing. If I didn't see it earlier with my own eyes, I would think him incapable of feeling. That being said, after hearing his words spoken this morning about all the lives that have been lost, perhaps he's buried them so deep down, he's no longer connected to them.

Reaching the bottom step, I come to a halt and continue to run my eyes over him. His arms are crossed behind his back giving him a confidence in his stance and I notice his boots are wet, but the rest of him appears to be dry.

"I take it the house is warded?" I inquire, keeping my own emotions in check and matching his pose.

"Yes, it will hold off the Gjinn so you can sleep easier tonight," he confirms as he glances to his left toward my room, then fixes his steely gaze back to me. "I did not intend to take so long. How are Kia and Rolland?" His tone holds nothing as usual, never giving anything more away than he intends to.

I keep my face straight and impassive. After many years of practice, it's easy to put on for Jack. "Much better. Rolland has some colour back in his face, and Kia is-" I pause as an idea comes to mind. Jack narrows his icy blue eyes at me just a fraction. "Kia is fine. I'm sure she will be happy to see you." My mask stays in place and I hope it remains there a while longer.

Jack studies me. Satisfied with his findings, he turns and strides to my room. I follow in his tracks, wondering how Kia will react to seeing him. When he turns into my room, he halts a few steps in. I come to stand beside him and find Rolland, Matt, and Kia sitting on the window seat with Kia on Matt's lap facing Rolland, her body turned so she can look out the bay window. Rolland and Matt are facing one another, deep in conversation about something, and they don't notice us standing there for a moment.

The sun is still setting, warming the room with its deep red and soft yellow rays.

Kia's back is looking even worse from all the movement earlier, but the bandages should be fine until morning, though they won't last much longer than that. An extensive line of blood is seeping through, with two other patches either side.

Kia turns in Matt's lap with a soft smile on her face. As she does, Rolland pulls in a breath and frowns at her. "Kia-" he stops whatever he was about to say, following her line of sight to see Jack. She doesn't get up straight away like she did when she saw Matt earlier. Instead, she turns fully to face him while Rolland looks back at Kia, narrowing his eyes at her.

"What are you-?" Rolland cuts himself off again, pulling his lips into his mouth, then sits back against the wall.

Matt frowns at Rolland with a confused look on his face, which I'm sure is mirrored on my own, as both of us wonder what's going on. Kia stands very slowly and takes a couple of steps forward before she stops at the foot of the bed so she's about a few metres away from where we stand.

I flick my eyes to watch Jack without turning my head and notice a small muscle work in his jaw, which he stops somehow. I look back to Kia as she moves her arms behind her back. I hear Rolland suck in a breath. Her posture shows as much confidence as Jack's and tension starts to build in the room. Matt's worried eyes flick from Rolland, to Kia, then to Jack, before they finally land on me.

"You are looking well, Kia." Jack's polished voice startles me slightly. A smile tugs at her lips as she gives a small nod but still doesn't blink. "And were there any complications when Brad removed the cuffs?" Jack asks. Kia moves her head to the side as a 'no' but continues not to blink. *How is she doing that?* "I am glad to hear it," Jack comments. *What is going on between these two?* Her eyes don't blink, but they seem to waver a fraction. Jack turns and strides out of the room.

Stunned as to what the hell just happened, I wait for a beat before I turn and follow after him. I still have a plan as to how to get information from Jack and I want to test it out. Picking up my steps quietly, I find Jack waiting at the bottom of the stairs. As soon as I reach his side, he starts going up. I walk along with him, but I don't speak, hoping we can have the privacy of his room to talk. We pass Gerry's room and no noise comes from inside. *Hopefully, he has turned in for the night and we won't have him poking about.*

We finally reach Jack's room, where he opens the door and waits for me to step through first. Unlike last time, I'm prepared for the sight my eyes want to feast on, but I drag my eyes away and focus on Jack. It's incredibly hard with so many colours sparkling around in my peripheral vision, but I want answers.

Jack takes his cloak off, hanging it on a hook on the back of the door and starts unbuttoning his undercoat. It fits snug to his body and looks incredibly warm with its long sleeves and low hem.

Deciding to just get on with it, I start talking. "Rolland took a shower with Kia to help remove the shirt that was sticking to her back, and he got pulled into her mind. He saw a flashback of Kia being whipped and felt her pain as though it was his own." Jack pauses for a fraction of a second, then continues to undress.

He takes out a cream coloured waistcoat from the cupboard and starts pulling it on as he talks. "You are from South Grandor, and your people call themselves Marbellows. Your race is known to have incredible healing abilities of the mind and body with minimal effort." My heart drops somewhere in my stomach. *He's known this all along and never said anything?*

Pushing my emotions down, I take a quiet, calming breath. "He got pulled in again when I bandaged her back and he had to watch her go through all the torture that was triggered in her mind." There's another pause in Jack's movements, but if I weren't looking, I would have missed it. *He wants to know more, but that isn't part of the game we're playing.*

He sits on a solid oak chair across from me while I stand leaning against his marble table, watching as he starts to unlace his leather boots. "Rolland is from North Grandor, and they called themselves Karbellows. Before we all got stuck here, your homelands were free of The Swarm and were thriving. My people were in good relations with both races in the North and South. After my homeland fell, we were taken in by both the Karbellows and Marbellows. We were received with more compassion and grace than any race could possibly have shown." He pulls his boot off and starts on the other.

My head starts to hurt, so I squeeze my eyes shut to rid myself of the pain. But as I do, a vision of trees sparkling white on the inside flashes within my mind, but it's gone so fast that I don't have time to study it. Shaking my head to clear it, I look up and find Jack observing me before he tugs off the other boot, then steps over to the wardrobe, taking a pair of shoes out. They look more formal, with the same details as those on the waistcoat he's put on. He sits down again and begins slipping the shoes on.

Come on, Sebastian, get your head together. Dropping my gaze down to the dark marble table I'm leaning on, I focus on the white lines running through it to help clear my head.

"When I healed Kia's knees, Rolland got stuck in her mind again. He took her place in getting tortured, and she had to stand and watch him go through it. I managed to wake her, but we couldn't wake Rolland. I stopped her from pulling him out, but somehow she took hold of my energy and used it to pull him out of her head." I don't look up this time. I wait. Silence follows my words, and I so desperately want to look at his face, to see how well his mask is holding up.

"My people are in the middle of building a craft that can withstand the conditions of the ice circle that keeps us here. It is only weeks away from completion and there is room for all those we have found," Jack reveals, his voice remaining steady. I look up without thinking and find he's already making his way back to the closet again.

"Matt was followed today in town and Kia seemed to know when she checked in on him," I divulge. Jack stops mid-step and turns to me. He wants to ask questions, but that isn't how this works.

He continues to the wardrobe, taking out a cream coloured cloak with more fine details around the hem, it looks incredibly light and soft, and I begin to wonder what it's made from. *Silk perhaps?* But it seems more durable.

"Ayrans do not have males in their species." Jack's crisp tone pings in my ears.

My mind seems to trip over on itself. I open my mouth to say something, but Jack raises his perfectly manicured blonde eyebrows at me. *Fucking arsehole. That pretty face needs to be punched.*

I take a deep breath and let it out. Finding a spot on the cream wall behind Jack, I stare at it. "Kia scaled the wall from my room and took a fair bit of interest in some of the paintings around the house." In my peripheral vision I see Jack stop what he's doing, so I flick my eyes over to him and find his jaw clenched, hard. *Good. Stew on that, dickhead.*

"I am heading out to meet with someone from Mid Gaia. Hopefully, they will be able to cleanse Kia enough to be able to take her deep within Mid Gaia, where she will be safe."

My face begins to heat and every part of my body tenses up. My heart is pounding in my ears and something feels like it's breaking inside of me. *I've nothing left to give him.*

"I will be back by sunrise," he adds, stepping over to the door, but I can't move.

"Sebastian, all I want is for Kia to be safe." I hear him let out a breath.

I turn and find his focus on the wall behind me, his eyes seeming to shine. *Fucking pompous prick.* All I want to do is remove his pretty head from his stiff shoulders and throw it deep into the ocean.

Forcing my arms to move, I pull away from the table and stand to face him completely. He hasn't opened the door yet, and there's still plenty of space between us.

"Rolland is feeling every emotion that runs through her, even when he's not trying with his gift," I urge. "He's hearing her talk in his mind, and when she was pulling my energy from me, I heard her too. I would advise you to reconsider, Jack, for the sake of them both." Stepping over to the door, I go to turn the handle with my left hand. But Jack's back is in the way, so I can't open it.

Jack drops his gaze down to his feet, seeming to hold a breath. "Ayrans are vegans by nature and do not need food to sustain themselves within their homeland. They have no hierarchy or systems of order as most races and species do. They do not require sleep but slip into a meditative state, where they speak to The Source as we call it. They usually only ever bear one child in each lifespan. On a few rare occasions, they have been known to bear two, but never in the same gestation. In very rare instances, some were able to bear three, though only from those who seemed to have a more profound knowledge of life.

She will be missed by her people and all I intend to do is get her back to where she belongs." He steps forward so that I can open the door, but I can't seem to process his words. My mind has gone blank and I can't get my head around eighty percent of what he just said.

"I apologise, Sebastian, but I really must be going." Jack's refined voice comes from my right, but it doesn't seem to register. I still don't move. Jack places his hand on my right shoulder and my body starts moving of its own accord. I try to fight his energy off, but it's useless.

As soon as we're out the door, he shuts it quietly behind him, then simply vanishes. *I think that round went to Jack....*

CHAPTER THIRTY-TWO

*G*erry

Opening my eyes reluctantly, darkness greets me. My brain is still wired up and restless from knowing there's a stranger in the house, and my anxiety is through the roof.

Glancing over at the clock, it reads just after one in the morning. I bury my head back into my pillow trying to find sleep, but it still eludes me. Grumbling, I haul myself out of bed thinking maybe a snack and a movie will help settle my mind.

Rubbing a hand over my face to rid my vision of blurriness, I skulk through the corridors and down the stairs toward the kitchen with sleep coating my eyes. Stopping at the bottom step, I turn my head toward Seb's room. The house is quiet, allowing my senses to tune into their heartbeats, all of which are beating steadily. Then my ears pick up on another that sounds somewhat erratic. Focusing my energy through my ears to see where the heartbeat is coming from, I find it slows down to a steady beat, and then it becomes barely audible. Curious as to what's causing the unusual rhythm, I tread toward the corridor that leads to Seb's room and listen again.

Nothing. Just the steady heartbeats of three people sleeping. Frowning to myself, I turn and make my way to the kitchen. Movement catches in the corner of my left eye from the stairs, so I thrust my energy into my senses, picking up on a body and legs coming toward me - but I'm not fast enough.

Weight slams into my neck, grabbing hold of my head. Steadying my legs, I grab hold of the body that's wrapped itself around my head as I feel the person force their weight on me to tip me back. Turning the momentum, I bring us down sideways slamming the body down with me. As I go to strike, I see a girl scrunching her face up in pain. The fraction of a second I take to slow down gives her the opportunity to retaliate and strike at my throat, cutting off the air supply to my windpipes - I falter again.

A shout comes from my right, but my focus remains on the girl as she begins to push my weight over. I make a grab for her throat as she gets a quick blow to my head, followed fast by a hit to my stomach. My weight tilts and I find myself on my back, so I reach for an arm, then feel a blade at my throat.

"STOP!!" Is yelled so loud, it nearly bursts my eardrums. The blade sinks lower but doesn't pierce the skin where it's held horizontally against my jugular.

"Kia. Don't." Rolland's voice comes from my left.

My eyes fly open as I go to push her off, except the bottomless pits I find staring back at me pin me to the spot. Black hair falls on either side of her face, darkening her features, which are intensified as she bares her teeth like she wants to take a chunk out of me. Pure rage is all I can see within her eyes.

"Gerry, don't move." Rolland's voice is beyond panic, which increases my heart rate.

Her eyes pulse and I can't see where the pupil starts or ends. The smell of blood hits my nose and I don't recognise it. I can't smell any fear from her, just a lot of pain and adrenaline coursing through her blood. Her heartbeat is erratic and seems to falter a few times. The hand holding the knife quivers ever so slightly, but her eyes remain steady, keeping my body locked in a state of paralysis. The blade pushes deeper piercing my skin and I begin to fight the energy that's keeping me held against my will.

"Kia, this is Gerry, he lives here. He means no harm to anyone," Rolland placates, but panic laces his words and it sounds as though he's trying to push against a wall.

A noise comes from somewhere in the girl's throat.

"Shit," Rolland says quietly. "It's not how you think, Kia, he would never hurt Matt," Rolland continues. My body moves in reaction to his words and the blade sinks deeper still.

"Gerry, what colour are her eyes?" Rolland's urgent voice comes through.

"WHAT THE FUCK, ROLLAND? THEY'RE BLACK! WHAT COLOUR SHOULD THEY BE?" I roar back to him in his head. Silence comes back.

"Kia, I know you think he means me harm, but I promise he won't hurt me or any of us here," Matt's gentle voice comes from behind Rolland to my left, sounding as though he's speaking to a child.

More blood drips down my neck as I continue looking into the black pits of her eyes. There's no life or feelings within them, but as I study them carefully, I see something toward the back of the pits. A single small star twinkles back as though it's lost in the night sky. Her eyes begin to waver.

251

"KIA!! STOP fighting me!" Rolland grunts as though someone has hit him. Her eyes waver again before her body is whipped off me quicker than my eyes can track.

I jump to my feet ready to strike back, adrenaline pumping through me, except I find Rolland cradling her into his arm while he sits on the floor, holding her head up so he can look at her face. She's completely limp like she's passed out.

"KIA!! Don't you DARE do this to me! I can't follow you in there!" Rolland shouts at her and I begin to think he's gone mad.

I run my eyes over her body to see her whole torso is wrapped in bandages, which are coated in blood. Guilt slams into me for being so rough on such a frail body. Even though she had a blade to my throat, she wouldn't have done any damage that Seb couldn't fix.

"KIA!!" Rolland roars at her. She lurches in his arms scrambling forward and pulling herself closer to him. "You're fine, you're fine. Just breathe." His voice has gone from anger to sympathy in a fraction of a second, and I feel like I've walked into another house.

Flicking my eyes over to Seb and Matt, I find they're looking down at them with a regard that makes my stomach turn. The girl seems to be struggling to breathe properly, with the rise and fall of her shoulders having no rhythm to them. But as Matt squats down next to Rolland, running his hand over the back of her head, she calms slightly. *What the fuck is going on?*

Seb stalks over to me, his focus remaining straight ahead as he pauses by my side. "I think the kitchen might be a better place to talk," he says tightly. His heart is pounding as rapidly as my own still is as he continues to the kitchen.

I look over at Matt and stare daggers into the side of his head. "Matt? Do you want to join us for some late-night cookies and milk?" My voice drips with sarcasm.

He drops his head in defeat, pulling himself up reluctantly to make his way to the kitchen. I hear the door open and close behind me but pause feeling like I should say something.

Rolland is still stroking her head and whispering into her ear, but as he peers up at me, I find his eyes are filled with remorse and unshed tears that pull at my heart. *How has a girl that he's only known for just over twenty-four hours burrowed her way into his heart?* Her black eyes flutter across my vision. *And why did he ask what colour her eyes were?* Remembering Brad's words about her back being touched and her having more demons than me, a deep part of me recognises her behaviour. No rational thought occurs when you're running on instinct, which is what drives my need to protect my Brothers. *The question remains, why did she think I was going to hurt Matt?*

"I'm sorry, Rolland, she came out of nowhere and I just reacted. I would never intentionally hurt her, you know that," I try explaining. *How can someone so small have taken down someone of my size?* There's nothing to her. She's tiny, and from the small amount of moonlight coming through the window above the stairs to my right, I can see so many bruises, cuts and other marks all the way up her trembling legs.

A faint smile tugs at Rolland's lips, which appears to have a calming affect on the girl, as I notice her trembling frame relaxes a little within his arms. "Trust me when I say, I know how that feels." The smile doesn't last long as his features pull down, as though he's concentrating on breathing. He dips his head into her right shoulder before continuing. "Go speak to Seb and Matt, tell them we're going back to bed." His voice is nothing like I'm used to hearing, it's laced with tiredness of the wrong kind, and with worry.

I turn, not knowing what to say and make my way to the kitchen, still feeling confused and guilty from the force she took to her back; my mind plays over how fast she moved and how she kept so quiet.

Stepping into the kitchen, I find Matt and Seb talking in hushed tones, though they stop as I move further in before closing the door behind me with a solid click. Deciding a distraction from the intensity of the situation would be helpful to everyone, I begin making sandwiches from the cold meat leftover from dinner.

"So, that was fun," I comment dryly. Matt tucks his head into his arms where he sits at the dinner table, but Seb remains standing at the breakfast bar, leaning his weight onto both hands looking as tired as I feel. "Rolland said they're going back to bed and he's right in doing so. He looks like shit," I say, taking out the bread and buttering slices for everyone.

"He actually looks better than he did a few hours ago, but we can discuss that when everyone is fully awake in a few hours." Seb takes a deep breath before continuing. "We don't know what happens when Kia turns like that, but Jack told us she's acting on instincts right now. So, most of what we are seeing isn't even her, it's a result of the months she's spent chained up. Whoever she is underneath that, is buried deep down under so much pain a part of me wonders if we will ever see it."

A small smile flitters across his lip. "Well maybe Rolland will, but the rest of us will have to be patient." His brow pulls down, and fear oozes from him. He realises I've picked up on it and lets a breath out. "Gerry, I know how bad that looked out there, but it was pure defence. Not that you attacked her, but whatever bond she has with Rolland, Matt and even me, is at the root of her losing it like that. The rest of the time she's either wrapping Rolland round her little finger, pulling at Matt's heart, giving Brad the jumps, or making Jack look like he's got emotions," he sighs, running a hand through his hair.

I finish putting the sandwiches together before placing them onto plates, then take a glance up at Seb again, as I'm still confused. "Why did Kia think I was going to harm you, Matt?" I question, walking over to the table and pushing a plate across to him, then set the other one at the top of the table for Seb to take. Matt grumbles as he lifts his head. He hasn't got his glasses on, and his grey eyes look red at the corners, no doubt from lack of sleep.

Feeling slightly bad, I give him a small playful smile. "What's so bad that you've got a girl sticking up for you?" I mock, trying to ease some more of the tension.

He narrows his eyes before slumping his head back down into his arms again. "I got followed," he finally admits through his arms, muffling his voice. My heart drops out, but I want him to open to me, not shut down.

"Did you get tagged?" I speak around a mouthful of food as Seb comes over to take a seat beside me and begins tucking into his sandwich. I flick my eyes at him and wink, to which he raises his eyebrows back, questioning my mood.

"Yes, but we removed it on our way home and destroyed it," Matt continues, still speaking into his arms. A slight relief comes from his words, but I feel like I'm missing something.

"Anything else I should know that can't wait until morning? I'm tired, and the boys are dropping by tomorrow lunch time to go over Intel." I take another large bite as my mind finally calls for sleep now that I've met the stranger. Not that I would call her harmless but knowing her defensive behaviour is what triggered her, a small part of me has relaxed. Yet her black eyes that held no life in them churns my gut.

"No, but I got an address from Aaron for another human trafficking institute. He wouldn't accept payment for the info as he's unsure of how it will play out. Every time he's gone to scope it out, he's always come away feeling as though he was being watched," he explains, his voice remaining neutral, not giving away his thoughts on the matter. He finally lifts his head up to look at me. "When I pulled up to meet him, he seemed more jittery than usual, and that's where I picked my tail up." He lets out a big sigh of relief, then grabs his sandwich before heading out of the kitchen saying, "Seb, I'm heading back to my room for a few hours, but I'll come straight to you to help as soon as I'm awake." He doesn't look back as he leaves.

Having a tail isn't unusual in our line of work, with some being more persistent than others, but with any luck it was scum following him, not the government.

Mulling Seb's words over about Kia, a part of me wants to see this other side of her.

All I want is for the guys to be safe and if that's what's fuelling her temper, then maybe we're not so different. As much as I want to tell myself she's harmless, the cut on my neck says otherwise. I raise my hand to touch it and find blood is still dripping a little.

I see Seb pull his mouth in to stop a smile spreading. "You got taken down by a girl," he taunts with a laugh. I smile back at him.

"Only because Rolland nearly blew my eardrums off," I counter.

"*Because* you got taken by a girl and she had a knife to your neck." He looks pointedly at me.

"*Because* I held back, BE-cause she's a girl," I emphasize. Seb laughs as he finishes his sandwich.

"She's got her wings clipped just now, so you have a massive advantage. Give her a few days." Seb winks before taking our plates over to the sink and rinsing them off.

"Her back looks-" I feel my gut twist as guilt runs through me again. Her small form is covered in blood and Seb says he's been healing her? *What was she like when they found her?*

We both make our way to the kitchen door, trying to find the right words. While I understand her anxiety and the stress she's gone through, my own instincts are to keep my Brothers safe from someone who could possibly turn on them.

"It's bad, Gerry, but the memories that come from it being touched are worse than the pain itself. It's a testament to her willpower that she really didn't stab you," Seb reveals from behind me. Seb's the calmest out of all of us, never appearing to get ruffled by anything. Yet, emotions seem to be coming through with his words, just like with Rolland's. There's depth to them and an underlying meaning.

I turn back to him, perplexed by what he's saying. "I've been on the receiving end of Kia turning like that and I was healing her at the time." He doesn't lift his head to talk to me as he looks down at the floor. My heart hurts for her, but concern for Rolland, Matt, and Seb overrides it, and I feel my temper rise.

"Seriously, Seb, why is she still here if she's that much of a threat?" I ask not understanding any of this.

He finally lifts his gaze, running his brandy eyes over me,

contemplating an idea. Then he nods, clearly coming to a decision. "Follow me but don't make any noise. Mask us if need be. Just don't talk, or react, okay?"

And just like that, his words cause my temper to fizzle, and is replaced by curiosity and a need for some answers. *This should be interesting....*

CHAPTER THIRTY-THREE

*S*ebastian

Hoping that I don't regret this, I make my way back to my room with Gerry behind me. I feel his energy creeping slowly around my legs, curling up them with the warmth of summer heat, masking us both.

Rounding the corner to my room, I keep my steps light so as not to disturb Rolland and Kia - with any luck they've fallen back to sleep. The door is open wide, giving us a good view into the room and with the small amount of light from the lamp on the near side, I can see Rolland's face. He appears to be sleeping, although the slight frown on his face would suggest otherwise.

They're laying like they were earlier today, with Kia flat across his chest and her arms tucked under his. Rolland has one hand resting on her head, which she has burrowed into his neck and the other laying low down on her hip. He has a sheen of sweat on his head again and I can see where a tear has dried on the corner of his right eye. The bandages on Kia's back are nearly covered entirely in her blood now, with only the sides and a few random patches remaining white.

How are we ever going to take those off, without one of them passing out?

I turn to Gerry, but I can't make out the look on his face. *"He's been slipping into her mind when I've been healing her, taking on her memories. She fights him for control of her pain and has woken him up when he's passed out twice,"* I explain.

Gerry pulls his gaze away, frowning at me heavily. *"And you let this continue? Why don't you stop it if you know it's hurting Rolland?"*

"You know how he is. He's never listened in the past when I've told him to stop, so he's certainly not going to now. Especially if it involves Kia."

Gerry nods in understanding before giving Kia another questioning look. *"She's welcome to stay as long as she needs or wants, as long as she doesn't hurt anyone else."* And with that, he turns and walks away.

Relieved I managed to avoid laying any more on him, I enter my room and climb into bed next to the sleeping forms. Sleep finds me quickly and I soon drop off as though I haven't slept in days.

A knocking stirs me from my sleep, proceeded by heavy footfalls thundering down the stairs.

"Shh, Kia, it's just someone at the door," Rolland mumbles, followed by a sharp intake of air. *Shit, the cleaner.*

Brad's voice can just be heard speaking and I hope he tells her we don't need her help today. The front door closes, and a few moments later a car starts. *That could have gone very, very badly.*

Lifting my head, I look over and find Kia watching me

with sad eyes, a frown across her forehead. *She must be so uncomfortable, even with Rolland taking her pain.*

"*Rolland, we need to heal Kia,*" I prompt through his mind. Silence follows my words, but Kia's frown deepens. "*Rolland, I know you're awake. She's uncomfortable, even without the pain,*" I push, knowing this is going to be hard. For the both of them. Kia narrows her eyes at me and I begin to wonder if she can hear me. "*Kia?*" I attempt, seeing if she can hear me telepathically. She turns her head into Rolland's chest, closing her eyes.

Dragging myself out of bed, I walk around it until I can see Rolland's face, which he still has turned in the direction of the door. I find his eyes shut, but I can't imagine he's sleeping with such a pained look running across his face. The dark circles have returned underneath his eyes and he's still got a fine sheen of sweat across his forehead.

They're both probably hungry but neither of them are going to be able to eat till after the bandages are off, so I forget the thought and move closer to Rolland, placing a hand on his head.

"Get. Off!!" he spits but continues to keep his eyes shut.

I release some energy into his head, to help ease the headache he's carrying from dehydration. Despite his grumbling I hear him let out a sigh of relief, as Kia turns her head in my direction to look up at me. Her eyes have softened, along with some of the tension that marred her face.

"I'm going to find Matt and some more bandages. Then we're going to take those off and see if I can heal the wounds." I turn and head out of the room, not waiting for a reply.

I head straight for Matt's room, but noise from the kitchen slows me as I pass the front door. I think it's Matt's voice I hear, so I poke my head into the kitchen to find Brad and

Gerry both digging into porridge, with Matt over at the sink. Matt looks up at me, looking slightly better than he did last night. Today he's wearing a black Henley that's rolled up to his elbows and a pair of cream cargo pants.

I head to the cupboard that stores the bandages then start piling them into my arms as I say, "if you're up for it, I think we could use some help when you're ready."

He dries his hands then takes some of the gauze pads and gel from my arms. When I look at his face, his anxiety is clearly written all over it. Words aren't needed anymore to portray how we both feel; his face reflects my own gut feeling on how bad this could go. I just hope I'm wrong. I glance over at Brad and Gerry, finding they're both looking at us with the same concern. Brad more so, though Gerry's face is full of guilt.

Feeling bad for him, I try to find words to ease his conscience. "She's just clipped, Gerry, just wait and see, she'll be running rings around you within hours." My words don't seem to have any effect, so I turn and head back to my room with Matt trailing behind me. Neither of us talks, both too caught up in our thoughts, both of us wondering how Kia will react and if Rolland will pass out.

Rounding the corner that brings us to my room, I hear Rolland's voice which sounds amused and pained at the same time. "This isn't going to work, Kia, not if you are pushing that on me. I can barely focus as it is."

Stepping into the room, Rolland is sitting up facing us, Kia's legs wrapped around his waist. She's holding his face in her hands, which leans against her left shoulder. I stand beside them and find Rolland's eyes shut as though deep in thought.

"Matt, if you would sit behind Rolland to support him, I'll get started on removing the bandages," I instruct, keeping as much emotion out of my voice as possible. Matt steps around the bed as I set the clean bandages down on the cabinet.

"Rolland, are you ready?" I ask him but look at Kia. She's got her eyes closed, though her face also looks deep in thought too.

"Just give us a second. I don't trust her just yet," he says with a slight tremble in his voice. Kia's eyes fly open as she leans back from him.

Rolland sucks in a breath, pulling back from her too. "Kia, just let me do this," he urges firmly. They stare each other down with glares and I can feel the tension growing between them.

"Fine, we do it together," he grumbles in what seems to be defeat. They both relax their bodies and move in unison, with a fluidity that makes it appear as if they've been practicing for months.

Rolland pulls her head toward his chest, stroking her hair, then eases both hands behind her lower back to support her. Kia turns her head, so she's tucked deep within his chest by his heart and clutches her hands under his legs.

Once they are settled, he nods, "let's do this."

CHAPTER THIRTY-FOUR

*R*olland

Focusing on something that will help me keep my sanity through this, I think of Kia's face when she pounced on me yesterday. Her smile was full of pride and pleasure, and her eyes sparkled with those stars that make you want to give your heart to her. Happiness comes from her as she hears my thoughts, but it's quickly drowned out by apprehension and fear. So, I pluck up another image into my mind - of her face when I made her laugh for the first time – and I feel another emotion come from her, one that's strangely like what I have for my farm.

Kia shows me the image of me wet in the pool when she pushed me in. I smile at her thoughts and she soaks up my pleasure. Pain suddenly pulls at her back, followed by a quick flash of a man's face. Fear starts to overwhelm her again. Needing to pull her out of it, I push to her another image of us kissing in the pool. She grabs onto it and I feel us being drawn into the memory as though we're back there.

I'm tracing her lips with my tongue; with heat pooling around my hardness, the will to hold back from her finally seems to snap. Drawing her up against me by her thighs, I dive deeper into her mouth, tugging her energy into me. Her legs tighten around my waist in response, causing her to grind up against my hardness, bringing a sweet moan from her mouth.

Needing to hear it again, I trail my hand up her legs to find her softness, but something strikes at my back, tearing a breath from me. Pain continues to lace up my back, making it hard to breathe.

Kia lifts my head to get me to look at her. I focus on those beautiful eyes that pulse from deep blue to silver, and then there's a flash of black.

Come on, Rolland, keep her focus on you.

Pain is still coursing down my back, but I ignore it as I take her mouth with mine again, tasting the sweetness that only belongs to her. I drink it in desperately, craving it like the madman I feel I have become around her. Small hands run up my chest, and it's as though she's touching my soul.

Another strike of pain hits my back making me falter in my movements. Kia looks away from me to what is causing my distraction.

No, Rolland, keep her looking at you.

I stand up in the pool and turn her around, so her butt is on the tiled edge of the pool before I begin nipping my way down her neck, bringing another deep moan from her lips, which makes my hardness jerk once again. Her hands find their way into my hair and she tugs, hard, asking for more.

Acid trickles down my back, but I focus on her body. Sucking at her flesh, drawing it into my mouth, rewarding me with another moan, followed by her nails digging into my shoulders.

Fire creeps down my back and I can't take anymore, so I

ease back, needing to take a breath. I find her eyes shining silver, so I focus on them, watching as they swirl steadily.

Something tears at my back and my body gives out.

A hard floor under my feet sends shivers along my skin, but the pain in my back has gone. Then movement to my right catches my eye and I see Kia being dragged by chains through a dark stone passageway. She's fighting her captor and manages to get a hard swipe to his neck, but the man is fast to respond, grabbing her by the throat, slamming her against the wall - a loud thud comes from the impact.

I stagger over to haul the man off of her, but I get sucked into her body instead. Kia now stands behind the man and is forced to watch as I get punched in the face. Pain strikes me, followed by pounding but it's nothing in comparison to what I was feeling earlier.

My shackles are yanked vigorously, and my head feels fuzzy, so I shake it from side to side, trying to clear it. A door opens to our right and I'm hauled through it into a large, dimly lit, grey-stone hall full of unusual beings, most of which have black eyes and a humanoid shape, though some look insect-like in appearance. I've just enough time to notice that they all sit at long steel tables before my focus is drawn like a magnet to a ten-foot tall reptilian humanoid that towers above everyone as it stands at the front of the hall, its yellow slitted eyes focused solely on me as I'm being forcibly dragged toward it.

As I get closer, I see that covering its colossal form are armoured green scales with hints of purples and yellows. Its three-fingered hands are covered in webbing and the long, sharp talons of its right-hand are grasping what looks to be a challis. Leathery bat-like wings are spread out and float high above its shoulders, casting deep shadows over the pointed features on its snake-like head as it tracks my movement.

The others in the room pay no attention, continuing to talk in clicks and buzzes. Kia runs in beside me, trying to pull me out of the memory, except I'm stuck here as she shouts something at me, but no sound comes out of her mouth. Tears streak down her face and the need to calm her forces me to move.

I heave at the shackles that grip my wrists, but feel pain strike at my back, causing a vice to clamp over my chest... I can't breathe.

Kia's shouting at me again, tugging at my arms, trying to get me to let go of the memory. As I try, I hear the reptilian creature making noises, which plucks at my attention. I turn to look at the nasty beast and manage to catch a glimpse of a massive needle filled with a black liquid just before it gets rammed into my neck. My body begins to weaken, but the clicking turns to words, and I start to understand a few of them. "Gjinn help weaken," a few more clicks, "not be tainted by your filth," more clicks, "must be whole or no deal." A few more clicks follow and my body weakens even more before I pass out.

"Rolland, please. You say we do together." Kia's silvery voice trickles through my ears, nudging at my awareness.

I edge myself up from the cold floor to find I'm trapped in her mind still. "Where are we?" I mumble as I open my eyes. I'm still Kia and she's watching me hang from the wall as she kneels by my side.

A door slams shut behind me and my stomach turns to ice from all the fear that pours through my body like hot lava. So much fear, it makes me nauseous.

"Rolland." Kia's voice wobbles from her emotions, causing a part of my heart to crumble away.

I turn my head to speak to her. "Kia, kiss me," I plead.

She moves forward, pressing her lips against mine just before acid whips at my back.

A man starts talking in a language I can't understand, and I feel the tears run down Kia's face, which is now mine. My gut retches as I can't free myself from the chains.

"Speak to me, tell me something about yourself?" I plead with her thickly. Metal spikes rip heat through my back, and I hear someone calling my name.

"I dream things that make heart hurt, but do not know what mean." Her words are spoken into my ear softly from where she's wedged herself between me and the wall, so her head is beside mine.

More acid followed by more words. The man's rough, gravely tone raises the hairs on my neck, causing more nausea to bubble up.

"What do you see in the dreams?" My voice is barely a whisper over the turmoil rising through my body.

Kia takes a sharp breath in, and more tears coat my cheeks, but the Kia that's in front of me wipes them away. The smell of putrid decay hits my nose, making my stomach roll even more.

"Flying. Flying above trees on something. Speaks to me, but I not hear words." Loss and sadness coat her whispers and I frown to myself, trying to think what she means, what she could be flying on. "I dream people dance, but I not see faces." Her voice breaks in front of me. I yank hard on the chains to comfort her, but the cuffs tighten around my wrists, sapping energy from me through my arms, draining me, causing my heart to stutter.

"Kia, we have to wake up." My words come out slurred. I feel her small hands move up my cheek.

"Try to wake. But it not stop," her voice cracks. "Then find Matt." Her voice has changed. A tiny amount of happi-

ness glides through her words. I open my eyes to see her attention is behind me. When I peer over my shoulder, I find Matt watching.

"Kia, listen to me." I try swallowing past the shards of glass that trickle down my throat. "I'm stuck and I can't shift from your mind." I force the words through the pain. Her eyes widen. "Wake up for me and pull me out," I say to her as more tears stream from her eyes. "I'll be right behind you," I whisper.

Her eyes search mine. "Promise?" she whispers back as more tears fall.

"Promise." She kisses me gently before she fades.

My head gets pulled back tightly and I get a look at the man's face that causes Kia's living nightmares. Every part of him looks human, except his rusty copper eyes, which have a look about them that makes me question it. Short, dark, buzzed hair shows his rigid features, and I can see a tattoo on his neck. Thinking it might be a key to figuring out who he is, I focus on it. Two spirals interlock with a line going through the middle. I mark his face, and the tattoo, in my memory, as I stare back at him. There's a small amount of stubble along his jaw and his skin looks rough and wind burnt.

He speaks to me, but his words are lost in my ears as a tube is forced down my throat, scraping against my wind-pipes. Panic drops into my heart and I can hear my blood pounding in my ears. I try to focus on my heartbeat instead of the tube crammed in my mouth, making it hard to breathe.

A voice calls my name from somewhere, but it's so faint.

I feel thick liquid start to slip down my throat. I pull hard at the chains to move away from the tube, but my head is held still by the man. I can feel the liquid from the tubes start to curl into my stomach, causing my insides to twist tightly.

I hear my name and it sounds like Kia's voice. I latch onto it, focusing every ounce of my soul on it. Warmth spreads through my chest and what feels like lips push against my cheek. I focus on the heat of her lips against my skin.

Slowly the feeling of the tube begins to fade, and I can feel my body, MY actual body, start to cough.

I drag air deep into my starved lungs and try to move, but lead fills every crack and crevice, so my muscles don't respond. Oxygen rushes through me as I take one more deep breath - then darkness claims me.

CHAPTER THIRTY-FIVE

*M*att

Seb tries to hold off a topless, struggling Kia as I try to wake Rolland but he's clean out.

"Seb, swap over, see if you can wake him, and I'll take Kia," I urge him as I watch Kia fight to pull herself from his arms. He nods even as he gets whacked in the chest by her elbow, so I put a shield up to stop her from getting to him. She flashes her eyes to me, pausing in her struggle to bare her teeth at me with a low growl.

"Kia, Seb is going to look at Rolland. He's not stuck in your head anymore, he woke up and is just unconscious," I say to her firmly but keep my voice soft. She relaxes a little but doesn't take her eyes from me as she continues to bare her teeth.

Seb moves over to Rolland but keeps Kia from reaching him by turning his body away.

"He's okay, Kia," I soothe, cupping her face as I move closer, trying to keep her focus on me. "He just needs rest," I console. Her eyes look so lost, but her mouth relaxes. She flashes those blue pools back over to Rolland. "I know you want to go to him, but just let Seb take care of him and I'll take care of you." As she brings her focus back to me, her eyes soften, so I pull her gently to me as I drop the shield, giving Seb his arms back so he can check Rolland. Kia buries her head into my neck and breathes me in while snaking her arms around my waist, easing herself further into my body.

"He's fine, just in need of a healing tank." Seb sounds relieved, but he will worry till Rolland wakes. His mahogany eyes, full of turmoil, rake over Kia. *"See if you can take her through to the pool, so I can get Brad to help me carry him through."*

I run my eyes over Kia's face. *I've not seen this look on her before, and it worries me.* She truly looks lost but with no trace of fear. "Kia, all Rolland needs is rest and he'll be fine. Seb is going to take care of him, okay?" I try to soothe her as I run my hand up her arm. She nods her head as her body begins to shiver. "How about we sit in the pool to ease the pain in your back?" She nods again, her body shaking as she begins to cry. Pulling her legs around so there's one on either side of me, being careful not to touch her back, I get to my feet. She's so light, her weight is easy to balance as I pull us up. I feel her look over my shoulder as we walk through the en-suite and her body shivers again. I begin to wonder if she's cold or in shock - or both.

Moving through the archway to the pool, I consider undressing but the notion seems irrelevant given the circumstance, so I make my way into the pool fully clothed. I feel the water hit my skin and it is pure bliss. The gel I make is a combination of aloe vera and other plant-based minerals.

Once I'm low enough that Kia's waist hits the water, I slow down to inch forward, but she's still trembling and hasn't moved her head from my shoulder.

"You ready?" I ask her quietly, but she doesn't acknowledge me. I turn until my lips are near her ear. "Kia, look at me." Slowly she pulls back so I can see her eyes, but they're becoming almost closed off. "He's fine. Just needs sleep. I promise."

Moving forward an inch so the water laps at her back, I still see no emotions show across her face. I shift left toward the ledge, feeling water lap higher along her back, but she doesn't flinch or take her eyes from me. I turn until the backs of my legs are against the ledge, then begin to lower us down slowly.

Kia eyes never leave my face, running them over my lips and eyes, seeming to take in every detail. Finally, they shut as she leans into my chest, releasing a heavy breath. I stroke her head, placing a kiss on her ear, trying to ease her worry. She's finally stopped shivering and I feel as though we've settled into a comfortable peace, the sound of the water moving between our body's like a soothing lullaby.

Footsteps pull me from my thoughts a while later and I turn to see Seb coming through the archway, his hands covered in the pink wax that the healing chambers contain. He's carrying two glasses and a jug of water with a stone in his hands. *Hopefully, she'll drink a little for us.*

"How is she?" Seb projects as he continues to make his way toward us.

"She hasn't moved since we got in the pool." A part of me is anxious, but she's breathing normally and resting for the most part. Seb squats down, placing the glasses and jug carefully on the tiles.

"Is Brad sitting in with Rolland?" I ask him, turning my focus back to Kia.

"Yeah, he cancelled his classes for the day."

I tip my head back to look at Seb to see him rubbing his hand over his mouth.

"Kia, Rolland is just sleeping, he'll be awake in just a few hours." Seb's refined voice bounces off the walls. "Can you take a drink for us?"

After a few moments, she lifts her head wearily from my chest and looks over to the glass. Seb pours some water before handing it carefully to her. She takes tentative sips to start with, then finishes the rest quickly before setting the empty glass back on the tiles. She turns to face me, and I notice that lost look is still swimming in her eyes. I want to see life back in them, to see them shine and swirl, to feel the pull of her energy.

Moving my hand to her face, I trace her round cheek with my thumb, wishing I could make her happy again. Pulling her head toward me gently, hoping I'm making the right move, she comes willing, and touches her lips to mine. I kiss her softly, coaxing her mouth to open for me. When she finally does, I taste her tongue and urge my feelings into the kiss, hoping she understands what I'm trying to say without words.

I feel Seb move into the water beside me. *"Don't stop kissing her, Matt, keep her attention on you."*

I continue working at her mouth, flicking my tongue over her lips, pulling on them to draw her into me. Her hands move up my chest, sliding up to my face, followed by her energy which begins to trickle from her mouth. I drink it in, letting it warm my throat before it makes its way down into my chest.

Tugging her closer to me by her waist, needing more contact, I feel myself growing harder each second. What I wasn't expecting was her fingers to dig hard into my neck, but the action encourages my hips to thrust, and I find my body grinding into her.

"Keep going, Matt, don't lose her attention or I'm screwed." I don't pay attention to Seb's rambles as I continue chasing her tongue with mine. Her breathing becomes ragged and noises come from deep within her - they pull harder on me and the need to be inside her pushes my desire higher, making my sense of right and wrong dwindle away. There's no rational thought.

Pausing for a split second, Kia drags in a deep breath before returning to plunder my mouth once again. Warmth starts to spread around my hardness like a gentle caress and I begin to wonder if I'm inside her. It tugs hard at me, pulling up a moan from somewhere in the depths of my core.

There's the distinct sound of moving water coming from somewhere behind Kia and she comes to a complete stop. Confused as to why she stopped, I lean back to look at her eyes. The deep blue has returned with the silver specs and they're swirling incredibly fast. Seeing that sign of life in her eyes brings a smile to my lips, which catches her eye. She smiles back and kisses me again, though more hesitantly this time.

The water sloshes once more, reminding me that Seb is still with us. Kia touches my lips softly one final time, then pulls slightly away, enticing me forward. I follow willingly, chasing her face which moves to the side. A mischievous smile suddenly lights up her face and I'm struck stupid in awe. Taking advantage of my distraction, she backs away slowly as she cups her hands under the water then lifts them up toward me, tossing huge handfuls of water at me, completely soaking my hair and face. Laughing quietly, she lunges from me toward Seb, pushing him under the water.

My glasses are now utterly useless, but I do my best to clear them by shaking them off gently. Putting the streaked glasses back on, my vision is still a bit obscured but it's better than having water pooling in them. I look around but I don't see anyone at first, then I catch sight of two figures swimming under the water. Seb resurfaces for air, but Kia remains below, floating behind him while he rubs the water from his eyes. Just as his vision seems to clear, he's pulled under again. I see Kia's figure swim to the steps as Seb turns in the other direction. Kia waits while his back is turned, looking for her. He can't seem to spot her in the water, though, so he resurfaces again, rubbing his eyes quickly to clear them as he keeps spinning, trying to search her out.

The little she-devil darts toward him, pulling him under again, and I can't help but laugh at her antics. As she finally resurfaces, she appears to be choking. Fear grabs me, so I surge toward her, but before I can reach her, Seb breaks through the water. She looks toward him with a massive smile on her face. My worry dissipates as I realise that she was merely laughing while trying to catch her breath. I relax, closing the remaining space between us. I take her into my arms as Seb rubs his eyes, mock-glaring in our direction, making her laugh harder.

"Just wait. Just wait till you're fully healed, then I won't go easy on you," Seb tells her, trying to be serious, but failing utterly. Kia laughs harder and pulls herself to me, trying to catch her breath. Seb runs his eyes over her back as he continues, "which won't be long, Little Bit, not at this rate." His smoky voice is full of determination as he steps forward in the water. She spins round to face him. Seb takes another step toward her, which makes her step back into me further and brings her back almost flush against my chest.

I look down and see Seb has managed to heal it remarkably well in such a short amount of time. The wounds are scabbed over and the skin around them have the soft pink glow of healing. Seb pushes closer in the water, a playful smile on his lips and a sparkling glint in his eye.

Oh dear, what is the he-devil going to do now?

CHAPTER THIRTY-SIX

*S*ebastian

I take another step closer to Kia, admiring the beautiful smile that shines in the deep blue pools of her eyes. Wanting to keep her happy, I loom ever closer, with every intention of finding a ticklish spot and exploiting it. Suddenly, something wraps around my left calf, tugging me to the side, hard. My balance tips as I hadn't been expecting an attack and I fall to my right but just manage to steady myself before my head slips under the surface.

Kia shoves herself from Matt's arms and makes a dive under the water when she sees the look of determination cross my face. I follow her under, chasing her sleek form, but I can't see anything through the haze of the water. I make off in the direction of the stone steps, but I still can't spot her. Rising from the pool to try and find where she swam to, I rub at my eyes and take a lung full of air as I turn to search her out. When my vision clears, she's nowhere to be found, but Matt is still standing in the same spot, trying desperately to hold off a laugh.

"Where did she go?" I demand playfully.

Matt shakes his head as he trudges past me. "We're so screwed, Seb," he says, the laugh finally bursting through his lips. "She sprung out of the water the second you dived under," he continues, his laughter echoing off of the stone steps as he moves toward them.

"What?" I ask, following him. "Where did she go?"

We reach the steps and Matt turns to me, shaking his head. "She literally sprang out of the pool, Seb." He's still smiling, but there's an odd seriousness in his words.

As we make our way through the en-suite and into the bedroom, I grab a few towels as we pass the heater. Stepping into my room, I spot Kia sitting in the window seat looking out at the gardens. I prowl over to her, wondering what she'll be capable of when she's fully healed.

Her back is so much better already, with the wounds scabbing over and looking a lot less inflamed. I drape a towel gently over her wet back then run a hand softly over her head. My thoughts turn to the markings that I spotted on her back. All roughly the same size but utterly different in shape and appearance. One looked like the number eight, and another appeared to resemble the yin-yang symbol.

Kia turns with a grateful smile to me, yet I can still see the sadness nestled in the depths of those beautiful orbs. Matt ambles up to my side, still completely drenched. I glance down to the floor and see all the puddles of water we've left everywhere.

"I'm going up to get changed," Matt's says before leaning forward over Kia, shaking his hair out onto her. She gasps as the chilled droplets land on her neck before she spins around lightning fast to grab Matt. But he's faster and jumps backwards, leaping over onto the bed with Kia hot on his tail. He doesn't get far though before she launches her weight onto his back, and they go down with a thump.

"Dammit!" Matt grumbles as Kia pulls herself to her feet looking down at him with a smile on her face that rivals the sunrise.

"Why would you try to run, Matt? I couldn't catch her in a pool, why would you think you're gonna get away from her when she's within spitting distance of you?" I question sarcastically as I stalk over to him.

Matt drags himself to his feet. "Seemed like a good idea at the time," he mutters, turning to face Kia. "You're trouble, is what you are. Definitely a little she-devil." He leans down and places a soft kiss on her forehead, then makes his way out of my room.

"I need to get changed, Kia, then maybe we can see about getting something to eat. How's that sound?" I see her nod, so I turn to grab some clothes from my drawers.

The summer heat is starting to beat through the house, so I opt for a pair of light shorts and a loose top. After getting changed and a quick tidy up in the en-suite, I head back to my room to find Kia sleeping in the bed with her face buried into one of the pillows she's hugging close to her chest. Glad to see her sleeping, the muscles all over my body that have been tense for what feels like days begin to release. Stepping over to the bed, I take a seat beside her to watch her sleeping form.

A few minutes later, I'm thinking how one small little bit of a being can have such a massive effect on those around them, when I hear Matt's soft footsteps pad through the hallway, returning to my room and pulling me from my lingering thoughts.

When he appears in the doorway, he's looking fresher and dry, but clearly still in need of sleep. "Get forty winks while she's resting, and I'll head through to check on Rolland and get us some late breakfast." Matt nods as he heads over to the other side of the bed, sliding in behind Kia.

Knowing she has Matt watching her, I make my way through the house to check on Rolland. *What does the little trouble maker have in store for us next, I wonder? I'm sure we'll find out soon enough. Now it's time to check on the big trouble maker.....*

CHAPTER THIRTY-SEVEN

*R*olland

Awareness crawls back to me slowly, along with the feeling of being tugged by an invisible string. Following where it takes me, I find Kia's presence and energy at rest, with very little pain. Memories filter back to me of what happened. Being caught in Kia's mind with no way of getting out. Making a promise to her, then not keeping it. *I'm in so much trouble.*

I feel a tug on the string that connects us as happiness runs through it, followed quickly by a flash of annoyance. *Shit. She's gonna kill me.* I make a noise of resignation, knowing her wrath is going to be hard to quell.

There's another draw on the connection and I get the feeling she's trying to find me. It won't take her long, not with the way she moves. I take a quick note of the state of my body before she destroys it - I feel rested and most of my energy seems to have been restored.

The aromatic wax drifts from the healing chamber, wafting toward me and easing my senses with its smooth undertones of frankincense, relaxing me. The candles that are dotted around the room almost make it feel like I'm in a chapel. There are four healing chambers, the size of large, deep baths, that run parallel against one another with seating for whoever's on watch duty. The whole area is a spacious place with several large heaters that line one wall, keeping everything warm, and a wide shower cubicle on the other. Dim red lighting softens the fully wood lined walls, adding extra comfort to the place.

Movement to my right catches my attention and I wonder who has been sent to watch over me.

"Rolland? You awake?" Brads timbre tone echoes off the walls. I keep myself as still as possible, focusing on my breathing.

Another tug on the string tells me she's seconds away. The corridors of the house must be slowing her down, otherwise I'm sure she would've been here by now. Frustration and more anger simmers through our connection, and I wonder if she's going to put a knife to my throat like she did Gerry. *So much passion squeezed into such a small body.*

The door crashes open and I hear the chair Brad was sitting on scrape back. "Whoa there, Kia, he's still-" his words are cut off.

Wondering if she's turned on him as she did on Gerry, I feel through the connection to find passion, anger and worry. *So much worry.* My hand twitches to go to her but I fight it knowing I need to bring her guard down if I'm ever to gain her forgiveness.

I feel her move closer, but I can't hear her. *How can she keep herself so quiet?* Brad's movements can be heard as his trousers brush against each other, but Kia remains completely silent. As she draws near, I take stock of her body, checking on her wounds and bruises. Her back feels as though its nearly healed, along with most of the bruising. *Well, Sebast-*

ian's been busy. I wonder how he managed it? Her throat is still raw, but she has a firm grip on the pain, so I don't attempt to pull on it yet, wanting to see if I can get the jump on her.

Kia's energy is right beside me now, filled with worry and remorse. Guilt starts to fill me, as her anger drifts away along with the happiness she was feeling. Her hand touches my cheek and I pounce, pulling her into the tank with me and immersing her in the wax. Her body lands on top of mine and I find her head, bringing her lips to mine. Not prepared for my attack, I have the upper hand. Finding my way into her mouth, I push my feelings into her, trying to tell her how sorry I am without speaking. She kisses me back, easing some of my worry.

"I'm so sorry, Kia."

She leans back from me, so I reluctantly open my eyes and find her silver eyes glowing from above me. *"Why?"* she asks, running her gaze over my face in puzzlement.

"For leaving you," I say, frowning a little at her question.

Kia mirrors my frown. *"You not leave me. I leave you. I angry at you being so stubborn."* I raise my brows at her accusation. She has more stubbornness in her little finger than I do in my whole body. A smile plays on her lips, though she tries to fight it.

Just then, the door crashes open and Matt comes rushing in. "You're fast," he says, then bends over to catch his breath. A few moments later Seb comes in too. "She was sleeping," Matt continues, while pushing his glasses up, panting a little. "Then sprang up like a jack-in-the-box and took off." He catches some of his breath.

Kia screws her face up as she looks over at Matt with absolute confusion, which sets me off laughing. She turns back, rewarding me with one of those rare full smiles that lights up her face.

"How are you feeling?" Seb's refined tone stirs through my ears as he walks over. He squats beside the tank, which is built low into the ground, running his deep-set eyes over my face. Happy with what he sees, his face relaxes.

"Pretty good to be honest. I'm just missing something," I tell him earnestly. He frowns down at me, so I begin pulling on that pain that Kia is keeping a firm grip on. It's seems to be mostly her throat and the bruises all over her body that are in continuous pain at the moment. Her back feels tender, but nothing emanates from it.

I keep my eyes on Seb as he continues to look at me oddly. I give another hard tug and feel Kia's arms give out a little from where she's leaning on my chest. She's using all her will against me, though she seems to be struggling this time. I turn my gaze on her, looking deep into her dark blue pulsing eyes. Focusing on the connection we have, I follow it all the way through her body, journeying through every inch of her. Her breathing picks up, causing her breasts to throb and drawing my attention to them. Using my desire to fuel my energy, I give a sharp tug and unable to hold me off any longer, her control snaps and all of the remaining pain flows to me.

"That's better," I smile, chuffed with myself. She blinks at me, sitting up straight.

"So, it seems you've all been busy bees," I smirk, turning to Seb. Matt and Brad are now standing behind him, both looking down with curious eyes. Brad's wearing his dark cargo pants and hoodie, but both Matt and Seb have put on shorts and t-shirts.

Amusement settles over Seb's face as he says, "yes, we had some fun in the pool. Then Kia got tired and took a nap."

He flicks his eyes over to Kia who watches him steadily. Defiance, strength, dominance and that something else that I don't recognise comes from her. The same emotions she pushed on Jack in Seb's room when she stared him down. The desire pulsing from her hits me, causing me to become even harder than I already was. It feels like she's testing him, to see if he'll stand his ground. She did the same with Jack, but she backed down at the last second for some reason. Seb moves to stand, not taking his eyes from her. Backing off, seemingly unsure of what she's doing, Kia pulls her gaze away to look down at me.

"Nope, not happening, Kia." *I know her games and I won't play them.* "Shower and food." She narrows her eyes at me, pushing more desire through me. "Nope," I chastise humorously as I stand, flinging her body over my shoulder before making my way over to the showers. Happiness and affection come from her as she rights herself, so I push my own pleasure to her.

Pushing the glass door of the large dimly lit tiled shower cubicle open, I turn a couple of the heads on and wait for them to heat. Easing her body down, I feel her skin stick to mine slightly from the wax. She curls her arms around me and more desire begins to work its way through my body. I'm nearly butt naked with just my boxers on, which is doing nothing to hide my erection.

Hot water runs over my head and down onto Kia, who's resting her head against my chest. I start to trail my hands up her lower back slowly, inching higher to get a careful feel her wounds. They're scabbed over nicely and with a little more of Seb's energy, they'll be gone entirely in no time. I move my hands higher on her back, testing her trust in me.

She kisses my chest and I feel her tongue flick across my skin, sending a bolt of pleasure through me. "You're relentless, Little Minx, and my willpower can only stretch so far," I murmur down to her, but she doesn't seem to listen to me as she continues working her way across my skin.

The door to the shower cubicle opens and the cold air hits my back and causes Kia's nipples to harden even more. Images of me nipping at them flick across my mind and I hear Kia suck in a breath.

"There are some clothes here for you both once you're done. I'm going to put something together for a late lunch. Neither of you has eaten since yesterday, so don't take too long. If you think Kia's up for it, Gerry and the boys are in the kitchen," Seb says, then closes the door behind him.

My stomach growls with the mention of food, startling Kia. I laugh at her before grabbing a bottle of shower gel and squeezing some into my hand. She steps back from me, eyeing me up like I'm crazy.

"It won't hurt you. It's just for cleaning the dirt and grease from your skin," I try to explain. She shakes her head at me, moving out from under the shower. I roll my eyes at her as I continue to lather up the gel, washing the remaining wax from me. The bubbles run into the drain and she watches them with disgust. "Kia, what is it with you and bubbles?"

"It not feel right."

"How so?" I ask, happy to hear her voice.

"I not explain it. Something deep in me. Same feeling have when Sebastian offer me roll. Part of me know not right."

"Fair enough. I say you listen to your instincts and go with what feels right," I reply with a smile, then turn off the shower before grabbing a towel. I wrap it around my waist, then take another and hold it out to Kia, who just stares at it. *You have got to be kidding me?*

"Step forward and lift your arms up," I explain gently,

trying to keep my face somewhat composed. Complete puzzlement crosses her features, but she steps forward and raises her arms a fraction from her body. I step up to her, pulling the towel around her, then tuck it in below her armpit. She watches with curiosity.

"Not practical, Rolland. I not keep on." Her silvery voice comes through slightly worried. I feel another smile pull at my lips.

"No, this is for taking the water off of your body. Seb has left us clothes to wear but it would uncomfortable and awkward to put them on over wet skin. Come, let's hope he's left you something flexible to move in," I encourage, running my eyes over her, taking in her face as she looks down at the towel.

I pull her by the hand over to the cabinet that Seb left the clothes on. I find a pair of comfortable jeans, a short-sleeved top, pants and socks for me in one pile and in another, there's a pair of swimming trunks, boxers, a vest, a short-sleeved top, and elasticized sweatpants with a drawstring top for Kia.

Turning my gaze to Kia, I find her features incredibly puzzled and lost. "Remember how Seb and I said your body is distracting?" I start. She looks over at me with a deep frown but nods. "This will help us *not* to be distracted," I explain, hoping I got that through to her.

"It just body, Rolland." Her sweet voice is perplexed and almost a bit worried.

Yes, but it's a damn fine one that calls to be worshipped, I think to myself.

Out loud I say, "yes, and all we can think about when we see it is touching it. If we keep touching you all of the time, we will never eat or leave this house. Though, now that I think about it, that really doesn't sound so bad..." I speak more to myself than to her. My words seem to spur her on and she takes the clothes and starts pulling at them, trying to figure out how they go on.

I grab the vest first and pull it over her head. "That okay?" I get a firm nod before she moves over to the door.

"Wait, wait-" She turns back to me with another frown. "How about some dry pants?" I suggest. *My brain can't handle this*. She looks down and starts to lift the vest up. I pull my eyes away and grab the boxers, holding them out to her.

"You face change colour, Rolland. You okay?" Her silken words are spoken with genuine concern as she tugs the boxers up her legs.

"I'm fine, absolutely fine," I say, trying to calm my body as it heats. I begin tugging my clothes on but stop when it comes to dropping my towel. *What the hell is wrong with me? Why am I so aware of my body around her right now?* I flick my gaze over to her, but she's looking at the cubical, taking it all in. Making quick work of my wet boxers, I pull them off and finish dressing.

Once done, I turn and find Kia waiting by the glass door, looking out at the chambers, deep in thought. "Ready?" She nods, so I push the door open for her to go through first, feeling more relaxed and at ease than I have been in what feels like weeks. As we make our way to the kitchen with Kia at my side, I send out a small prayer that she doesn't have a bad reaction to Gerry's boys.

As well as an additional prayer that this not so little issue in my pants goes away by then, cuz that wouldn't be awkward....

CHAPTER THIRTY-EIGHT

*B*rad
   The kitchen is buzzing with noise and I wonder how Kia is going to handle it. Seb's making what looks to be a fruit salad, while Gerry has pans cooking with what I think are chicken and onions. I'm not a fussy eater - so long as it's edible and relatively fresh, I'll eat it.

Gerry is going over the plans with Ant for scoping out the address Matt gave him earlier. Ant's a kind-hearted guy who wears his heart on his sleeve - unlike Gerry. Gerry picked Ant up a few years back when we were tracking a shipment of people. The military had been monitoring it too, but was made to pull out at the last minute due to orders from higher up. Ant had every detail and strategy in place for getting them all out, only to be told their hands were tied. We continued with our plan anyway and freed forty innocent people that night. As Ant returned to his desk after everyone else had left, he spotted Rolland and decided to check out what we were doing. Poor guy nearly lost his head that night for trying to sneak up on Seb. He explained who he was, and Gerry seemed to take an interest in him. A few months later,

Gerry had Ant pulled out of the military, followed by Ben and Ryan.

To look at them, you can see that Gerry and Ant have very similar appearances, but Gerry's shoulders are more well-built and broader than Ant's. They both have a few inches of thick hair that never seems to look like it's been brushed, and a constant growth of stubble. Strangely, they could pass for brothers without batting an eyelid.

Ben, who handles most of the technical side, sits at the opposite end of the breakfast bar with Matt looking over his shoulder. They're going over as much CTV footage as they can find on the place we're scoping out. Ben is incredibly lean and tall, with sandy blonde hair that he's continuously flicking out of his face.

Jason is pacing as he speaks to someone on the phone just outside the patio doors. He's smiling, so I'm guessing it's his wife. He's as big as me in build and always fun to spar with, never holding back on his punches. Tattoos cover his arms and trace all the way up his neck, similar to mine. I've spent more time with him than I have with any of Gerry's other boys - getting tattoos together and meeting his wife and kids. A beautiful family, full of so much love and passion. His eyes flash up and find mine before he laughs and winks at me, most likely from a comment his wife made about me and my fascination with dragons.

Mike is pulling out glasses for Seb, asking him about an 'Accuracy International AWM', which I'm pretty sure is a gun, but it could be a sword for all I know. Mike is from Wales originally, although his accent seems to have faded. He's a very reserved guy but seems okay opening up around Seb. The only other time you see him relax is when he's with his wife, who I've only met a handful of times over the past ten years. She's quieter than he is, if that's even possible.

Then there's Ryan. I look over at him and notice he seems slightly lost today. His eyes flick over to the door every few minutes, clearly waiting for Rolland to come through. If there were ever a bigger kid than Rolland, it would be Ryan. His ash blonde hair is shaved at the sides but still has some length to it at the top. His green eyes are always full of life and never seem to lose focus, while his mind, and his mouth, seem to move at a million miles an hour most days. Sometimes I wonder if it's because he doesn't have a filter that he gets on so well with Rolland - the pair are a recipe for trouble. The last time we spoke he was just about to propose to his girlfriend. I wonder how it went? *I should ask him.*

The kitchen door opens and Rolland's broad form steps through. A hush seems to fall around the kitchen, although Mike doesn't seem to notice as he carries on yapping away to Seb about whatever weapon it is that he's currently obsessing over. Ben continues to tap away on the laptop, and Jason's voice quietly filters in through the door. Seb's cutting slows down significantly, causing Mike to slack in his chatter a little. I hear Ryan's chair scrape back as he stands to go over to the door, then Rolland steps in further followed by Kia's small frame. She's wearing one of Rolland's vests that hangs low over her legs, so you can just see that she's also wearing boxers, although nothing else. Her eyes scan over all the new people, taking each of them in as her gaze moves around the room.

Mike stops talking, but Ben keeps tapping and Jason's voice still drifts through, both unaware of who has walked in the kitchen.

"Kia, these are Gerry's Boys-" Rolland begins as he glances around the room. A frown pulls down on her face as she looks up to Rolland. He goes to continue but stops when he sees Kia's face. He appears to be struggling to form words and I wonder if she thinks he meant Gerry's sons. He takes a deep breath as he seemingly communicates something with her, then looks over to Seb. The silence stretches on for too long, and Ben finally catches on and stops his tapping.

Seb seems to consider something and then laughs, causing Rolland to frown at him.

"I'll start again. Kia, these are guys that Gerry has found over-" he pauses again, glaring a little at her. *What's up with him?*

"Fine, this is Mike," he points in Mike's direction. Kia looks over at him and Mike lifts a hand. "This is Ant," Rolland says.

Ant leans over the counter to offer her a hand to shake, which she just looks at. "Pleasure to meet you," Ant offers kindly.

Kia flicks her eyes up at Rolland, who closes his eyes to her. He's still not looked away from her and he seems to struggle with his composure, though whether from trying to keep his patience or not to laugh, I can't tell.

Kia steps forward and puts her hand in Ant's, who shakes it lightly, though there is a slightly perplexed look on his face when he takes his hand back.

"That's Ben over there next to Matt," Rolland directs, continuing to watch her. She looks over at Ben and a small smile appears on her face but turns to a frown when she seems to sniff.

"And this is Ryan." Rolland turns finally away from Kia to look at Ryan with a big smile. Kia pulls her attention away from whatever was bothering her and smiles when she looks at Ryan. *Interesting*. Ryan and Rolland step into each other and embrace, whacking each other on the back.

"How did it go?" Rolland asks Ryan.

Tapping picks up from Ben and chopping continues from

Seb, who's keeping his eye on Kia. She makes her way over to see what Gerry's doing, frowning deeply at the pans, then turns to Rolland again, who's still busy talking to Ryan about his recent engagement to his girlfriend. Mid-sentence, his attention gets pulled away from Ryan.

"Hold on, Ryan," Rolland says, sounding puzzled.

Gerry's looking at her curiously, but Seb's face begins to pale slightly as he flicks his eyes over to Rolland, who falters in his step, then seems to pale a little too as he turns to Seb. Kia becomes alarmed and moves over to Rolland tugging at his arm. But he doesn't turn to face her, seeming to struggle with something.

"What is it, Rolland?" I ask. *It can't be that bad, surely.*

"Her whole race is vegan, and she will know if I lie to her."

"It's protein-based, Kia. I very much doubt you'd like it," I tell her.

Rolland's whole body relaxes, and he takes her hand, pulling her along as he returns to speak to Ryan. *"Thank you, Brad."*

I look over at the patio door and see Jason finish his call. He spots Kia as he walks into the kitchen, flicking his eyes over to me as he bobs his head. "Gale says hi and that she has another book for you; I'll bring it over with me next time we drop in," Jason offers.

I nod, "thanks." I smile at her thoughtfulness as I think back to the two books she's found on mythology in the last few years, both of which are over three hundred years old.

Jason skates his eyes over Rolland, honing in on where he's joined hands with Kia. "This must be Kia." He steps forward, offering his hand to her, which she shakes without hesitation this time. "My name's Jason."

Earlier we gave the boys a general debrief on how we

picked up a girl who's in weak physical and mental health, and in need of a roof over her head. Seb also explained that her vocal cords are severely damaged, so she's unable to talk.

"Gale was asking if any of you have found anyone special yet. I told her that you're all too wrapped up in your work to even see what's past your nose, but perhaps Rolland has eyes after all." Kia frowns at Jason's words, not understanding most of them. I don't say anything, feeling as though it's better to leave it to those more involved.

Seb, Mike and Ant begin dishing up the plates, working together like a well-oiled machine. They've done this many times before, so everyone knows their role in the kitchen. I take my drink with me as I make my way over to the table to find a seat. Everyone else begins taking chairs too, with Kia and Rolland the last to join as they sit at the top of the table. As Kia takes in the abundance of food, she finds my eyes watching her and holds me with her gaze for few seconds before I smile and wink at her. She smiles back and looks down at her plate.

Poor girl looks like a lost sheep amongst the wolves, but I have a feeling she's made of much heartier stock than that. Probably best not to underestimate this little squirt.

CHAPTER THIRTY-NINE

*M*att
      Kia is sitting to my left between Rolland and me, with Ryan on his other side. Next to Ryan sits Mike who's speaking to Seb quietly to his left about more firearms, blades and other weapons that he's trying to locate. Seb only seems half focused on the conversation, as he keeps glancing over at Kia eating.

Ryan and Rolland are deep in debate over machinery, and I've wrapped up as much information with Gerry and Ben as possible regarding the footage, deliveries, employees and what little building maps we could find. Thankfully Ben had a few more ideas than I did with finding the maps. His attention is on his phone, so I turn to Kia to see how she's coping with her fruit salad.

The fork seems cumbersome in her fingers as she tries to stab at a tomato with it. I lean into her ear and whisper, "just use your hands, we don't care." I lean back and watch as a beautiful smile spreads across her face. I smile back at her, pleased with myself. Quick as lightning, Kia leans over and kisses me gently on the lips, then turns back to her food and starts tucking in, this time using her hands. Gratification is clear now that she can enjoy the food without having to bother working the cutlery.

A little moan escapes her as she pops three grapes into her mouth, drawing Rolland's attention to her. Then she makes another noise from the back of her throat. I don't think she realises she's doing it and only me and Rolland seem to be able to hear her. She polishes off her plate, then looks around to find Seb watching her with affection. He heads to refill her plate, bringing her a glass of water back with it.

After watching her tuck into her third helping, she looks incredibly content as her eyes start searching the room for something. Rolland stops speaking to Ryan and turns to whisper something in Kia's ear, which earns him a confused look. Rolland lets out a deep breath and lays his head on the table in defeat.

"What's the matter?" I ask him.

"How do you explain time to someone," he grumbles, not lifting his head from the table. *Crap*.

Kia runs her hand over his head looking worried. "If you're too long, I'll come find you," he finally says and a smile spreads across her face. Rolland sits up fast and turns slowly to her. "No," he says, mock glaring at her. She winks at him, before pushing her chair back quietly and stepping out of the room.

"Where's she going?" I ask him.

"Toilet," he mutters, peering over his shoulder toward the door. "I told her if she's not back in five minutes, then I'll come looking for her. She had no clue what I was on about."

"You look a lot better than you did a few hours ago," I say, running my eyes over his face.

"I feel it," he sighs, shaking his head. "But I'd do it again in a heartbeat." He flicks his eyes to me for a beat, then to Ben. "Everything set for you guys and Gerry tonight?"

Ben looks up from his phone when he senses Rolland's voice is aimed at him. He pushes his glasses up and brushes his long fringe away from his eyes. "Yeah, there's no more I can do from a screen till they touch down tonight." Ben looks up the table and back to Rolland. "They're not planning on going in, it's just to get a feel for the place. We need to get the timing right between the pick-up and drop-off points. Once we have that down, we'll go in together next week."

Rolland nods and looks over at Gerry. "Gerry?" At the sound of his name, Gerry looks over from where he sits between Ant and Brad. "No contact, yeah? Just scope the place out." It's not a question. He wants confirmation.

Gerry rolls his eyes. "Don't worry. I just want to get a feel for the streets, public contact, exit points and see what vantage points Mike can get," he confirms. Satisfied with his answer. Rolland stands and begins clearing the table, which seems to have a domino effect, causing everyone else to do the same.

G erry and the boys have left, leaving the house quiet once again. I've just spent the last hour trying to get a hold of Gregg to see if he's got any results from the sample I gave him, except he's not answering any of my calls or messages.

Making my way down the steps to the kitchen, I hear the sound of pans moving around coming from behind the door. As I push in, I find Seb cooking yet again, though he doesn't seem to be happy about it. "You okay?" I query, ambling into the room.

He's rifling through the fridge, hunting like a madman. "I'll be fine, though I'm glad you're here." His voice is off, as though he's barely containing his temper.

"What can I do?" I ask with concern, watching him continue to pull ingredients from the fridge, setting them aside next to the hob.

"There's not much you can do, but," he lets out a breath, "Rolland should hear this too, though I'm just not sure how I'm going to speak to him without Kia about."

My stomach starts to churn. "I'm listening," I encourage, stepping over to the breakfast bar to take a seat, making it clear he has my full attention.

"I spoke to Jack last night, before Kia jumped on Gerry," Seb starts, a small smile playing around his mouth, though it quickly falls away. "I gave him a rundown of the day's events in return for some information that he would rather not have told me, given the choice."

After our last conversation regarding Jack, and what he told Seb, the feeling of dread increases.

"He told me where Rolland and I are from, plus a small part of our history," he continues as he begins chopping lettuce, putting it into a colander as he goes. "Then he shared with me a few details about the Ayran species."

Something about his words raises the hairs on the back of my neck. My mind starts coming up with scenarios of various ways they could be seen to be bad, but I can't seem to fit Kia into any of them.

"They have no hierarchy or systems in place like those here on Gaia. They're vegans by nature, don't need food to survive and usually bear only one child." My mind seems to snag on the one child part for some reason. "It's incredibly rare, but they have been known to bear two or three, and even then it's only been known to happen a few times."

Which would mean she has no siblings; her parents must be so worried about her. Guilt settles into my stomach. *To have only one child and then to have that child go missing - it would be heartbreaking*. I pull myself out of my thoughts to find Seb watching me. It as though he's reading my thoughts, even though I'm not projecting them.

"They have no males in their species," he finishes.

"What??" I puzzle, frowning hard. *I know I didn't hear him right because that's impossible. Well not totally impossible as jellyfish, snakes and other animals are known to be asexual. But not a human, not that she's human.* My head starts spinning. "Did I hear you right?" I ask looking back to Seb, but find he's already resumed his chopping. "Sebastian?"

He stops what he's doing, though doesn't look over at me as he says, "Jack went to meet with some Atlantians last night to see if they would cleanse Kia so that she can enter into Mid Gaia." He stands motionless, staring at the chopping board.

My ears are ringing, and I can't seem to take oxygen into my lungs. My rational mind knows she must go, yet my heart and some deeper part of me screams that I can't let her.

Blinking my eyes to clear them from stinging, I manage to pull myself together. "Thank you for telling me, Seb," my words are barely audible.

Silence follows as Seb continues to stare at the chopping board. "I don't know if I can let him take her, Matt," his voice raw. *Neither do I, but what choice do we have? Can we really protect her? She's already nearly healed and our time is running out.*

My thoughts return to the pool. The taste of her lips. The feel of her body and the way her eyes change with her emotions. There's still so much I want to know about her, and I've not even had the pleasure of hearing her speak yet.

Like a madman fighting for his crazy pills, she's become an addiction you can't bring yourself to admit to. Admitting to it would mean you had to face facts.

Facing the fact that you care about someone so deeply, that even though you've never heard them speak, and know nothing about them, you would still be willing to give your life for them.

"How are you going to tell Rolland?" I manage.

Seb has finished cutting and is now washing the salad with the purified water. He doesn't answer for ages, and I'm beginning to think he won't, when he finally speaks up.

"I'm not."

CHAPTER FORTY

*J*ack

After conversing with Hiliarchian, and returning from Russia once again, I head off in search of Jerhaner in hopes of sharing some more of my thoughts and concerns regarding Kia.

Heading straight for his office, I am fortunate to find him there without the need to search the entirety of the mountain. He appears to be studying a book, of which the pages look to be Tyrian made.

Feeling my presence as I enter his study, he straightens then turns to face me. A small nod grants me permission to close the door for privacy. I feel energy sealing the door from behind, giving me some comfort.

"Jack, I have never known you to question yourself so much," Jerhaner muses, his tone curious and light. *Is it that clear to see?*

Questions plague my mind after Sebastian's and Matt's revelations over the last twenty-four hours. I would have returned sooner to check on Kia's recovery if Kerboran had not obtained me when I had finished speaking with

Hiliarchian. I cannot say I entirely regret assisting him, as my aid in helping him at the cut off points in a Russian mountain meant he was able to corner a stranded Brahducas, a shapeshifter that had been stranded by himself for four hundred years, with no contact except that of animals. Whether the twins will ever be able to get him to shift back into his humanoid form is another matter.

"Kia. She questions all my logical thoughts every time I step into the room with her," I begin. Jerhaner holds my gaze steady. "When I returned home after speaking with you yesterday morning, I encountered a Gjinn." Jerhaner's eyes flicker ever so slightly at my words. "There is also the possibility she has a Draconian after her." *Not all Draconians are malevolent, but most on Gaia are.* My stomach churns at the thought of them.

"How certain are you?" Jerhaner queries, his features remaining steady, though his thoughts do not.

Far too many lives have been lost to them. Just like The Swarm, they feed on the essence of life around them. An Ayrans life force is the equivalent of a hundred human lives. Undiluted, untampered, pure of corruption from other influences, it is not so easy to take the life force, or essence, from an Ayran as it would be from a human.

"It was through a vision Matt had of her," I confide in him.

"Do you think Matt is getting his abilities back?" he asks pensively. This question has run through my own thoughts after what we have come to learn about Matt and his powers. Our knowledge was already limited, and with Matt being the only one of his species to aid in the war, it has left us with very little information regarding his abilities and power.

"I would not like to say, though Kia was able to manipulate his shield and turn it into more of an Ayran's cocoon barrier," I disclose, keeping my eyes on him for a second longer, before I turn to pace slowly - something I usually only do in his presence. "She is also displaying Tyrian type behaviour," I continue, glad to have someone to voice my thoughts to. "Sebastian informed me she is speaking through Rolland's mind and is becoming attached to him." I tilt my head to look at Jerhaner, although his face does not reflect shock as I had assumed it would. *What is he not telling me?*

"Jerhaner, would you care to enlighten me as to what is running through your mind right now?" I ask curiously.

"I would not like to hinder the path that has been set for that which is already a precarious balance." His eyes hold mine and I begin to wonder if he refers to Kia or me.

"Hiliarchian is willing to administer the serum into Kia once she is at full health. Her advice was to shelter her here, where the mountain can cloak her energy," I confirm, watching as a fine line, unnoticeable to those with average eyesight, appears across his brow. His mind seems torn between two choices. A part of him wants to tell me, yet something holds him back.

"Would you be willing to acquaint me with Kia, before she arrives here?" he requests.

My thoughts turn to Rolland and Sebastian, although Rolland is more in the forefront. His connection with Kia has deepened far past any kinship I have ever witnessed between an Ayran and another race before. Then again, her last display of dominance would suggest that she would not allow him to defend her *if* she is in full health.

"I see no reason to deny you once she has fully recovered physically," I grant him.

Perhaps he could shed some light on her mind or, at the very least, her behaviour. *Will Kia display the same Tyrian display of dominance to Jerhaner?* The thought curls my insides, setting a deep frown upon my face, which I cannot conceal.

"Jack?" Jerhaner's voice stirs something within me. Shaking the thought away, I turn my gaze back to him, finding his features drawn in. "What happened just now?" he asks, slightly concerned.

"I am sure it is inconsequential," I try to deflect, still not willing to acknowledge my feelings.

"Perhaps it is. Then again, I have not seen that reaction from you in a very long time, not since our last attempt at using the serum," he says with understanding. The last time we tried cleansing someone, they did not pull through, nor did the several before them. Their hearts were too infected, and with such little energy remaining within them, their minds gave out. Any hope of freeing those of us left was annihilated, putting more pressure into finding any remaining survivors and rebuilding the craft.

"I must return to England to check on Kia's recovery. I shall let you know as soon as she is stable enough," I inform him with a heavy breath.

The energy on the door at my back disperses and Jerhaner nods in a sign of acceptance. I return his nod, then make my way out of the central part of the mountain so that I can teleport to the house in England.

Back within the comfort of my own room in England, I change into something lighter. As I pull on a loose, silk tunic, I feel Kia's energy move closer. Her power and energy are exceptionally strong, and it feels as though she has fully recovered. I pause, getting a better sense of it, and discover it to be a stronger energy than I have ever felt from any fully matured Ayran. Her mind prods at my awareness, the dormant imprint I left within her simply waiting to see if she falls into her mind again.

Her presence moves steadier toward my door. *Is she looking for something?* I trace along the connection that joins us in order to get a read on her thoughts and emotions. Like Rolland, I can pick up on some thought patterns, but it is not stable enough to distinguish a complete train of thought.

Finishing the button on my tunic, I step over to the door, opening it slowly. Her thought patterns do not change, so I wonder if she did not hear it. *A dim-witted thought to pacify my own tortured mind - of course she heard it.*

Stepping through the doorway, I keep my eyes up, focusing on the walls until I have the door secured, its seal in place. Once that is done, I push some energy through, fortifying the wards and charms that are in place. Those who reside in the house can see the door, yet not open it. Any intruder would merely walk past, thinking it just another wall.

Turning down the hallway, I find Kia studying a painting. The one she is appraising caught my interest many years ago, in Sweden, and it had been painted many years even before that. I pace over, pausing on her left, taking in the painting that has always brought me such pleasure. A unicorn, or as Ayrans know them, Erkenstar, is grazing in a woodland much like those found on Gaia, yet it has such profound colours that it leads the mind to think it could be from another place. The artist either had insight or a very vivid imagination.

Fallen into mythology along with the dragons that Brad craves the knowledge of, they were once known to many races and species, much like the wild deer of Gaia. Ellusive by nature, sure-footed on any terrain, and can move at speeds that would outrun any other land animal known. They roamed the lands freely, healing and nurturing life, keeping the balance of free will, that which every living entity has the right to. Long ago, they had something close to kinship with all sentient beings, but after the invasion of The Swarm, their trust and discernment of us changed, leading the way to them becoming no more than memories, even to those who knew they really existed.

Wishing I could ask Kia what thoughts play through her mind, I settle for studying her face, taking in her skin that seems so much more vibrant than it did just hours ago. A small frown skims across her forehead as though she is concentrating hard. Checking in on her thought patterns, I find that it feels as though she is chasing something within her mind. A blockage causes her to falter; she pulls back from the painting, as though the thought causes her pain.

"Are you well, Kia?" I ask, concerned. *Is she unable to access her memories?*

She straightens at the sound of my voice, mirroring my posture into a stance of confidence, then takes a small step back from me. Her energy hits me, driving through me, just like a Tyrian would when testing for power to find a suitable partner. She pushes hard, but I stand my ground, pushing back at her. A small flicker crosses over her eyes at my response. Thankfully, she pulls back on her energy and I feel a small relief from her retreat.

Her eyes pulse from sapphire blue to silver, then begin to swirl. Energy creeps up my root chakra, which is entirely open to her. Drawing down on my shields to close her off, I feel them struggle as her energy slips further up into my sacral chakra, warming it through. I feel a tug, followed by my desire to take her lips, claiming them, marking her with my essence. Thoughts of keeping her by my side, in my homeland, as my partner, surface. That idea triggers some rationality to return to my mind, so I slam my shields down hard, and push her out completely.

Kia takes an audible breath, which tugs at my heart. She blinks slowly, then pulls her gaze away from me to look back at the painting. My mind feels abused by what just happened. She steps forward to resume her appraisal of the picture, and her thoughts have wholly returned to the way they were before I interrupted her, as though I had never spoken.

"I have more paintings of the same nature if you would like to look at them?" I try to ameliorate. She turns to me, offering a smile with a small nod. Relieved to have reconciled things for now, I offer a small smile in return.

"I need to speak with Sebastian first, and then it would be my great pleasure to share them with you," I offer, running my eyes over her small frame. Sebastian has done remarkably well in healing her considering the amount of pain she endured and the damage she has sustained. I expected it to take him far longer to heal the broken bones along with her back. It would undoubtedly have used more energy from her to recover than anything. Guilt simmers within me for not being here more, though I wonder what her reaction to my presence would have been if I had, in fact, stayed.

Kia nods to my offer, returning her gaze once more to the painting in front of her. Leaving her where she is, I continue on through the house to find Sebastian, who's energy stirs within the kitchen.

CHAPTER FORTY-ONE

*S*ebastian

Matt still sits at the breakfast bar, deep in thought after my last words. Neither of us have spoken since I said I wouldn't talk to Rolland about Jack's plans to take Kia to Mid Gaia.

Kia's fruit salad is complete, though I wish I had more of a variety to give her. The fridge is barely stocked since Matt had to abandon the shopping, plus our cleaner who usually brings in fresh produce from our local market wasn't able to leave anything since Brad had to send her away. *I'll need to make a trip myself tomorrow morning, perhaps some exotic fruits would suit her pallet better than what I have stocked.* My thoughts turn to how we will explain the guys eating meat to her. *A whole race of vegans is mind-boggling, and Jack says they're more powerful than any other race?*

How are we going to keep her safe from all those that seek her out? Perhaps we could take the serum. Chance it that we pull through. It stands as our only option right now if we want to stay with her. Take the serum and hope we all pull through, or let Kia go and stay here waiting for the craft to be finished. Perhaps we can find her once we have passed the ice circle. Would we still be infected once we crossed the storms that surround Gaia? My head buzzes with questions.

I glance over at Matt to see his head bowed deep in thought. He's known of Kia the longest from the visions that he was having of her. It explains so much of his behaviour over the last few months, though I mistakenly put it down to work. A part of me knew there was more, yet I didn't listen to my instincts. Instead, I pushed them aside and buried my head in my own work.

The kitchen door opens and Jack steps through wearing his usual stoic mask. He's changed back into the comfortable, light cotton clothing he wears when he's home. *Perhaps he intends to stay for a few hours?* His gaze flicks from me to Matt, then back to me again, making me wonder if he's come to share more information, but is unsure if he should do so with Matt in the room.

He closes the door behind him, then turns fully, pauses, shuts his eyes, then lowers his head as he did outside the house, and in my room, to activate the stones. Most likely he's soundproofing the room. Matt looks up and over, obviously just as intrigued as I am as to what Jack plans to share.

I want to play a different game with Jack this evening, so I grab the opportunity before he can start. "I want to offer you some information, Jack. You can ask a question about it if I get to ask my own questions," I offer in an even tone, continuing to prep the vegetables but keeping my eyes on him for a few moments. His eyes flicker minutely, trying to follow my thoughts, no doubt.

"I will only agree once you have parted with the information." His tone is flat and careful.

He's at a disadvantage for once when it comes to knowledge and he clearly doesn't like it. Yet he's not so desperate to trust that what I know could be valuable. *Let's put his theory to the test.*

"I found something on Kia's back," I say as I finally pull my eyes away, giving him a moment to digest my words. As much as I want to watch his every movement, a part of me knows he'll be more compliant without the intensity of my eyes on him, so I continue chopping at the vegetables for the guys' dinner.

"Deal," Jack finally says with a slight tone to his voice, sparking my interest. I skim my eyes over to him to find he's standing with his arms behind his back and his feet shoulder width apart, giving him an air of openness that I'm not sure I've ever seen from him.

"Why don't Ayrans have males in their species?" I ask, turning my attention to the mushrooms.

There's a small pause before he answers. "I do not know the answer to that, Sebastian. The Haoghvans have only given that information to a select few," Jack's voice is steady once again. *Huh, Jack doesn't know the answer to something. That's new.*

"That's not an answer, Jack," I say in an even tone of my own, before I look up to him. His eyes catch mine, and he stares back.

"Fine. Ask another," he relents.

"How do Ayrans procreate?" I ask curiously as I move on to cutting the peppers. I find that keeping my hands occupied helps my mind stay focused.

"It is done when they are in a deep meditative state, though the time frame in which it takes to complete, and the gestation of the fetus are both unknown," Jack reveals, still keeping his tone steady.

My brain can't seem to process what he's saying. *How*

can you make a life through meditation? That's absurd. Surely there must be more to it?

My mind starts going through various possibilities as to how that could even happen, but Jack's voice pulls me from my internal dialogue. "What did you see on Kia's back?" he asks with just a slight eagerness to his tone.

I look up, holding his gaze this time. I wish I knew just how much I could be jeopardising any possibility of us staying by Kia's side by telling him.

"Markings, like the one behind her ear. What is the process of cleansing the body so that you can enter into Mid Gaia?" I fire back at him, hoping to take him off guard. His eyes bulge slightly at my revelation about Kia's markings, followed by a slight grinding of his jaw from my question. *Now, this is fun. I could stand here all day, watching him squirm.*

"The cleansing of the body can be done by ridding it of toxins through diet and meditation, but it takes years to complete. There is also, however, a serum that can be administered. Most bodies that have been exposed to the infection over a prolonged amount of time fail to pull through. The mind is too weak to resurface, and the heart usually fails in the battle over the body. How many marks did you see?" His voice sounds off, as though he's trying very hard to keep his tone even, which he usually does without much effort.

Something in me feels like it's dying. *How long has he known this? And why has he not told us before?* I can feel my heart pounding in my ears, and I feel like I'm back in my room with the Gjinn. Paralysed, yet completely aware of my surroundings. Fear grips my heart, making it hard to breathe, and the knife in my hand trembles slightly. Jack raises his eyebrows a fraction, and his piercing blue eyes hold mine, daring me to move.

"Five could be seen on her skin that have fully healed, but more could be seen where the skin is healing. Why is Kia expressing desire, if her species doesn't procreate with males?" I spit out through clenched teeth, keeping my eyes pinned to his. I watch for every detail that might show on his pretty face, that pretty face that is just asking to be hit – preferable with a sledgehammer.

"I do not know. I have never seen an Ayran behave as Kia does," he reveals, keeping his piercing eyes on mine but doesn't ask his own question, knowing that his answer wasn't enough to grant him one. *That's twice he's failed to answer my questions. How has she got him so perplexed when he said he spent many years of his childhood growing up with them?*

Pulling myself back to the questions I have, I intend to drag this out as long as possible. "How is Rolland speaking telepathically with her?" I eventually ask. Jack's eyes bulge again, and I see Matt move a fraction in my peripheral vision. He is just as worried about them as I am. Jack's reaction turns my stomach slightly.

"They are exchanging energy through thought, body, and what is known as 'life' that runs through us all, which is sometimes referred to as our soul or spirit. Their spirits are recognising each other, and in doing so, forming a bond. Has Kia turned on anyone else?" Jack's voice is becoming edgy, causing my already churning stomach to drop like a dead weight.

"Yes, she turned on Gerry thinking he meant Matt harm. What will happen if Rolland and Kia are separated?" I demand, needing to know the answer as much as I need my next breath. Silence follows my words. Jack's eyes glare back at me, demanding I ask another question, yet he knows there is no other question that will pacify me. He wants more

313

answers to Kia's back, I'm sure of it. But either he doesn't know the answer or isn't prepared to give it to me.

Jack moves, turning his back on me and walks out of the kitchen. Matt quickly scrambles out of his seat just as I turn the off the cooker, and we both chase after Jack, knowing he will search out Kia to get the answers he wants.

Fuck that. He's a dead man if he thinks he can walk away from me and not tell me what the fuck could happen to them if they're separated. Game. On.

CHAPTER FORTY-TWO

*R*olland

As I saunter up the stairs to my room, I relish in the knowledge that I can feel Kia's emotions and take her pain, no matter where she is in the house. Happiness, peace and whatever that other feeling is that I still can't put my finger on yet, flows back through the connection which joins us.

Coming to a stop at my door, I find her sitting on the window seat in the cocoon she's made out of my duvet, looking out at the back gardens that encompass the vast lake.

I walk over to her with a playful smile bouncing around on my lips, wanting to see her face. She knows I'm here, so I can't get the jump on her, and she knows my thoughts and intentions. She pulls down the duvet as I near her so that I can see her face. Eyes that are so full of life, wonderment and happiness shine back at me, with the deep blue pulling me further to her, enticing me forward. I let my eyes roam over her shiny ebony hair that seems to have a life all of its own. Its smooth and wild as it's been pushed up in crazy angles by the duvet. Her already tiny face looks even smaller where it's hidden within the folds. And then there's that fucking smile - the one that draws my attention to her beautiful mouth like a moth to a flame, the one that reaches her eyes making them as bright as the sun, the one that lights up the entire room like fireworks in the night sky.

Taking a seat next to her, I begin to bury my head in the duvet, trying to find my way deep into its folds, searching for her belly so I can nip at it. She giggles at my antics, encouraging me on. I lift her onto my lap and as she settles down, she pulls the duvet up around us, creating a shelter with it. Darkness encloses us both in its thickness, and I start a trail of nipping and kissing at her skin through the vest she's wearing. I can sense that she wants to drop the duvet so she can feel me but also doesn't want to let go of it just yet. The thought makes me laugh, fueling and spreading her desire.

"Drop it, Kia," I dare her, my voice coming muffled against her skin. "You can't hold onto it forever," I taunt, kissing my way up her neck to her ear. She doesn't drop it, but her energy begins to slip into me. "That's not fair, Kia. I don't have magic mojo like you," I moan into her shoulder. The duvet drops slightly, giving some light back to our eyes. Inching back from her, I find her head is entirely out of the duvet, but she keeps a tight hold of the rest, pulling it up around my own neck, so we're both under it.

Her eyes flick over my face. *"Your heart so beautiful, Rolland."* Her accent is Norwegian or maybe Swedish, but very light in places.

"And your soul is too pure for my thoughts," I tell her with meaning. Puzzlement washes over her, so I show her an image of me sucking on her nipples while running my hands up her legs, sharing with her my intentions of feeling and doing more. She sucks in a breath as her eyes deepen and begin to swirl before she moves forward toward my lips. I

keep track of her mouth, needing the taste of her on my tongue more than I need my next breath. Her lips touch mine gently, just as her emotions change from desire to worry in a fraction of a second. I pull back to see what has her so concerned and find her eyes are fixed, not moving as they were a seconds ago.

"What is it, Kia?" I ask confused examining her face. Annoyance, anger, and a shitload of dominance hits me, followed by a huge dose of rage before she pulls it all back, muffling it slightly but not cutting it off entirely. I frown, not understanding what has her so worked up.

"Kia? What's wrong?" I ask again. Frustration simmers up before she muffles that too. "Kia!" I demand a little louder.

Noise from the hallway pulls at my attention, but I keep my focus on her, wondering if she's about to go into another bout of rage. Jack appears at my door, but I refuse to look away as another wave of dominance slams through me. *What is it with her and Jack?* Her eyes remain a steady blue, studying something as she considers my face, but not seeming to see me.

"Kia, could I trouble you to see your back?" Jack asks in his usual flat tone.

Possessiveness rears heavily up in me and my arms tighten around her small waist, drawing her a fraction closer to me. Her eyes soften and begin swirling again. So many emotions course within my own body at once they feel like they're slightly suffocating me. The undeniable need to protect her from any visions, thoughts, and feelings runs like fire through my veins. *He shouldn't even get to fucking look at her, let alone get anywhere near her back.* Kia's hand moves up my neck to my face, pushing comfort through to me and easing some of my worries.

317

I hear more noise coming down the hallway, then make its way into my room, but I don't hear any more voices.

"Jack need answer Sebastian's question first." Kia's voice comes through my mind sounding worried.

"I don't want him looking at or touching you, Kia," I tell her firmly. My hands draw her closer to me, and my heart feels as though something is crawling around in it, looking for an escape. Something coils within me, like snake ready to strike at any movement. Vengeance needs to be served for what they did to her and someone is going to pay for it.

Something flashes in Kia's eyes before her lips descend fiercely upon mine. She trickles energy down my throat, pushing the feelings away and soothing them like a wave from the ocean crashing over a sandy beach. Her lips pull at mine, encouraging them to open, and I feel my shoulders relax as I reflexively open my mouth to her, discovering her tongue and tasting it. Relief flows through me from Kia and my lungs seem to start functioning again. She inches back from me, looking me in the eyes with compassion and understanding.

"Ask, Rolland. Ask to answer Sebastian's question, and I finish that," she says playfully, her eyes shining with silver stars. My heart warms at her games, knowing she's using my own tricks against me. I feel a smile tug at the corner of my mouth.

"Answer Sebastian's question, Jack," I finally relent, but don't take my eyes from Kia. I can't. I'm not sure what I'll do if I look away right now.

Silence comes from behind Kia. *I don't care - so long as she's in my arms, where she needs to be, where she belongs, I just don't care.* I run my eyes over her lips, thinking about my reward for doing as she asked.

"Wait, Rolland. You need hear what Jack answers. Sebas-

tian and Matt worry you and me." Concern laces her voice and I don't like it. A frown pulls my lips down at hearing that note of concern. *"It not matter what he answers. I here. With you,"* she soothes. I relax again, finally dragging my gaze away from Kia's to look behind her at Jack. His jaw is clenched so hard I'm surprised he hasn't cracked any teeth and there's a definite line etched across his forehead. *Huh, I didn't think he had facial expressions - guess you really do learn something new each day.*

His study is on the back of Kia's head like he's trying to penetrate her thoughts. I flick my gaze over to Matt and Seb, who can't seem to decide who to watch. Kia, me, or Jack. It's amusing to watch and brings the smile back to my face. Happiness floods to me from Kia, so I soak it up, using it to fuel my own feelings.

"I do not know what will happen, Sebastian. Kia needs to return to her homeland, where she belongs and will be safe. Her energy has already returned and is still increasing, attracting more of those that mean her harm." Jack's voice doesn't sound right. He sounds lost, confused perhaps, and maybe even worried. Shit, Jack never sounds worried. Except when it comes to Kia. Then his words begin to sink in.

Kia return home? She IS home. What is he on about? Something about her energy returning and attracting those that wish her harm. I look over to Seb, who has got his face to the ceiling with his eyes closed.

Deciding to keep Kia in the loop, I speak aloud with him. "Seb, what's he on about?"

Kia's emotions are completely muffled, though not cut off completely. She's giving me room to feel without her own feelings distracting me. I flick my eyes to her, finding a frown that mirrors my own until she seems to realise, or hear, something. Her head moves round to Matt, as though she's trying to concentrate on him. Matt notices her looking at him, and narrows his eyes slightly at her, causing her to turn back to me.

Seb finally brings his focus down to look at me - his eyes are full of remorse and guilt. *What the hell?*

"I was trying to tell you before I healed Kia's knees. When Kia reaches her full potential, it will be like having ten of us standing in the same room. Jack wants to get Kia somewhere safe, where her energy can be masked until-" Seb pauses his words. *Why is he hesitating?* His hesitation churns my stomach, causing my fingers to dig deeper into Kia's hips.

Feeling Kia's small hand tug at my face, I turn my gaze to hers. *"I here, Rolland. In arms. Listen my voice."* I feel her lips on my head and relax my shoulders again. She pulls back, turning her attention to Seb, waiting. I look over at him and raise my eyebrows, waiting for him to continue as well.

"Like us, she's not from here. She's from a land far outside of the ice circle," Seb forces out, then swallows hard, trying to find his words. "Jack wants to get her back to her people, who will be missing her dearly, Rolland." His voice breaks at the end and I know there's so much he's leaving out.

An image flits through my mind, sent from Kia. Trees higher than skyscrapers, full of colour and life, followed by a searing pain that races through my head. I suck in a deep breath before Kia tries taking control of the pain. My eyes flash back to her, glaring at her for even thinking of doing so. She sticks her tongue out at me, which pulls a smile from my lips.

Kia takes a deep breath, before kissing me on the lips again, releasing more energy through me and warming my heart. Then she slowly removes herself from my lap, running her hands up my face, pushing comfort, the feeling of home, and peace heavily through my body, making me feel sated and relaxed. I let her go, wishing I had the strength to fight her and pull her back into my arms.

Instead, I sit and admire her form as she rights herself, straightening up with determination. I feel her tug at my energy where her hand is still touching my face. Unable to deny her anything, I give her my energy more than willingly. Someone pulls in a breath. *I think it may have been Jack.*

Kia turns from me and stalks incredibly slowly in the direction of Jack. I keep a trace on her emotions, watching as she repeats the process of what she did in Seb's room to Jack again. Dominance thunders through her with need, desire, and a shit load of frustration coursing through her. I move my eyes to Jack as I lean forward onto my knees, watching her handy work. *So small. So full of life. She's incredible.*

More dominance flows from her and I feel a tug on the connection that joins us. She's asking for more energy, so I push some through to her, giving it to her freely. Jack takes another audible breath but doesn't move. His eyes have widened considerably as he works his jaw hard. Kia comes to a stop in front of him, holding the energy that I've given her, poised, ready to do what she needs to do. Jack's eyes waver ever so slightly.

Kia lets go of my energy, returning it slowly to me as she walks around Jack to leave the room. Jack is left stunned, which is slightly unnerving, but I keep my eyes on him, wondering what's going on in his head.

His mask has slipped, revealing an array of emotions. Frustration, desire, need, and a whole bunch of confusion is written over his face before he closes his eyes, pulling himself together then takes a deep calming breath. "If she continues to gain energy like that, she will be felt within a hundred-mile radius. We need to leave by first light to get to Greenland if we are to stand a chance of keeping her safe."

Jack's words are ground out before he reopens his eyes and looks over at Seb. "Pack plenty of warm clothing for everyone," he finishes before turning and leaving the room.

My mind flits back to Kia needing to return to her homeland. *The simple answer is, where she goes, I go. It's pretty simple really.* With my mind made up, I move from the window seat to the closet and notice Seb and Matt are still standing there. They both look like their expecting me to break down or something. *What's their problem?*

"What?" I ask in pure puzzlement as I step into the closet and pull down a bag from the shelf. I begin filling it with jumpers, thermal tops and extra layers. I feel the guys' presence behind me, but I ignore them and carry on packing the bag.

"Are you okay, Rolland?" Seb's voice sounds confused and concerned as he speaks to me from the doorway to the closet. Most likely because he feels badly for keeping shit from me, though I can hardly blame him. It's not easy to have a conversation with a distraction like Kia in your arms, not to mention her ability to pick up on every little feeling of mine.

"Yeah, of course. Don't worry about it, Seb. We've both had our minds occupied. I can hardly hold a grudge against you for not speaking sooner given the circumstances," I say lightly as I finish putting some socks into the bag. All I have left to grab is a pair of boots and some toiletries for the road.

"Rolland. You know it's not that easy to just leave Gaia," Matt's tentative voice comes from behind me.

That crawling feeling seems to resurface, making its way up through my stomach and burrowing itself somewhere deep within me. A feeling of rage comes from somewhere, though I can't track its origin. The thought of Kia leaving and never getting to see that brilliant smile again seems to snap something inside of me. A noise from behind me plucks at my awareness, and I want to kill whatever it is that's threatening to take her from me. Small hands pull at my face and Kia's eyes fill my vision, but I can't escape the need to destroy something, to rip it to pieces till the words can never be spoken again.

Lips find mine and warmth trickles down my throat, fighting the feelings that are rising within me. *"Feel me, Rolland, I here with you. Put hands on me. I here,"* Kia's urgent voice pierces through my mind, taking over my own thoughts. My body relaxes, giving me control of it once more. Taking a breath, I inhale the distinct smell that is Kia - that clean crisp smell of the forest after its rained. Her tongue pushes for entrance as she tugs on my head so that I lower myself down to her, way down, to meet her tiny body. As her tongue touches mine, her unique and never changing taste explodes into my mouth like a goddamn ray of sunshine. And as she continues to pour her energy into me, I feel like I'm drinking from the Holy Grail, like life itself is working its way through my veins.

Grabbing her by the butt, I lift her up so I'm supporting her weight. *"Kia. I need you."* My words are desperate as I rain kisses down her neck. Comfort, reassurance and happiness flow from her, as her hands pull at my head so that I'm looking at her. She runs her eyes over my face, looking for something, though I have no idea what. Happy with her findings, she offers me a smile before encouraging my head to her chest so she can stroke my hair. I continue to breathe her in, filling my lungs with her scent and letting it calm me.

Slowly rational thought begins to return, along with the realisation that I still need toiletries. I kiss Kia's ear as I slide her down my body, then grab the bag I dropped on the floor. When I turn, I find Seb and Matt staring at me with a look I can't decipher.

"What?" I ask them bewildered. *What's up with them?* "Shouldn't you guys be packing?" I suggest.

Matt turns and heads out, but Seb remains standing there, looking at me. His eyes flick over to Kia, then back to me.

"Seriously, Seb? If you need to say something, just say it," I bite out a little sharply. I don't mean to be harsh to him, but he's just standing there as though he's waiting for something. His eyes flicker to Kia again, who's standing to my right, holding onto my arm, still pushing comfort and reassurance through me. I wait, knowing I have to finish getting ready, but hoping he'll spit out whatever the fuck is on his mind.

CHAPTER FORTY-THREE

*S*ebastian
What the hell just happened? I could feel his rage boiling and it felt like being in the same room as Kia when she snaps. Then she appeared, grabbed hold of Rolland's face and started kissing him. Slowly he began to relax, till the bad energy left him altogether. The glare she gave Matt and me, you'd think she was going to stab us. She stared Matt down till he finally looked away, but I kept my gaze till my eyes stung and I couldn't hold them open anymore.

As soon as I blinked, her focus had moved from me, back to Rolland. Now he's behaving as though nothing happened. *Does he seriously not remember? Or is he choosing not to acknowledge it?* His eyes look entirely normal. Full of life, though slightly dopey from whatever she's pushing on him.

Deciding to leave telling him any more till perhaps we're on the road tomorrow, I flick my gaze to Kia, to see her eyes finally returning to some sense of calm too. It's as if she knows I'm relenting, giving him some space. I offer a minute nod, acknowledging our truce.

"Nothing, Rolland. You're right, I should be packing. I'll finish dinner, then get to it," I say to him gently. Rolland shakes his head, rolling his eyes a little. I turn and make my way out of his room and head toward the kitchen to finish dinner.

Just as I finish up dinner, Brad walks in and makes his way over to the fridge, grabbing himself a beer.

"You want one?" he offers, waving a beer in my direction. More of a red wine drinker, I decline by shaking my head.

I'm still deep in thought about Kia and Rolland and worrying about how the hell I'm ever going to get through half the information that Jack has shared. *Perhaps he just won't care, though that doesn't mean her people won't.* The main obstacle is getting out of here alive without being sucked alive by a Gjinn or killed off by a Dragonian or whatever they're called. Once we make it to Greenland, then perhaps getting out of here will be something worth contemplating. *But how do you tell the guy she's a virgin and never been touched by a man till us?* I can feel my head begin to pound as I serve up the dinner.

"What's up?" Brad's baritone voice comes from the breakfast bar to my right. *Shit. He knows nothing either.* Though then again, he doesn't need to know anything more than we're all heading off tomorrow, him included.

Letting a breath of air out, I pause in what I'm doing. "Kia's energy has already returned to max and is still increasing apparently. Jack wants to head off at first light for Greenland. The mountain there will mask her energy. Then they're going to administer a serum to cleanse her of the infection so that she can pass into Mid Gaia," I try to summarise. "Jack wants us all to pack suitable clothing, including you," I say reluctantly, knowing he has commitments of his own. He frowns as he considers my words, so I continue to finish serving, then begin taking the plates over to the table.

"I'm sure I can move stuff about with my clients. How long do ya think we'll be gone?" Brad queries lightly. *Fuck. I pause in my tracks slightly and hope he doesn't notice. How the fucking hell am I going to explain this shit to him? I'm pretty sure he's seen Rolland and Kia together. Does he think it's just a fling?*

Rolland and Kia step through the kitchen door before I can say anymore, so I leave it for now. *Is this how Jack feels? Always needing to keep a mask in place, afraid of revealing truths that could upset the balance of the house?* I keep my eyes down, as I continue taking the plates over to the long solid wood table.

Turning with the last dish which just happens to be Kia's, I find her standing in front of me, her head bowed low, so I can't see her eyes. I flick mine up to Rolland, who's sitting at the top of the table with his back to me, digging into his dinner already. I look back down at Kia, my eyes catching on her head of hair that shines much like my own. *You would think it would be full of knots as it's not been brushed, but it just seems to fall gently with a natural wave to it.*

Using the hand that's free, I tilt her face up, so I can see her eyes, but she keeps them shut while chewing on her lip. *How frustrating must it be not being able to talk? With the only means of communicating being through someone else, giving you no privacy or independence?* Her eyes flash open at me, showing me her deep blue sapphire eyes, that pulse once again remaining steady, continuing to swirl like they always do. *Shit. Can she hear me?* She blinks once. Then pulls her face away, taking her plate from my hand, before reaching up on her toes and kissing me on the lips. Stunned as to what the hell just happened, I stand there, watching her make her way back to the table to sit beside Rolland on his left. *What the fuck?*

The kitchen door opens again and Matt walks through. I turn to him but catch Brad watching in my peripheral vision. Matt still seems a little shaken from Kia's stare down earlier, as he rubs the back of his neck, flicking his eyes over to her and then to me.

"You're okay, Matt. I think she feels bad for it. And I'm confident she was just protecting Rolland. Again," I try to explain. Matt takes a visible breath, then heads over to his place at the table which is to the right of Rolland. I turn my gaze to Brad, who's looking at me with incredibly raised eyebrows. *Why? Why me? Why do I get left with the heavy shit to explain?* This is definitely a conversation that needs to be spoken aloud, not one done through thought, at the dinner table.

"Later," I say to him. He nods before making his way over to sit on the other side of Matt, while I take my seat to Kia's left.

The table is surrounded in a heavy silence as I take my seat and I do a quick assessment of everyone. Rolland looks more or less back to his usual self, with just a ghost of a shadow under his eyes. Matt has his head down, focusing his attention solely on his dinner. *Poor guy must feel entirely out of his depth with how to handle Kia's mood.* Kia's leg brushes up against mine, but no energy flows from it, so I ignore it and continue studying everyone. Brad looks as relaxed as Rolland, though his gaze keeps flicking up to Kia a little more than the usual. But then again, it's Kia.

I turn my attention to her, watching as she picks at her food, not seeming to be as keen as she was earlier today. She lets out a breath, slouching a bit then leans into me, so her head is resting on my right bicep. I glance up to Rolland who polishes off his food but skates his eyes up to Kia before resuming his focus on his now empty plate. He stretches his muscles out before standing to take his dish to the sink and begins clearing up. I move my arm carefully around Kia's back, tentatively placing it over her as I watch Rolland's movements. As my arm rests down on her back, he pauses, seeming to compose himself, then carries on with the dishes. Kia turns into me further, sliding her arms around my body. I finally feel her energy working its way up through my veins and a part of me feels like I'm taking a breath for the first time in hours. Using my free hand, I continue to eat my dinner.

Matt peeks up at us and I know he wants to be doing the same with her. Brad finishes his dinner next, even though he had a double size portion of everything. He takes his plate over to Rolland and begins helping him tidy up the kitchen.

"Come sit with us once you're done, Matt," I say to him. His eyes flick over her, then up to me before giving me a nod. I watch Rolland to see if I can get a read on him, but his focus is on the dishes, though his shoulders appear tense from behind.

Matt finally finishes, brings his plate to Rolland to rinse, then comes back. He sits on Kia's right side, taking Rolland's seat, looking incredibly awkward and unsure of what to do. *All he wants to do is pull her into his arms, but he won't, as he's too afraid of hurting or upsetting her.*

Kia eases herself from me slowly, then turns to Matt, her head still low. Matt creeps his arm back in invitation, yet still unsure of what to do. Kia seems to decide for him, as she shifts herself so she's sitting sideways on his lap, with her back to me, tucking her head into his neck before taking a deep breath and relaxing as though falling asleep. I see Rolland relax completely, as he looks up at the ceiling as though he's thanking the heavens. He puts down the cloth in his hand and walks over to us with a content look on his face, before placing a kiss on Kia's crown, then turns and heads out of the kitchen.

"Seb's room, Matt, when you're ready for bed," Rolland calls before closing the door after him.

Brad frowns, confused, as he stands at the kitchen door, obviously not understanding any of this, then raises his brow at me in the hope of getting some kind of explanation.

"She kinda... grows attached to you. Then there's the small part where she doesn't have any understanding of the male species," I offer, flicking my eyes to Kia's back for a beat. "She may have glared a little at Matt earlier and now they're making up. Rolland's just content because she's finally at peace, though I'm pretty sure she's not sleeping," I explain. Brad's eyebrows go up to his hairline and then drop into a deep furrow, as he tries to process everything I just said.

"So, how long am I rescheduling for?" he asks simply, as he puts away the last few pans. *Shit. I think it's about time I start telling him stuff.*

Taking a deep breath, I try to keep it as simple as possible. "Jack says his people have built a craft, strong enough to get through the storms that circle Gaia. It's due to be completed within the next few weeks. It's in the same mountain that we're heading to at first light," I say, keeping my tone as neutral as possible, folding my arms over one another as I lean on the table.

Brad raises an eyebrow at me again. "And he just told you this today?" he clarifies, before heading over to the fridge.

"No, last night before he left to speak with the Atlantians, just after I spoke to you," I justify, knowing he won't be pleased that he didn't hear this sooner. "He went to see if they would cleanse Kia so that she can pass through to Mid Gaia," I tell him, hoping he understands what I'm trying to say, without saying it.

He moves back over toward the table. "And?" he questions.

"He hasn't said. The conversation went off course slightly when he wouldn't answer my question regarding Kia and Rolland becoming more attached." My tone turns a little sharp at the end.

Brad's eyes flicker over to Kia, then back to me. His eyes soften as a thought occurs to him. He takes the lid off the beer, then takes a long swig before placing it down on the table in front of him, leaning his weight forward. "From what I've seen, I'd say she has become attached to not just Rolland, but you and Matt as well. So why the extreme worry over him and not all of you?" he asks curiously, as his eyes deepen slightly, giving me the sense of safety in his presence.

"Kia has become far more attached with Rolland than she has with us. Jack says they're sharing energy as their souls recognise each other. But he doesn't know what would happen if they're separated," I tell him heavily. "I've never seen anything like the way he looks at her, and her him. You have to see it to know what I mean. Then there's her rage that she slips into when one of us is being threatened, and I'm pretty sure I saw Rolland go into that same kind of rage earlier, but Kia seemed to pull him out before he lost himself to it," I try explaining. "I have feelings for her myself, though there's not an ounce of jealousy toward Rolland or Matt when I see them touching her. My sole focus just seems to fixate on making her smile. The rest becomes inconsequential."

His gaze that has been steadily on me now moves to Kia. He takes another pull of his beer before speaking. "So, is this a case of playing it by ear? Or do I need to start wrapping stuff up in preparation for the possibility of leaving Gaia?" His deep voice sounds rational, as though we're discussing what mode of transport to take on holiday. He must read my thoughts on my face as he continues to talk.

"It's pretty clear to see, Seb. It's always been just a matter of time. We know we don't belong here, though I never thought I'd ever get off this forsaken plane. Yes, I have commitments, but they're there to fill a void. Just like you can't explain much of what you see happening around ya with Kia, I can't explain why I need to get out of here. It's always been a matter of time, Sebastian. That's all." His words carry so much meaning, even though his tone remains steady as does the look in his deep amber eyes.

And just like that, I feel a weight lift from my shoulders, and I lean back in my chair, finally able to relax somewhat.

"I would say that once we reach Greenland and we know if Kia can be cleansed, we can then talk time frame of how long we have left here. Though I guess that once we get there, internet and phone reception is going to be poor, so I would advise you to wrap up as much stuff up as possible with the expectation it will be at least several weeks." My words feel right as I say them, and I pull my gaze away from Brad to look at Kia's back.

Her breathing is completely even, as though she's sleeping. Knowing I still need to pack, I stand and conclude my conversation with Brad. "I'm going to pack a bag, so I'm ready in the morning, though I just realised Jack never said if we're taking the chopper or what."

Brad stands and begins making his way to the door with me. "It would make sense to take the chopper as it's faster. Which mountain did he say we're going to?" he asks before taking another swig of his beer.

"He hasn't. He was a little shaken by Kia's display of...

whatever it is she does to him," I say, smiling as I think about Jack being taken down a peg or two. I see Brad frowning at my smile. "Trust me. You have to see it," I say with a laugh.

Turning back to look at Matt and Kia before I walk through the kitchen door, I see he's still got her curled up in his lap, her head tucked comfortably into his neck. He looks to be sleeping himself as he rests his own face on her head. Happy that they've reconciled things, I head off to my room to get ready.

CHAPTER FORTY-FOUR

*M*att

I hope never again to see Kia look at me the way she did earlier. I didn't want to upset Rolland, yet he needed to know that Kia has to go home to her people and the chances of us surviving the serum are abysmal. The only alternative is to stay here and wait for the craft to be complete, then go look for her after. Though what are the chances we would find her? There are no maps of how to get in and out of Mid Gaia unless Jack knows the routes.

Kia still sits within my arms, her nose tucked into my neck, and if my body would allow it, I'd sit here all night till we had to leave. *Though I wouldn't be much good flying the chopper half asleep.* With that thought of encouragement, I stand slowly, sliding an arm under Kia's legs to support her weight. She shifts herself slightly with my movements and I begin to wonder if I'm hurting her back. Her energy flows from where her cheek now rests against my chest, seeming to ease some of my worries.

Thankfully, Seb's left the kitchen door open, so I don't need to juggle her about trying to open it. I make my way to

Seb's room wondering if I can just keep her like this and pack in the morning. Just set the alarm and get up before the rest of the house.

Rounding the corridor that takes me through to Seb's room, I find Rolland sitting up against the headboard in his usual spot closest to the door on the bed, studying his phone - most likely going through emails regarding the farm, or maybe looking for possible stopping off points.

Seb is to my right, quietly packing a bag at his chest of drawers but stops when he sees us. He runs his eyes over her and a small smile appears on his face.

"You're not going to put her down to pack, are you?" His voice is full of mirth. A smile plays along my own lips as I head over to the other side of the bed. Rolland still hasn't looked up as he continues to study his phone.

Sitting carefully so as to not wake her, I ease myself down as though I'm holding a newborn baby that's just fallen asleep.

"She won't wake, Matt." Rolland's voice comes from behind me, though it sounds like he's only giving me half his attention as he speaks. "She's not sleeping per se, but she won't stir if you move her either. Just be careful of your movements near her back," he finishes, still sounding distracted.

Unsure of how to move her without causing her pain, I turn my back to the headboard, as I swing my legs up. *There, that wasn't so bad.*

Rolland finally turns his head to me, his eyes full of humour and life. Glad to see him smiling again, I give him one of my own. Silently, I wish never to see such a tortured look on his face ever again. He returns his focus to his phone just as Seb appears from the bathroom with a few bits to go in his bag.

Deciding to get more comfortable, I pluck my phone from my pocket and settle in. I need to check if Gregg has replied yet but there's nothing. Putting it to the side, I slide my feet under the duvet before pulling it up to cover Kia's shoulders. I run my eyes over her face, taking in the dark eyelashes that fan against her fine lightly bronzed skin, which is looking slightly lighter tonight, with the depth of colour fading around her neckline. My eyes take in her pink lips that darken and swell as they do after being kissed. Her round face and delicate features are so unique to her - I doubt I'll ever see anything like them again. I move my eyes over her black ebony hair, wondering how it shines and doesn't mat without brushing it. Dipping my head forward to breathe her in, I fill my lungs with her scent. My gel has faded, leaving just her own unique essence, which I haven't been able to pinpoint. At first, I thought she smelt like the forest after it has rained – fresh and clean but with the hint of wet wood. Then it changed to something exotic, almost fruit-like, with the undertones of sweetness to it. As I breathe her in now, I can smell the sea, as though it's pooling around my feet, calming me into a state of tranquillity.

My body unwinds with each breath, pulling me deeper into relaxation. I ease our bodies down the headboard, turning onto my left side to curl her deeper into me, then bury my face in her hair. Snaking my arms around her waist to hold her against me, sleep finds me fast, knowing she's safe in my arms.

CHAPTER FORTY-FIVE

*R*olland

    Something stirs me awake, but my ears don't pick up on any sounds, so I have no idea what it could be. I feel for the connection to Kia and find it's strong and steady, except she's not next to Matt where she fell asleep. I feel for her emotions to find curiousness and worry flow back to me. Following the connection, I find it leads through to the front of the house. *What is she up to now? The little minx can't keep out of trouble for more than five minutes.*

Forcing my eyes open, I let them adjust for a few seconds to the light coming from the lamp. More worry flows from Kia, prodding at my senses and waking me up further.

"Kia, what are you doing?" I ask her curiously, sitting up before swinging my legs off the bed. She doesn't reply, concerning me more, but after a few more seconds of trying to wake my stiff eyes up, her feathery voice trickles through.

"Something not right, Rolland." Her voice is full of apprehension, raising the hairs on my neck.

"You not being here in my arms is what is not right," I try reassuring her, making my way to Seb's door.

Pain fires through my stomach, pulling a breath from me and causing me to falter in my step, followed by another shot of pain, forcing me to double over, folding myself in half and falling to my knees. I try to drag air into my lungs, but I can't. Another blast of pain hits me again, nearly rendering me unconscious. Putting my hands on my stomach, I find no blood, but the pain is still there. KIA!

I can't take air into my lungs to call the guys and my body feels like it's caving in from the pain that's spreading up my body.

"SEBASTIAN! MATT!" I shout into their minds.

The pain continues to spread, then stops as she pulls it back into herself. Dragging air in desperately, I yell at the top of my voice, "SEB! MATT!!"

Tugging hard on our connection, the pain returns to me, but with it, the inability to speak or move. I hear Seb jump off the bed and he's by my side in a fraction of a second.

"KIA. FRONT DOOR!" I shout again through their minds, still curled up on my knees. They both scramble from the room as Kia pulls on the connection, grasping for control of the pain, while she tries to shut me out of her feelings. Remorse soaks every inch of her and it's as though she's drowning in it. Anger seeps through, followed by more guilt as I see Matt's and Seb's faces flash across my vision from her own thoughts. She tugs hard and I lose my grip on it.

Hauling myself to my feet, I drag more air into my starved lungs, gaining some strength back in my limbs. I manage a few steps into the hallway, then stagger right, heading toward the front door. Feeling along our connection, I find her drowning in pain and darkness, lost to all other feelings. I yank hard on the link and pain covers me like a suffocating blanket. Heat, acid and something else crawls in my stomach, making me stumble over my feet but I grab for the wall to balance myself. I blunder a few more steps before she pulls the pain back, freeing me again. A couple of more steps and I see her as I round the corner. Seb has her in his arms, speaking to her as she curls her body in tight from the pain. I yank hard once more on the thread, and the pain returns, but I can't feel her emotions - the connection is fading.

Kia relaxes as the pain leaves her and comes to me. I force myself up on my feet, filled with determination after seeing her, but as I move toward her, the pain is pulled from me once more, allowing me to take a lung full of air. I stagger the last bit of the way, feeling for our connection to drag her pain back, but there's nothing there.

Taking her out of Seb's arms, I cradle her head in my hands. "KIA! DON'T YOU DARE DO THIS!" I scream at her.

Light catches in my peripheral vision from my right, but I don't turn to look. All my focus is on Kia, who has gone completely limp - I feel no emotions, no pain and no connection to her.

"KIA, PLEASE DON'T. DON'T SHUT ME OUT!!!" I scream at her. My heart is pounding in my ears and the world begins to fade out.

I need to feel her, any emotion, something. Any-fucking-thing. "Please, Kia, baby, just let me feel you, sweetheart," I whisper into her ear, but it comes out garbled through my emotions. Unchecked tears coat my cheeks and my heart feels like it's being squeezed tight by some unknown vice.

Seb's voice floats through to me, but I can't hear his words. Everything around me has been muted, leaving only Kia's face in focus in my hands. As I look down at her small lifeless frame, I find it soaked in blood. *So much blood.* Lifting her head to my chest, I still feel nothing.

"Rolland, she's still alive." Seb's intense voice simmers somewhere.

I ease her head back to look at her face. "I can't feel her," I hoarsely whisper to him. "Kia, please," I try one last time. Nothing.

Something begins to crawl its way up inside me. A darkness that's looking for revenge for taking something so innocent, pure, and beautiful from this world. She's suffered so much, only to be allowed a few hours of freedom before her life was taken from her. *Why?* The crawling feeling within me spreads, tracking its way through my limbs, fuelling my need to destroy something. I feel a hand on my shoulder, followed by a shit load of calming energy, immobilising me completely.

But I can't just sit here. I want to destroy something. I NEED to destroy something.

Kia's face still lays within my hands. *She deserves to be avenged. Every single one of them and anyone who stands in my way. They need to be removed from existence.*

The noise around me has faded out, leaving the only sound of my own pounding heart within my ears. Kia is pulled from my arms, but I'm still left paralysed by whoever has their hand on my shoulder. *Someone has taken her from my hands and they're going to die. Slowly. Painfully. With no remorse.*

Calmness is forced on me, but I push back on it, hard, not willing to allow anyone to stand between Kia and me. Someone has taken her from me. *How. Fucking. Dare. They. Her place is in my heart. And I can't feel her anymore.* Rage fills me and I begin to push against the hand that's holding me paralysed with the calming energy. *It needs to be removed.*

Fixating on the image of Kia's face in my mind, I lift my

hand slowly to the one that's resting on my shoulder. Some of the noise around me begins to filter in, but my focus remains on whoever stopped me from keeping Kia in my arms. Letting the rage take over, I allow it to do its work. I move to my feet fast and push the body belonging to said hand against the wall, my hand around its throat, squeezing hard. A pretty face stares back at me, and a small part of me recognises that face, but I don't care for it. The owner of it needs to die. Slowly. I begin tightening my fingers. The eyes I see flash blue and something within my mind tries to nudge at me to stop.

Why would I want to stop? That's a stupid thought. The pretty face needs to be demolished into smithereens. So, I squeeze harder as I'm encouraged on by the darkness that's fuelling my energy. It craves death, just as I do.

Energy moves up my arm from the pretty face and I'm pushed back slightly. My hand begins to loosen as the blue light from the pretty face starts to get brighter.

I'm forced back hard and thrown against the wall behind me and as my head hits the wall hard, fall into unconscious.

CHAPTER FORTY-SIX

*S*ebastian
    "SEB! MATT!!" Rolland's shouts pull me from my sleep. I'm up off the bed and by his side in a fraction of a second. Rolland's curled up on his knees, not far from the bedroom door. *"KIA. FRONT DOOR!"* he roars in my head.

Matt scrabbles off the bed and is at my heels as I sprint to the front door. Time slows the closer I get to it as I spot Kia's form laying limp by the open front door, her stomach covered in blood from what must be gunshot wounds. Her body seems to come to life, as she curls herself into a fetal position, sucking in a desperate breath. Sinking to my knees, I pull her to me, taking a quick glance out the front door - and I find our front garden is swarming with beings.

Matt throws up a shield to hold them off, so I turn my gaze back to Kia, drawing her further into my arms as I try getting her to open her body up so that I can look at the wounds.

"Kia, sweetie, I need to get to your stomach, so I can heal you," I try coaxing her while pushing my hand against her side, but she curls in tighter, turning into me. There's so much

342

blood seeping from her, but I can't get my hand to the wounds.

"Come on, Kia, let me take the bullets out, so I can heal you. Just listen to my voice, sweetheart," I encourage. Her body finally relaxes, giving me a chance to lift her vest up, but before I can get to work, she pulls herself back in tight, curling up in pain again.

I lift her face up to mine to study her. She opens her eyes a fraction, allowing me to see her pupils. Blackness is fighting the silver within them and as they find mine, I catch the silver winning before she goes completely limp. I check for a pulse which beats steadily, thankful that she's just passed out from the pain.

Rolland yanks her roughly from my arms, then shouts, "KIA! DON'T YOU DARE DO THIS!" His face is covered in tears and he's looking half-crazed. My heart breaks for him, knowing how deep his feelings go for her.

Matt's shield pulses, growing considerably, which catches my eye and I turn to find it looking like it did after the Gjinn attacked. It's translucent and multicoloured swirling energy pulses, forcing the beings back.

"KIA, PLEASE DON'T. DON'T SHUT ME OUT" Rolland screams at her in front of me. I look back to Rolland as he draws her closer to his head and whispers to her, "please, Kia, baby… just… let me… feel you… sweetheart." His voice breaks as he tries to get his words out.

"Rolland, she's still alive. I need to get the bullets out and heal her. Let me get to her, Brother," I appeal to him, trying to get to her stomach, but he doesn't seem to hear me. He's breaking apart before my very eyes, and the life within him that brings so much happiness when he's around is fading.

"Rolland, she's still alive," I explain, trying to use a more demanding tone in order to get through to him.

"I can't feel her," he whispers, but doesn't raise his head from her ear.

"Kia, please." My heart feels like it's been torn up through my throat. Hearing the agony in those two words, I feel my own eyes begin to sting. *I know she's still alive. I felt her pulse. She's just gone under.*

Jack appears to my right as Brad's feet thunder down the stairs. I peer up at Jack, having no clue whether to heal Kia or fight off whoever is out the front. Jack stares out the front door, taking in the number of beings out there and Matt's shield, then fixates his eyes on me. When he finally starts talking, he uses a tone that leaves no room for questions or doubt. "Brad, take Kia and get her out of here. Sebastian, go with him so you can heal Kia," he commands, then places his right hand on Rolland's shoulder. I watch as Rolland's face becomes impassive. "NOW!!" Jack shouts through clenched teeth, shining with a madness of their own.

Brad bends low, easing Kia from Rolland's arms, as an explosion comes from the roof, shaking the whole house. The sound of glass shattering fills my ears as pictures fall from the walls and the few lights that remain on flicker.

"Use the truck, Brad. We will be right behind you, just make sure to WAIT FOR MATT," Jack grinds out, his focus remaining on Rolland beneath his hand. "GO!" he roars.

My heart wants to stay by Rolland, but the influence behind Jack's command forces my body to follow Brad, who's making his way through the house to the back. More explosions come from above, vibrating the walls but they remain steady. I keep my eyes glued to Brad's broad back as I feel a tear slip down my cheek. I don't bother to chase it away, but take a steadying breath, trying to stay focused. *Kia needs me. If I crack now, I'll never have enough energy to heal her.*

We hurry past the door that leads to the gym then pass the corridor that leads to the healing chamber. Kia's face when Matt referred to her as, 'springing up like a jack-in-the-box' comes to mind, pulling another tear from me. I take another steadying breath as we round the corner to the garage that Brad works in. The house shakes again from another explosion and all the lights go out. A section of the garage roof collapses, but my quick reflexes kick in. I leap back avoiding the debris, but catch Brad curling himself into a ball, Kia tight within his arms, as chunks of wood, plaster and floorboards fall onto them, burying them. My heart sinks as I take in all the debris covering them and I fear the weight of it is crushing them.

Movement stirs within the rubble, then Brad pops up, shakes the dust off his head and continues on as though someone had just laid a light blanket over him, not the tons of cement, plaster and wood that I know was there. *This is the reason why Jack had Brad take Kia; he's basically indestructible.* Brad trudges through the gap that was made in the wall from the explosion, so I leap over the debris to follow him.

He waits by his Range Rover at the back-passenger door for me to take Kia from him. When I catch up, he eases her into my arms then opens the door for me. I climb in, drawing Kia further into my body, running my eyes over her small form which is still steadily bleeding.

Holding her head in my left arm, I lift her top up to see three gunshot wounds in her gut. Pushing my finger into a hole, I begin searching for the bullet, but with each movement my finger makes within her, more blood flows from her. Brad's door slams shut, and he starts the engine.

"Brad, I need you to pull the bullets out," I say desperately. He turns in his seat and takes in the amount of blood that's seeping from her. He swallows deeply - not from the sight of blood, even though there's just so much of it, but from fear, his fear for her life. He gently places his large left hand over her stomach and gets to work extracting the metal bullets from her. He retrieves the first one, dropping it to the floor, then pulls the remaining two out, dropping them too before running his eyes over me, looking concerned.

He turns back to the steering wheel as I get to work healing her, intent on knitting all the tissue, muscles, stomach lining and skin back together. Once done, I pull her closer, checking for her pulse once again. Her heart beats strong and steady and it's almost as though she's just sleeping. As I stay focused on her, I feel her pulse falter, just once, and my own heart follows the same pattern. But just like that, the anomaly is gone and her heart returns to its even cadence. I turn her head to me and hold her close, wondering what the fuck we do now. Just then, Jack's parting words begin to ring through my head on repeat. *JUST WAIT FOR MATT.....*

CHAPTER FORTY-SEVEN

*M*att
Kia's body lays covered in blood by the wide-open front door and moonlight pours in, illuminating her body. My legs can't seem to move fast enough to get to her. Seb pulls her into his arms as I instinctively throw a shield up outside the house. Energy pushes against the barrier, testing its strength, but I hold strong.

Seb tries to speak to Kia, but she curls herself tighter into a ball. More energy dives against my shield, harder, drawing my attention away from them. I turn my focus out the front door and my heart falters. They haven't reached the stone drive, but they are swarming the grass that surrounds it. I see three Gjinns, a dozen black-eyed humanoid beings that I recognise from my visions with Kia, with relatively normal looking men bringing up the rear. And, in at the centre of it all, is one of the men that tortured Kia. He's as tall as Rolland, though his build isn't as broad around the shoulders and he doesn't have the chiseled look that defines Rolland. He has a slight dip in his step as he prowls toward my shield, smiling venomously like he's already got Kia within his grasp. I rake my eyes over him, taking in his short buzzed dark hair and clean-cut face that shows his rough skin in the glow of the moonlight. Dark eyes find mine, looking for weakness.

I thrust more energy into my shield, spurred on by his taunting look. Too many months have I stood by and watched this piece of scum touch Kia, unable to do anything about it. The only way he'll get to her now is over my dead body. I hear Seb behind me, but I keep my focus on the man trying to get to Kia. I can feel the Gjinn's combined energy pushing at my shield, trying to force their way through, working with the black-eyed beings who are trying to suck power from it.

Rolland's voice shouts from behind, but I still don't turn my attention away from what's happening outside, keeping my focus purely on holding them off. More energy is sucked from my shield, yanking at my hand as the dark-haired man runs his fingers over it as though he's tasting it through touch. Energy slams into me from my back, moving through my arms, down my legs, comforting me with reassurance. It flows through my hand, pulling hard and, using me as a conduit, it shoots out from me, adding to my shield.

The shield changes from its translucent white, to the multicoloured, swirling brightness that Kia made when she transferred her energy through it before. The extra power in the shield shoves all the beings at least ten yards back from the stone drive. As I feel the power stir within me, it calms my racing heart and eases the tension from round my shoulders. I immediately recognise it as Kia's, which confuses me, making me want to turn to see her, but I can't as my body feels like it's hardening to stone.

"I sorry, Matt." I'm finally hearing her, which causes my heart to race. *Why is she sorry?*

"You have nothing to be sorry for, Kia. It's us who have failed you," I point out.

"I lonely." Her silvery tone slips through my mind, reminding me of softly lapping waves. I feel her emotions leak through to my heart as though she was standing inside me - remorse and sadness engulfs us.

"So much darkness. I thought I would lose myself to it." Her voice sounds foreign, curling in certain places as it trickles through my mind, raising the hairs on my neck. *What is she talking about?*

"It never stops. Never. I needed-" Kia tries to continue, but it sounds like she's struggling. More of her emotions course into my heart and it feels almost like guilt.

"Needed comfort. Something hold onto." Her words still don't make sense.

Is this why she came to the front door? To look for comfort?

"Searched everywhere. But everything dark and shut off."

I frown, trying to figure out her words. *"Kia, what are you talking about?"* I ask tentatively.

"Then I find you." Her voice is so quiet, but I grab onto her words like a lifeline.

Then a vision floats across my mind - it's me, sleeping in my bed and I see what could be described as perhaps the ghostly shape of Kia stepping up to me. She sits beside me on the bed, running her small fingers through my hair.

"Your mind beautiful, open, full- same need have in me." Her voice lightens slightly, then more remorse falls over me like someone has poured a bucket of it over my head, trying to drown me.

"Kia, it's okay," I try to ease gently.

"Went in you and found comfort I look for." Her voice becomes a little steadier, though her emotions are still heavy,

weighing my heart down. The vision she's showing me moves as the ghost-like shape of her seeps into my head, caressing it, then dissipates, along with the image.

"Feeling you, everything darkness and pain, made breath work," her voice breaks again, curling with her unusual accent. Another vision slides across my mind, showing one of the times I stood and watched her being burnt with a branding iron. Her scream pierces my ears and I feel tears begin to slide unbidden down my cheeks.

"Kia, it's me who did wrong, not you, I should've spoken to the guys sooner. Got you out of there sooner. It's my fault you suffered for so long," I elucidate, feeling more tears slide down my cheeks. *"Let me make it up to you!"* I appeal, hoping she'll forgive me.

"There much pain, Matt," her voice begs me to listen to her. More tears pour out and I'm not sure if I'm breathing anymore.

"Sebastian will heal you, but you need to stay with us and go back to your body," I implore with every ounce of my soul.

"He not keep heal me. Every count, more his energy flow in me, connect deeper, like you and Rolland. I hear thoughts, then he hear me, like Rolland," her voice urges me to understand.

"Kia, it doesn't matter, all we want is for you to be safe, healed, and to get you home," I tell her desperately.

"I not remember home or any people there." I feel her heartbreak as she confesses to me. *"All I know you. Rolland, Sebastian, Jack, Brad. Even Gerry. He cares you all and sits heavy in his mind when he dreams."* Her words become slightly cracked as her emotions overwhelm her.

"Kia, Rolland needs you. I need you. Sebastian would not

think twice to heal you, even if it meant him being connected to you for the rest of his existence." Keeping my tone firm, I try to rein in some of my own emotions, but with the treacherous tears flowing, I fool no one.

But she doesn't listen to my words as she continues pouring her heart out into mine. *"I feel spreading, Matt. And now spreads through Rolland."* My heart falls into my stomach at her words.

Like a puppet, she turns my head from the mob outside the front door to look inside the house. To my right, Rolland has Jack pinned up against the wall, strangling him. Rolland's eyes are black with no light left within them. He looks demented, his sole thought being to kill Jack. Kia shows me another image of Rolland's eyes turning black before Kia's face looms within his view, settling his eyes back to their usual deep blue. Guilt and sadness are all Kia feels as she blames herself for Rolland's behaviour.

She turns my head back to the beings outside, drawing my focus back to the man who runs his hand over my shield again. He isn't smiling anymore though. The house shakes beneath my feet, and a look of determination crosses over the man's face.

"If stay. They come. I not take Rolland from me. It is he part of me, like you. Feelings for you, Rolland and Sebastian too much. You all I know. If take you, my mind and heart not accept, if do to you, what they to me." Kia's words become desperate, pleading almost.

"I DON'T CARE, KIA!" I shout back to her, trying to get her to see sense. *"All I know is that I need you, Rolland needs you. You can't leave us!"*

I can feel her intentions. She's leaving to go somewhere that she can't be followed.

"KIA!!!" I can't breathe. Her energy stays within me, keeping the shield up, but her presence within my mind disperses, leaving a silence in its wake. I feel empty, even though her energy still flows through my hand, keeping the shield up.

The house shakes again under my feet and noise returns to my ears.

"Matt," Jack's crackling voice comes from my right. I turn and find him carrying Rolland over his right shoulder. Red fingerprints mark his neck deeply from where Rolland strangled him, and his eyes are slightly red too, full of emotions that make my stomach turn.

My hand begins to tremble from the onslaught of reality. Rolland losing it with Jack. Jack breaking his mask. Kia leaving. And the beings that will stop at nothing to get to her.

Jack speaks clearly to me, knowing I'm desperately holding on to my last thread of sanity. "We need to get to Brad's truck, Matt. Rolland is fine and so are you. Just take a deep breath and focus on each step, alright?" Jack requests tentatively.

I've never heard him speak like that before, but I nod as more tears keep flowing like an unattended water faucet. I drag air into my lungs and focus on moving my feet. Jack passes me, stepping out of the front door, so I follow him. My shield changes colour as I feel more of Kia's energy flow through it.

Suddenly the colours of my shield stop swirling, deepening into a dense blue, and obscuring the beings from seeing us. Jack's head lifts to watch the shield change as he continues down the stone steps, then turns right toward the back of the house. The house has been destroyed on either side from explosions, and I feel something hit the shield hard, but it doesn't falter.

Keeping my focus on Jack's back, I take a steadying breath to calm my pounding heart. Moving my hand to pull the shield with us, it doesn't budge, but stays in place at the front of the house, holding the beings back. As we round the last corner and I spot Brad's truck waiting.

CHAPTER FORTY-EIGHT

*B*rad
Keeping an eye on the side mirror, my foot is twitching, ready to get the hell out of here. It's one thing talking about fighting a Gjinn; it's another seeing three of them outside your front door. Not to mention the hoard of creepy black-eyed beings that look similar to the one I was fighting at the building Rolland found Kia in.

I glance to my right at the house, taking in the damage made by the grenades that managed to get passed Matt's shield from above. Rolland's room on the second floor has crumbled down within itself, the majority of being what fell on Kia and me. Moving my gaze to look at Seb in the rear-view mirror, I find he's calmed slightly since healing Kia. For a minute there, I honestly wondered if he had completely cracked. Not that he's an unemotional guy, but he holds his feelings close to his chest, much like Jack does, hiding them behind a mask. To see Seb breaking as he did was downright concerning. I watch him as he tucks Kia tight to his chest, before kissing her crown then burying his nose deep in her hair. His face has calmed, but not his eyes. He worries for

Rolland and about Jack's words - w*ait for Matt; he didn't say wait for the rest of us.*

Movement catches my eyes in the side mirror, and I see two figures illuminated by the light, just visible from the moon behind the clouds. One looks a lot taller and broader at the shoulder than the other. My heart begins to pound slightly and my grip on the steering wheel tightens a fraction, but Matt hasn't returned, so we can't leave. Silver hair catches in the moonlight, easing my heart slightly as I make out Jack, who has Rolland slumped over his shoulder. *Shit. What the fuck happened?*

As they draw nearer, Matt leaves Jack's side and heads around to the passenger front seat. Jack continues to the driver's side and opens the door behind me, setting Rolland's body down inside, as Matt opens the passenger door and climbs in. After Rolland is settled, Jack pauses for a few moments before speaking to Seb in a voice that sounds strained, almost as though he's got a sore throat. "Keep them together, and within sight of each other. I do not think she will wake. If she does, tell her to stay with him." Jack sucks in a breath as though he's struggling to breathe. He closes the door before opening mine and his face looks... wrong. His eyes are slightly red, not the cool crisp blue I know them to be, his neck is sporting a heavy red bruise that looks to be getting worse, and there's a roughness around his features that just doesn't look right on him.

"Head to Rolland's farm. Only stop for fuel. I will grab your bags and find you along the route." His voice strains as he forces each word out with intention, purpose, and past the pain in his throat. I nod in acknowledgement, ready to get heck out of here. "Take the dirt road you had put in." With those final scratchy words, he closes the door and vanishes.

Putting the truck into four-wheel drive, I start across the

back garden, heading to the dirt road that leads to the back roads. Matt's uneven breathing beside me catches my attention, but I keep my focus on finding the dirt road. After a few minutes, my mind starts wondering if maybe those creepy beings might have blocked our back exit too. But then I find the bumpy dirt road and fortunately we don't run into anyone. The road finally opens onto a single-track back road, allowing me to pick up some speed.

My thoughts turn from Jack's throat, to Rolland's unconscious form in the back, and finally settle on Matt's erratic breathing which he can't seem to get under control, even though he's trying his hardest. It's worrisome. I flick my gaze to Seb in the back, but he's settled so far back into the shadows that I can't see his face.

"Matt, there's a bottle of water in the glove box, try and have a drink for me, Brother," I encourage, keeping my eyes on the road. He doesn't move for a few moments but eventually leans forward to find the bottle. His hands are shaking badly, though it's uncertain whether it's from shock or the amount of energy he used to hold the shield in place around the house.

Wishing I had something to calm his nerves, I try talking to him in the tone I've used with Gerry in the past. "Kia is in the back in Seb's arms, not in theirs. The bullets are out, and he has already healed the wounds, she just needs rest." I glance over at him as he screws the lid back on the bottle. "Rolland's fine. He just needs to wake up. Nothing changed." I push as much energy into my voice as possible, trying to ease some of his shaking.

"Rolland tried to kill Jack." Matt's whisper is barely audible as it rushes out of his trembling body. "He filled up with rage like Kia does and strangled him." Matt tries to pull a breath in to calm his body, but it refuses to listen to him.

"She thinks it's her fault," he grits out, still leaning forward in his chair. *What? When did he speak to her? Rolland tried to strangle Jack? Rolland enjoys a good fight, but I'd never imagine him throttling someone.* I scrunch my face up in response to Matt's words.

But he's not done sharing. "She doesn't remember anything or anyone from her home. All she knows is us." He tries to even his voice out as he talks, but his breath pulls in at the end. "Every time Seb heals her, he's connecting to her more deeply, strengthening and growing it, like the connection she has with Rolland." He takes another breath in. "And me." He rests his head into his hands, leaning over his knees.

Glancing up to Seb in the mirror, I still can't make out his face where it remains hidden in the shadows. I reach over to Matt and place a hand on his back, hoping to give him a bit of reassurance. Luckily, it seems to help as I hear his breathing finally calm and feel some of the tension ease in his back. After a few miles, Matt finally sits back in his seat, turning to face the window.

I decide to mind-speak so as not to disturb Matt. *"How's Rolland?"* I ask.

"Just passed out. He had a bad bash to the back of his head, but I've already healed it. He may have a bit of a headache when he wakes, but that's about it," he comments with an even tone.

"And Kia?" Silence follows for a long time.

"Her heart is steady but it's as though she's in a deep sleep. Every few minutes it flutters slightly, like hummingbird wings, then evens back out." Seb's smoky voice remains even, though it sounds worn out and tired.

"Try and get some sleep, Seb. It may be your only chance." With those last words, I turn my full attention back to the road. Worry for Rolland and Kia settles in as my

SARAH B MEADOWS

thoughts turn to our home which has been demolished, and I wonder about what actually happened back there between Jack and Rolland. Concern for my Brothers, and Kia, weighs heavily on my shoulders as I begin to question how long we can keep those that hunt her off of our backs.

With Rolland and Kia both unconscious, Seb full of emotions that are seldom seen on him, Matt having a breakdown, Jack looking like shit, and Gerry still scouting with the boys in London and completely unaware of what's happened... what a cluster fuck we all find ourselves in.

As I continue on down the road, I can't help but wonder how Gerry's going to react when the news of what went down hits him. Then I begin to wonder... how much more can we all really take?

I guess we'll find out....

ACKNOWLEDGMENTS

Model cover picture supplied by Darren Birks - Covers Unleashed
Stock images used for cover:
Depositphotos/Avella2011
Shutterstock/Happetr
Shutterstock/Peerapat Lekkla

ABOUT THE AUTHOR

My pen name is Sarah B Meadows and I was born in Peterborough (England), and grew up in a large family. While I was young, I moved to Essex to live with my dad. We moved around a fair bit – Romford, Colirow, Southend-on-sea, Leigh-on-sea.

I later moved to Scotland with my eldest son who was just one at the time. I currently live with my husband and three children, within our twelve acres of land by the coast of Scotland. We have three horses and a cat.

I have always had a passion for nature, drawing and writing. I love taking hikes, be them short or long, listening to music, drawing and of course writing. I was always encouraged to use my imagination, and now I am using it to write Fantasy books. My debut book will be out on March 28, 2019, I hope you enjoy it. Please follow me on the following social media platforms:

Printed in Great Britain
by Amazon